Praise for Millie Criswell's previous work, *Temptation's Fire*:

"Millie Criswell's *Temptation's Fire* snaps with the speed of lightning, crackles with sensuality, and pops with surprises. A highly entertaining, well-crafted read."
—Kathe Robin, *Romantic Times*

"Five stars. Millie Criswell is fantastic! She is destined to become one of the greats in this genre."
—*Affaire de Coeur*

PASSION'S REBIRTH

Eden entered the dark interior of the barn and climbed the ladder that led to the hayloft. When she reached the top rung, she paused, sucking in her breath at the sight that greeted her. Clay was naked from the waist up. The sunlight streaming in through the small hexagonal window bathed his muscular torso in filtered beams of light. He looked like a golden bronze statue, all sinew and muscle, his biceps thickly knotted, as he heaved the heavy bales into neat stacks. His chest glistened with the sweat of his labors, and droplets clung to the dark patch of curls swirling over his broad chest.

Eden swallowed, trying to still the rapid beating of her heart. She hadn't seen so much of Clay in a long time, hadn't remembered his body looking quite so . . . so virile, and it took her breath away.

She felt like a Peeping Tom and cleared her throat. When Clay saw her, he merely nodded in greeting. She completed her climb until she was standing in close proximity. The loft had an intimate, cloistered feel to it, reminding her of the times they'd spent in her father's barn.

As if Clay could read her mind, he smiled knowingly. "Just like old times, huh, angel eyes?" He set down the bale he held, never taking his eyes off her.

Like a wary animal caught in the sight of a hunter's gun, Eden stood transfixed. Before she could protest, Clay smothered her lips with his own, demanding, seeking a response. He was not disappointed.

ANOTHER TIME... ANOTHER PLACE... ANOTHER LOVE—
Let Pinnacle Historical Romances take you there!

LOVE'S STOLEN PROMISES (631, $5.99/$6.99)
by Sylvie F. Sommerfield

Mitchell Flannery and Whitney Clayborn are two star-crossed lovers, who defy social conventions. He's a dirt-poor farm boy, and she's a South Carolina society belle. On the eve of the Civil War, they come together joyously, and are quickly and cruelly wrenched apart. After making a suitable marriage, Whitney imagines that she will never feel the soaring heights of passion again. Then, Mitchell returns home seven years after marching away....

VELVET IS THE NIGHT (598, $4.99/$5.99)
by Elizabeth Thornton

To save her family from the guillotine, Claire Devereux agrees to become the mistress of the evil, corrupt commissioner, Phillipe Duhet. She agrees to give her body to him, but she swears that her spirit will remain untouched. To her astonishment, Claire finds herself responding body and soul to Duhet's expert caresses. Little does Claire know but Duhet has been abducted and she has been falling under the spell of his American twin brother, Adam Dillon!

ALWAYS AND FOREVER (647, $4.99/$5.99)
by Gina Robins

Shipwrecked when she was a child, Candeliera Caron is unaware of her wealthy family in New Orleans. She is content with her life on the tropical island, surrounded by lush vegetation and natives who call her their princess. Suddenly, sea captain Nick Tiger sails into her life, and she blooms beneath his bold caresses. Adrift in a sea of rapture, this passionate couple longs to spend eternity under the blazing Caribbean sky.

PIRATE'S KISS (612, $4.99/$5.99)
by Diana Haviland

When Sybilla Thornton arrives at her brother's Jamaican sugar plantation, she immediately falls under the spell of Gavin Broderick. Broderick is an American pirate who is determined to claim Sybilla as forcefully as the ships he has conquered. Sybilla finds herself floating upside down in a strange land of passion, lust, and power. She willingly drowns in the heat of this pirate's kiss.

SWEET FOREVER (604, $4.99/$5.99)
by Becky Lee Weyrich

At fifteen, Julianna Doran plays with a Ouija board and catches the glimpse of a handsome sea captain Brom Vanderzee. This ghostly vision haunts her dreams for years. About to be wed, she returns to the Hudson River mansion where she first encountered this apparition. She experiences one night of actual ecstasy with her spectral swain. Afterwards, he vanishes. Julianna crosses the boundaries of her world to join him in a love that knows no end.

Available wherever paperbacks are sold, or order direct from the Publisher. Send cover price plus 50¢ per copy for mailing and handling to Pinnacle Books, Dept.778, 475 Park Avenue South, New York, N.Y. 10016. Residents of New York and Tennessee must include sales tax. DO NOT SEND CASH. For a free Zebra/Pinnacle catalog please write to the above address.

Promise of Eden
Millie Criswell

PINNACLE BOOKS
WINDSOR PUBLISHING CORP.

This book is dedicated to
Tommye Ring Morton

Sometime sister, sometime mother, full-time friend.
A genuine Southern belle, who rings true every time.

PINNACLE BOOKS are published by

Windsor Publishing Corp.
475 Park Avenue South
New York, NY 10016

Copyright © 1993 by Millie Criswell

All rights reserved. No part of this book may be reproduced in any form or by any means without the prior written consent of the Publisher, excepting brief quotes used in reviews.

If you purchased this book without a cover, you should be aware that this book is stolen property. It was reported as "unsold and destroyed" to the Publisher and neither the Author nor the Publisher has received any payment for this "stripped book."

The P logo Reg. U.S. Pat. & TM Off. Pinnacle is a trademark of Windsor Publishing Corp.

First Printing: December, 1993

Printed in the United States of America

One

"Hellfire and perdition! What on earth am I going to do now?" Eden Fairchild muttered, untying the black silk strings of her cottage bonnet as she crossed the room to gaze out the window of the plantation office. Her eyes clouded in anger and frustration as she stared at the majestic oaks that graced Beauclaire's front lawn and the white, waxy blossoms of the dogwood trees that bordered the split rail fence.

She hated surprises! She always had, even as a child. And her father had just reached up from the grave to deal her the biggest surprise of her life.

She had just returned from town and the reading of her father's will and was unprepared for the tumult of emotion pounding within her breast. Anger and bitterness, alien to her before, penetrated as deeply as a knife plunging into her back.

Her father had betrayed her.

Toying with the sash that held back the gold

damask drapery, she thought of Lawrence Fairchild. The tall, strapping individual with the deep-set blue eyes had withered these past two years, like an apple left out to dry in the harsh sun. His illness had eroded his brawn and brashness, leaving only an empty shell and a weakened heart. He had died six weeks ago, and the reading of his will had produced few surprises save one.

As his only living heir, Eden had inherited Beauclaire Plantation, the stately brick Georgian manor house; one hundred slaves; and over seven hundred acres of land bordering the Rappahannock River in Essex County, Virginia.

She had also inherited a massive debt; Beauclaire had been mortgaged.

Even kind old Mr. Tayloe, the white-haired, soft-spoken solicitor, had been embarrassed to reveal that she was up to her ears in debt. Though he had spoken with kindness and concern this afternoon during the unpleasant proceedings, there was a grim note of finality in his voice that spoke of hardship and financial ruin.

Tossing her bonnet carelessly aside, Eden seated herself behind her father's battered oak desk and sifted through the pile of unpaid bills which lay atop the blotter. Deep lines bracketed her mouth as she picked up and read the contents of a copy of the promissory note made out to their neighbor Charles Braxton in the amount of twenty thousand dollars.

Twenty thousand dollars! It might as well have been a million, Eden thought dejectedly.

There was no mistaking the handwriting.

Lawrence Fairchild's distinctive strokes, as bold and audacious as he had been, filled the paper. She shook her head, thinking of the odd legacy her father had bequeathed his only daughter. But then, why should she be so surprised? As with everything else in his life, her papa'd had the last word.

Wondering what other surprises were in store for her, Eden searched through the various drawers of the desk to find sealing wax, her father's gold signet ring, and a stack of stationery, but not much else.

The right bottom drawer was difficult to open, and she yanked on it several times before it gave way. Another stack of papers greeted her, filling her with dread. If these proved to be another pile of unpaid debts, Beauclaire was doomed.

Quickly scanning the documents, she discovered correspondence relating to the factoring of the tobacco crop. Relieved, she moved to replace the papers when the edge of a leather book caught her eye. Reaching further into the drawer, she pulled it from its hiding place, dusting off what appeared to be an old journal.

Wrinkling her nose as the musty, neglected smell rose up to assault her senses, she opened the leather volume, her eyes widening in disbelief when she read: *Private Journal of Charlotte Peters Fairchild.*

"Mama's journal," Eden murmured, quickly turning the page, eager to find out more about the woman who had died shortly before Eden's fifteenth birthday.

Beauclaire, May 3rd, 1826. My wedding day, and I am to be joined in the holiest of institutions with my beloved Mr. Fairchild. Surely my heart cannot contain the joy of such a union. I am, most certainly, the luckiest of women.

Gazing at the elegant script that filled the yellowed page, she sucked in her breath. The notation, penned some twenty-four years before, came as quite a shock, for it revealed that her mother had actually harbored deep feelings for her father; the revelation brought a lump to her throat.

An estrangement had existed between her parents for as long as Eden could remember. She knew the cause of it—the deep, dark secret that had eroded the once happy marriage of Charlotte Fairchild to her beloved Lawrence. But it had never been spoken of, never acknowledged. It had been hidden away beneath layers of hurt and covered up by false pride, and was now deeply buried in the graves of her parents.

Gliding her fingers over the rough-grained leather, she experienced a closeness to her mother that she hadn't felt when Charlotte was alive. "You and Papa are both gone now, Mama, and I am left to face an uncertain future and a pile of debts." Heaving a sigh that held all the pent-up frustration and desolation she felt at the moment, she set the journal carefully aside, wishing she could read further, but knowing she had little time for such idle pleasures at the moment.

Now, she was pressed with the problem of finding the resources to manage Beauclaire, the Virginia plantation that had been in her family for over two hundred years.

A knock on the door interrupted Eden's disquieting thoughts, and she looked up to find Aunt Agnes marching through the doorway like a one-woman army. She smiled softly as she observed the older woman's outrageous attire.

Agnes, her mother's sister and Eden's only surviving relative, was dressed in the shocking new style that female advocate Amelia Bloomer had designed. *Bloomers*, they were called. Full harem-type pants with long, tunic blouses worn over them. They had been dyed black, in deference to Eden's father, but it was the only concession the older woman was willing to make. Aunt Agnes refused to wear a dress; she refused to wear a corset; she refused to "truss herself up like a turkey ready for roasting," as she so aptly put it. Fortunately, she possessed a tall, wiry frame, making the added accouterment unnecessary.

"Come in, Agnes," Eden called out, eyeing the comfort of the outfit with something akin to envy as she motioned her forward. Her own dress made of heavy, black bombazine was vastly uncomfortable. And even without the hoops and crinolines, which she'd had the good sense to discard this morning, she was hot and sticky.

The present fashion standards could only have been dictated by a man, Eden decided, a man who had an inherent dislike of women.

"Mercy me, child!" Agnes cast Eden a baleful glance. "It's like an inferno in this room." Crossing to the double-hung window, the older woman pulled back the drapery, pushing up on the sash to open it, then repeated the steps with the casement on her right.

The room was immediately bathed in the golden glow of sunlight, the rays bouncing off the white-plastered walls and dark, pine-planked flooring, while the cooling breeze of the late afternoon wafted in, admitting the distinctive odor of boxwood and bringing relief to the stifling room.

Wiping her hands briskly together, Agnes wagged her head, clucking her tongue in disapproval. "I declare, you have no more sense than that bluejay out on yonder limb."

Eden smiled weakly, thinking that at least the bird had sense enough to be outside, enjoying the freshness of the spring day. "I was just looking over Papa's books," she explained, hoping the excuse would be enough to forestall one of her aunt's lectures, which she was in no mood to listen to right now.

Aunt Agnes had a penchant for lecturing. In fact, Eden was quite positive that had Agnes not been summoned home to care for Lawrence Fairchild, she'd have spent the remainder of her days touring the country on behalf of the newly formed women's movement.

Having participated in the women's rights convention, held two years before in Seneca Falls, New York, Agnes had become an ardent follower of Elizabeth Cady Stanton and Lucretia Mott, the country's most outspoken female advocates.

Deprived of the privilege of lecturing to the

masses on the equality of women, Agnes had repeatedly expounded her views to the Fairchilds and anyone else who would listen. Her conduct had served only to widen the rift between Eden's father and her outspoken aunt. The two had never gotten along. Hate might have been too strong a word to describe their feelings for one another, but dislike certainly was not.

Knowing how Agnes felt about her father, Eden had been surprised when her aunt had answered her summons to come home to care for him. But then, knowing that Agnes's sense of familial duty far outweighed her animosity, Eden expected no less. Aunt Agnes was one of a kind.

"From that look on your face, child, it would appear things are not as they should be." Agnes seated herself in the sturdy oak chair that rested in front of the desk. "I suppose Lawrence was his usual inept self when it came to handling the management of this place. I told him planting those additional acres in tobacco was going to be the ruin of us all."

"You mustn't speak unkindly of Papa, Agnes," Eden replied, quick to defend her father's actions. "He did what he thought was best."

"*Hmph!* Lawrence always did what *he* thought best, with never a care to anyone else. He was the autocratic despot to the very end. Why, I truly think he thought he could order God to let him live. The man was insufferable."

Eden smiled at her aunt's criticism, harsh though it was, for it described her father to perfection. She might have loved her father, but she hadn't been blind to his faults; they'd all suffered because of them at one time or another. And it would do little good to take offense at anything Agnes had to say; she was going to give her opinion, whether or not you wanted to listen to it.

"Beauclaire has been mortgaged," Eden finally explained, watching her aunt's bright blue eyes, as sharp and assessing as the woman herself, widen in shock. She was surprised by the reaction, for Agnes wore her feelings on her sleeve, and there were few things that took the older woman unaware.

"It seems Father borrowed a great deal of money from Mr. Braxton, securing the note with the deed to this plantation. I'm at a loss as to what I should do."

Agnes was ever ready with one of the trite phrases she was so fond of spouting. " *'A change of fortune hurts a wise man no more than a change of the moon.'* " At Eden's groan, she added, "You still have the tobacco crop."

True, Eden thought, but it was a long way from becoming marketable, and when it was, there were no guarantees that they would turn a profit. Tobacco plantations in the Virginia Tidewater had suffered of late, for a variety of reasons—weather, insects, depletion of the soil—and Beauclaire had been no exception. They'd been holding on by a fragile thread, and it now looked as if that thread was about to snap.

"This year's crop won't be ready for months yet. With the drought we've experienced the past two years, coupled with the blight, I don't hold out much hope that there will be enough profit to pay off the debt."

"We've only one alternative, then, though it grieves me to say it," her aunt stated, brushing impatiently at the annoying strands of graying black hair that had escaped the confines of her bun.

Eden knew what her aunt was about to suggest. Selling off slaves had become an accepted practice in Virginia, as had the hiring out of extra laborers. Eden thought the practice of separating families quite barbaric, and she let her aunt know it. "I won't sell any of our people, and I'm shocked that you'd even consider such a thing, Aunt Agnes. Why, you're practically an abolitionist!"

"Don't go narrowing those violet eyes at me, child. My personal convictions matter little when your future is at stake. Remember, my dear, *There are no gains without pains.*'

"If your father hadn't been ill these past two years, you can be sure he'd have had little compunction about selling his slaves south. He viewed them as chattel, never people." Her face reflected the disgust in her voice. "I'm surprised he didn't order that overseer Mr. Wakefield to perform the foul deed. It was so like Lawrence not to dirty his own hands with anything sordid. The benevolent patriarch, that's how he thought of himself."

"I'll not sell any of our people, and that's final!" Eden's tone softened as she sought to explain her position. "Now that Papa's dead, I propose to institute a plan whereby the slaves will be able to purchase their freedom."

"Your idea is a noble one, Eden. And I'm proud of you for saying it. But it's impractical even to think it. Where would you get the money to pay them?"

Tiny lines of uncertainty creased Eden's forehead. She had wondered the same thing, but she wasn't about to give up the idea. A feeling of unrest was sweeping over the land. Slavery was a popular issue with the Northern abolitionists who vigorously sought its end. The publication of Frederick Douglass's narrative on the life of a slave had already incited men to action. And only two months ago, the rescue of the slave Shadrach from a Boston jail had added more fuel to the furor.

Times were changing, and it was time for men and women of good conscience to change with them.

"I wouldn't be able to pay the slaves a wage, but they could work off their time at a set rate, so much per week. I think it would increase productivity, if they knew that their efforts would result in freedom. I proposed the idea to Papa over a year ago; but, of course, he denounced it as sentimental impracticality."

"I'm vehemently opposed to this peculiar institution of slavery, as you well know," Agnes said. "I guess I've spent too much time up north not to have had some of those Yankee views rub off on me. But I can see no other alternative than to sell some of the newer field hands south to the cotton states. They're clamoring for labor down there and paying handsomely."

Noting the despair on her young niece's face, Agnes's heart grew heavy. How cruel to shatter such innocence and idealism, she thought. Eden reminded Agnes of herself at that age—headstrong, impetuous, filled with vitality that only youth could provide. She hated to fracture her illusions—to crush the independent spirit that was so much a part of her nature—but reality had a strange way of doing just that.

Hadn't Agnes learned that painful lesson early on? Hadn't Lawrence Fairchild been an excellent teacher?

Swallowing the angry bile that rose thickly to her throat whenever she thought of Beauclaire's former master, Agnes added, "You've done your best, Eden, trying to take over the running of this place when your father took ill and before that, taking over for your mother when she died. I told your father that a child of fifteen was too young to assume the mistress's responsibilities of such a large plantation.

"But that was eight years ago, and this is now. It's time you let someone else shoulder the responsibility. I want to help, if you'll let me. Selling the slaves is the only way."

Without replying, Eden pushed herself up from the desk, crossing the room to stare morosely out the window. The plantation office sat at the front of the house, affording a commanding view of the Rappahannock River. Across the expanse of lush green lawn that comprised the yard, she observed Hattie and Lulu's boys swinging from a rope tied to a venerable oak—the same tree she herself had swung from as a child. They didn't seem to have a care in the world, and she envied them that.

She had grown up quickly after her mother's death, and it had cost her much of her childhood. The mistress's duties had consumed her every waking moment, leaving little time for frivolity and pleasurable pursuits. Menus needed writing, foodstuffs needed doling out. There were sick slaves to tend, clothing to be sewn . . . the list of chores was endless. And now, with this added responsibility on her shoulders, she felt as old as Methuselah, or at least as old as Agnes's fifty-five years.

But observing the children's antics, Eden blossomed with renewed determination. Hattie and Lulu had been born on Beauclaire, as had their children, Ephraim and Lucius. There was no way she was going to break up families, or sell off any of her people.

There had to be another way to get the money to pay back Charles Braxton. She didn't know how, but she was determined to find it.

"What you mean, you is goin' visitin'? It ain't proper for a young lady to go calling on no gentleman by herself."

Standing in front of Beauclaire's six-paneled entry door, looking every bit as formidable as that solid piece of oak, Eden's housekeeper crossed her beefy black arms across an equally ample chest, thrust out her chin, and dared Eden to step around her.

"Now, Aunt Ruby," Eden cajoled, pulling on her gloves as she spoke. "There's no call to worry. I'm just driving to Mr. Long's plantation." She glanced into the swan-necked gold mirror, smoothing back the tendrils of hair that had escaped her chignon. "I won't be long." She stepped forward, but Ruby held her ground, forcing Eden to retreat.

"Mista Long is trash as far as I'se concerned, and no decent woman is goin' to go a'visitin' the likes of him alone."

Eden's chin notched higher as she stared into the ebony eyes of her mammy. "Need I remind you that I am mistress here?"

Recognizing the spark of stubbornness in Miss Eden's eyes, Ruby stood fast. She had promised Miss Charlotte on her deathbed that she would look out for Miss Eden, and by all that was holy, that's just what she intended to do.

"You might be mistress of dis heah plantation, Miss Eden, but I'se the one that suckled you when you was just a babe, and I ain't about to let no harm come to my baby."

Eden stared at the benevolent tyrant before her and bit back her retort, for she knew that Aunt Ruby had only her best interests at heart.

Aunt Ruby, with her husband, Uncle Beevis, had lived at Beauclaire since before Eden was born. Their daughter Jewel, only two years her senior, had been her playmate when they were children. They were all part of her family, strange as it might seem to those Northern abolitionists who portrayed all slave-holding Southerners as whip-yielding tyrants. Yankees were always quick to condemn what they didn't understand.

Aunt Ruby had been more mother to Eden than Charlotte Fairchild. It was Ruby who had tended her hurts, sung lullabies to sooth her nightmares, comforted her when her mama had died. And she loved the black woman dearly. But Ruby was as overprotective as she was kind, and Eden had to make her understand that this trip to Long Acres—Cyrus Long's plantation in Port Royal—was extremely important.

It had come to her in her sleep last night, like an inspiration from the heavens, that Cyrus Long, a former business associate of her father's, would be the perfect one to lend her the money she needed. Cyrus had expressed a fondness for her—had even attempted to press his suit some time ago. Surely she could convince him to make her the loan.

But first, she had to convince Aunt Ruby.

"It's very important that I visit Mr. Long, Aunt Ruby. The future of Beauclaire . . . of all of us . . . depends on it."

Ruby said nothing at first, pretending to study the pink rosebuds that repeated over the papered walls of the entry hall. Finally removing the starched white apron from around her waist and setting it down on the mahogany side table, she declared, "Then I goes wid you."

"That's not really nec . . ." Noting the black

woman's implacable features, and the way she crossed her arms over her chest as if the matter was already settled, Eden knew it was useless to argue; she'd won few arguments with Ruby over the last twenty-two years. "You'd best get your shawl, then, if you're going with me. There's a nip in the air this morning."

"And you best fetch your bonnet, Miss Eden. We wouldn't want that pretty white skin to get all freckled, now would we?"

Defiance flared briefly in the depths of the violet eyes. Plopping the black satin bonnet atop her head, Eden tied the grosgrain ribbons beneath her chin, and wondered, not for the first time, who was really in charge of Beauclaire. Judging by the self-satisfied smirk on Aunt Ruby's face, she thought she knew the answer.

A short time later, seated on a lumpy horsehair sofa in the parlor of Cyrus Long's house, a cup of oolong tea balanced on her lap, Eden pondered the wisdom of coming to Long Acres for a visit, and was suddenly grateful for the comforting presence of Aunt Ruby, who waited outside in the carriage.

Though she had never seen the inside of a brothel, after viewing the inside of Cyrus Long's parlor, Eden thought she knew what one might look like.

Garish red velvet drapery, fringed with gold tassels, hung at the two large palladian windows. The fabric was repeated on the sofa and side chairs, while two ornate crystal chandeliers hung suspended from the ceiling; their candles reflecting off the red-flocked wallpaper which covered the walls from top to bottom. Over the fireplace hung a portrait of a half-naked, well-endowed, nymphlike creature whom Eden supposed was Cyrus's vision of the ideal woman.

Observing Cyrus Long's taste firsthand brought to mind something Eden's mother always said: "Breeding tells, Eden. Remember that." And in Cyrus's case, lack of breeding told, too.

The object of Eden's consideration was at the moment seated across from her on the opposite end of the sofa, his adoring brown eyes snaking over her person in reptilian fashion, making her skin crawl at the close scrutiny, as if the man could see beneath the heavy mourning dress she wore.

Whatever Cyrus Long was thinking had an excitable effect on his nature, for his round face was flushed as crimson as his furnishings, and his forehead and balding pate were dewy with nervous perspiration.

He was a short, stocky man—not fat enough to be considered obese—but definitely corpulent. He had long, graying side-whiskers, nearly reaching his chin—muttonchops, they were called—but Eden thought he looked more like a pig than a lamb.

"I'm delighted that you've honored me with a visit, Miss Fairchild. Though I must confess, I *am* surprised that you're out making calls so soon after your father's funeral."

Eden didn't need, or want, to be reminded of

the impropriety of her visit, and she attempted to mask her annoyance with a small smile. "My visit is directly related to my father's passing, Mr. Long, or I would not have ventured beyond my home at such an inappropriate time."

"Of course, of course," he responded quickly, reaching out to pat her hand in a consoling gesture. "Please accept my deepest condolences at your loss."

She fought the urge to pull back her hand and was grateful for the gloves she wore that prevented direct contact with his sweaty palm. "I have a problem, Mr. Long, and thought perhaps you might be inclined to offer me some assistance."

"You have only to ask, dear lady. Never let it be said that Cyrus Long did not come to the aid of a damsel in distress." He smiled then, tightening his grip on her hand, revealing teeth that were badly yellowed by the ever-present cigars he smoked; the odor clinging to his person was as offensive as the man himself.

Easing her hand out of his grasp, Eden made a great pretense of sipping her tea, then said, "You're very kind, Mr. Long" noting how he preened under her flattery like a fat, waddling duck who'd just laid the largest egg in the barnyard.

"I hope I can rely on your discretion. I don't wish my personal travails to become common knowledge."

"Of course, my dear. Think of me as a trusted friend. A dear, dear trusted friend."

She swallowed her disgust. "I've recently discovered that Beauclaire has been mortgaged. I need a loan to pay off the debt."

At once the lazy, indolent look grew sharp and assessing. "You say Beauclaire is mortgaged? For how much?"

"I'm in need of twenty thousand dollars."

A sharp whistle flew out between Cyrus's lips before he pushed himself to his feet and began pacing across the red and gold Aubusson carpet. At last the chance he'd been waiting for was within his grasp: Beauclaire was in financial trouble. The high and mighty Fairchilds were not unassailable after all.

"That's a substantial amount, Miss Fairchild. What type of collateral do you offer in return for the investment?"

"Collateral?" She had never even considered that he would want some type of security for the loan. How completely naive and stupid she must be not to have thought of it.

"Surely you must realize that in matters of business, one must expect something to be given in return," he continued, his gaze wandering over her person in a frankly assessing manner. "I'm sure we could work something out, Miss Fairchild. You are not without assets."

His grin held the deviousness of a naughty child, and he wondered again at his good fortune. Beauclaire was one of the richest plantations in the Tidewater, even with the reverses it had suffered of late. That, coupled with the beauteous belle of the county—the elusive Eden Fairchild—

would make him the richest man in Virginia, not to mention the luckiest.

Setting her china cup down on the tea table in front of her, Eden pushed herself to her feet. "I'm afraid I don't understand what you mean, Mr. Long. I've just explained that Beauclaire is already mortgaged. My assets are encumbered at the moment. I had hoped you would loan me the money on good faith. I assure you, in a year or two, providing Beauclaire has a good tobacco crop, I'll be able to repay you."

He stepped forward, his warm, fetid breath brushing her cheeks as he spoke. "Your plantation is not the only thing I covet, Miss Fairchild. You yourself have much to recommend."

As she recognized the lascivious glint in his eyes, his words suddenly became all too clear, prompting hers to grow as frigid as a winter's day. "I am not for sale, Mr. Long. I'm sorry if I gave you the impression that I was." Picking up the voluminous folds of her skirts, she turned to leave, but his words halted her in her tracks.

"I'm making you an honest proposal, Miss Fairchild. I'm asking you to be my wife."

She spun on her heel, her eyes widening. "Your wife? You're asking me to marry you?" The thought was preposterous—downright comical. But she could see by his earnest expression he was dead serious.

"Indeed. I find the prospect highly exciting." Stepping forward, he closed the distance between them. "Surely you must know how I feel about you. It was only your father's illness that prevented me from pursuing my suit more aggressively. It's no secret that I desire you . . . for my wife," he amended quickly.

She hadn't missed the slip and shudders of revulsion darted through her, but she kept her mask of civility firmly in place. "I'm flattered, Mr. Long, but I'm not interested in marriage." She had made that point quite clear to her father several years ago, when Cyrus had first pressed his suit. Fortunately, Papa had agreed with her.

Like a dog suddenly deprived of his bone, Cyrus snarled as he barked his disapproval. "Because of what happened between you and that Braxton boy? Well, I can tell you, missy, I'm more of a man than that young whelp."

Eden gasped, her hand flying to the cameo brooch at her throat before her lips compressed into a thin line. *How dare this pompous bore bring up her relationship with Clay?* Straightening her spine, she impaled him with eyes that had darkened to purple in their anger. "You overstep your bounds, Mr. Long. What was between Clay Braxton and myself is none of your concern."

"It is if it's keeping you from marrying me."

"I assure you, it has nothing to do with my reasons for not wanting to marry you—or anyone else, for that matter." She had no wish to marry. Not now, not ever. Marriage was a death sentence. Her mother had died at age thirty-five. And Eden, knowing that Charlotte Fairchild's miserable marriage had hastened her death, had no plans to follow in her footsteps.

"My reasons are my own, and I intend to keep

them that way." *And she certainly had no intention of revealing them to this fat, little toad!*

"Well, I'd think on those reasons long and hard before you turn down a very respectable offer, Miss Fairchild. I'm not without assets. I could offer you a very comfortable life here at Long Acres."

She fought to keep her temper in check, though the effort was costing her dearly. Already a dull ache had formed at her temples. "I really must be going, Mr. Long, though I do appreciate your hospitality."

Before she could reach the door, he grabbed on to her arm, restraining her, shocking her with his boldness. "A high-spirited filly like you needs a strong hand, Miss Fairchild. You need to be ridden long and hard, learn who your master is."

"Let go of me, sir!" She yanked her arm free, breathing deeply from the exertion and her own anger. "If you ever think to lay a hand on me again, be prepared to die, Mr. Long, for I will shoot you down for the dog that you are."

Throwing open the door, Eden ran from the room and out of the house. But she could still hear the man's sinister laughter long after she had reached the safety of her carriage.

Two

Racing across the open meadow, tossing up large clumps of dirt in their wake, horse and rider appeared as one, their black manes flying, their breathing deep and uneven as they pulled up at the edge of the newly planted field of tobacco to catch their breath.

Eden dismounted, patting the sleek stallion's lathered neck, wiping gently at the foam with her gloved hand. The scent of leather and horseflesh, offensive to some, had a balming effect on her soul.

"You're a good boy, Othello, you black beast," she cooed into the horse's ear. "If all men possessed your dignity and loyalty, the world would be a better place." But they didn't. Men wanted to be in control—to strip every ounce of independence from a woman's nature. And she'd vowed long ago it would never happen to her.

There was a heaviness to the late afternoon air, and it caused droplets of perspiration to form on Eden's upper lip. She wiped at them with the back of her hand, then loosened the top button of her blouse. Lifting up her hair, which hung down her back in riotous disarray, she fanned it against her neck, trying to cool herself off. She was hot under the collar. But her discomfort had more to do with this morning's encounter with Cyrus Long than with the weather.

How dare the despicable, odious man speak to her in such a fashion! To think he'd actually had the audacity to ask for her hand in marriage. It was unconscionable. Long's cruel treatment of his slaves was a well-known fact in the Tidewater; she doubted a wife would fare much better.

Oh, to be a man, she thought, slapping her riding crop against the purple velvet skirt of her habit. To be spared the Cyrus Longs of this world.

Striding over to where Isaac, her slave foreman, stood, Eden observed the large black man as he supervised the field hands in the transplanting of the tobacco seedlings—a time-consuming job that required much attention.

The tobacco hills had already been laid out in neat rows, and the slaves were now in the process of transferring the seedlings to the small mounds. She watched them, their sweat-soaked shirts sticking to the broadness of their backs as they hunched over to perform her labor, and it filled her with shame.

The system was wrong, and she knew it, though it would be difficult to grow tobacco without the use of slave labor. It was a formidable crop, requiring constant care and hours of manpower.

The song the slaves sang while they worked

sounded mournful to her ears, and she suddenly realized how misguided her father had been to perpetrate the lie that "a singing darky was a happy darky." Well, the slaves were singing, but they weren't happy. How could they be when their souls were owned by another? Wasn't that the very reason she'd chosen to be free and independent herself?

"Afternoon, Miz Eden? Sumpin' I can help you wid?" The black man, dressed in drab nankeen britches and shirt, snatched the straw hat from his head, clutching it to his chest. He bowed his head in deference, lowering his eyes to stare at the ground, as was expected of him.

As foreman, it was Isaac's job to see that the field hands' assigned tasks were completed with maximum efficiency and a minimum of grumbling. He had been elevated from the lowly position as fieldhand nigger because of his intelligence and respectful nature, and he would do what ever he had to to retain his exalted position, even if it meant bowing and scraping to the white folks.

Eden turned toward the foreman and smiled. "Good afternoon, Isaac. Do you know where Mr. Wakefield is?"

"Yes'm, Miz Eden, he be over to da other field. Dere was a problem wid some of the seedlings we done planted the other day. Mista Wakefield, he went to check on dem."

"A problem?" Eden's brow creased, her lips turning down into a frown, before she offered her thanks and remounted Othello, heading toward the south field, and praying the entire time she rode that the new seedlings would be all right.

As precarious as her financial situation was at the moment, she couldn't afford to lose this year's crop. She needed the cash to pay off existing debts and purchase supplies for next year's planting.

Spotting her overseer as he bent over a small mound of dirt, his wheat-colored hair glinting like gold in the sunlight, Eden called out, waving as she approached.

"Afternoon, Miss Fairchild," James Wakefield stated, pushing himself to his feet. "What brings you to the fields today?" The man spoke in a clipped British accent, his six-year residency in Virginia doing nothing to soften the intonation of his speech.

Without waiting for his assistance, Eden slid off the saddle with the agility and ease of an experienced horsewoman and rushed over to the newly planted mounds, bending down to examine them. She frowned at what she saw. Many of the seedlings had wilted under last night's unexpected frost. The leaves were a sickly brownish color, appearing as shriveled as her hopes at the moment.

"Have we lost many tobacco plants, Mr. Wakefield? It appears last night's turn in temperature hasn't been kind to our seedlings."

"No need to worry, Miss Fairchild. It's only twenty or so that we've lost. It won't be of much consequence."

Eden's sigh of relief was almost audible, and

she smiled gratefully at the tall man at her side. James Wakefield had worked at Beauclaire almost three years now, hiring on within a year of the onset of her father's illness.

He'd been a conscientious supervisor, though not overly harsh to the slaves—Eden would never have sanctioned that—and his assistance had proven invaluable during her father's long illness. He'd given advice when asked—never usurping her authority as owner, even though he'd been forced to take orders from a woman—and possessed the manners and breeding of a gentleman, traits foreign to most overseers. She deemed herself fortunate to have such an able-bodied, loyal individual in her employ.

"That's a relief," she finally replied. "I don't know what we'll do if we can't bring this crop in."

Taking hold of her gloved hand in a solicitous fashion, James led her away from the eager ears of the field hands to stand beneath a showy white catalpa tree. "You shouldn't concern yourself about such things. That's what I'm here for. I'll take care of everything. Haven't I always?"

Staring into eyes as cerulean blue as the sky overhead, Eden nodded. "You've been a godsend, James." They'd been on a first-name basis for over a year, but did not speak familiarly in front of the slaves, James feeling it would undermine both his and Eden's authority if the slaves thought they were getting too friendly with each other.

"I know you've had a difficult time these past two years, Eden, with your father's illness and the poor showing of the crop. But rest assured, I'll always be here to help and offer guidance, if you need it."

His eyes traveled over the supple curves, the full roundness of Eden's very ample breasts, and he felt a familiar yearning low in his belly, but did his best to hide the attraction. She was vulnerable, but she wasn't ready. Not yet.

"You've been a good friend, James, as well as a good employee. I hesitate to burden you with my troubles."

"A burden shared is always lighter, my dear."

Eden smiled, going on to disclose what she had discovered among her father's papers. "I tried to borrow the money from Cyrus Long, but his terms were not acceptable." She fought to keep the aversion out of her voice, but it did not go undetected.

Knowing Cyrus as well as he did, James could well imagine what the old fool's terms were. He smiled inwardly. Any man with feeling between his legs wanted to get beneath Eden's skirts, no matter if the cost was twenty thousand dollars.

He had dreamt many times of those supple white thighs wrapped around his waist. God, how he wanted the silly little virgin—wanted all that she possessed, namely, Beauclaire. And she didn't have a clue in the world as to his feelings.

As unobtrusively as he could, James removed his hat, wiping his hand across his brow, before repositioning the piece of felt in front of him to hide the burgeoning evidence of his desire. "I'm sure there's a way out of this predicament, Eden. You're not to worry. I'll put my thoughts to it this evening and see what kind of solution I can come up with." He was pleased by her look of gratitude. He'd done his best to ingratiate himself with the Fairchilds. It seemed his efforts were finally beginning to pay off.

Escorting her back to her mount, James frowned when he noticed the shape of the saddle. "I see you've been riding astride again. What's Aunt Ruby going to say if she finds out?"

Eden grinned impishly, displaying two charming dimples. "You'll not reveal my secret, will you, James?"

Placing his hands about her small waist, he lifted her effortlessly onto her mount, staring enviously as she wrapped her legs about the flanks of the big, black beast.

"I'll keep your secret this time, Eden, and hope you'll be more circumspect in the future." No wife of his was going to behave in such an unladylike fashion, and he had definitely decided to make Eden his wife.

The Wakefields might have fallen on hard times in America, necessitating his employment as a common laborer, but in England they'd been landed gentry. And would be again, if he had anything to say about it.

Waving his farewells as Eden galloped away, James suddenly felt the pressing need to relieve himself of the rock-hard bulge between his legs, thanks to Miss Eden Fairchild. Deciding that a visit to the slave quarters was in order, he hurried over to the dun-colored mare he'd left tied to a scraggly cedar.

Belle's thighs might not be as white as Eden's, he thought, but her breasts were just as large. She was a comely wench, for a nigger.

As the horse picked his way along the marshy edge of the riverbank, Eden reveled in the beauty surrounding her. The blossoms of the azalea bushes splashed pink and white against the green velvet landscape, while the fragrance of lilac perfumed the air. She inhaled the heady aroma, welcoming the warming rays of the sun against her cheeks.

Her riding hat hung dejectedly from the pommel of her saddle, and Aunt Ruby would have had a fit to see Eden tanning herself so. The whiteness of a woman's skin was the mark of a true lady, according to the old black woman.

But Eden had given up on the idea of becoming a true lady years ago, having found the thrill of riding astride, the comfort of discarding her corset, and the pleasure of feeling the sun on her face much more enjoyable.

Here in the South, beauty was measured on a standard of facial pallor. Her skin was still white enough to be considered fashionable—thanks to Ruby's diligent applications of buttermilk—but a few freckles did sprout across the bridge of her nose on occasion, much to the old woman's consternation.

There was much to recommend being a hoyden, as Aunt Ruby frequently called her. And Eden knew she'd grown every bit as independent as her outspoken aunt. She chafed at society's constraints, unwilling to be bound by convention and rules that had been designed by men to keep women in their place.

Her mother would roll over in her grave if she knew how Eden had changed. Charlotte Fairchild had been a stickler for the proprieties. One would never have seen Charlotte without a corset to accentuate the smallness of her waist, or a bonnet to protect her lily-white skin. No. Eden's mother was a lady through and through. But not a very happy one, Eden reflected.

There'd been a great sadness hovering about her mother—a terrible loneliness, as if she had somehow become disconnected from her life at Beauclaire.

Perhaps reading more of the journal would give her some insight into what kind of person Charlotte Fairchild really had been. There had to be more than the socially correct, unfailingly polite woman Eden had known. Surely there had once been a warmth—a plethora of emotions that bubbled up effervescently. There'd been a hint of it in that first journal passage she'd read—the joy and wonder of a bride coming to her new home.

How had Charlotte really felt about Beauclaire? Had she loved the vast plantation as much as Eden did?

Gazing back up the hill toward the two-story manor house, Eden smiled proudly. No one owning such a magnificent home could fail to love it. The warm bricks, once bright red, had mellowed with age, like fine red wine. The four columns supporting the porch overhang gleamed white in the afternoon sunlight. There was a wide center hall slicing through the middle of the house, with two sets of double doors at both front and back. The formal rooms led off on either side of the hallway, and a large, winding staircase of black walnut swept up to the top floor bedchambers.

The house was flanked on either side by two immense oak trees, and a long, double row of boxwood lined the oyster-shell path leading to Beauclaire's front doors.

Behind the main house stood the kitchen, also made of brick, which was connected to the house by a covered walkway. Beyond the kitchen stood two neat rows of whitewashed slave cabins.

"*Beauclaire*–'beautiful light,' " Eden whispered, thinking it had been aptly named by her great-grandfather, William Fairchild, over two hundred years ago.

There was no way she was going to lose her ancestral home, she resolved. Tomorrow she would ride over to Briarwood, the home of Charles Braxton, and pay him a visit.

He had nearly been her father-in-law once. But that had been a lifetime ago. Things had changed since her breakup with Clay. Relationships, once close, had strained near to snapping, and she had been the cause.

She hadn't seen Charles Braxton since Eulalie Braxton's funeral, held some eight months ago at the Methodist Church in town. His younger son, Richard, and daughter-in-law, Lucy, had paid their respects at her father's funeral, though. She'd learned from them that Mr. Braxton had been ill.

Had Charles Braxton turned into a bitter, irascible old man? Would he blame her for Clay's sudden departure five years ago?

No! she decided, shaking her head. Charles Braxton was a good man—a kind man. He would be reasonable. He had to be. The future of Beauclaire depended on his good graces.

But standing on the slate porch of the two-story white clapboard house the next morning, Eden wasn't quite as confident as she'd been the day before.

Coming to Briarwood had brought back a rush of memories and feelings long since forgotten. Staring at the blue painted front door, a feeling of déjà vu swept over her.

It had been five years ago in May, one month before she was to wed Clay Braxton, that she'd last come to Briarwood, picnic basket in hand, to lure Clay away from his work. The sun had been shining, much as it did now. But then, she had been filled with the youthful exuberance of loving Clay—a woman in love on the eve of her wedding. Now, she had only her memories to cling to and no one to blame for her loneliness but herself.

Five years. Had it been that long? She worried her lower lip, her hand poised on the brass pineapple knocker. The pineapple—a symbol of hospitality here in Virginia. Would she still be welcome?

Her fears were abolished a moment later when the door swung open and Rufus, Mr. Braxton's majordomo, smiled warmly, his brown eyes sparkling.

"Well, Miss Eden, ain't you a sight for these tired, old eyes?"

"Hello, Rufus, it's good to see you again." A tide of nostalgia swept over her. Seeing Rufus, being at Briarwood again, brought a lump the size of an orange to her throat. She swallowed, entering the familiar hallway as the old slave ushered her inside.

Rufus explained that Master Richard and Miss Lucy had gone visitin' and wouldn't be back for hours. Eden offered a quick, thankful prayer at the news. She had no wish to confide her problems to those two, especially Lucy, who would no doubt be overjoyed to learn that Eden was in trouble. Acquaintances they might have been the past six years, but friends, never!

Glancing quickly about, Eden noted that everything looked the same as it had when Clay's mother had been alive. Bluebirds still perched on gold-papered walls, and the walnut tall-case clock, once belonging to Eulalie Braxton's mother, still ticked off the seconds and minutes.

Eden's heart kept time to the swing of the brass pendulum as she entered Charles Braxton's study. It took a moment for her eyes to adjust to the darkness of the room. The windows had been shuttered closed and only a single oil lamp was left burning on the desk. As she scanned the area, she spotted Charles Braxton seated in a wheelchair near the fireplace.

Though the day was warm, the fire had been lit, the burning logs crackling loudly in the hearth, making the room dreadfully uncomfortable. Droplets of perspiration trickled down between Eden's breasts; her palms, dry moments ago, were suddenly moist.

Charles Braxton sat hunched over in his chair, a green crocheted throw covering his bony shoulders, and she was stunned by the change in his appearance. He had seemed wan at his wife's funeral those many months ago, but now he looked deathly white and horribly feeble.

"Mr. Braxton," she said softly, relieved when she saw him raise his head and turn to look in her direction. "It's Eden . . . Eden Fairchild. Rufus said I might speak to you for a few moments, if you're feeling up to it." The light of recognition entered his eyes, then a semblance of a smile crossed his lips.

"Come in, my dear. Don't let my appearance alarm you. I'm not quite ready to greet the grim reaper yet, though he's done his best to entice me." His attempt at laughter resulted in a strangled, choking cough.

Alarmed, Eden stepped toward him to offer assistance, but noting his embarrassment, she thought better of it and seated herself in the embroidered wing chair next to him instead. "I had no idea you were feeling so poorly, Mr. Braxton. I would have called sooner, had I known."

From Richard's description, she had thought perhaps the elder Braxton suffered from the ague, but now she could see that his condition was far more serious than that.

Charles smiled kindly. "You've had your own burdens to bear, child. I'm sorry I was unable to attend Lawrence's funeral. Lucy told me he was given a fine send-off. I'll miss the opinionated old fool."

The corners of Eden's mouth twitched, and she almost smiled at his remark. Charles Braxton and her father had been friends for years. But there were never two men with more divergent opinions. They disagreed on just about everything, including the proper time for harvesting the tobacco, and whether or not to rotate the crops—her father had been dead set against it—and sometimes they argued about whether or not the sun would shine on a particular day.

"What brings you to Briarwood, my dear? I confess I'm surprised by your visit, though it brings back memories of good times past." A faraway look entered his eyes, and Eden shifted uncomfortably in her chair, unsure of how to broach the subject uppermost on her mind.

"I've only just learned of the debt my father owes you, Mr. Braxton."

He reached for the pipe that lay on the table next to him. "Yes, Lawrence felt the need to plant additional acreage in tobacco, though I advised against it. He asked me for a loan and I obliged."

"I realize that I owe you a substantial amount of money, Mr. Braxton, and I want to assure you that I intend to pay back every bit of it." She paused, taking a deep breath, inhaling the pungent aroma of his tobacco. "But I'm afraid that I won't possess the funds by the due date on the note. According to the terms my father agreed to, the note is due in full by the first day of June. I find that deadline impossible to keep."

Eden watched the concentric swirls of smoke circle above the older man's white-haired head while he absorbed everything she had to say. Nervous droplets of perspiration dotted her upper lip and brow, and the heat from the fire did nothing to lessen her discomfort. Removing a linen handkerchief from the pocket of her gown, she wiped at the moisture and waited, gnawing her lower lip apprehensively.

"I would like to help you, child, really I would."

A flicker of hope ignited in her breast and she was quick to respond, "I promise to pay you back every cent I owe, Mr. Braxton, if you'll just allow me an extension on the loan."

"I'm afraid that I'm not in a position to do that, Eden, though I would if I could."

Her forehead creased in confusion. "I don't understand."

"I no longer own the controlling interest in Briarwood, Eden. After Eulalie died, and I took ill with the malaria, I decided that the only sensible thing to do was to turn the plantation over to my son."

"Then it's Richard I should speak to?" He shook his head, and a deep feeling of dread swept over her.

"No, my dear, it's not Richard you need deal with, it's Clay. He holds the note to your property now."

"Clay." The name exploded like a gunshot within her head but came out as a whisper.

Clay held the note to her plantation. Clay—her former fiancé—the man she had jilted two days before their wedding—the man who despised the very ground she walked on.

"My God!" The blood siphoned from her face, prompting Charles to pat her hand in a comforting gesture.

"You mustn't fret so, my dear. I'm sure once Clay hears of your predicament . . ."

"Hears!" she blurted, jumping to her feet. "I thought he was in Texas, fighting Mexicans. You mean he's back?"

Charles's hazel eyes lit with pleasure; a bloom of color touched the hollow of his cheeks. "Yes, Eden, Clay arrived home late last evening. I never doubted that my son would one day return to claim his birthright. The ownership papers, which I had prepared long ago in anticipation of his return, were signed last night, giving him legal ownership of Briarwood."

Eden fell back down in her seat, the breath rushing out of her, as if she'd just been kicked in the stomach by a mule.

Clay was home.

Clay, of the bright green eyes and the dimpled cheeks.

Clay, who had made her heart race and her toes tingle.

Clay, who hated every fiber of her being.

She swallowed hard. "I'm sure you must be very happy," she said at last, forcing a smile to her lips. She knew how glad the old man was to have his eldest son back. It had nearly destroyed him when Clay had left Briarwood . . . left because of her.

"Indeed. I felt some of my former strength return, flow into my veins at the sight of him. Wait until you see him, Eden. I hardly recognized my own boy, his skin has darkened so from the sun. I told him he was going to be mistaken for one of the darkies, if he wasn't careful." He shook his head, chuckling softly at his witticism.

Eden's smile was more of a grimace as she turned her head to stare into the flames of the fire and became lost in her own misery. The study door opened, but she didn't realize someone else was in the room until the shutters were unfolded and a shaft of light danced into the room, landing brightly in her lap.

Turning her head in the direction of the window, her pale skin was bleached even whiter, her eyes rounded at the sight of the brown-haired man who stood bathed in the golden glow of the early morning sunshine.

"Clay," she whispered.

Three

"Hello, angel eyes." The nickname came easily to Clay's lips, as if it had only been yesterday, not five long years, since he had uttered it.

The sight of Eden, even garbed in mourning, took his breath away. The black hair he'd remembered sifting his fingers through looked soft and thick as a piece of velvet as it cascaded down her back in luxurious waves. And her large, violet eyes—angel eyes, he had called them, for he'd always said she'd been sent to him from the heavens—still sparkled like amethysts.

Eden had always been lovely, but time had rendered her beautiful.

Beautiful and stubborn.

And fickle, he reminded himself.

Forcing his hands into the pockets of his trousers, lest he betray his reeling emotions, he strode across the room to face her.

"Clay." Eden mouthed his name stupidly again, staring at the man who had haunted her dreams so many nights during the past five years.

He was even more handsome than she'd remembered, if that was possible. His skin was indeed darkly tanned, making him appear more virile, more rugged. His chestnut-colored hair, resting just above the collar of his shirt, was streaked with golden highlights. He was bigger than she'd remembered, though still lean; his arms and legs were heavily muscled; and his broad chest was accentuated by the clothing he wore.

He dressed in the garments of a gentleman—black cutaway coat, white ruffled shirt, green brocade, double-breasted waistcoat—but she could see beneath the polite exterior that the gentleman had changed. She sensed it in his commanding stride when he crossed the room; in his stance, which contained just a hint of arrogance; in his eyes, which were as cold and hard as two jade stones.

"Have I sprouted two heads, Eden? Is that why you study me so closely?" Clay smiled at the blush on her cheeks, but the smile held no kindness.

"No! I'm sorry." She rose from her chair and held out her hand, which he took, much to her relief. Currents of emotion surged though her veins at his touch. Even through the glove she wore, she felt scalded and fought the urge to pull her hand away. "It's good to see you again, Clay. It's just . . . such a surprise, that's all."

"A wonderful surprise," Charles interjected, noting the exchange between the two with something more than casual interest. "Come closer, son, let me get another look at you. I was just telling Eden that you've turned as black as old Rufus."

Clay stepped toward his father, an affectionate smile on his lips, and leaned his elbow casually against the mantel of the fireplace as he spoke. "That's what being out in the sun for twelve to fifteen hours a day does to a body."

"You're referring to your sojourn in Texas, I believe." Charles was unable to keep the bitterness out of his voice, but if Clay noticed the animosity, he made no mention of it.

"The Mexicans weren't easily convinced to part with their territory."

"I've read several accounts of the Texans' struggle in the newspaper," Eden remarked. "Of the fight at Buena Vista."

Clay turned away then to stare into the flames of the fire. He didn't want to be reminded of Buena Vista, of the shrieks and wails of the dying, of the innocent Mexican women and children who'd been killed during the bombardment of the city.

At least some good had come of it. Santa Anna's army had been defeated, and Zachary Taylor's victory had boosted him into the President's chair, where he presently sat, though the nation was now embroiled in dispute over the future of the lands won. The North wanted them brought into the Union as free states, the South, as slave states.

"The war is over. The United States was victorious. It's best to let the memories rest, the wounds heal."

Eden noticed the pain in Clay's eyes when he turned to face her. She had seen that raw pain one time before, five years ago, and it drove into her heart like a bullet. Would she always feel guilt where Clay was concerned?

"What brings you to Briarwood, Eden? Father tells me that you've been an infrequent visitor at best."

A slow heat crept up Eden's long white neck to land on her cheeks. She glanced over at Clay's father, who smiled in encouragement rather than condemnation. "I've just learned of Mr. Braxton's illness. I came to pay my regards."

"Is that the only reason?"

Was there a hint of hope in the question? But noting the opacity of Clay's green eyes, Eden knew she was just being fanciful.

Before she could reply, Charles spoke up. "Eden came over to discuss some business, Clay. But we won't speak of it now. Why don't you ring for Rufus; have him bring in some tea."

"I can't stay, Mr. Braxton, though I appreciate your thoughtfulness. I promised Aunt Agnes I'd assist her with the mending this afternoon."

"How is your aunt, Eden? I haven't set my sights on Agnes Peters in years. Does she still swagger about in men's clothing, smoking those hideous cigars? Damned peculiar, if you ask me."

Hearing the condemnation in Mr. Braxton's voice, Eden smiled politely. Few people understood Agnes's eccentricities, not that her aunt gave a hoot about what anyone thought. Eden admired that about her.

It wasn't easy to flout Southern propriety, especially if you were a woman. It was thought that correct comportment was the foundation for social order in the South. Compliant behavior made it that much easier for men to exercise their absolute authority over women. Independent nature such as Agnes's were frowned upon, even ridiculed.

"Agnes has forgone male attire for bloomers, though she still smokes a cheroot on occasion."

Charles shook his head, looking as if he were about to say more on the subject, but only repeated, "Damned peculiar."

Holding out her hand to the older man as she made to leave, Eden extended her wishes for a speedy recovery.

"What's this? No kiss? I'm far too old to put up with a handshake from a pretty young woman."

Smiling shyly, Eden obliged, bending over to place a kiss on the old man's grizzled cheek. As her head came up, her eyes locked with Clay's, and the anger she saw reflected in their depths gave her pause.

Her fate rested with this bitter man—her fate and the lives of every man, woman, and child at Beauclaire. She smiled bravely and straightened, ignoring the ache deep within her chest at the distressing thought.

"Goodbye, Clay." Her farewell was met by silence. And as she made her way to the door, she felt his piercing eyes boring into her back. *Bullets again.*

Clay fought for composure as he watched Eden depart. How easily she had walked out of his life, then back in. He hadn't been prepared for the cauldron of emotion she'd stirred up: hate mingled with bittersweet memories of what they'd once shared.

And love.

No lust.

For surely it was lust he felt battling freely with the revenge that was uppermost on his mind.

"Eden's turned into a beautiful woman, hasn't she?" his father probed, forcing Clay's attention back.

Clay shrugged. "I hadn't noticed. I suppose she's pleasing to the eye." His voice reflected none of the anguish Eden's visit had evoked.

Liar, Charles thought, staring intently at his son, who chafed uncomfortably under the scrutiny. Clay was never very good at hiding his emotions. He'd have thought five years long enough to heal the hurt Eden's betrayal had caused, but apparently Clay's wound still festered.

"What did she come over for, anyway?"

Charles relit his pipe, puffing repeatedly on the stem, creating billows of white smoke to cloud the air with a licorice aroma. "Much has happened since you've been gone, son."

Clay grew defensive. "You're not going to lecture me again on my hasty departure, are you?"

"Your temper's grown quick and your manners have waned, my boy."

Noting the sudden pain in his father's eyes, Clay felt a stab of guilt. He had brought enough pain to the old man over the last five years; he wanted only peace between them now. "You're right." He gently squeezed his father's shoulder. "Living in the wilds of Texas did nothing to improve my manners, nor my disposition. The Texans are a wild bunch. I'll relate some of my adventures when you're feeling up to it."

Charles smiled, reaching up to pat Clay's hand. He had missed the boy—missed him almost as much as his dear Eulalie. It was good to have his family home with him again. "I look forward to it. And now, I will tell you about Eden's predicament."

Clay seated himself in the chair recently occupied by Eden and waited. He didn't really want to talk about Eden—to think about her—but he could see by the set expression on his father's face, there'd be no escaping the interview.

"As we discussed last evening," Charles began, "Lawrence Fairchild is dead. Eden has inherited Beauclaire and all of Lawrence's other property, including, I'm afraid, his debts."

Clay withdrew a cheroot from the inside front pocket of his coat, lighting it. "I see nothing unusual in that."

"What we didn't discuss," Charles continued, ignoring the interruption, "is the fact that Lawrence's largest debt is to me, or more specifically, to you."

A puzzled frown creased Clay's brow. "I'm not quite sure I follow you."

Charles went on to relate the details concerning his loan to Lawrence Fairchild and the subsequent note secured by the deed to Beauclaire Plantation.

"So what you're saying is that unless Eden pays me back the money by the first of June, Beauclaire is mine?" A calculating gleam entered his green eyes, which Charles didn't miss.

"Technically, that's correct, but I have no intention of forcing Eden and her family off their land."

"But that's not your call to make; it's mine, is it not?"

Charles could see Clay's mind working to formulate all the possible ways he could gain his retribution against Eden and was determined to put a stop to it. "You know perfectly well that I've turned Briarwood over to you." At great expense to my sanity, he added silently, thinking of the tantrum Richard and Lucy had thrown when he'd made the announcement. "But as the new retainer of this estate, I would expect you to conduct yourself as a gentleman of honor. And no gentleman would throw an innocent woman out into the streets."

"I haven't played the role of gentleman for five years," Clay argued, his expression turning smug as he inhaled deeply on his cigar, stretching his long legs out in front of him. Retribution was at hand, and he'd see to it that Eden paid for the hell she'd put him through these past five years.

"I think you're forgetting about that little stipulation in my will."

Clay's voice hardened ever so slightly. "You're

referring, of course, to the clause that states I must marry within a year of your death?"

"If you do, you will retain three-fourths ownership of Briarwood; if not, Richard will claim an equal share. Your brother and sister-in-law are sorely vexed with me for turning Briarwood over to you. They feel slighted, since they stayed on to manage the plantation in your prolonged absence, and claim a grave injustice has been done them.

"Perhaps there is some validity to their complaints, but as eldest son, Briarwood must pass to you, and to your son."

Clay took a moment to digest his father's words. He should have expected that Richard and Lucy would not take kindly to his acquisition of Briarwood. The prospect of dealing reasonably with Richard was not entirely distasteful to Clay. He was sure they could deal well together as partners. But Lucy . . . the woman was a shrewish harpy. There would be no peace between the brothers if she had her say.

"You've backed me into a corner, Father. It's not a very comfortable position to be in."

"I'm no longer a young man, Clay. My health is failing, which is why Briarwood was turned over to your care. I want to go to my grave knowing that your wanderlust is a thing of the past. That you will remain here at Briarwood for the remainder of your life. Richard has convinced me of his desire to control Briarwood. And he already has a wife."

A bitch of one, Clay thought silently, but aloud he replied, "Why tell me this now?"

"Fate has a way of dealing a strange hand. Perhaps Lawrence's death and mine will be the catalyst to bring you and Eden together again."

Clay's mouth dropped open, then snapped shut, a red flush suffusing his face. "Your faculties have dulled, Father. Perhaps you have forgotten that it was I who was jilted five years ago. That Eden had no desire to wed." He hadn't forgotten and never would.

"Things have changed; circumstances have altered."

Clay shook his head, pushing himself to his feet. "I fear you are overly tired, Father. You're not making any sense."

Charles smiled at his eldest son. The boy was stubborn, always had been. But he'd come around. Damned if he wouldn't see to it that he did.

"When you take the time to consider all the options, you'll see that I make perfect sense. Go—reacquaint yourself with Briarwood. Walk the fields, smell the air, feel the dirt between your fingers. You will find that I'm not as senile as you think."

Charles watched Clay leave the room and stared pensively at the shut door. Was he being foolish to think that Clay and Eden could have a life together? That they could rekindle what they once had? They'd been deeply in love once. A love like theirs could not have died so easily.

He clicked the pipe stem against his teeth. He hadn't imagined their reaction to one another.

There were still embers smoldering deep within their souls. They just needed a little spark to get them going again.

Well, hell, he had enough fuel left in his tired old bones to get an entire forest ablaze, he thought, his hazel eyes sparkling. It shouldn't take too much to ignite two stubborn young people who belonged together.

It was one of the few things that he and Lawrence had agreed upon: Clay and Eden belonged together.

Now the only trick was to get them that way.

Seated at the edge of the river, his back propped up against the thick trunk of an oak, Clay stared into the placid water, tossing the stones he held, one at a time, into the murky depths. A swarm of bees on a branch high above his head hovered about their hive.

He had discarded his coat and waistcoat; they lay neglected at his feet. His shirt sleeves were rolled up, and the blond hairs on his tanned forearms glittered in the sunlight as he pondered the recent conversation he'd had with his father. Recalling the old man's words, *". . . You and Eden together again,"* he frowned deeply.

Had his father lost his faculties? Had Charles Braxton's illness rendered him feebleminded?

It was preposterous to think that he and Eden would eventually marry. Too much had happened, too many bitter feelings had formed. And besides, Eden had made her feelings on marriage perfectly clear that day in the barn, five years ago. He closed his eyes as the painful memory resurfaced.

They had just returned from their morning ride, a daily ritual for them. He had been eager to get back to the privacy of the barn, to crawl up into their special hiding place in the loft to share a few kisses and caresses, as they'd done so many times before. But Eden had been sullen, almost withdrawn, that morning. When he'd attempted to kiss her, she'd pulled back, pushing out of his embrace. It was then she'd told him she was breaking off their engagement.

"I can't marry you, Clay. I'm just not ready to make a lifelong commitment to you."

If she had hit him over the head with a pitchfork, Clay couldn't have been more stunned. It was the last thing he'd expected Eden to say, and his response reflected his surprise. "Not marry me! But why? You know I love you; I thought you loved me."

"I do," she vowed. "Never doubt it. But . . . but I'm not sure that marriage is the right thing for me."

"Not right? What are you saying? All women must marry. It is the natural order of things."

She took a deep breath, then said, "I'm not ready to give up my freedom."

"You act as if you'll be treated no better than a slave. I love you, Eden. As my wife you'll be treated well—put on a pedestal—catered to."

"I don't want to be put on a pedestal, Clay. I want to be free and independent. To do what I want, when I want. A wife is nothing more than her husband's possession—a piece of chattel."

A piece of chattel. The words still burned in his head, in his heart. Had she thought so little of him, loved him so little, that she'd feared marriage to him?

Five years, and still the hurt of her betrayal lingered. He had thought many times of gaining his revenge, of hurting her as she had hurt him.

The opportunity was at hand, but his father's edict prevented him from acting.

Or did it?

Marriage, the old man had said. *Marriage*—the one thing Eden feared, even abhorred. Clay smiled. Marriage could definitely be a suitable revenge. And he needed to marry to satisfy the stipulation in his father's will to retain complete control of Briarwood.

Eden was at his mercy now. He held all the cards, not to mention the note to her precious plantation. He knew Eden well enough to know that she would never do anything to jeopardize Beauclaire. Her alternatives were few. Her visit to Briarwood had proven that. Fairchilds didn't beg. They were too proud, and Eden possessed the largest dose of pride of any woman he'd ever met.

And he'd met quite a few, but they weren't all ladies. His smiled deepened at the thought. There were some lovely *señoritas* back in Texas who had warmed his bed and his blood quite nicely. He felt an unwelcome stiffening between his legs.

Damn! But it had been a long time since he'd

had a woman. And Eden's visit this morning only reminded him of that fact. Images of Eden's lush breasts, soft lips, milky white thighs resurrected from his memory. And they were painful recollections. Not only to his heart, but to other parts of his anatomy—parts that cried out for some womanly attention.

Damn! He pulled off his boots, then started to unbutton his pants. The river looked cold, but it was just the cure for what ailed him at the moment.

He wasn't one to frequent the slave quarters; no one at Briarwood ever had, to the best of his knowledge. And Eden's soft, supple body wasn't available to him . . . at least, not yet. The thought of her made his pulse race.

"Damn!" he cursed, aloud this time, pushing himself to his feet, stepping gingerly into the water, his toes turning numb.

That woman had caused him nothing but grief for the past five years. Maybe, just maybe, it was time to pay Miss Eden Fairchild back.

Four

Using her fingers like a hoe, Eden scraped at the dirt surrounding the small heads of lettuce, trying to dislodge the stubborn weeds that grew around and between the neat rows of vegetables.

She'd come out to the garden at first light to perform the first of many arduous tasks she'd set for herself that day. For in work there was solace, and the opportunity to avoid thinking about Clay and the present set of circumstances she found herself in.

Clay. The memories of him had seared a path to her soul, leaving indelible impressions: her sixteenth birthday when he'd given her her first, real grown-up kiss; the caresses they'd shared in the loft of her father's barn; the glorious plans they'd made for the building of their new home. She'd thought marriage to Clay would be the answer to her dream. But as her wedding day approached, fears of losing her identity had magnified, the memories of her mother's unhappiness had plagued her, until she decided her only means of avoiding the same fate was to cancel her plans to wed.

Tears obscured her vision, but she brushed them away with the back of her hand, and along with them, the bittersweet memories.

Clay's return had already caused her a great deal of anguish and heartache. She'd thought of little else since arriving home from the Braxtons' yesterday. She had only to close her eyes to conjure up his handsome face—the anger in his cold green eyes, the hardness in his voice.

She was doomed; they all were. For Clay would never find it in his heart—the heart she had stomped on—to allow her an extension on the loan.

Yanking on a particularly stubborn root, she tossed it aside, wishing she could eliminate Clay's bitterness toward her as easily.

"You want I should cut more of de lettuce, Miz Eden?"

Eden looked up, startled to find Belle standing just behind her left shoulder. She'd been so alone in her thoughts, she'd hadn't realized the young slave woman had come out to the garden to assist her.

"Just cut one or two more, Belle. I'd rather pick it fresh tomorrow than have it wilt in the root cellar." Eden turned to stare Belle full in the face, and when she did, her eyes widened in alarm at the sight of the purplish bruises on the black woman's face. Belle's left eye was swollen shut, and there was a nasty cut on her upper lip.

"Lord have mercy! What happened, Belle?"

Eden pushed herself to her feet, coming to stand in front of her. "Who has treated you in such a vile manner? Was it Sam?"

Belle stared down at the bare toes she scraped self-consciously through the dirt, unwilling to let her mistress see the fear in her eyes. "I fell, Miz Eden. No one done touched me."

Tilting up Belle's chin with the tip of her index finger, Eden examined the bruises more closely, her eyes darkening with compassion and anger when the young girl winced in pain. Eden knew Belle was lying, most likely to protect Sam, whom she was to wed in a month's time.

Slave marriages, rare in the South, had been permitted at Beauclaire, especially when the parties involved were as much in love as Belle and Sam seemed to be. Had she been wrong to agree to the union?

"You've been beaten, and don't try to tell me differently. If Sam has done this to you, then he must be punished." Belle's Sam was a big man, well over six feet tall, with a barrel chest and arms the size of tree trunks. He put his size to good use as Beauclaire's blacksmith. Had he also used it to mistreat Belle?

Belle shook her head, her eyes filling with tears. "It weren't my Sam, Miz Eden. Sam would never hurt me. Dat man loves me sumpin' powerful."

Eden wasn't entirely convinced and her eyes glared bright with suspicion. "Then who?"

Plucking nervously at the folds of her soiled apron, Belle insisted, "I tell you, I fell. Please leave it go, Miz Eden. I'm just a little sore, but I'll be all right."

It was then Eden noticed the red welts on the woman's forearms, the deep rope burns on her wrists. She gasped, revulsion rushing through her at the sight. Had Belle been tied up before being beaten? What monster had done such a horrible thing? Surely no one at Beauclaire, for all who worked here knew Eden would never countenance corporal punishment, for any reason.

Noting the panic in the young girl's eyes, Eden didn't press her further, but vowed silently to find out just who had perpetrated such a heinous act. If it was Sam, she would break her own rule and have him flogged; no one, black or white, could be allowed to get away with what had been done to Belle.

"I want you to go into the kitchen and have Sukie tend to your injuries. And if this happens again, you're to come tell me, you hear? I won't have any of my people mistreated."

Belle nodded, then walked off toward the kitchen to let Sukie tend the wounds that were visible, though no one could treat the hurt inside, she thought bitterly.

Was Miss Eden so blind that she couldn't see what was going on right under her nose? What had been going on since the devil's own spawn, Master Wakefield, had come to work the slaves at Beauclaire?

Belle wiped at the tears running down her cheeks as she thought of the shame the overseer had heaped upon her time and time again.

"Spread your legs, you black bitch. Let me show you what a real man fucks like," he'd taunted, pushing her down on the bed, driving into her over and over.

Belle had tried to protest, had begged for mercy, telling him of her impending marriage to Sam, but Master Wakefield had only laughed.

"That black buck's dick can't compare with mine, can it, Belle? Tell me, Belle. Tell me how much you want it inside of you."

When she'd refused, he'd whipped her. But first he had bound her spreadeagled on his bed, tying her wrists and ankles to the brass head and footboards.

"You're a comely wench, for a nigger, Belle," he said, pinching her nipples hard with his fingers. "You like it rough, don't you? All niggers like it rough." He slapped her then, driving into her soft core, driving and slapping until she thought she would faint from the pain.

But she wouldn't cry; she wouldn't scream. She wouldn't give the white bastard the pleasure of knowing how he'd hurt her. For if he'd known, he'd have been all the more brutal.

When he'd finally gained his pleasure, he had cried out in ecstasy. But it hadn't been her name on his lips, and her blood had run cold.

"You're sweet. You're so goddamn sweet, Eden."

And Belle's heart had filled with fear for her kind mistress.

The young missus had unlocked the gates of hell—had allowed the devil to enter her home—

and she had no idea that she would be the one consumed by the fires of Satan.

The long mahogany table, covered by a white damask cloth and set with Eulalie Braxton's heirloom rose Canton china and Waterford crystal, stood in readiness for the evening meal. Around it, Clay, Richard, and Lucy waited to begin the first course of peanut soup until the elder Braxton arrived.

Outside, the whirr of locusts, the insistent chirping of crickets, could be heard through the open window, but inside there was only silence.

Clay sipped thoughtfully on his wine, unaware of the animosity cast in his direction by his brother and sister-in-law. He was apprised of it moments later, when Richard, bolstered by several glasses of Bordeaux and a few swift kicks in the shin from his wife, shifted nervously in his seat, cleared his throat, and said in a voice filled with bitterness, "You always manage to come out on top, don't you, Clay?"

Clay's glance shifted from the hurt in his brother's eyes to the animosity in his sister-in-law's. Snood-shrouded brown hair framed Lucy Braxton's heart-shaped face, and the wax tapers in the brass chandelier overhead glowed softly, illuminating the displeasure there.

Sighing inwardly, Clay wished for the moment that he was back in the midst of the war with Mexico, rather than facing the petty jealousies and rivalries that confronted him now. Being shot at seemed the lesser of the two evils.

"Richard deserves to inherit all of Briarwood," Lucy drawled, in a whiny voice that was all too familiar to Clay. "He's the one who stayed behind to manage things, care for your father, while you were off licking your wounded pride."

Her barb hit, and Clay stiffened for an instant.

"Lucy, that's enough!" Richard snapped, casting his wife a quelling look, though he knew he would pay for it later. He had no desire to pick a fight with a man who outweighed him by fifty pounds, and whose years of outdoor living had rendered him whipcord-lean and tough as horse leather.

Clay held up his hand in a conciliatory gesture. "Let her speak, Richard. She's got five years of animosity to get out of her system. Obviously her spleen is in need of venting." He inclined his head toward the spiteful woman as if to say, "please continue," before taking a sip of his wine.

"You really can't blame us for being upset, Clay. No one expected Father to make the announcement that he did, and no one expected you to heed his demand that you return home."

Clay stared at his brother, who, at thirty, was two years his junior. Richard's resemblance to his father was striking. He had Charles's hazel eyes and possessed the same even temperament. That is, when he wasn't influenced by his shrewish wife.

Gulping down the rest of his wine, Clay tried to explain his position. "There are certain benefits and obligations to being the firstborn son. I have inherited both, thus I was forced to return and assume my rightful position as owner of this plantation. I did not influence Father's decision, nor could I possibly refuse his request to return. I had hoped that we could deal amicably with one another over this recent turn of events and work together to keep Briarwood running smoothly."

Lucy pushed back her chair and stood so abruptly, the crystal goblets threatened to overturn. "Well, I declare! Of all the unmitigated gall. You sashay in here, pretty as you please, after being gone for five years, and expect us to grin and bear it. I think not, Brother dear. I, for one, do not intend to welcome you with open arms." The small brown eyes glared intently at Clay before the short woman threw down her napkin and exited the room in a flurry of taffeta, lace, and indignation.

Richard stared openmouthed after his wife, a warm flush covering his cheeks. He noted the pity in Clay's eyes, and his flush deepened as he pushed back his chair. "I apologize for my wife's rudeness. I'd best see to her. Lucy's unbearable when she's in a high temper."

Clay shook his head as he stared at Richard's retreating back. High temper, indeed! The woman was in a terminal state of bitchiness. What did his brother see in that thin stick-of-a-woman, anyway? Lucy was far from pretty. Her nose was hawkish, her lips always pursed in displeasure. He couldn't imagine what she'd be like in bed and shuddered at the thought.

Marriage to the wrong woman could definitely be hell. But marriage to the right one . . . Well, there certainly could be some advantages.

"I hope that red flush on your face is caused by that wine and not by the loud commotion I've just heard."

Clay looked up to find his father being wheeled into the room by Rufus. He smiled ruefully. "So you heard?"

"A man would have to be deaf not to," Charles returned, unfolding his napkin and placing it on his lap.

"Lucy is unhappy with me at the moment." Clay refilled his glass with more wine, pouring his father some. "She'll get over her pique, once Richard gets done smoothing down her feathers."

The old man's eyes filled with sadness. "I've no doubt they're more put out with me than with you, Clay. I'm the one who made the decision to have you return."

Clay reached out, patting the older man's hand. His father had aged in his absence. There was a permanent stoop to his shoulders, and his face was well mapped with lines of fatigue. His hands, which were once strong and held the reins of the plantation so securely, were spotted and gnarled with age and infirmity.

"I'm glad you did, though I didn't appreciate it at the time I received your letter." At least it had come, Clay thought. The one informing him of his mother's death had not caught up with him until weeks after her funeral. It was still difficult to believe she was gone.

Charles's right eyebrow shot up, and his voice filled with childish pleasure. "You're glad to be home?"

Clay's attention returned. "It's where I belong. I'm no rough-and-tumble Texan, though I enjoyed the hell out of myself while I was there. I did a lot of growing up, and now find that I'm ready to settle down and face my responsibilities."

The elder Braxton beamed. "Would this have anything to do with the lovely Eden?"

"Perhaps. Marriage to Eden would satisfy many things." Including the bulge in his pants, he added silently. Not to mention his desire to get even.

"You still love her?" his father probed.

"Let's just say, there are many feelings I have for Eden that need to be sorted out, and leave it at that."

"You could do much worse. Eden is a beautiful woman. And Beauclaire would make a handsome addition to your holdings."

"I've already thought of the practical aspects of such a union." And the fact that Eden would never willingly part with her beloved Beauclaire. He'd already figured out a way to get around that little predicament, and he smiled widely at the thought.

"You seem pleased with your decision, Clay. When do you plan to propose?"

"The sooner the better. There's less than a week left for Eden to fulfill her father's obligation. She's already indicated to you that she's unable to do so. I see no reason to prolong her agony. I'll speak with her tomorrow."

"That's very big of you, son, considering all that's passed between you. I'm proud of you."

Clay had the grace to blush, and took another swallow of wine to hide his discomfort. "No sense getting your hopes up. Eden is a stubborn woman. She's refused me in the past. There's no guarantee that she'll be receptive to my proposition."

"I have no doubt you'll convince her. You can be quite persuasive when you need to be."

Clay's smile never reached his eyes. "Yes. I intend to be just that."

"How could you just sit there and let Clay lord it all over you?" Lucy berated when Richard walked into the room. She quit pacing and threw herself into the Windsor chair. The oil lamp on the dresser revealed high color in her usually pasty white cheeks and a puckerish purse to her lips. "Really, Richard, sometimes I wonder what kind of man you are!"

Untying his stock, Richard threw it on the table next to where his wife sat, stifling the urge to strangle her with it. Lucy's bad temper was nothing new, and neither was their present discussion. It had been her favorite topic of conversation since the day she'd learned Clay was coming home.

"Clay is my brother. What would you have me do? Challenge him to a duel?"

"At least there is honor in that."

He gave her a sidelong glance of utter disbelief before replying, "I fear you are becoming hysterical, madam. Perhaps a dose of laudanum would be in order." Ripping forcefully at the onyx studs that held his shirt closed, he watched them scatter over the hardwood floor, then directed his attention back at his wife, who was staring at him with something close to astonishment on her face.

He didn't lose his temper often, but Lucy had pushed him to the brink of his patience this time. She could be such a shrew when she set her mind to it. But she could also be wanton in bed, on those rare occasions when she let him touch her. He felt himself growing harder by the minute.

Richard stepped toward her, holding out his hand. "Come, let me soothe your frayed nerves with kisses," he said, pulling her up and into his arms. "I don't wish to discuss my brother or my father's edict at the moment; rather, we could occupy our time much more pleasantly." He attempted to kiss her, but she pushed him away.

"You think to pet and paw me like a rutting dog in heat. Well, I won't let you touch me, Richard. I'm much too upset *at the moment,*" she parroted, her smile venomous.

Dropping his arms, Richard rubbed his neck in agitation and frustration. A headache was beginning to grow—one of many he'd had over the last six years, since he'd married eighteen-year-old Lucy Ambrose, only daughter of Percy Ambrose, his father's solicitor. It had been a marriage conceived in heaven and born in hell.

"Perhaps if you had let me touch you a little more often," he complained, "you'd have had the grandchild my father always wanted. Then he might have been more inclined to turn Briarwood over to me."

Richard smiled inwardly, noting the calculating gleam flaring in his wife's eyes. Lucy wasn't the only one who was greedy, but his greed derived from a much baser instinct.

"What makes you think that would work?" she asked.

Turning her around, he unfastened the hooks on the back of her gown as he spoke. "You know how much the old man wants a grandchild. He's asked you often enough over the years if you are yet with child."

"That's true enough." It had been a sore subject between her and Charles, one she'd tried assiduously to avoid. She had no desire to risk her life and ruin her figure bearing Richard's brats.

Pushing the gown down about her waist, he untied the strings of her corset, brushing her neck with soft, feathery kisses. "You need no device to enhance your figure, my sweet . . . you are perfection." He pulled off her silk chemise to reveal pert breasts, small but well formed.

Lucy preened under his flattery, throwing her arms about his neck, pressing her bosom into his chest. Excitement lit her eyes, but it wasn't of a sexual nature. "You truly think a grandchild would appease your father enough to allow him to reconsider his decision?"

Cupping her breasts, he rubbed the swollen

nubs until they hardened with desire. "We must produce an heir, my sweet. Only then will we have the means to obtain Briarwood."

Lucy's brown eyes glazed with the passion of her quest as Richard led her to the bed, pushing her back onto it. "But Richard, how long will it take to conceive this child? You know I am not overjoyed when it comes to matters of the flesh."

"These things take time, my sweet," he said, his voice thickening with hunger as he pulled off the remainder of her clothes, then quickly discarded his own. Positioning himself over her, he separated her legs to accommodate the implement of his desire.

"We must work at it day and night, my sweet. We must endeavor to plant my seed deep inside you, or else Clay could end up with our plantation. We wouldn't want that to happen, now, would we?" At the shake of her head, he plunged inside her, smiling in fulfillment at her look of surprise and then satisfaction.

It had taken him six long years to unlock the secret to his wife's sexual ardor. Now that he'd found it, there was a lot of time to make up for. Silently he thanked Clay for his good fortune.

Five

Eden rose early the next morning, as was her custom. The sky was a pinkish, predawn gray, but though the sun had yet to make its appearance, she wasn't foolish enough to think it wouldn't be hot as Hades later in the day.

May was melting into June with a vengeance of sizzling temperatures and rising humidity. She dressed in a lightweight lavender, sprigged-muslin day gown, over which she wore a starched white apron. The promise of warm weather seemed as good an excuse as any to forgo the traditional black of mourning; and besides, she was getting darn tired of looking like a crow.

Eden didn't stop to question whether her sudden interest in her appearance had anything to do with the fact that Clay Braxton was back at Briarwood.

After a hearty breakfast of bacon, ham, hotcakes, and fried eggs, she discussed this evening's menu with Sukie, wandered about the house to make certain it had been put to rights by Aunt

Ruby and Jewel, and was now on her way out to the smokehouse.

Once a month, a full inventory was made to determine what supplies were on hand and what items needed to be purchased or bartered for through their tobacco factor over in England. Then an order was placed which was filled in exchange for a predetermined number of hands of tobacco.

Only those items that couldn't be produced on the plantation, or bought in Tappahannock, like the exquisite cherry tester bed her father had acquired for her birthday two years before, or the literary works of Charlotte Brontë and Sir Walter Scott, were purchased.

Taking the key from the chatelaine about her waist, Eden unlocked the door to the smokehouse. The smell of smoke and hickory immediately assaulted her senses as she stepped into the dark, dank building. Hams and shoulders, curing on large hooks, hung from beams overhead, as did slabs of bacon. Several of the ham shoulders and bacon flanks were housed in barrels of brine to be corned.

Withdrawing a scrap of paper and a pencil from her pocket, she made note of their numbers, then moved into the adjacent storeroom where the majority of the supplies were kept.

Barrels of flour stood against the far wall. She counted out six loaves of sugar and made a notation to order more. Cases of wine and brandy, consumed in abundance when her father had been alive, were neatly stacked beneath the shelves that held tins of tea, coffee, and various spices.

Finishing her task, she locked the door and made her way toward the slave quarters to perform her daily rounds.

The slave cabins stood off the ground in two neat rows on either side of a wide lane. Each boasted two rooms, a fireplace, wood floors, and several windows. The cabins were scrubbed and whitewashed four times a year to prevent disease and to enhance their appearance, which instilled a measure of pride in the slaves, as did the wearing of new clothing twice a year. Each family tended its own garden to supplement the weekly rations of pork, cornmeal, and molasses with fresh fruits and vegetables.

It was Eden's responsibility, as it had been her mother's before her, to tend to the sick and injured slaves. She had learned from Aunt Agnes, who was very adept at healing, various recipes for potions effective in treating ague, chilblains, night sweats, and a host of other ailments She took her role of healer seriously. The lives of many people rested in her hands.

A short time later, after having administered a large dose of castor oil to Ephraim, who had indulged too freely in the cherry orchard, and applying a poultice to the grooms, Caleb's, infected big toe, Eden, satisfied that everyone else was fit, headed toward the washhouse to supervise the laundering of the clothes.

It was well past noon when the mistress of

Beauclaire trudged wearily back to the main house to change her clothes for dinner.

Clay sat in one of the white wicker rockers that graced the front porch, waiting for her, sipping slowly on a glass of lemonade which the slave girl Jewel had provided. His eyes followed Eden's approach and remained riveted as she climbed slowly up the wide front steps.

She was achingly lovely, he thought, watching as she removed her apron, then arched from the waist to rub at the small of her back; her large, firm breasts thrust out provocatively, until his fingers fairly itched with want to touch them.

He shifted uncomfortably in his chair, trying to remember what had brought him to Beauclaire in the first place. But it was damned hard. Eden had definitely matured in the five years he'd been gone.

As she bent over to retrieve a slip of paper that had fallen out of her pocket, her breasts came dangerously close to falling out of their confinement, and Clay nearly choked on his lemonade, alerting her to his presence.

Eden glanced up to find Clay's eyes trained on her bosom. She blushed furiously, and her hand immediately flew up to cover herself as she straightened. "Clay, what on earth are you doing here?" she asked, climbing the remaining steps of the porch.

He rose when she approached, arching a dark eyebrow. "Aren't I welcome, Eden?"

Her color deepened, and she stammered, "Of . . . of course. How . . . how rude you must think me. I shall go in and change out of this soiled gown; I shan't be a moment."

He smiled suggestively, gazing at the low décolletage. "Why change, when this gown is so utterly charming on you?"

She chafed under his scrutiny, cursing herself inwardly for having worn the coolest, but oldest, gown in her wardrobe, which was a good deal too small in the bodice and necessitated the wearing of an apron. Of course, she hadn't expected to be entertaining guests this afternoon. And certainly not Clay Braxton!

"Very well," she finally conceded, taking a seat in the other wicker rocker, folding her hands demurely on her lap. She wouldn't give Clay the satisfaction of knowing how humiliated she was to have been found looking like something one of Agnes's cats had dragged in from the fields, with most of her bosom on public display.

Clay resumed his seat, pouring a second glass of lemonade and handing it to her.

Condensation had formed on the bottom of the glass, and as Eden took a swallow of the liquid, several droplets of moisture dribbled down. Clay's eyes followed the liquid as it slid down Eden's chest, onto her left breast, and disappeared somewhere into the deep crevice.

"Was there something you needed to speak to me about?"

An unwelcome warmth crept up Clay's neck, and he felt as naughty as a boy of thirteen when he'd been caught sipping whiskey behind his father's barn. He forced his eyes up to her face.

"Actually, there was. Perhaps we should go into your office where we could concen . . . speak more privately."

Eden's heart sank. Clay had come to discuss the money she owed. The moment she had dreaded was upon her. Taking a deep breath, she forced a small smile to her lips. "Of course."

Aunt Ruby opened the door as they approached and smiled widely at Clay. Her white teeth, like the ivory keys of the pianoforte, contrasted brightly with the black of her skin.

"It sure does my heart good to see you again, Master Clay. I done missed your handsome face." She pinched his cheek and was rewarded with a kiss, causing her to chuckle. "Mercy me, Master Clay, you gots the devil's own charm."

Clay laughed, and Eden frowned deeply before saying, "We'll be in the study, Aunt Ruby, and we don't wish to be disturbed."

A look of uncertainty passed over the old woman's face. "Now, Miss Eden, you know it ain't fittin' for no single lady to be closed up in a room with no single gentleman. Of course, seeing as how it's Master Clay, I guess it'll be all right. You just leave the door open, you heah?"

Heaving a sigh, Eden motioned for Clay, who was grinning at her like a hyena, to follow her into her father's office, then slammed the door as loudly as she could, hoping Aunt Ruby had heard it. *It would serve the traitorous old woman right!*

Clay chuckled at Eden's display of temper. "Aunt Ruby's only trying to protect your chastity."

"I can protect my own chastity, thank you very much!"

Her comment brought a frown to his lips. "I'm well aware of that fact, Eden."

She blushed all the way down to the tips of her toes before asking, "What is it you wish to speak to me about?" She leaned back against the desk, bracing herself with her hands.

"Father and I had a very interesting discussion after you left yesterday, Eden. I was quite surprised, actually stunned would be a better word, to learn that you are now in debt."

"I'm well aware that I owe your father a substantial sum of money."

"Actually, you owe *me* a substantial amount of money. Briarwood has been turned over to me, as has its debts, one of which is yours."

Eden straightened, embarrassment coloring her words when she replied, "I'm sure your father also told you that I am unable to fulfill the agreement that my father made with yours. I do not have twenty thousand dollars, nor do I anticipate having it by the first of June."

Her eyes followed his hands as he picked up the silverplated letter opener off the desk and began toying with it, as he was toying with her. She remembered the strength in his hands, the gentleness of his touch, remembered holding his hand when they walked through fields of clover and new-mown hay, remembered his fingers, so gentle, as they caressed her cheek. A lump caught in her throat but quickly dissolved when his next words jolted her out of the joyful past back into the painful present.

"It would be a pity if you were to lose Beauclaire."

Her face whitened. "Surely you don't mean to foreclose on my plantation!"

"You owe a debt of honor, Eden—one that I assume you are more than willing to satisfy."

She grew instantly wary. "Of course, I'm willing to satisfy the debt; but as I told you, I'm not in a position to do so just now."

"Ah, but that's where you're wrong, angel eyes." She flinched at the endearment, but he continued as if he hadn't noticed. "I think you're in a very excellent position to fulfill your father's debt."

"I don't understand."

"It's quite simple, really. My father has placed a stipulation in his will that I must marry within one year of his death or divide Briarwood equally with Richard, something I'm not willing to do. As you know, Father's health is failing, and he is quite eager to see that stipulation satisfied."

She wiped her sweating palms on the skirt of her gown. "But what does that have to do with me?"

"Five years ago, you robbed me of the chance to satisfy that stipulation. I think it's time you made amends."

Intense astonishment touched her pale face. Absently she shook her head, not believing what she was hearing. "You want to marry me?"

"More precisely, I want you to marry me. If you

do, I will tear up the note that is owed on this property."

Eden felt her knees go weak, and she plopped herself down into the green-tufted leather wing chair by the hearth. Why was she suddenly inundated with marriage proposals? The one thing she had sought to avoid was being thrust at her from every direction. Fighting for composure, she tried to explain in a voice as calm as she could muster, "I have no wish to marry."

His lips flattened. "Yes, I know. But you really have no choice. Either you marry me, or I will foreclose on this property and take Beauclaire from you."

Like a cocked rifle ready to explode, she sprang from the chair to stand before him. "That's despicable! Never in a million years would I have believed you capable of sinking so low."

Was this hard, bitter individual standing before her the same man she had given her heart to so many years ago? She knew she deserved Clay's contempt, even his dislike, but she never thought he would hate her, not after everything they had shared. Tears burned behind her eyes, but she blinked them back, refusing to let him see how deeply he had hurt her.

"Despicable is a rather harsh word, don't you think? I prefer to think of this as a business arrangement."

"But why would you want to marry me after everything that has happened? Surely you don't still love me."

"Love?" He laughed and the sound went into

Eden's heart like another one of those damned bullets. "Love is for fools and poets, angel. I'm a practical man; you have something I want."

She stiffened, her hands clenching into fists. "You're referring to my body, of course." Her eyes narrowed at the smug smile on his lips. "I saw the way you looked at me before, with desire in your eyes."

He stepped toward her and reached out his hand, running his finger down her neck, until it rested at the top of her breast. He could feel her heart pounding beneath his hand, and it pleased him to know that his touch still excited her.

"I'm a man and you're a beautiful woman." He traced his finger over the fullness of her breast, drawing it dangerously close to her nipple. At her sharp intake of breath, he withdrew.

Eden's nipples, hard and pulsing, pushed painfully against the fabric of her gown. She turned to avoid Clay's knowing smile. Damn Clay to hell! He still had the power to arouse her, to turn her insides to mush. She sucked in her breath, strengthening her resolve. Well, it wouldn't work. She wouldn't give in to seductive smiles and practiced charms.

Marriage was man's way of subjugating woman. She had seen it done to her mother and had no desire to live under any man's thumb, especially Clay's. And she was just about to tell him so when he said, "Though your body is quite lovely, Eden, quite developed," he leered at the swell of her breasts, then smiled at her outrage, "it is not what motivates this proposition."

"I don't believe you. Men are always motivated by lust." It had been the downfall of Adam, of her very own father!

Clay shrugged. "Believe what you will. I've had any number of women over the years. What you have between your legs is nothing special," he paused at her gasp, "though I admit, there was a time when I could think of little else except planting my flesh deep within the velvety confines of your . . ."

"Stop!" The blood rushing through her veins was making her light-headed; fearful she would faint on the spot, she took a deep breath. "This is utterly outrageous. Your conduct is ungentlemanly, not to mention downright vile. I am appalled that you would speak to me as if I were nothing more than a strumpet. If I were a man, I would demand satisfaction."

Looking into her eyes, he tipped up her chin. His voice was as smooth and hot as maple syrup. "You should always demand satisfaction, angel eyes. I certainly do."

The flame in her cheeks intensified at the implication of his words, and she jerked her head away. "I think you had better leave."

"I think not," he countered, falling into the other wing chair. "We haven't finished our discussion."

"*Oooh!*" was all she said, before throwing herself back down into the chair. The leather cushion made a swooshing sound as she landed.

"What I'm proposing is merely a business arrangement—a marriage in name only. There is no need to consummate it. I have other avenues of fulfillment open to me."

"Whores, you mean!"

He smiled. "Whores, and ladies whose legs are not drawn as tightly closed as yours seem to be. What are you saving yourself for, anyway? If you're not careful, you'll end up a dried-up old prune like that aunt of yours."

Eden was so outraged she could barely speak. When she finally did find her voice, it was as sharp, her words as pointed, as a double-edged sword. "You leave Aunt Agnes out of this, you . . . you bastard!"

He laughed aloud at that. "I'd completely forgotten how diverting you can be on occasion, Eden. Life with you would never be dull, that's for certain."

"Well, you'll never have the opportunity to find out, Clay Braxton. I refused your hand in marriage five years ago, and I do so again now. I will not marry you. I will not sell myself like some poor piece of white trash. I have my pride, even if you do not."

The vein in Clay's neck throbbed ominously, but he fought to keep his temper under control. Eden would not get the best of him this time. He would conquer the willful little piece of baggage, no matter what it took.

"Your pride could very well be your ruination, Eden. Will you let it stand in the way of saving your plantation, of keeping your family intact, of preventing the sale of all those slaves who look to you for care and comfort?" He pushed himself to his feet and gazed down at her, saw the tears in her eyes, but still did not relent.

"You have always been a stubborn, headstrong minx. I believe it's what kept you from marrying me in the first place. You wanted your freedom; you've had it. And what has it gotten you? What will you do when you're free and independent and living on the streets, like the poor white trash you revile?"

"Please." She shook her head, covering her ears.

"I will go, but know this—you have seventy-two hours to change your mind and agree to this marriage. It's more time than you gave me when you left me standing at the altar on the eve of our wedding."

Her head shot up, the light of understanding bright in her eyes. "It's revenge, isn't it? You're doing this for revenge. All because of what I did to you five years ago."

Walking to the door, he opened it, then paused, looking back at her. "Seventy-two hours, angel eyes. And not a second more."

He walked out then without a backward glance, as surely and stubbornly as she had walked out on him five years before, and it sent a cold shiver of fear careening down her spine.

Six

"I won't do it! He can't make me do it!"

Eden's vows were punctuated by a loud boom of thunder that rattled the windows of her bedroom and sent her flying out of the rocker and scurrying into her bed. She burrowed under the green-quilted counterpane, pulling it up and over her head. Another boom sounded, and then another, followed by the sound of raindrops pelting the glass.

She hated thunderstorms! She hated Clay! She hated everything about her life at the moment!

A few minutes later the noise abated, and she peered out from the covers into the lamplit room, breathing a sigh of relief. Beyond the multipaned windows, the rain still fell in torrents, but mercifully, the thunder had ceased.

Coward! she told herself, pushing back the counterpane before propping herself against the headboard. How can you fight Clay, when you can't even conquer a childhood fear of thunder? she thought.

A quiet conscience sleeps in thunder, but rest and guilt live far asunder.

"Damn Agnes's trite phrases!" she muttered under her breath, hating how close it was to the mark.

Gazing up at the ormolu clock on the mantel to find that it was nearly one in the morning, Eden groaned aloud. No wonder she felt so awful. She'd been sitting in the rocker by the hearth, reading Charlotte Brontë's *Shirley,* and had dozed off. She'd been dreaming—about Clay and his imperious demands—when the thunderstorm started. It was more a nightmare than a dream, she realized, fidgeting with the folds of her white lawn night rail.

What on earth was she going to do? Since their awful confrontation this afternoon, she had tried to think of a way to solve her dilemma, but had found no suitable solution. She couldn't marry Clay knowing what she knew about his thirst for vengeance. Why, she'd be nothing more than his white slave—his chattel. She'd have no control over Beauclaire, no say in anything he did. Clay would rule absolutely over her, as her father had ruled over her mother.

Thinking of the frail, unhappy woman brought to mind the journal. Leaning over the side of the bed toward the nightstand, Eden reached into the drawer, retrieving the leather volume.

Perhaps she would find an answer to her predicament within the pages of her mother's diary. Opening it, she turned to the second journal entry.

May 4th, 1826. The horror of it all. I am filled with revulsion about what transpired within these walls last night. Mr. Fairchild, the brute, as I shall now refer to him, has taken my most precious gift and torn it asunder. The pain, oh, the pain; it is not to be borne. I am reviled. I am shamed by the acts I was forced to endure, all in the name of wifely duty. Surely this is not seemly behavior for a married couple, though "the beast" assures me that it is. Gone are my girlish dreams of romantic bliss. Gone with the unspeakable act of fornication. Save me, Lord, for I am truly doomed.

Staring at the passage, Eden swallowed the lump in her throat, hardly able to comprehend what she'd just read. She felt like a voyeur, peeking into her parent's inner sanctum. Obviously, her mother had never intended for anyone to read her personal thoughts, but here they were in black and white, a tormented tale of a marriage which hadn't lived up to her expectations.

The disillusionment had started much earlier than Eden had believed, hours after their vows had been spoken—on their wedding night.

Reading further, she discovered more entries detailing normal household routine, parties they'd attended, but no other mention of marital trouble.

The gong on the clock chimed the half hour, making Eden realize the lateness of the hour; she needed to get some sleep.

Obviously, there were no answers to be found within her mother's journal. The passage she'd read had only created more insecurity, more apprehension about marriage. She was more determined than ever to avoid the institution, especially to Clay Braxton.

At least she would be spared the *"horror of it all"* her mother had described. Clay had said a business arrangement—a marriage in name only. She wouldn't have to perform any unspeakable acts.

Funny, though, she'd never considered what she and Clay had done all that unspeakable. It had been quite pleasurable, really. They'd never actually consummated their relationship, but they'd come darn close on several occasions. Clay's lips on her mouth and body hadn't been revolting at all. Quite the contrary! She had wished, more times than not, that his control had been slightly less than resolute.

Experiencing a strange tingling sensation between her legs, a tautness in her nipples, Eden grew instantly annoyed at where her thoughts were taking her. Tossing the book back into the drawer, she turned out the lamp and turned over to go to sleep. But it was several more hours before she accomplished that feat.

"Good heavens, Eden! You look like the last rose of summer that's been left on the bushes to wilt," Agnes declared, eyeing her niece across the dining room table and frowning deeply. "Are you ill? Shall I fetch my medicinal herbs?"

Stifling a wide yawn, Eden shook her head. "No, really, I'm fine, Agnes, just a bit tired."

"That's an understatement. The flesh beneath

your eyes is almost as purple as the orbs themselves. You look as haggard as my Thomasina after she delivered her last litter of kittens."

"Thank you very much!" Eden declared, before taking a sip of the strong black coffee Agnes pushed in front of her, feeling instantly revived.

"Lord have mercy!" Aunt Ruby cried, bustling into the dining room with a silver tray piled high with slices of warm, juicy ham and piping-hot buttermilk biscuits. Setting the food down on the table, she clucked her tongue. "*Mmm, mmm, mmm.* What you been doing to yourself, child?" Placing her hand on Eden's forehead, she sighed in relief. "Well, leastways you ain't got no fever."

"I'm fine, everyone," Eden said, exasperated. "I stayed up too late reading."

Aunt Ruby muttered under her breath about white folks being stupid as sin, reading at night when they could read just as easily in the afternoon, before marching out of the room to fetch the rest of the breakfast dishes.

Agnes leveled a glance at her niece. Eden's wan appearance didn't fool her one little bit. The child was sorely vexed, and it didn't take a genius to figure out why. "I know Clay was here yesterday, Eden, so you might as well tell me everything."

Slathering a biscuit with a dollop of strawberry jam before taking a bite, Eden hesitated to unburden herself. Agnes's only solution to their dilemma was to sell off the slaves; something Eden could not allow.

And she hated the thought of placing more

burdens on her aunt's shoulders, strong though they were. Caring for Papa had been burden enough. The last few months of his life had been trying. He'd been unable to perform even the most rudimentary of personal acts, and Agnes had administered to him without complaint, refusing all offers of assistance, making Eden silently and guiltily thankful.

Gazing up, Eden found her aunt's bright blue eyes still trained on her and sighed. "Clay holds the note to Beauclaire. He's proposed an arrangement of sorts."

Agnes's eyebrows nearly rose to her hairline. "Nothing improper, I hope. Shoo, shoo, you naughty cat," Agnes said to the calico who had climbed on top of the table. "If Aunt Ruby sees you, she'll skin you alive, Desdemona." Seemingly unimpressed with the threat, Desdemona curled up into a ball and went to sleep.

Agnes's preoccupation with her cats was nothing new to Eden, and therefore did not require comment. What did was the *improper* aspect of Agnes's question regarding Clay.

"If you consider marriage improper," which Eden thought was highly possible, considering Agnes's feminist views, "then I guess it is."

"Marriage! Lord have mercy!"

"Well, I have no doubt the good Lord will be merciful, but Clay . . ." Eden shook her head. "He's out for revenge."

"Are you so sure about that? After all, you were engaged to be married once. Perhaps Clay still harbors a deep affection for you. *'Men and melons are hard to know.'* "

Eden felt her cheeks warm as she recalled their recent conversation about love. "Trust me, Clay doesn't harbor any such thing. What he harbors is a grudge. He holds the note to Beauclaire, he needs a wife to satisfy some stupid stipulation in his father's will . . ."

"Charles Braxton was ever the fool. *'Half wits talk much but say little.'* Why, I often wondered how Eulalie could even stand the man." Agnes shook her head. "His spine's so stiff it's a wonder he can sit down."

"Clay wants to marry me for revenge," Eden finished, ignoring her aunt's outburst.

Stirring a teaspoonful of honey into her tea, Agnes was thoughtful for a moment. "Does he desire an heir? Is that the reason?"

"Thankfully, no. He's assured me that the marriage would be in name only. The reason has something to do with retaining ownership of Briarwood."

"And if you agree to this marriage?"

"He will tear up the note he holds on Beauclaire."

"But as your husband, he will retain ownership of the plantation anyway. *'Good wives and good plantations are made by good husbands.'* "

Eden sighed at Agnes's use of the familiar adage. "Exactly."

"And I'm assuming your views on marriage have not changed."

"I've no desire to become an extension of my

husband. I want to be my own person, make my own decisions."

"I fear my views have rubbed off on you, Eden."

"Perhaps. But there is also the fact of my mother's unhappy marriage, and the circumstances surrounding it."

"Your mother wasn't entirely innocent of blame, but we won't talk of that now. Now we must decide what to do about Clay Braxton." Clay was a very handsome man; he and Eden made a splendid-looking couple, Agnes thought, before adding, "You know, Eden, spinsterhood can be a very lonely existence. *'Nothing gives more pain than too much pleasure; nothing more bondage than too much liberty.'* I have you, and therefore, am not alone in my declining years. But who will you have when you're old and gray? It's something you need to consider."

Eden couldn't believe what she was hearing from her independent aunt. Her voice held a note of incredulity when she asked, "You think I should marry Clay?"

"I don't believe you have much choice. You either marry Clay or lose Beauclaire. Remember, *'Pride goeth before the fall.'* "

"But it's blackmail!"

Heaving a sigh full of resignation and regret, she said, "My dear, I would never presume to tell you what to do. You're a woman grown, after all. Since your mother died, I've tried to give guidance, be here for you when you needed me."

"And you have, Agnes. You've been wonderful."

"You might not think me so wonderful when you hear what I have to say."

Eden stiffened in her seat, bracing herself for what was to come. Aunt Agnes never minced words. It was the one quality she loved about the woman, and also the one that she feared the most.

"You shouldn't pattern your life after an old woman like me." At Eden's protest, Agnes raised her hand. "Let me finish. You think I'm noble for not marrying, for living my life without a man. But it hasn't been easy, Eden. I have regrets about the course my life has taken. I would hope to spare you that. I think you should marry Clay Braxton. You were friends once. You can build on that friendship, see where it takes you."

"But he only wants me out of revenge. To pay me back for jilting him five years ago." There was definitely nothing *friendly* about Clay's demeanor toward her, quite the opposite.

"Perhaps. But *'Still waters run deep,'* Eden. There's always more than meets the eye where men are concerned."

Frustrated by her aunt's perversity in quoting maxims to fit every objection, Eden countered with one of her own. " *'Necessity never made a good bargain.'* "

Smiling softly, Agnes replied, " *'The most exquisite folly is made of wisdom spun too fine.'* You would be marrying a man with whom you have a lot in common, Eden. Have you forgotten what brought you and Clay together in the first place?"

"Our love of the land." They had spent countless hours walking over every acre of land, exploring its beauty, finding secret hideaways, like their favorite swimming spot down by the river. They'd had such dreams back then.

"Beauclaire and Briarwood joined together would make an impressive plantation."

"But I wouldn't control it. Clay would make all the decisions. He would put me up on a pedestal, as he threatened to do five years ago, and leave me to collect dust." She looked toward the window, watching dust motes riding into the room on a wave of sunlight.

"Then you must make him see that you're no porcelain doll, but a flesh-and-blood woman. A woman with brains as well as beauty."

"But how?"

Agnes smiled confidently. "My dear, you're a very clever woman. I have no doubt in my mind that you'll have Clay Braxton wrapped around your little finger before the honeymoon is at an end. *'A spoonful of honey will catch more flies than vinegar.'*"

"But he hates me!"

Wiping her lips on her napkin, Agnes folded it carefully, placing it on the table. Pushing her chair back, she rose. "*There's more than one way to skin a cat.'* My apologies, Desdemona," Agnes said to the cat, who was now curled up on the windowsill.

Leaning her elbows on the table in a very unladylike posture, Eden held her head in her hands as she watched her aunt depart the room.

She felt utterly defeated at the moment and wanted to do nothing more than crawl back beneath her covers and go to sleep.

Sighing, she pushed herself out of the chair, eyeing the ham and biscuits longingly, before shaking her head. "Damn Clay Braxton! He's not only ruining my life, he's ruining my breakfast."

"What's that you say, child?" Aunt Ruby asked as she bustled back into the room, carrying more delectable dishes that made Eden's stomach rumble.

Was that sausage gravy she smelled?

She shrugged dejectedly, tasting gall, not gravy, and ordered, "Have Sukie's boy run out to the stable, Aunt Ruby. Have him tell Caleb to saddle Othello for me."

"Where you goin' in such an all-fired hurry, Miss Eden? You ain't had your vittles yet, and you're too skinny, by far, to go off without eatin'."

"Well, you can blame Clay Braxton for my lack of sustenance. I have to ride to Briarwood right away. I have pressing business to discuss with Clay."

"You is goin' to see Master Clay?" A dark eyebrow arched.

"Yes, Master Clay. That blackmailing, blackhearted son of a . . ." She paused at the old woman's gasp. "Clay Braxton will rue the day he decided to force me into marriage, Aunt Ruby. You mark my words."

But as Eden spun on her heel and stormed out of the room, Aunt Ruby couldn't quite contain the smile of satisfaction creasing her leathery face, nor the chuckle emanating from her chest.

"Yes, sir, we is goin' to have us a wedding," she declared. "And it's about time, too!"

Eden rode the short distance from the main house of Briarwood to the large whitewashed barn where Clay was presently engaged. Dismounting, she handed the small black boy, who identified himself as Will, Othello's reins before removing both her riding jacket and hat and tying them securely to the horse's saddle.

"If you'd walk him around a bit, then give him some water, Will, I'd be mighty grateful," she said, noting the boy's eager grin. Will couldn't have been more than nine or ten, but he seemed to know his way around horses. Othello, who was a pretty good judge of human character, had already sized the boy up and snorted his approval.

"Yessum, be glad to. He surely is one fine piece of horseflesh." Will eyed the horse with an appreciative eye.

"If you take real good care of Othello while I'm gone, I just might have some peppermint candy in my saddlebag." At his broad grin, she smiled and asked, "Do you happen to know where Master Clay is? I was told I could find him in the barn."

"He be up in the loft, stacking the hay bales, mistress. And don't worry none; me and this horse is going to get along jes' fine."

Eden entered the dark interior of the barn, inhaling the sweet scent of hay and molasses-covered oats. She was greeted with snorts and whinnies as she passed four of Briarwood's prized stock. The elder Braxton had had a passion for horseracing in days gone by.

Recognizing Clay's buckskin stallion in the far stall brought back long-forgotten memories of all the wild races that she and Clay had participated in. Though Othello was big, standing almost sixteen hands high, Clay's mount Tempest was even bigger and faster. And it was Clay who usually came out ahead. She frowned fiercely. *Like now.*

Climbing the ladder that led to the hayloft, she was grateful for the riding habit she wore. She couldn't have maneuvered as easily in cumbersome petticoats and hoops, and most likely would have fallen on her backside with her skirts billowed up and over her head.

When she reached the top rung, she paused, sucking in her breath at the sight that greeted her. Clay was naked from the waist up. The sunlight streaming in through the small hexagonal window bathed his muscular torso in filtered beams of light. He looked like a golden bronze statue, all sinew and muscle, his biceps thickly knotted, as he heaved the heavy bales into neat stacks. His chest glistened with the sweat of his labors, and droplets clung to the dark patch of curls swirling over his broad chest, then dipping down to a vee before disappearing into the waistband of his tight black breeches.

Eden swallowed, trying to still the rapid beating of her heart. She hadn't seen so much of Clay in a long time, hadn't remembered his body looking quite so . . . so virile, and it took her breath away.

She felt like a Peeping Tom and cleared her throat, waiting until Clay looked up. When he saw who it was, he merely nodded in greeting and kept on working, making Eden feel less important than a bunch of smelly hay.

"Good morning, Clay." She completed her climb until she was standing in close proximity. The loft had an intimate, cloistered feel to it, reminding her of the times they'd spent in her father's barn.

As if Clay could read her mind, he smiled knowingly. "Just like old times, huh, angel eyes?" He set down the bale he held, removing a handkerchief from the waistband of his pants, never taking his eyes off her for a moment, while he wiped at the sweat staining his face and chest.

Eden looked damned appealing in that white cotton blouse she wore, he thought. He knew she wore no corset; she never did. Just a camisole covered those ripe, luscious mounds he remembered so well. The light in his eyes was sensual, challenging, as they raked over her appreciatively.

Like a wary animal caught in the sight of a hunter's gun, Eden stood transfixed, afraid to move a muscle. Clay's reminder of days past made her feel suddenly uncomfortable and terribly vulnerable. She swallowed again, the lump in her throat much larger this time.

"Did you wish to speak to me about something?" he asked.

Remembering why she had come forced all of Eden's anger to the forefront, leaving behind all the unwanted feelings and recollections. "You know darn well why I've come, Clay Braxton."

His smile was wildly erotic. "I thought perhaps you had come to resume one of our former pastimes." Wishful thinking on his part, Clay decided. Eden came to torture him, to leave him in a permanent state of unfilled desire, as she had left him so many times before. Back then, he had thought fulfillment close at hand and had played the role of gentleman. Now, he had no such intention.

Red splotches of color rose instantly to Eden's cheeks. "You are absolutely vile! I have come because you have left me no choice in the matter."

"We all have choices, Eden; sometimes we just make the wrong ones."

She knew he was referring to her decision not to marry him five years ago, but she refused to let him bait her. "Well, no doubt I have made the wrong one this time, but I have come to the decision that I will marry you, provided you agree to a small concession."

He put his hand over his heart. "My dear, I am overcome by your affectionate proposal. Just what is this concession you're referring to?"

Her lips thinned. "You know very well that this marriage was not my idea, Clay. You are the one who did the proposing. And," she added, "my concession is that I wish to have a say in the management of Beauclaire."

Eden sucked in her breath, waiting to hear what

his reaction would be. It was important that she be treated as Clay's equal—his partner. Beauclaire was her life. And if she was forced to share it, then she wanted to share it equally.

"A say in the management?" He rubbed his chin, as if considering her request, while formulating a reply that was sure to lull her into a sense of security. "I think that could be arranged, providing you defer to me before all decisions are made final."

"Spoken like a true *husband.*" She spit the word out as if it were a curse.

"Then you've decided to accept my proposal?"

"Yes, damn you! I'll marry you."

"So you've decided to sell yourself to me for the sum of twenty thousand dollars? I'm flattered. I hope you'll be worth it."

She gasped, bringing her hand up to slap the smug smile off his face, but he was quicker and grabbed her wrist. "Now is that any way for a proper fiancée to treat her adoring husband-to-be?" he asked, before pulling her into his chest. "I think we need to seal this betrothal with a kiss." Before Eden could protest, Clay smothered her lips with his own, demanding, seeking the response that he so desired. He was not disappointed.

The touch of Clay's lips sent Eden's senses spiraling. Her heart began to pound, her blood heating to liquid fire. When she felt his thrusting tongue go deep within her mouth, she groaned in surrender, melting into him. Her fingers came up to explore the thick mat of curls on his chest, as blood continued to pound in her brain and butterflies danced a wild rhythm in her stomach.

She felt hot lips against her neck, against the exposed flesh of her breast as his mouth burned a searing path down her body, and a delicious lethargy filled her being, weighting her arms and legs. The protest that came to her lips as he undid the buttons of her blouse took too much effort to utter.

Untying the ribbons of her camisole, he pushed back the material, gazing reverently at the perfection before him. Cradling Eden's large breasts, Clay felt the weight of them, the satiny smoothness of her skin, the rigidity of her nipples as he laved his tongue over them. He took one breast into his mouth, sucking, devouring, like a starving man unable to get his fill.

Eden groaned in mindless ecstasy as Clay's mouth closed over her nipple and his hands reached down to cup her buttocks, pressing her venus mound into the rock hardness of his manhood. Mindless with passion, she made no protest when he lowered her to the soft pile of hay, nor when his questing hands moved up her skirt to explore the smoothness of her calf and thigh. Slowly, his fingers inched toward the moist, aching center of her being, touching the soft nest of curls, now dewy with desire.

"Clay," she whispered, her voice a harsh whisper as she pressed against his hand, wanting more, needing more. But just as the ache intensified, growing unbearable, Clay withdrew. She moaned in protest, feeling suddenly bereft. Slowly

Eden opened her eyes to find Clay's mocking smile upon her. Her stomach clenched, but not in pleasure this time.

"As much as I would like to continue our little tryst, angel eyes, I won't, for I have promised that this marriage will be in name only. And I honor my vows, though others do not."

As if a pail of cold water had been dumped on her head, Eden's ardor quickly dissipated. Rolling out of Clay's embrace lest he see the mortification his words elicited, she rose to her feet, buttoning her blouse as quickly as her fingers could perform the formidable task.

With heat staining her cheeks and the feel of Clay's hands and lips firmly imprinted on her flesh, she descended the ladder without so much as a word and fled the barn as quickly as her wobbly legs would carry her.

Clay stared after her, an agonized expression replacing the mocking smile of moments before. "Damn it, Eden," he muttered to the empty barn, feeling the unsatisfied bulge of his manhood pressing painfully against his pants. "I still want you. Damn you to hell for that!"

Seven

As if the trying episode she'd experienced yesterday at Clay's hands hadn't been enough, this afternoon Eden was beset with yet another, when Clay's sister-in-law came to call.

Lucy had shown up shortly after dinner, dressed in a deeply flounced, jonquil-yellow taffeta gown with matching mantle, looking very much, in Eden's opinion, like a perfectly arrayed lemon. Of course, the sour purse to her lips only enhanced the assessment.

They were seated in the parlor, or blue room, as Eden's mother had always referred to it—blue wainscoted walls surrounded it on all four sides, topped by a charming blue and red floral paper design. The women perched in two matching blue velvet Chippendale loveseats, sharing a pot of orange pekoe tea and a plate of freshly baked scones, which rested on the Queen Anne-style tea table in front of them.

The windows behind them, overlooking the rear yard, were open, allowing a delightful breeze to enter. Not that they needed it. Lucy's constant babbling had emitted enough air to circulate, hot though it was.

"I was just so surprised when Clay told us of your engagement, Eden. Wasn't this rather sudden? He's been home less than a week." Lucy smoothed the folds of her gown, then folded her hands primly in her lap, while her prying eyes rested on Eden's face.

Eden cursed inwardly at Lucy's probing question, hoping that the heat creeping into her face would be attributed to the tea, and vowing with every breath she took to get even with Clay if it was the last thing she did. Seducing her was one thing. But to inflict Lucy on her . . . It was the final straw!

Not knowing how much of their agreement Clay had divulged to his family, Eden smiled sweetly—though the effort cost her dearly—and chose her words carefully. "We found that, after seeing each other again, we still had feelings for one another." *Hate. Anger. Resentment. Lust.* The latter brought the scene in the barn to mind and a full-blown red stain to her cheeks.

"Why, Eden Fairchild, I do declare! You're blushing like a schoolgirl. How charming."

There was something about the way Lucy said *charming* which made Eden realize that the woman felt quite the opposite. There wasn't enough honey in Lucy Braxton's Southern simper to hide the resentment in her voice. She resented her upcoming marriage to Clay. But why?

About to make some inane remark that would

satisfy Lucy's unending curiosity, Eden was saved from answering when Jewel entered the room to refill the teapot.

"Would y'all care for more scones, Miss Eden? Miss Lucy?" the young girl asked, pausing expectantly.

Smiling kindly at Jewel, Eden allowed her gaze to linger on the petite black woman. With her café au lait complexion and refined features, Jewel was a lovely woman. But it wasn't just her outward appearance which made Ruby's daughter lovely, it was the girl's sweet, self-effacing demeanor. Eden couldn't remember a time when Jewel had uttered a harsh word to anyone. She was definitely a rarity—and well named.

"No, thank you, Jewel. These will be quite enough," Eden felt safe to reply, since Lucy hadn't partaken of any cakes up 'til now.

"You sure, Miss Eden? Mama says you need plumpin'." Jewel winked, making Eden laugh before the servant slipped out of the room.

Lucy's face contorted in outrage. "How can you stand for that nigger wench to speak to you in that fashion, Eden? Why, she was positively insolent!"

Her spine stiffening against the back of the loveseat, Eden sighed inwardly. How could she explain the give-and-take relationship she had with a slave to a woman like Lucy? Lucy would never understand. But Eden attempted to try anyway. "Jewel is family. We grew up together. Besides, she loves to tease me."

"Tease you!" She gasped, her hand flying to

her chest. "I declare, Eden," Lucy admonished, shaking her head, her brown ringlets bobbing every which way, "darkies need a strong hand, lest they become uppity. It's hard enough having those smelly, lazy creatures around . . . but to make them uppity . . . it's too horrid to consider." She fanned herself briskly with the ivory sticks she'd pulled out of her reticule, looking as if she were about to suffer an attack of the vapors.

Eden felt heat rush through her veins, but it wasn't embarrassment, or the vapors, that set her blood to boiling. She fought to keep her temper in check, trying hard to remember that Lucy was a small-minded, mealy-mouthed brat, who was soon to be her sister-in-law. With that in mind, she counted to ten, then quickly changed the subject.

"Have you done something different with your hair, Lucy? It's very becoming."

The woman preened under Eden's flattery, patting her curls, smiling, and forgetting all about their recent conversation.

"Why, yes! Do you like it? Richard says it makes me look like a Greek goddess." Lucy giggled, and the sound frayed every one of Eden's nerve endings.

"Really? I wonder which one he had in mind?" Medusa, most likely, Eden deduced uncharitably.

A soft blush suffused Lucy's cheeks, and she leaned close to Eden in a conspiratorial fashion. "I have a secret to confide, and since we're practically sisters . . ." Eden winced at the word.

". . . I'd love to share it with you. Richard and I are going to have a baby."

A genuine smile of happiness crossed Eden's lips. A baby. She adored children and asked eagerly, "Really? When?"

"Oh, it hasn't happened yet," Lucy confessed, "but we're still trying. I didn't really like . . . Well . . . you know . . . all that groping and grunting. But I've found it can be quite pleasurable, if I have one or two glasses of sherry beforehand."

Eden stared openmouthed, not quite believing that this woman had just revealed the most intimate aspects of her relationship with her husband, and not quite certain how she should respond to them. After a moment, she replied, "I'm so pleased for both of you."

"Well, you'll be experiencing the carnal side of marriage soon enough, Eden dear. Clay's got quite the reputation when it comes to the ladies." Covering her mouth in mock mortification, she said, "How indelicate of me to have said that," then waved her hand airily, as if it really was no matter. "But surely Clay can't be faulted for what he does before marriage. Men have their needs, barbaric as they may seem."

Eden had sampled some of Clay's *need* and had no desire to partake of more, and the same went for this conversation. Was the woman catty, or merely obtuse? Eden wasn't quite certain.

At that moment, the parlor door slid open and Aunt Agnes arrived carrying Desdemona in her arms. Eden could have jumped for joy, so relieved was she to see a familiar face.

But that relief suddenly turned to consternation when the cat leapt out of Agnes's hands—or was she thrown? Eden couldn't quite decide—and fairly flew across the room to land smack dab in Lucy's lap.

A shriek that could have awakened the dead erupted from the frightened woman's lips, and it was all Eden could do to keep from smiling, especially when she glanced across the room and caught the mischievous twinkle in Aunt Agnes's eyes.

"Good heavens! Come back here, you naughty cat," her aunt cried out.

Agnes lunged forward, but succeeded only in scaring Desdemona, who landed with such force on top of the tea table that she knocked over the pot of tea in the process. The brown liquid poured over the hem of Lucy's skirt, and the distraught woman screamed again.

"Get out of here, you stupid cat!" Lucy shrieked, swiping after Desdemona with her hand, but the cat successfully managed to elude the blow and hastened her retreat out of the room.

It only took a few moments for Lucy to regain her composure, bid her farewells, and exit the room and the house, much to Eden's relief.

Turning toward her aunt, who was munching on a scone and had the most innocent expression on her face, Eden shook her head. "You're a treasure, Agnes. I don't know what I'd do without you. That woman makes me crazed. To think we're actually going to be related." She shuddered. "It gives me the willies."

Agnes nodded, quite matter-of-factly. "I feared as much. *'People who are wrapped up themselves make small packages,'* " she said, as if to explain her actions.

For once, Eden felt grateful for Agnes's maxims and crossed the room to give the older woman a heartfelt hug. "Thank you."

" *'If you'd lose a troublesome visitor, lend him money.'* " Agnes's mouth twitched at the corners. "I had no money, only Desdemona."

Kissing the older woman's wrinkled cheek, Eden replied, "A worthy exchange, dear Agnes. A very worthy exchange."

Troublesome visitors seemed to have no end this day as Eden looked down the dusty road from her seat on the rear porch and noted Clay's approach on the big, golden buckskin. She felt panic rise within her.

What on earth did he want now? And how could she face him, after what had happened between them yesterday?

The sun had melted into the horizon, leaving only a purplish cast to the evening sky. It was still comfortably warm, and a gentle breeze ruffled the leaves of the oaks and elms that graced the yard. The sound of barking interrupted the stillness, and Eden frowned when she noticed the two Irish setters trotting up the drive alongside Clay's horse. Thomasina and Desdemona, Aunt Agnes's cats, were sure to take exception to those four-legged creatures.

Clay was dressed more formally than he'd been yesterday, but she still sensed an air of wildness about him. Or was that cocky grin he sported just part of her imagination? She clenched her fists, forcing a smile to her lips as he dismounted and climbed the steps to take a seat next to her on the swing. The dogs sprawled at his feet and immediately went to sleep.

"Evening, angel eyes," he drawled. "What are you sewing?" He gazed at the lump of coarse cotton material in her lap and cocked a questioning eyebrow at her.

"Just hemming some dishcloths." She bit the thread, then tied it off, trying to act nonchalant in his presence. "Is there something I can do for you?" She knew it was the wrong question to ask as soon as she saw the erotic smile twist his lips.

"Sure thing, Eden. But maybe we'd better wait until after we're married." He winked, relishing the blush that crept steadily to her cheeks.

Her voice rose sharply. "There won't be any marriage, Clay Braxton, if you don't desist in making such outrageous statements. It's hardly proper, and most unseemly of you."

"I'll try to keep that in mind. What I actually came over for is to let you know that the plans for the engagement party are all set."

"Engagement party?" She shook her head in denial. "There'll be no such thing. I'll not dignify this farce of a marriage with a formal announcement."

"You will, if you're going to marry me." The

implied threat hung in the air as he held her gaze and saw the multitude of emotions flitting across her face: anger, worry, and finally resignation.

"Why must we parade our problems before the whole county? I'm going to be a laughingstock as it is."

"You're wrong, Eden. No one knows of our arrangement except you, me, and my father. Everyone will just assume it's a love match."

Deep lines bracketed her mouth. "I'm sure that's what your sister-in-law thinks. She was here today with her probing questions and ceaseless chatter."

Clay chuckled. "Yes, I heard. Lucy was quite put out about the cat. She really did look like something the cat had dragged in when she walked into the house."

Eden joined in Clay's laughter, realizing that it was the first time since he'd come back that they'd shared an amusement. Once, they had laughed easily together . . . She shook herself, unwilling to think of the past.

"Tell me more about this engagement party. Where are you planning to hold it?" Eden asked.

"Here, if you're agreeable. Father's not well, and I don't trust Lucy not to sabotage the entire event."

"Here? But we can ill afford . . ."

Clay held up his hand. "I'll pay for everything. I just need you and your aunt to organize the party."

Eden mulled over Clay's request. She did love

parties, and they hadn't had one in such a very long time. "When were you planning to hold this party?"

"I thought perhaps at the end of the month. That should give you enough time to plan your menu, hire the musicians . . ."

"Musicians! You mean there's going to be dancing?"

Eden clapped in childish delight and Clay smiled indulgently, suddenly realizing that there hadn't been much fun or excitement in Eden's life over the past five years. Even before that, since she'd always put her plantation duties before her pleasures.

"Of course. And spare no expense. In fact, I want you to buy yourself a new gown. You'll have to buy one ready made. There isn't enough time for you to have one sewn."

Her face fell. "Oh, I couldn't. What would people say? It's one thing to forgo mourning attire here at home where no one can see me. But to go out in public . . . It just isn't done."

He turned and placed the tip of his finger under her chin, turning her to face him. "Your father wouldn't have wanted you to spend your days dressed up like a crow, mooning over him. Lawrence was full of life. I expect he'd want you to be the same way. And besides, you can wear lavender, if you're so determined to please society. It's perfectly suitable, and you look quite lovely in it."

She blushed, fidgeting nervously with the folds

of the lavender cambric gown she had on. "Thank you."

"So, is it agreed?" he asked, pushing himself to his feet.

Eden followed him to the end of the porch. "I suppose, but I'll have to check with Agnes. I'm going to need her assistance for such a large undertaking."

Reaching into the inside front pocket of his coat, he pulled out his wallet and handed her a thick wad of money. "This will get you started. If you need more, you know where to reach me."

She stared wide-eyed, her voice filled with incredulity. "But there's over five hundred dollars here!"

"Isn't it enough?"

"Why, yes. More than enough. But don't you think it's a bit extravagant?"

He put his arm around her waist, pulling her close to his chest in a very possessive gesture. "You're to be my wife, Eden. I want the world to know what that means to me . . . for outward appearances, of course."

She swallowed, gazing into the bright green eyes so full of promise. "Of course."

He lowered his head and kissed her, and all thought of parties, money, and refusal died on those very lips he plundered so thoroughly.

Eden felt her knees weaken as his tongue found its way into her mouth, and it was necessary to wrap her arms about Clay's neck to keep herself from melting into the floor boards. The kiss continued for several minutes, and just when she thought she would faint from the breathless ecstasy of it, he released her and stepped back.

She had felt the insistent bulge of his desire against her stomach, heard the ragged sound of his breathing, and was happy to know she wasn't the only one affected by the intimacy.

There was an undefinable look in Clay's eyes when he announced, "I'll be back soon, angel eyes. Try not to miss me too much."

Clay's arrogant laughter broke Eden's trance, and she spun on her heel, heat burning her cheeks, outraged that she had once again fallen under his spell. Slamming the door behind her as she entered the house, she vowed it was never going to happen again.

Clay wasn't the only visitor who called at Beauclaire that evening. Seated in the overseer's cottage on a frayed and torn blue velvet wing chair which had once graced the parlor of the main house, Cyrus Long looked very smug as he sipped on his bourbon and related recent events to his friend James Wakefield.

"I tell you, Wakefield, I got the news straight from my nigger's mouth. It seems one of Eden's field hands come over to Long Acres to pay a visit to a prime wench I just purchased. She said he was her husband, but I didn't believe that for a minute. Anyways, it appears that the lovely Miss Fairchild has found a way to get her hands on that twenty thousand dollars."

"You're daft, Long. Where on earth would

Eden get that much money? She told me herself that you refused to loan it to her."

Cyrus studied the amber liquor in his glass. Eden's rejection had hurt, and he wasn't likely to forget about it for a good long while. "She wasn't agreeable to my terms."

"And I can just imagine what those terms entailed." James laughed. "Don't deny that you'd like to get beneath the lady's skirts."

A sinister smile curved the older man's mouth. "She's a prime piece of meat, all right. I don't deny that I'd like to stick it to her a time or two. God, who wouldn't? It makes my dick hard just thinking about it."

James shook his head in disgust. "That's your problem, Long. You think with that miserable piece of flesh you've got between your legs, and not with your head."

"And I suppose you don't fancy a fuck with the wench."

"I've got bigger, more permanent plans for Miss Fairchild."

"Well, if you're thinking about marrying her, you can forget it. I've already tried that ploy. It didn't work."

James smiled confidently. "I don't mean to be rude, old man, but you and I are hardly in the same league."

"I doubt you'll be smiling, Wakefield, when you hear what I came over here to tell you."

"And what, pray tell, is that?"

"Just that Eden and that old beau of hers, Braxton, are fixin' to marry. It was nigger gossip, true enough. But the darkies are usually privy to the goings on in the big house." Cyrus was pleased to see the flush of anger now covering the overseer's face. The good-looking bastard wasn't quite so conceited now.

"You lie!" James jumped to his feet from the settle bench and began to pace the room. "I don't believe it. I've seen the chap here a time or two, but I had no idea she was entertaining the idea of marrying him."

"She was engaged to him once, before you began working here."

James slammed his fist down so hard on the wooden table, he nearly upset the oil lamp centered there. "There'll be no wedding. Mark my words."

Grabbing his hat, Cyrus stood and walked toward the door. He'd witnessed Wakefield's temper a time or two and had no intention of remaining in the same room with him when it let loose.

"I don't know what it is you've got in mind, Wakefield. But I'd be pleased to lend a hand. I'm no fan of the Fairchilds, nor of the Braxtons, for that matter."

James didn't acknowledge the offer before the older man shut the door behind him. Seething with uncontrollable fury, he picked up his glass, filled it to the brim with brandy, and gulped it down. The brandy burned, but it was no match for his temper.

"There will be no wedding," he repeated, throwing the empty glass against the wall, watching it smash into shards. "Not as long as I've got a breath left in my body."

Eight

The town of Tappahannock was a bustling center of activity when Eden and Agnes, with Aunt Ruby following close behind, toting a parasol to shade the "white folks' delicate skin," made their way down the main street the next day.

The seaport community boasted four mercantile stores, two hotels, a jeweler, a mantua maker, various other establishments, and of course, a milliner's, where the trio was now headed.

Much to Eden's amusement and surprise, Agnes was all atwitter about the engagement party, which was quite out of character, considering Agnes's views on marriage.

"I think it was terribly kind of Clay to suggest this party, don't you, Eden?" Agnes asked, as they entered the small brick building, where colorful bolts of cloth lined the shelves and fashion dolls stood in rows upon the glass counters like a chorus line of dancers.

Eden was spared from voicing her less-than-enthusiastic opinion regarding Clay's kindness when Clarice Willowby, the reed-thin, bespectacled proprietress of the shop, hurried forward to greet them. She was grinning from ear to ear, doing a remarkable impersonation of a hungry cat with a full bowl of cream. Unfortunately, her unsightly chin whiskers only added to the image.

"Ladies, ladies, welcome," she gushed enthusiastically, making Eden wonder if those were really dollar signs she saw reflected in the woman's eyeglasses. She had to blink to assure herself that they weren't.

"Good day, Miss Willowby," Agnes replied, her manner instantly reserved as she addressed the avaricious merchant. "We'd like to see some evening dresses. My niece is in need of something . . ." Agnes tapped her finger against her cheek, trying to decide just what that *something* was, while Eden mentally supplied her own list of possibilities to complete the sentence.

Modest. Inexpensive. Lavender.

"Spectacular," Agnes proclaimed, causing Eden's mouth to drop open. "And spare no expense. Her fiancé wants her to look stunning for their engagement ball."

"Aunt Agnes!" Eden stared at her aunt with something akin to shock on her face.

Agnes waved away her objection with a flick of her wrist. " *'There's more than one way to skin a cat,'* my dear. And your fiancé has supplied you with the means to do it."

Clarice Willowby didn't know a thing about cats, being a dog lover, but she did know about making a tidy profit, and so rushed to the rear of her shop to return a moment later with the most exquisite gown Eden had ever laid eyes on.

It was white tulle, deeply flounced, embroidered with dozens of tiny violets on the skirts and bodice, and Eden sucked in her breath at the beauty of it. Of course, it was totally out of the question, and totally inappropriate, due to her current state of mourning. But still . . .

"This dress was made for Lydia Pendergast of Port Royal," Miss Willowby explained. "But the poor dear suffers from consumption and is literally wasting away. Alas, the dress no longer fits her."

"Oh, child, it's lovely," Agnes stated, running her hands over the fabric, her eyes sparkling with delight. "You must get it; the tiny violets will bring out the color of your eyes."

Excusing herself, Eden grasped her aunt firmly by the elbow and led her to a corner of the room, away from Clarice Willowby's eager ears. "You know that's out of the question, Aunt Agnes. I'm still in mourning for Papa. What would people say if I showed up wearing something like that?"

"My dear, I learned long ago not to listen to what others say. Their opinions don't matter. Be true to yourself. I'm sure if Lawrence were here, he'd advise you to purchase the gown. And, of course, there's still the matter of your future husband."

"Clay?"

Agnes nodded. "If Clay Braxton is blackmailing you into marriage, then that constitutes a declaration of war, don't you think? A woman has only so many weapons she can use, child."

Eden gasped. "Aunt Agnes! Shame on you! What you're suggesting is . . . is . . . Well, it just is. And besides, I told you . . ." Her voice lowered to a whisper. "Our marriage is to be in name only. I have no intention of bedding Clay Braxton."

"Perhaps not. But there's nothing that says you can't make him suffer for what he's putting you through."

Make Clay suffer. What a delicious notion, though she wasn't sure how she could accomplish that feat. But the idea certainly had some merit, and she smiled wickedly. "Come, Aunt Agnes, we have some shopping to do."

The blue eyes sparked with mischief. "How much money did you say we have to spend?"

"Over five hundred dollars."

Hmmm. Then we'd best get started. It will take us the better part of the afternoon to disburse such a sizable sum."

Grinning, the two co-conspirators locked arms and rejoined the proprietress, who mentally calculated her good fortune.

"I don't know why I let you talk me into going on this picnic, Clay. With all I have to do, and the party only a few days away . . ." Eden shook her head, sighing in exasperation as she trudged down the dirt path, across the open field, toward the copse of pine trees that would lead them to the river. She had to take two steps to every one of Clay's to keep up with his longer stride.

We have to have a courtship, Eden, if we're going to convince people that we're truly in love. Or so Clay had explained when he'd shown up at the kitchen door this morning, while she was in the midst of preserving pickles and up to her elbows in brine.

"I thought I'd explained all of that this morning," Clay now said. "Besides," he added, grinning, "you used to love our picnics."

Eden colored fiercely. Those "picnics" were nothing more than excuses for two young lovers to spend time alone, away from prying eyes, and she hadn't forgotten how they had whiled away the hours together. And neither had Clay, from the erotic glimmer in his eyes.

"If you think I'm going skinny-dippin' with you, Clay Braxton, you've got another think coming."

They had reached the small outcropping of rocks, and Clay took a moment to spread out the quilt and set down the wicker basket before answering. There was amusement in his voice when he said, "You weren't quite so modest five years ago, angel eyes. Why the sudden shyness? After all, we're to be married soon."

Plopping down on the blanket, a mask of indignation on her face, Eden smoothed the folds of her cotton skirt with quick, nervous strokes. "I was a mere child then," she explained. "I've matured, in case you hadn't noticed. I don't indulge in such frivolous pursuits anymore."

Clay's gaze raked her from head to the tips of

her bare toes, which were peeking out from beneath the hem of her dress, bringing more color to her cheeks. Apparently, Eden was still childlike enough in her thinking to have shed her shoes and stockings this morning. He chuckled to himself, thinking of all the times she'd been reprimanded by Aunt Ruby for the very same thing. Shoes were too confining, she had wailed. She wanted to be free . . . free as a bird.

He frowned, suddenly realizing that Eden's desire for freedom had cost him dearly.

"I have noticed that you've matured, Eden." His voice was seductively low as he dropped to the blanket beside her. "I didn't think it possible that you could grow more beautiful, but you have." He picked up her hand, placing a kiss in the center of her palm, delighting in the way the violet orbs darkened to deep purple. She was such an innocent. Or was she?

The thought that Eden might not still be the innocent she was five years ago tortured him. Five years was a long time, and Eden was a beautiful woman. Perhaps he'd be getting used goods. Perhaps he needed to find that out.

Currents of desire rushed through Eden's veins at the kiss, and she wondered how the nerve endings in the lower portion of her body could possibly be connected to her hand.

The sensations she was feeling rendered her speechless for the moment, and she stared at Clay's lips as if mesmerized.

"You look a bit flushed, angel. Perhaps a cool dip in the river is just what you need."

When she didn't respond to his goad, Clay shrugged and began to remove his boots.

"What are you doing?" she demanded, finally realizing his intention as his hands went to the buttons on his shirt. She gasped aloud.

"What's it look like, angel? I'm stripping down for a swim. Care to join me?" There was a definite challenge in his eyes.

Eden shook her head, her eyes widening when he began to unfasten his trousers. "This is highly improper, Clay. What if someone should happen by? What if someone sees you naked?"

At that moment his pants dropped down around his ankles and he kicked them aside along with his modesty, grinning. "I think that *someone* is just you, angel eyes. And you've already seen me without a stitch on. But if you're truly offended, I guess you could cover your eyes." With that, he jumped into the river, emitting a loud yelp as he hit the chilly water.

Eden stared, mouth agape, as Clay's firm flanks sliced through the sparkling water. His buttocks were as tanned as his back, and she didn't want to dwell on why that was so. The thought of covering her eyes had never entered her mind, and she didn't want to dwell on why that was so, either.

Sighing, she lay back on the blanket, hands clasped behind her head, to stare up at the tree branches. Sunlight filtered through oak leaves and pine needles, casting lacy patterns over the ground. Two plump robins trilled happily to each other, and a persistent gray squirrel tugged determinedly at a stubborn acorn.

It was so peaceful here, so quiet. She closed her eyes and thought of all the times she and Clay had come to this secluded spot to steal a few moments alone, to plan their future, to share kisses and embraces.

"You must be thinking about something wonderful, Eden. You've got the naughtiest grin on your face."

Eden's eyes flew open and she gasped at the sight of Clay standing over her, stark naked and dripping wet. Droplets of water glistened like diamonds on his chest hair, and the sheen of moisture on his flesh made him appear sleek and smooth as an otter. She did cover her eyes this time, but the memory of his long, thick shaft, hard, yet velvety smooth, would forever be embedded in her mind.

"Please," she choked out, "put on some clothes." A moment later she heard Clay laugh, then say, "You can look now, angel; I'm decent."

Just barely, she thought, opening her eyes to find his chest still bare. He reclined next to her, only inches away, and she swallowed hard at his nearness. She inhaled the spicy cologne he always wore, and the scent made tiny butterflies dance in her stomach. She clutched at it.

"Are you hungry?" he asked, mistaking her reaction. "I brought some fried chicken. And Mammy Mae tossed in a couple of pieces of chocolate cake." Eden's stomach rumbled in response, causing Clay to laugh. "I guess you are."

He handed her a leg, then asked, "Is everything all set for the party?" while nibbling on a breast of chicken.

Eden never knew the sight of someone eating a piece of chicken could be so erotic. She nodded, gulping. "Yes. Sukie has been cooking for days already. And Mr. Tayloe and his two brothers have agreed to provide the music." He sucked on his fingers, one at a time, and Eden experienced a definite response, unable to forget the way his lips had felt on her breasts.

"Sounds like you've got everything under control."

She fought for composure. "I thought we'd have the party outside in the yard. It's so much cooler, and Caleb and Otis said they could build us a dance floor."

"Whatever you think is best," he said, reaching back into the basket for a slice of cake. He broke off a piece, bringing it to her mouth. "Have a bite. Mae will be beside herself if I tell her you didn't eat any of her cake." He placed both the cake and the tips of his fingers into her mouth, so that her lips and her tongue came in contact with his flesh; his eyes darkened in response to the touch.

Why did her touch still have the power to excite him? Why, after everything she had done did he still want her so damn much?

Eden had difficulty swallowing the cake, so large was the lump in her throat. Her heart thundered in her breast and she was certain he could hear it.

"Remember when I used to put a piece of cake in my mouth and feed it to you?" he asked.

She nodded mutely, watching in horror as he placed another piece of the chocolate confection into his mouth and leaned forward to touch her mouth with it. She had no alternative but to nibble at it.

His lips tasted as sweet as the cake, no sweeter, as her tongue licked at the gooey icing. It seemed a natural progression for his tongue to meet hers, and soon she found herself on her back again, Clay leaning over her, and his tongue deeply embedded in her mouth.

Her hands came up of their own volition to glide across the smooth muscles of his back. His flesh felt like velvet steel—smooth, yet hard. His hands seemed to be everywhere at once—in her hair, on her breasts, on her face, while his mouth remained firmly fixed on her own.

She could feel Clay's hard erection pressing into her soft woman's mound, and though she knew it was wrong—quite insane—she couldn't prevent her hips from arching up to meet it, to grind against its pulsing warmth in a most primitive way. It seemed so right to be in Clay's arms again. And so good. So very good.

The scent of lilac filled Clay's nostrils as his hands were filled with the soft flesh of the woman beneath him. He reached down to pull up the skirt of her dress, and when no protest was forthcoming, slid his fingers into the open seam of her drawers to caress her womanhood. She wanted him; she was ready for him. And that knowledge filled him with satisfaction, anger, and a yearning so powerful it was painful. Her ardent response only confirmed his suspicions: she was no virgin.

"Clay." Eden breathed his name, unsure if she had spoken his name aloud or merely shouted it out silently. However, there was no mistaking her moans of ecstasy as his fingers plied the slick folds, toying with the hard bud of her passion until it throbbed painfully.

Engrossed in their lovemaking, the couple failed to notice the pair of cerulean blue eyes that watched them from behind a thick stand of cedars.

James Wakefield had stumbled upon the passionate duo quite by accident, and the sight of Braxton's hands on Eden's creamy white flesh filled him with mindless rage.

But he couldn't keep his eyes off the sight, couldn't prevent himself from growing hard at the vision of her nakedness, and his hands reached down into his pants to cup his thick, swollen shaft.

With every moan and sigh from Eden's lips, he imagined that it was his hands that touched her, his lips that caressed her.

Then he slunk away quietly, so as not to be heard. They would feel his presence soon.

But not now.

The only thing Eden felt at the moment was ecstasy as Clay's mouth trailed down her neck.

He kissed the exposed flesh above her breasts, then suckled at her nipples through the thin lawn material of her gown.

She was fire—hot and all-consuming. As his fingers continued their magic, she could feel herself growing taut. She arched her back—reaching—reaching, not knowing what she sought, pushing herself into Clay's hands as she held his head firmly to her breast.

"Oh! Oh!" she cried out as she exploded, her climaxed cries smothered by his mouth.

Wonder filled her being at what had just occurred, and she heaved a deep sigh of contentment, feeling wonderfully relaxed. But when she opened her eyes, that contentment fled. Clay, elbow bent, was leaning on his hand, staring down at her, a sardonic expression on his face that brought a bright stain to her cheeks.

"Did you enjoy that, angel eyes?" Though his voice was soft, his eyes were not.

"I . . . I . . ."

"*You* at a loss for words, Eden? I don't believe it." He pushed himself to his knees and began to repack the basket, as if what they'd just shared mattered nothing to him. She lowered her dress, embarrassed now to have him see her so exposed.

"This time was your turn, angel. Next time it will be mine."

That comment brought her bolting upright to a sitting position. "Next time?"

His smile was nasty. "Do you really think we can live in the same house, sleep in the same bed, and not touch each other? I think I've just proved that theory wrong."

Eden pushed herself to her feet; her hands balled into fists as she stared down at him. "You don't know me at all, Clay, if you think me so weak."

"How can you deny your weakness, when the smell of you still lingers on my hands, in my nostrils?"

Tears formed behind her lids. Hurt and angry, she cried out, "I hate you! You're vile, despicable! I never want to see you again."

Clay's laughter was mocking. "Oh, but you will, angel eyes. You're going to see a whole lot more of me, as I am of you."

She was trapped, and he knew it. And she hated him for it. And for making her feel things she didn't want to feel. He was wrapping silken threads of bondage around her, attempting to imprison her heart and then her body. Well, it wouldn't work.

"You won't win, Clay. You won't," she said, before spinning on her heel. She was about to walk away when his next words halted her in her tracks.

"Oh, but I already have, Eden. I already have."

Nine

He wouldn't win! Eden vowed, tugging on the bodice of her new gown as she readied herself for the engagement party. Aunt Agnes was right. This was war. Clay might have won the first skirmish, but she was going to win the battle.

She looked at her reflection in the mirror and her frown deepened. Why on earth hadn't she tried this gown on before tonight? she wondered. It was at least two sizes too small in the bust, and her bosom was hanging out of the dress rather indecently. Well, there was no help for it now, she thought. It was too late to take a needle to it. She'd just have to refrain from taking any deep breaths.

"What you frowning about, Miss Eden?" Jewel asked, as she approached the dressing table. "I'd think you'd be happy about your party this evening. You look like a perfect *angel* in that dress."

"Don't call me that," Eden snapped, growing suddenly contrite when she noted the hurt on the young girl's face. "I'm sorry, Jewel. I guess I'm just having a case of the jitters."

"That's all right, honey," the maid said, taking the silver-handled hairbrush off the dresser to fashion Eden's hair into long, spiral curls. "You is to be married soon, and new brides are always a bit on edge."

Yes. Especially when they're forced to marry a despicable, blackmailing rogue like Clay Braxton, Eden thought silently, but aloud replied, "I suppose you're right, Jewel. Did Aunt Agnes say if any of our guests had arrived?" It was going to be next to impossible to carry out this charade of the happy engaged couple tonight, especially in light of what had happened the other day down by the river.

Eden had spent the better part of each day since, chastising herself for her behavior. Fortunately, Clay had kept his distance and she hadn't had to face him again. But she would tonight. And she was dreading it with every fiber of her being.

"Your aunt says that the Tayloe brothers are here, tuning up their fiddles," Jewel replied, fastening a silver amethyst clip into the side of Eden's hair. She stepped back to admire her handiwork before adding, "Miss Agnes done said that if Mr. Phinneas Tayloe gets as drunk as he did at the last party and plays off-key, she's goin' to box his ears in."

Eden couldn't help but smile at that. Agnes might succumb to her own vices of cigar smoking and an occasional glass of sherry, but she didn't tolerate improper behavior in others. Perhaps Eden should confide what Clay had done to her.

Maybe Agnes would box his ears in, too. On second thought, she'd better keep her own counsel where Clay was concerned. She had enough trouble at the moment as it was, and Aunt Agnes could be downright militant when she set her mind to it.

Picking up her fan off the table, Eden flicked it open, waving it in front of her face in a coquettish manner, batting her eyelashes at Jewel. "I do declare, Miss Jewel, I guess I'm ready to go down and face the music," she drawled in her best Southern simper.

Giggling, Jewel opened the door, shaking her head as she watched her mistress depart. Miss Eden had the devil's own look in her eyes tonight. And she pitied Mr. Clay Braxton something fierce.

Mr. Clay Braxton was standing at the refreshment table, indulging in his third glass of champagne punch. The need to fortify himself for the evening ahead seemed to take top priority at the moment.

He'd been "on edge," as his father had politely put it, since his encounter with Eden down at the river. Just thinking about her response, about the way she had felt, tasted, brought a tightening to his loins. "Damn the minx!" he cursed, downing yet another glass of punch.

Clay smiled politely, inclining his head as the Fortesque sisters, Edwina and Rowena, strolled by, batting their lashes at him. Good God! How could there be two such ugly creatures in one family? he wondered unkindly, staring at the two horse-faced women before his attention was stolen away by the arrival of his fiancée.

There were many well-wishers gathered around Eden—mostly men, he noted unhappily. When they parted to make a path for her, he could only stare, mouth agape, and a deep red flush suffused his face that had nothing to do with the punch he'd been drinking.

The gown she had on was positively indecent! Her lush breasts overflowed the bodice, and she looked as if she might spill out of it at any moment. She was conversing with Brad Townsend, that wet-behind-the-ears banker's son, and though she had her eyes trained on his face, he had his locked on her bosom. And who could blame him, with the blatant invitation she issued?

His blood began to boil, and with long, commanding strides, he crossed the yard to stand before her, nodding at Brad, a warning note in his eyes that made the younger man flush.

"If you'll excuse me, Miss Eden, I think my mother needs my assistance," Brad babbled, before taking his leave rather hurriedly.

Eden, perplexed by Brad's nervousness, inclined her head, before turning to stare at her fiancé, who hovered over her left shoulder. "Do you always have that effect on people, Clay? Why I thought poor Brad was going to faint dead away."

"No doubt from the sight of your breasts, which the young pup has been drooling over like a rabid dog," Clay ground out, annoyed by her smug smile. Grasping her elbow, Clay led Eden to a secluded corner of the yard.

"Let go, Clay," Eden protested, rubbing her arm when they'd stopped. "You're hurting me."

"I suggest that you go back into the house and change your gown at once, Eden. The one you have on is totally inappropriate for tonight's fête."

Biting the inside of her cheek to keep from smiling at Clay's obvious jealousy, Eden replied innocently, staring down at her gown, "Don't you like it, Clay? Aunt Agnes thought it was stunning."

"Aunt Agnes doesn't have a pair of breasts the size of watermelons," Clay mumbled under his breath.

"What was that?"

"Nothing. Your gown is cut rather low, don't you think? Now that we're to be married, I'd prefer that you save your charms for my eyes alone."

She flicked open her fan and waved it in front of her face. Clay's ardent expression was searing her right down to her drawers. "Oh, Clay, don't be so provincial. After all, our marriage is to be in name only; you said so yourself. And there are plenty of other women here—Stephanie Dupree, for one—who wear their gowns cut equally as low. We women don't set the fashion standards, Clay; we leave that up to the men. After all, men always know what's best." She smiled sweetly at him.

"Don't push me, Eden. You are treading on thin ice, right now."

"In the middle of summer! Why, I hardly think that's possible, Clay."

Eden's name was being called, and both she and Clay looked over to find James Wakefield strolling in their direction. Eden couldn't have been happier at the arrival of the overseer, especially when she looked over to find the pulse in Clay's neck throbbing violently.

"Why, James," Eden gushed, more for Clay's benefit than anyone else's, "how nice to see you. My, don't you look handsome this evening." He was wearing a suit of black superfine with a snowy white ruffled shirt and stock. Latching on to the Englishman's arm, she said, "James Wakefield, this is my fiancé, Clay Braxton. James is my overseer," Eden explained. "He's been a tremendous help to me, and I don't know how I would have gotten along without him."

Clay fought to keep his temper in check as he watched Eden fawning over the Englishman. The blond man seemed to be enjoying the attention, and Clay hadn't missed where his gaze had traveled—to Eden's breasts.

"I believe this is our dance, Eden," Clay announced, reaching for her hand, which was still glued to Wakefield's forearm.

"Don't be silly, Clay. I'm going to dance with James. Isn't that right, James?"

Clay didn't miss the informality with which Eden addressed her employee. Just how familiar was she with James Wakefield? he wondered.

"I'd be honored, Miss Eden," the overseer said, nodding politely at Clay before leading Eden out to the makeshift dance floor, leaving Clay to stare helplessly, furiously, at the retreating couple.

The dance floor was lit by several strategically placed torches, and Clay had an excellent view of the dancing couple. His fingers curled into claws when Wakefield's hand came up to rest possessively on the small of Eden's back. She was smiling up at the blond bastard, whispering something that brought a grin to his lips, and Clay felt an unwanted surge of jealousy rush through his veins. "Damn the faithless bitch!" he muttered through clenched teeth. Damn them both!

"You dance divinely, James. Thank you for rescuing me from Clay," Eden said, as she twirled about the floor in James's arms.

Wakefield's eyebrow arched. "Why would you need rescuing from your fiancé, Eden? Isn't this a love match?" He watched her carefully, and saw the uncertainty in her eyes. Perhaps there was still time to remedy the situation, he decided. Eden and Braxton weren't married yet.

"You know how lovers quarrel, James. And Clay and I have been doing an inordinate amount of it lately." *That was an understatement.* "Prenuptial jitters, I suppose."

"I must say, I was quite taken aback when informed of your upcoming marriage, Eden. It was rather sudden, was it not?"

Eden swallowed, wishing she could confide in James, but knowing she could not. "Clay and I were engaged years ago. He left to fight for Texas independence. I thought we were through. Apparently, fate had a different plan in store for us."

James was unimpressed by the romantic tale, and when the music stopped, led her off the dance floor. "Shall we go for a stroll? All that dancing has made me quite warm." When she agreed, he led her down the oyster-shell path toward the river.

Eden wondered briefly if Clay would notice her absence. But the need to escape the party and Clay was too strong to ignore, and so she tossed caution to the wind and followed.

The night air was scented with jasmine and boxwood. The roar of the cicada seemed deafening as they moved farther and farther away from the music and the lights of the house. She could tell they were nearing the river, for the temperature had dropped and she could smell the brackishness of the water. They stopped under the bower of a tall linden tree.

"You look beautiful tonight, Eden," Wakefield remarked, unable to tear his eyes away from her breasts. They were lush and white, and he could almost imagine he saw the pink tops of her nipples. He turned quickly to face the river, lest she see his arousal.

Her cheeks dimpled prettily. "Thank you, James. It's been such a long time since I've dressed for a party . . . and danced. I'd almost forgotten how."

He turned back to face her, once again under control. "You've had a great burden to shoulder, Eden. And you've handled it remarkably well. I don't know of another woman who could have managed as well as you have."

His praise warmed her and she smiled gratefully, placing her hand on his forearm. "You've been a good friend, James, and I thank you for your kindness."

"I had hoped to be more than just your friend, Eden," he said, his arms reaching out to pull her into his embrace.

Stunned by the declaration, Eden stared up at him, as if in invitation, and James's mouth closed over hers. For a brief instant, she let him kiss her. She'd always wondered what it would be like to kiss the handsome Englishman. It was pleasant, but there were no fireworks, no explosions within her, as there were with Clay.

When his tongue pressed against the seam of her lips, and his hands moved up to touch her breasts, Eden pulled out of his grasp, shaking her head. "Stop, James! You mustn't. I am engaged to be married."

Wakefield backed away immediately, realizing his mistake. He couldn't afford to lose his position at Beauclaire. Not now. Not when his future and Eden's were so irrevocably entwined. He must exercise caution and wait. Though the memory of the way her soft breasts felt in his palms would make the waiting as hard as his cock.

Swallowing his anguish, he said, "I'm sorry, Eden; I don't know what came over me. Possibly too much champagne punch. I'm not used to drinking spirits."

Embarrassed, Eden replied, "Speak no more of this, James. It is forgotten. I must go. Clay will be searching for me." She spun on her heel and departed.

James watched her go, rubbing his crotch as he did. He would have the teasing bitch one day. He would spread her open and thrust his cock deep inside her. It was a promise he had made himself. One he intended to keep.

"Where the hell have you been?" Clay demanded, when Eden made her way back to the party. Throwing down his cheroot, he grabbed her roughly by the arm, dragging her away from prying eyes. "And where's Wakefield? I saw you leave with him, Eden."

Eden's face grew hot and she was thankful for the darkness that hid her humiliation. It had been a mistake to leave with James. She had no idea he possessed feelings for her; she had never meant to lead him on. "We went for a stroll. He must have found someone else to dance with," she lied.

"Stay away from him. I don't like the way he looks at you."

His high-handedness annoyed her. "And which way is that, Clay? The same way you look at me, with lust in your eyes?"

He grabbed her then, his mouth grinding down on hers, his tongue thrusting deeply, while he clutched at her buttocks, pulling her into his groin. When he felt her go limp, he released her and she stumbled. He took several deep breaths before speaking.

"You're mine, angel. I bought you lock, stock, and barrel. If you think differently, think again. I learned some pretty nasty tricks living in the wilds of Texas. Don't push me."

Eden had never seen Clay's anger unleashed before, and it frightened her. "I swear nothing happened."

"You always were a tease, Eden, leading a man on until . . ." He pulled her toward him, taking her hand and placing it on his crotch. It was hard and throbbing. At her gasp, he said, "If you want it bad enough, angel, you know where you can get it."

Clay stalked off in the direction of the party, and Eden sucked in huge gulps of air, trying to restore her equilibrium.

This was not the same Clay Braxton she was once engaged to.

This man was an animal—a stranger.

This man was going to be her husband.

" *'What's good for the goose is good for the gander.'* " Agnes whispered, sidling up next to Eden a short time later. She had spotted her niece standing at the edge of the dance floor, looking very much alone and very disturbed about something. When Agnes had spied Clay in the arms of Stephanie Dupree, she knew why.

Eden blushed at her aunt's knowing look as she turned to face her. "I'm sure I don't know what you mean, Aunt Agnes."

"This is your engagement party, child. It's you

who should be dancing with Clay, not that cheap bit of fluff Stephanie Dupree." Nobody had hair that red! Agnes decided. Henna was the only possible answer.

"Why look how shamelessly she smiles up at Clay."

Eden did, and her eyes narrowed.

"And they're dancing much too close. People are bound to talk. *'Glass, china, and reputation are easily cracked and never well mended.'* You must do something, Eden."

"Do something?" Eden's eyes widened as she stared at the determined woman's face. "What would you have me do? If Clay wants to dance with another woman . . ." She shrugged, her words trailing off.

"You know darn well that you provoked him, Eden. And I'm not faulting you for it. God knows the man needs a comeuppance. Though it was wrong of you to slip away with that odious overseer. Tongues could wag and Clay could very well refuse to marry you. Then where would you be, child? No husband—no plantation."

The reminder was painful, and Eden winced. "What would you have me do? Act the jealous woman?" She crossed her arms over her chest, her chin tilting up defiantly. "I assure you, I couldn't care less who Clay chooses to dally with."

Agnes didn't believe that for an instant, but she refrained from voicing her opinion, saying instead, "If you want to be made the laughingstock of Essex County, then so be it. Personally,

I thought you were made of sterner stuff. Swallow your pride, child, and cut in. *As pride increases, fortune declines.* You have much to lose, Eden."

Realizing the truth of her aunt's words, Eden nodded solemnly and made her way onto the dance floor, looking like a prisoner on her way to the gallows as she approached the laughing couple. Clay seemed to be enjoying himself immensely, right down to ogling Stephanie's generous proportions. And Stephanie had a look seen only on the face of a man-hungry piranha.

Ignoring Clay's raised eyebrow and Stephanie's pique, she tapped the redhead on the shoulder. "I believe this is my dance, Stephanie. Do be a dear and find another partner."

The woman's smile was painfully polite. "Of course . . . if Clay wishes me to leave."

Both women looked at Clay expectantly—one in self-assured smugness, one biting her lower lip apprehensively—but Clay's face was as unreadable as a blank newspaper.

Would Clay denounce her? Eden wondered. Humiliate her in front of their friends and neighbors?

Curious eyes were trained on the couple, ears attuned to the conversation on the dance floor, while murmurs of speculation buzzed all about them. Bowing politely, Clay released his hold on Stephanie's waist and reached for Eden's hand. A collective sigh of relief went up, not the least of which was Eden's.

Her face as red as her hair, Stephanie stalked

off, disappearing into the crowd, but Eden barely noticed; her eyes were trained on Clay.

"Is this our dance, angel eyes?" Clay asked, smiling.

"It would seem so, and you needn't look so smug. It is *our* party, after all. Our guests expect us to act the happy couple."

His smile disappeared, and there was a bitter edge to his words as he twirled her about. "Oh, so this is all for their benefit? I should have guessed."

"Not entirely. I've always enjoyed dancing with you, and I'm pleased to find that your skills were not diminished by your sojourn in Texas."

"Angel," he whispered for her ears alone, pulling her into his chest, "my time spent in Texas only served to enhance my talents. Didn't I prove that to you the other day?"

His warm breath tickled her ear, creating chills over her bare arms, quite in contrast to her heated face. "A gentleman would not bring that up."

"I ceased being a *gentle* man five years ago, angel eyes. Have you ceased being a lady?"

She gasped, quickly turning about to see if anyone else had heard his offensive question. "Of course not! How could you ask such a thing?"

The high color in her cheeks seemed to indicate otherwise, and Clay's grip tightened reflexively. "Five years is a long time, Eden. I'd be a fool to think that you'd saved yourself for me."

She noted the burning question in his eyes, but she'd be damned before she admitted such a thing to Clay. Let him think what he wanted; he'd hear no reassurances about her innocence from her lips.

Her silence was damning. And at the end of the dance, Clay bowed politely and stomped off in the direction of the punch bowl, fury lighting the jade of his eyes to emeralds.

Eden stared after him, wondering if she should go to him, tell him what he wanted to hear.

But she could not.

Her pride would not allow it. Declining fortune or not.

"Clay looks fit to be tied, Eden. What on earth has happened?"

Eden groaned inwardly at the sound of the familiar drawl. She stared at her soon-to-be sister-in-law and resisted the very great urge to smack the stupid woman.

Lucy was obviously pleased to find that Eden and Clay had been arguing, though she did her best to hide it behind that all-too-sweet smile of concern she always wore. "I'm sure I don't know what you mean, Lucy," Eden lied. "Clay and I were merely chatting about the wedding."

"More likely you were discussing his liaison with that Dupree woman," Lucy countered maliciously. "I can't blame you for being upset with him, Eden. After all, the woman was Clay's paramour at one time."

Eden did her best to hide her shock, unsure whether or not to believe the gossipy woman.

Lucy was a troublemaker, and she would no doubt like to create trouble for both Eden and Clay. Clay had confided that Lucy was unhappy about his father's decision to turn Briarwood over to him. No doubt she would like to see Clay's efforts to find a wife thwarted at every turn.

"What Clay did in the past is none of my concern, Lucy. And, anyway, you're quite off the mark. We weren't discussing Miss Dupree."

"I'm so relieved. I'd hate for anything to come between you and Clay."

"Thank you, Lucy. I can only imagine how heartfelt your concern is." She smiled at the flustered woman's blush.

Not one to give up, Lucy sought a different bone of contention. "I declare, Eden! That dress you have on is totally inappropriate, don't you agree? To show so much bosom so soon after your father's funeral . . . Why, it just isn't done, my dear."

Eden let her gaze flow over Lucy's slight form. And when it landed on the catty woman's unremarkable bosom, she shook her head sadly. "It's a pity that you are so . . . so lacking in some of the more desirous feminine traits, Lucy dear. Does Richard mind that your bosom is so small?" She waved her hand airily. "Probably not. Men are happy with even the smallest of tidbits one is eager to share with them."

Lucy gasped, flushing hotly. "Why, I never! How dare you!" She stuttered so, Eden was sure the poor woman was about to have an apoplectic fit.

"Aunt Ruby says that if you rub goose fat on your breasts, it makes them as large as melons." Gesturing at her own generous mounds, Eden added, "Perhaps you should try that, my dear. It's done wonders for me."

With a shriek of outrage, Lucy lifted her skirts and hurried away. Eden could barely control the laughter that bubbled up in her throat as she watched the spiteful woman depart. Brushing her hands together as if she'd just completed some arduous task, Eden smiled happily and headed back to the party, remarking under her breath, "One Braxton down, and one to go."

Ten

June 15, 1826. I am finally with child. I pray to the almighty God that Mr. Fairchild will find it in his heart to abstain from his perverted pleasures and leave me in peace. I can find no solace at Beauclaire, only misery. How I wish for days gone by, to be reunited with my beloved Papa and Mama, and never have to submit to the horrors of the marriage bed. Modesty prevents me from putting into words the unspeakable acts I have committed, all in the name of love. Ha! As if that lovely intangible existed.

Eden gasped in surprise as she stared at the passage, stunned by the revelation that her mother had borne another child. No one had thought to mention that she'd once had a brother or sister. What had happened to the baby? Had it died?

Consumed by curiosity, Eden was determined to find out more about this mysterious child and vowed to speak to her aunt first thing in the morning.

Her eyes drifted over the passage again and she

shook her head sadly. Mama had not found the love she had wanted. Her marriage had been plagued with unhappiness from the beginning.

Was history merely repeating itself with her upcoming marriage to Clay?

She slammed the book shut. Damn, what a wretched state her life was in! In two days' time she was to be joined in holy matrimony to a man who was marrying her for revenge. To a man she was marrying to save her beloved plantation. Where was the joy she was supposed to know? Where was the love? The respect?

It had been nearly three weeks since that fateful night of the engagement party. She had seen Clay infrequently. They'd gone riding a few times, played bridge with Richard and Lucy one evening—Eden swore she could smell goose fat emanating from Lucy's direction—but there'd been no repeat of passionate kisses, or of ugly scenes such as the one that had been played out the night of the party, and no further mention of James Wakefield.

In fact, as far as James's behavior went, Eden might have dreamt the unfortunate encounter between them. He'd been pleasant and respectful, and it had been business as usual between her and the overseer, much to her very great relief. At least that was one problem she needn't worry about. Lord knew, she had plenty of others to occupy her mind.

Heaving a discontented sigh, she tossed the diary onto the floor and leaned her head back against the pillow, staring up at the crocheted canopy overhead. The threads were entwined to form a lacy design, and she marveled at the intricacy of the pattern. But one snip, one strong pull, and the whole carefully wrought design would unravel, come apart.

How like the canopy her life was at the moment. It wouldn't take much to tear her and Clay's marriage apart. Based on selfish motivations, it had no solid foundation upon which to build.

Tears welled up in her eyes, blurring her vision, until the intricate pattern was obscured—eclipsed by her pain. She wanted no loveless marriage. She wanted no marriage at all. But if she was to have one, then she wanted to be happy, content, not grow miserable and bitter, like her mother.

Two days. She had two more days before she would become Mrs. Clay Braxton. And that thought was nearly as terrifying as it had been five years ago . . .

Seventeen-year-old Eden stared at her reflection in the mirror and felt panic rise within her. Two days. Two more days and she would be Mrs. Clay Braxton. Her hands began to sweat as she smoothed the white satin skirt of her wedding gown.

"You look lovely, daughter," Lawrence Fairchild said. "Clay Braxton is a lucky man."

Eden spun around, thrusting her shaking hands behind her back at the sight of her father standing just inside the doorway of her room. "Thank you, Papa."

Lawrence cleared his throat, shifting his feet uncomfortably. "I'm sure your aunt has spoken to you of your duty to your husband."

Her cheeks pinkened, and she nodded.

"It is a wife's duty to submit." He couldn't keep the aversion out of his voice and Eden wondered at it, even as she chafed at the implication of his words. "It is the wife's role to service her husband and make him happy in all things. Men were put upon this earth to protect; women to serve. It is the natural order of things. Do you understand what I'm saying, Eden?"

"No!" she wanted to scream. No! She didn't understand why women must be subjugated into a servile position, to turn their heads at their husband's infidelities, as her mother had turned hers so many times. But she didn't scream. Instead, she blinked back the tears behind her lids and nodded, replying in a small voice, "Yes, Papa, I understand."

"You're young, Eden, but Clay will take you in hand, teach you all there is to know about being a proper wife. Don't disappoint me, daughter."

He spun on his heel and walked out, and Eden knew at that moment that there would be no marriage to Clay Braxton. Her father's words confirmed her worst fears, turning her dream of happiness into a nightmare. Marriage meant bondage, and she would never give up her freedom. Not for Clay, not for any man.

Eden shook herself, wiping her sweating palms against the counterpane, pushing the old, unwelcome memories to the back of her mind. Two more days, she thought, swallowing, hard. Two more days.

Clay shielded his eyes, gazing out at the long rows of tobacco plants silhouetted against a clear blue summer sky. Some of the laborers were bent over their hoes, weeding around the individual plants, while most of the field hands were in the process of topping the young plants, which required removing the top of the plant to prevent the tobacco from flowering, thus channeling the plant's energies into the twelve leaves that had formed. Once done, they would then remove the suckers, or secondary shoots, that would rob the developing leaves of important nutrients.

Charles Braxton had always told his sons that putting up a tobacco crop was a lot harder than raising two sons to adulthood. Clay was beginning to believe him. He'd forgotten how time-consuming the whole operation was, how a successful crop was dependent on so many variables—the weather, the slaves' cooperation, the soil.

Tobacco had a way of depleting the soil, much the same way an amorous woman could drain a man of his energies, sap his potency until he was putty in her hands.

He frowned. Eden was an amorous woman. But he'd be damned before he'd let her sap his strength. There was only going to be one master in charge of Beauclaire. And that master was him.

"Clay! Clay!"

At the sound of his name, Clay looked up to find Richard riding toward him, waving what appeared to be a copy of a newspaper. When he dismounted, Clay stepped forward to greet him, a worried frown on his face. "What's the problem, Richard? It's not Father, is it?" With all the excitement of the wedding, Charles had not rested as much as he should. His cough had worsened, and his appetite had declined.

Richard's voice was filled with excitement. "Word's just arrived that President Taylor is dead. I thought you'd want to know, seeing as how you served with him in Mexico."

Clay grabbed the newspaper, the *Rural Southerner*, out of his brother's hands and read the disturbing report of President Zachary Taylor's death due to cholera. It was hard to believe that "Old Rough-and-Ready," as he was often called, was really dead. Clay could still picture him sitting astride his horse in a broad-rim straw hat, blue-checked gingham duster, and pantaloons. He'd been one hell of a fighter, Clay thought, looking up to find Richard's intense gaze upon him.

"I guess you'll have to postpone the wedding, huh? It wouldn't look right to be married on the heels of such a traumatic event," Richard advised.

Wiping the sweat from his brow with the back of his hand, Clay shook his head and replied, "I hear Lucy speaking now, Richard, not you." He saw color rise to the younger man's cheeks and knew he had hit the nail on the head. "Well, you may advise your charming wife that I have no intention of postponing my marriage to Eden. It goes on tomorrow as planned, come hell or high water."

"I assure you, our motives were purely unselfish, Clay. Lucy wants only your happiness, as do I."

"And half of Briarwood?" Clay added, his right eyebrow arching in question as he observed his brother's flushed face deepen to crimson.

"I don't deny it. I've worked hard to make this plantation a success. It hardly seems fair that you should waltz in and take over after all my hard work. Briarwood prospers, thanks to me."

"*Tsk, tsk, tsk.* I hear sweet Lucy again, brother dear."

Richard grabbed the paper out of Clay's hands and remounted, furious at the knowing smile hovering about his older brother's lips. "You won't be wearing a smile much longer, Clay. Not when you're married and have to appease your wife. Trust me, hell is preferable to the miserable institution of marriage."

Richard rode off, leaving Clay to ponder the younger man's words. He had no doubt that Richard's marriage to Lucy was hell. Christ! The woman was a spawn of the devil herself.

But though Eden would attempt to make his life a living hell, Clay had no doubt that marriage to the passionate, stubborn woman was going to give him nothing but pleasure, and a taste of heaven most men find only after they're dead.

* * *

Eden gazed at her reflection in the long cheval mirror, and her hands started to sweat. The antique satin wedding gown she wore signified that her marriage to Clay was a reality she could not escape from this time. Taking a deep breath, she filled herself with calm acceptance of what was to come and returned her attention to the fitting at hand.

The dress, which had been her mother's, was belted at the waist, and had huge, puffy sleeves and a low-cut bodice worn off the shoulder. It was a stunning creation of satin and lace, with seed pearls sewn onto the bodice and skirt. A row of tiny hooks marched all the way down her back to her waist.

Holding out the sides of the full, bell-shaped skirt, she twirled about, feeling like a fairy princess. And from the approving expressions on Agnes's and Clarice Willowby's faces, they thought so, too.

Miss Willowby had arrived first thing this morning to oversee the final fitting of the bridal gown. Eden's mother had been shorter, as well as a great deal smaller in the waist and bust, necessitating a complete alteration of the gown. It had taken the talented dressmaker the better part of two weeks to complete it, but the wait had been well worth it.

"Well, that should do it, Miss Eden," Clarice said proudly. "I don't believe I've ever seen a lovelier bride." Surprising both of them, she bussed Eden on the cheek. "I hope you and Mr. Braxton will be very happy."

"Thank you, Miss Willowby," Eden replied, forcing a smile to her lips. She might look like a lovely bride, but she was definitely not a very happy one.

Agnes escorted the dressmaker to the door, then shut it behind her, leaning against the solid oak as she faced her young niece, her blue eyes clouded with concern. "Are you going to tell me what's wrong, child? Your face is longer than Reverend Sproull's sermons. Do you want to talk about it? I sense it's more than just tomorrow's wedding."

Eden crossed to the window and stared out. The sun was at its zenith. The fragrance of lilac drifted in, and she inhaled deeply of the sweet scent. Several of the slave children played on the lawn under the towering oaks, and there was a continual drone of activity as everyone prepared for tomorrow's event.

Everything appeared as it should. But nothing was the same. After tomorrow nothing would ever be the same again. And as Eden glanced down at the lovely dress, she thought of her mother, who'd worn the same garment, had the same fears, and had lived a life of misery and despair after experiencing the joy of her wedding day.

Turning to face her aunt, Eden finally spoke. "Mama wore this very gown, Aunt Agnes, when she married Papa."

"That's right, child. Charlotte was a lovely bride, though not quite as stunning as you." Agnes smiled. "You do your mother proud in that gown, my dear."

"Why was she so unhappy, Agnes? Why did she hate her life at Beauclaire?"

Uncertainty marred the older woman's features; she chose her words carefully. "You mustn't think of unpleasantness on the eve of your wedding, Eden. It's bad luck."

Eden smiled ruefully. "That's a joke. I've had nothing but bad luck since Papa died and Clay Braxton returned. I doubt a little more will hurt anything."

Taking a deep breath, Agnes explained. "Charlotte wasn't like you, Eden. She was weak, frail, too sheltered. She wasn't able to accept the harsh realities of life."

"Like the loss of a child?"

A look of surprise passed over Agnes's face, and then she paled slightly. "You know? How?"

"I found Mama's diary the day Papa's will was read. Though I haven't read it all, the parts I've read reveal a woman who despaired of ever finding happiness."

Agnes took a seat on the edge of the bed, trying to still the nervous shaking of her hands. *Charlotte's diary*. What if . . . ? She forced the unwanted thought from her mind. "Did the diary mention me?"

Eden was puzzled by her aunt's nervousness. "I don't believe so. There's been no mention of you, not yet, anyway. Why? What has upset you so?"

Agnes's mouth pinched tight, and there was pain in her eyes. "It's nothing we can discuss now, Eden. Now is not the proper time to address such things. But I promise you, I will reveal all when the time is right."

"You're scaring me, Aunt Agnes," Eden admitted, coming to sit next to her aunt on the bed, reaching for her hand, which was cold and clammy.

"There's nothing to worry about, my dear," Agnes reassured her, squeezing Eden's hand gently. "The past should be left dead and buried. It only conjures up painful memories best forgotten."

"Like Mama's dead child?"

Agnes nodded. "It was a boy, named after your father. He was born dead. Your mama never fully recovered from the loss of that child. He's buried next to her in the cemetery, but there is no headstone to mark his existence, only a rose bush to lend beauty to an otherwise gruesome occurrence."

"But that's terrible! Poor Mama."

"It's the way your father wanted it. Lawrence didn't want your mother to dwell in the past. He felt that if there was no headstone, Charlotte would get over the death of their son sooner. He was wrong."

"I feel so sorry for Mama. She seemed like such a lost soul."

Agnes drew Eden to her bosom. "Your mama is dead, child. Let her rest in peace. Don't delve into things you know nothing about; it will only bring you unhappiness." And me, as well, she thought, smoothing back the dark tendrils of hair from Eden's face as she had done so many times when Eden was a child.

"But I want to know more about my mother. She always kept me at a distance. Reading her diary brings me closer to her."

Agnes's voice filled with determination and she set Eden from her, staring her straight in the eye. "You must promise me something, child. You must promise not to read any more of the diary until we've had a chance to talk.

"You have to prepare for a wedding. Tomorrow begins a new chapter of your life. Close this old chapter, Eden, and begin anew. Give yourself a chance at happiness."

Tears misted the violet eyes and Eden's voice was choked with despair when she said, "What if I can't find happiness with Clay? What if I end up just like my mother? That fear has haunted me for years. I saw what marriage did to Mama; I don't want to end up like her."

Agnes's voice was vehement. "You won't, child! You have my word. Trust me and trust yourself. Clay Braxton is an honorable man. And though he has taken advantage of your misfortune, he is nothing like your father. There was love between you once." Her voice softened. "Nurture those feelings, child. They will come again. *Neither a fortress nor a maidenhead will hold out long after they begin to parley.*'"

"Aunt Agnes!" Eden blushed to the tips of her toes and she shook her head, wondering, not for the first time, if Agnes knew a saying to fit every occasion. It appeared, much to Eden's great consternation, that she did!

The pounding on the slave cabin door grew louder, as did the drunken roar of James Wakefield's voice. "Get your black ass out here, Belle. I've some work for you to do."

The slave's heart pounded in dread. "It's Mr. Wakefield," Belle whispered to her husband Sam. "I gots to go and see what he wants."

The burly black man pulled his wife back down onto the cornhusk mattress, his eyes filling with fury. "You knows what he wants, Belle. The same thing he always want. You'se my wife now. I can't let you go to him."

"Hush, now," Belle said, patting his cheek as she made to rise. "I gots to go; you knows that. We gots no choice. Iff'n I don't, Mr. Wakefield will make our lives plumb miserable."

Sam snorted. "Like they ain't already."

"It don't matter none, Sam. You is my man. Mr. Wakefield can take my body, but you has my heart."

"But it ain't right."

"You gots to promise me you'll stay in this cabin, Sam. I'll be back as soon as I can. Wakefield's drunk. No doubt he'll pass out before long." But she knew that was a lie. Spirits only made Master Wakefield virile, more mean.

"I'll go to the young missus. Miss Eden will help us," Sam said, attempting to rise, but Belle pushed him back down.

"Miss Eden is getting married tomorrow; she can't be bothering about the likes of us. Promise me you'll stay."

When Sam grudgingly agreed, Belle drew on her cotton shift to cover her nudity and answered the summons.

"It's about time, bitch," Wakefield yelled, reaching out to pull her out the door. He cupped her breasts with both hands, squeezing painfully until she winced. "Get your black ass over to my house. I got some chores for you to do."

"But it's the middle of the night, Master Wakefield. Can't it wait till morning?"

Wakefield grabbed her hand and rubbed it against his crotch. She felt the rigidity, the fullness of his desire, and bitter bile rose to her throat.

"I got a powerful hunger tonight, Belle. I need you to take care of it."

"But I'se married now, Master. I gots me a husband."

His upper lip snarled. "You won't if I sell that big buck downriver, now, will you?"

Belle's eyes filled with fear and hatred. The threat was familiar, having been made many times before. And she had no doubt in her mind that the overseer would carry it out without Miss Eden's knowledge. She pulled the door behind her, so Sam couldn't witness her shame.

Yanking the slave woman by the hand, Wakefield pulled her along in the direction of the barn. "I changed my mind, wench. No need to dirty the sheets when the barn's full of freshly mown hay. And soft, too."

When they reached the barn's black interior, he locked the door behind him and panic, once again, blossomed in Belle's chest. "Get on up that ladder, Belle. We'll go up to the loft. No one will disturb us there."

"Please, Master Wakefield, don't hurt me none," Belle pleaded, as she started to climb up the ladder, Wakefield right behind her. When they reached the top, she felt his hands on her legs and she gasped.

He wouldn't hurt her, Wakefield thought. Not tonight. Tonight it would be Eden's body he took, Eden's breasts he held tenderly in his hands. "Now, why would I want to hurt you, Belle," he said softly, running his hands up her thighs, squeezing her mound. "Climb up there and take that dress off. Get on your hands and knees." When she did as he ordered, he gazed down at her and chuckled. "You look like a cow ready for milking with those big tits of yours hanging down. I wonder, do you give black milk or white?" Leaning over her from the rear, he unfastened his breeches, then cupped the pendulous globes.

"Next to Eden, you got the biggest tits I've ever seen, girl. Spread your legs." Belle gasped at the mention of Eden's name, then did as instructed.

"Since we're in a barn, it's only fitting that we should fuck like animals," he slurred, grasping her buttocks with both hands, sliding his fingers into the crevice. "You're slick, Belle. You want it, don't you? Tell me you do, Belle."

With tears clouding her vision, Belle swallowed, then lied, "Yes, master, I want you something fierce." *She didn't want to be beat; she didn't want to be tied up like some dog. God forgive her!*

"Do you think Eden will want it when I plant my cock deep inside of her?" He plunged into her then, and her cry saved her from answering.

"Eden, Eden," he moaned, as he drove in to the hilt, rocking back and forth, bringing forth a gasp of pain from Belle's lips. He clutched the bud of her desire. Belle forced herself to think of other things.

Biting her lower lip as Wakefield's shudders of pleasure shook her, Belle felt her shame knew no bounds, and she silently cursed him. And with every powerful thrust of his manhood, she vowed that one day she would get even. No matter how long it took.

Eleven

She had promised to *love, honor and obey*, but as she gazed across the black and white tiled ballroom of the mansion to where her husband stood in conversation with his father, Eden knew she had no intention of doing any such thing.

The wedding ceremony was over, the reception all but done. All that remained was the wedding night.

She swallowed hard, wondering why she had nearly forgotten about it. She'd been so preoccupied with the actual ceremony, she had forced to the back of her mind what came after.

A marriage in name only. Would it be? she wondered, as she watched her husband cross the room with long, purposeful strides in her direction. Clay looked so handsome in his formal black attire. The emerald stickpin in his snowy white cravat matched the color of his eyes exactly. Her heart fluttered as she caught his smile, which she returned in kind.

"Father wishes to bid you good night, Eden,"

Clay said, coming to stand before her. "He'll be leaving now, as will Lucy and Richard."

"And you? Will you be leaving, too?" She held her breath, wondering what his answer would be. But when his smile turned blatantly sensual, she knew, and her heart sank.

"What do you think, angel eyes? How could I leave such a beautiful bride on our wedding night?" he whispered, reaching for the curl that lay against her breast.

The feel of his hand against her flesh brought warmth to her cheeks, and other, lower, regions of her body. "We had an agreement, remember?" she reminded him.

"I won't force you, Eden. But then, I really don't think I'll have to." He said the words with such confidence, such arrogance, Eden became immediately incensed; her eyes flashed fire.

"You're . . ."

"Ssh," he warned, grasping her waist. "My father is approaching. Let's keep our affairs of the bedroom private. It's no one else's business what goes on there."

"Or doesn't go on," she countered, glad she was able to wipe away his smug smile before pasting on one of her own to greet her new father-in-law as he wheeled himself toward them.

"You made quite a beautiful bride, my dear," Charles said, his eyes brimming with unshed tears of joy. "I'm so happy that you and Clay have finally gotten together after all these years. I can go to my grave in peace now."

Eden smiled at the man's confession and was

about to respond when Agnes whirled into the room, breathing fire like a dragon as she turned on Charles Braxton with a vehemence Eden thought excessive. She was stunned by her aunt's outlandish behavior.

"I see you haven't changed a bit, Charles Braxton. Still moaning and groaning about your deathbed. And on your son's wedding day, of all things. You should be ashamed."

Charles looked up at the gray-haired woman he remembered quite distinctly, a red flush suffusing his cheeks. "Well, well, Agnes. I should have known. No one else at this plantation was ever as rude."

"No one else had the guts to speak the truth but me, you mean."

The hazel eyes traveled over Agnes's form insultingly before they returned to her face, which was masked with indignation. "You'd think on your niece's wedding day that you would have the decency to wear something feminine and appropriate," Charles accused, "instead of those disgusting pant things you're so fond of wearing. You'll never be a man, Agnes Peters, no matter how hard you try."

Observing the two, Eden had the distinct feeling that there was more to this argument than met the eye, but she didn't have time to ponder it now. Exchanging a worried look with Clay, who just shrugged and shook his head as if to say, "There's nothing we can do about a long-standing feud," Eden stepped forward to intervene. She didn't trust the stubborn glint in her aunt's eye, nor the way her hands were clenched into fists.

"Come, come, let's be friends," Eden cajoled. "After all, we're related now. Surely you two can bury the hatchet."

"Hmph!" Agnes said, crossing her arms over her chest, looking like she'd very much like to bury the hatchet in Charles Braxton's back.

"Hmph!" Charles mimicked, needing no explanation as to why Agnes Peters was still a spinster.

For once in his life, Clay was relieved to see Richard and Lucy crossing the room in his direction; though he had to admit, he hadn't seen his father this animated in weeks.

"Here comes Richard now, Father. I think you should bid these lovely ladies goodnight. I fear you are overly tired."

There was no mistaking the warning note in Clay's voice. Charles smiled apologetically at Eden, ignoring Agnes altogether, and bade his new daughter-in-law goodnight with a farewell kiss, before departing with his other son.

When Charles was out of earshot, Agnes, who looked as if she was ready to spit nails, blurted, "Well, of all the unmitigated . . ."

"I think perhaps we're all a bit tired, don't you, Aunt Agnes?" Eden butted in, before the outspoken woman could voice another rude comment. Clay had returned from escorting his family out, and she had no intention of refereeing a shouting match between those two.

Clay and Aunt Agnes had been tiptoeing around each other all day, and Eden feared it was only the solemnity of the occasion that had prevented either of them from voicing their true opinions of each other. Agnes might think Clay an honorable man, but she wasn't quite ready to forgive him for taking unfair advantage of her niece. And now that their marriage was sealed, she'd have no qualms about saying so.

"I suspect you're right, child," Agnes replied, casting Clay a hostile look. "I bid you a good evening." With that, she spun on her heel and disappeared out of the room, leaving Eden and Clay quite alone.

"Whew!" Clay remarked, shaking his head. "I feel like I've just ridden on the tail end of a hurricane."

Eden laughed, for that was as good a description of Agnes as any. "I guess you can see who I take after in temperament."

Pouring two glasses of champagne, Clay handed Eden one and smiled. "I like my women with a little fire. I just don't want to be incinerated by it."

The flames of desire were already licking at Eden's flesh and she gulped down her drink, wishing there was some way she could douse the heat that burned within her every time Clay drew near.

But she knew there was not. There was an attraction between them that neither suffering nor time had lessened. She wanted him. He wanted her. And their joining was an eventuality that was going to pass, no matter how hard she tried to avoid it.

"You've grown very quiet, angel eyes." He refilled her glass, the intensity of his jade eyes searing her.

"I guess I'm just tired."

"Shall we go up to bed, then?"

There was a wealth of uncertainty, of desire, in his voice as he posed the question, and Eden knew how important her answer would be to both of them. She swallowed the contents of her glass in one gulp, a denial forming on her lips; but before she could utter it, Clay took the glass from her hands, redepositing it on the table, and swept her up in his arms.

"I believe it is customary for the groom to carry his bride over the threshold."

"But . . ." He swept out of the room and into the hall before she could protest, climbing the wide staircase to the second floor, and Eden's heart pounded with every step he took. "Clay," she began again, unsure of just what it was she was going to say. For some reason, her thinking had become quite muddled.

"Don't fight it, Eden," he said, kicking open the door to her room. "We both want it; you know it's true. We're married now."

Eden felt hot. Her head was spinning, as was the room. The champagne had rendered her lightheaded, and she wrapped her arms about Clay's neck, clutching him close, hoping to regain her equilibrium.

Mistaking her reaction for acquiescence, Clay smiled triumphantly and strolled to the bed, lowering Eden onto the feather mattress.

"I feel so dizzy," she confessed, unable to stifle a giggle.

"Roll over, let me help you with your hooks." She did as he ordered and soon his deft fingers had unfastened each and every one of the tiny hooks. He eased her dress down, removing her petticoats and stockings until only her corset and chemise remained.

"Why on earth do you women wear such hideous things?" he scolded, untying the laces, noting the harsh red marks the corset had left.

"Mama's dress would never have fit without it," Eden confessed, filling her lungs with air when Clay removed the constricting garment.

"Feel better?" he asked, his eyes drinking in the sight of her smooth white flesh. Only the thin chemise hid her ample charms, and he would have that removed shortly.

"Much. But aren't you going to get undressed? Surely you don't plan to sleep in your clothing." She giggled at the absurd thought, bringing a smile to Clay's lips.

Eden was tipsy, he thought, stripping quickly out of his clothes. He'd never seen her imbibe more than half a glass of sherry before. And obviously, the champagne had gone straight to her head. Hopefully, she wouldn't be too drunk to enjoy what he was going to do to her tonight. Completely naked, he approached the bed. "I'm undressed now, Eden."

Eden, who had closed her eyes for a moment, opened them quickly and gasped. Clay was completely and deliciously naked. His huge member stuck out like some fierce warrior's sword. Without thinking, she reached her hand out and stroked the velvet hardness, hearing his sharp intake of breath.

"Did I hurt you?" she asked, pulling her hand quickly away.

He climbed onto the bed, easing himself down next to her, pulling at the ribbons of her chemise until they were undone. "You did once, angel eyes, a long time ago. But we're going to make up for that tonight."

Eden felt confused. She couldn't quite decide what Clay was talking about, and when his hand reached out to cup her breast, she just didn't care any longer.

"You're incredibly beautiful, Eden. I've dreamt of this moment for a long time."

Clay's voice cast a seductive web over her, and Eden couldn't form a response, for he was sucking on her nipples, first the right one, then the left. Soon her chemise was lying on the pillow next to her head and she was completely naked.

"I want you, Eden. I've always wanted you," Clay confessed, before thrusting his tongue deep within her mouth. The fingers of his right hand trailed up her legs, her thighs, coming to rest on the apex between them. He cupped her mound, grinding the heel of his hand over the soft, springy curls. When he felt her moist response, heard her moan of desire, he inserted his finger into her cleft, moving in and out in replicated rhythmic motion with his tongue.

Eden felt incredible heat center between her thighs.

She moved against his hand, knowing what pleasure awaited her.

When the hard weight of him settled over her, she didn't protest. Not until the butterflies in her stomach turned to wildly flapping bat wings and the bed beneath her began to spin.

"Clay!" she choked. "Clay." Panic rose in her throat.

"I know, sweetheart. I know," Clay said, easing himself between Eden's outstretched legs. Mistaking her paleness for fear, he mumbled soothing words in her ear, ready to drive his manhood home, when Eden pushed forcefully against his chest, opened her eyes wide, covered her mouth with her hand, and leaned over the side of the bed.

Clay's heart shriveled, as did his erection. There was no mistaking the sound of Eden's retching, nor the offensive odor that rose up to inform him that Eden had just given up her champagne and most of her dinner.

With a groan, he held her head until all that was left in her stomach were dry heaves of air. Easing her back down on the pillow, he procured a wet washcloth from the marble-topped washstand and placed it on her forehead; then, gathering up more towels, he cleaned up the mess on the floor, dumping it all out the window onto an unsuspecting crape myrtle bush, which would, no doubt, think twice before blooming this year.

Climbing back on the bed, Clay tucked his now

sleeping wife under the covers, blew out the oil lamp, and smiled ruefully into the darkness. "Well, angel," he whispered, "I've had many reactions to my lovemaking over the years, but never quite like the one you gave me tonight."

With a chaste peck on her cheek, he settled in next to her and prepared himself mentally for what was sure to be a totally miserable night's sleep.

The next morning Eden awoke with her temples pounding louder than Wilbur Tayloe's drum and a godawful taste in her mouth. Cocking one eye open, she spied her husband's smiling face gazing down at her. He was propped up on his elbow, staring at her intently, as if she were the most interesting specimen in the world. She smiled weakly.

"Morning, angel eyes. How are you feeling?"

Her answer was a moan, and Clay immediately summed up the situation. With gentle hands, he applied pressure to her temples and massaged the throbbing area with small, circular motions, smiling at the contented sigh that escaped her lips.

Eden had never felt anything more wonderful in her life. Well, maybe that wasn't *quite* accurate, she reconsidered, feeling heat rise to her cheeks.

"Better?"

She smiled gratefully in response. "Yes."

"I have just the thing to fix you up." Without a thought to his nakedness, or the soft gasp that escaped Eden's lips, Clay bounded out of bed, returning a moment later with a cup of hot coffee that Jewel had brought in moments earlier. The familiar aroma sent Eden's stomach rumbling in response.

"Drink this. You'll feel better."

She did, but wasn't quite as optimistic about his prognosis. "I doubt that I'll ever feel better again."

He laughed. "A whole sentence this time. You *are* on the mend."

"It's bad of you to joke at a time like this, Clay. I'm dying. At least you could take pity on me."

"And who's going to pity me, Mrs. Braxton? At least you slept like the dead. I was awake most of the night."

It was then she noted the dark circles under his eyes, the shadow of a beard on his face; and the memory of what they'd been doing came crashing over her like a tidal wave. Her cheeks flamed and she stared down at her lap. It was then she noticed that she was completely naked. "Oh!" Her hands moved so quickly to cover herself, she nearly spilled the hot coffee.

Clay removed the cup from her hands before she could burn herself, then settled down next to her. "We have some unfinished business, you and I," he said, his finger trailing up her arm.

Tingles of awareness darted through her, but she refused to acknowledge them, clutching the sheet tight about her. "Whatever do you mean, Clay? It's broad daylight out! And . . . and . . . Well, I wasn't myself last night."

"I thought you were wonderful." His hand

moved up to cup her breast and Eden's heart thudded in response as he eased the sheet out of her hands. "Don't cover yourself. Your breasts are much too lovely to hide." He leaned over and quickly kissed each nipple.

Eden sucked in her breath, grasping Clay's head. She wanted to hold him to her breast, allow him to continue creating the delicious sensations, but she couldn't. Reason demanded that she put an end to his seduction. "You mustn't." She tried to push him away.

"Oh, but I must," he whispered, ignoring her attempts to stop him, sucking furiously, creating fire wherever his lips touched. All of Eden was throbbing now, not just her temples.

Grabbing Eden's leg, Clay tugged her down until she was lying flat on the mattress. "I want you on your back, Eden. I want you looking up at me. I want to see your eyes darken with passion when I enter you." He placed his hand between her thighs and began massaging the ache there. "Better?" he said, smiling at her blush as she recalled his earlier question. She was wet. And hot. The heat from her pulsing mound was driving him wild.

Eden felt powerless to refuse. Clay's mouth seemed to be everywhere at once. He tortured her nipples with quick, teasing strokes, then trailed down to lick at her navel. Every muscle in Eden's stomach tensed as he moved from her stomach, lower, ever lower, until his head rested between her thighs.

"Clay," Eden moaned, as his tongue entered

her. All thoughts of resistance fled, and Eden arched up, opening her legs wider to give him access.

"You're so lovely, angel. Pink and soft, and sweet as spun sugar." He tongued her a few moments longer, then settled himself on top of her, easing his turgid member between her legs. "Open for me, sweetheart. That's right." His mouth found her lips and he kissed her hard, plunging into the depths of her tight, virginal canal.

Eden winced at the brief moment of pain, then relaxed and gave herself into the rhythm of Clay's movements. She clutched at his hips, pulling his long staff fully into her. She heard his moan of pleasure and felt joy that she had pleased him.

Harder and harder Clay pumped into her, entering then receding, over and over as they climbed to the pinnacle of their fulfillment. As she neared the edge of the precipice, her body began to quiver; every nerve ending in her body seemed to be centered at the juncture of her legs. With one final, hard thrust, everything exploded and she cried out as their bodies melded together and became one entity.

Eden had never felt so totally relaxed, so contented; she was deliriously happy. So much so, in fact, that she couldn't contain the satisfied smile that crossed her lips. Her heart was full to bursting. All the niggling doubts about marriage to

Clay had just been erased by their beautiful act of consummation.

They were now man and wife; their marriage would work. She would see to it that it did, for she realized that her love for Clay, which had lain dormant for five long years, had blossomed fully within her heart.

Opening her eyes, she gazed into Clay's green orbs, searching out his feelings for her. But other than the passion that still rode him hard, she could find no love light shining within them.

"You were wonderful, angel," Clay finally said, heaving a contented sigh of his own.

And a virgin! He hadn't dared hope that she was still an innocent, and the pleasure he felt at the knowledge was overwhelming. He'd been the first; he'd be the last!

"It was well worth all the pain and the waiting I had to endure to experience the total satisfaction you've just given me. Thank you." He kissed her lips tenderly, then rolled off her, not seeing the hurt in her eyes.

Eden couldn't believe what she was hearing. Thank you. Thank you, he had said. Not, I love you, Eden. I've missed you, Eden. Just, Thanks for the satisfaction.

Eden's blossoming love was wilting quickly. She bit her lower lip to keep from screaming all the awful things she wanted to say.

"Was it good for you, sweetheart? Did I please you?"

She swallowed her tears and her disappointment. Clay would never know how she felt; she wouldn't give him another weapon to use against her. Taking a deep breath, she said, "It hurt." *God, how it hurt.*

Tenderly, he caressed her cheek. "It always hurts the first time. Next time . . ."

Her voice hardened, her words coated with bitterness. "There won't be a next time. I've more than fulfilled my part of the agreement, though you weren't gentlemanly enough to keep your end of the bargain. Kindly return my note to me. I believe you've been paid in full."

Clay reeled as if he'd been slapped. His face whitened, then his lips slashed thin across his face, his eyes hardening to green ice. The calculating little bitch, he thought. Here he'd believed that she had formed some feelings for him, that the love they'd once shared had been rekindled. But all she wanted was her damn note back. All she cared about was her damn plantation!

Jumping out of bed, as if he couldn't abide being next to her one moment longer, Clay retrieved his evening jacket from the floor and pulled out a sealed envelope. Pulling on his breeches, he tossed the envelope in her lap.

"I was saving this—as a surprise wedding gift." He laughed sardonically. "Foolish me. Here—take it. Clutch it to your breast. See if it brings you the same satisfaction our lovemaking did."

Ignoring her shocked gasp, he continued, "If I thought I could stay away from you, I would ride back to Briarwood and never see you again. But I can't. And I won't. For I paid twenty thousand dollars for the privilege of thrusting between those milky, white thighs of yours, angel. And I aim to get my money's worth."

Eden paled as white as the sheets, sinking back into the pillows.

"You sold yourself like a whore, sweetheart, and I'm going to ride you until I get my fill." He paused by the door to look back at her over his shoulder with an expression that was chilling. "And, angel, I'm a hard man to satisfy!" With that, he slammed out the door so hard the Chippendale mirror on the wall shook.

With tears blurring her vision and an ache in her heart that hurt to the depths of her soul, Eden tore open the envelope. Inside rested the promissory note. Another piece of paper fell out, written in Clay's distinctive handwriting: "For my wife Eden on our wedding day. *What God hath joined together, let no man put asunder.*"

She wept. For Clay already had.

Twelve

"Lordy, be. The sun might be shining as bright as a baby's smile, but there is black clouds on de horizon. Yes, sir!" Aunt Ruby complained to her daughter Jewel, as they finished putting the last coat of beeswax on the parlor furniture. "These past two weeks have been plumb miserable."

Jewel paused, dustrag in hand, a secretive smile curving her lips as she thought of Eden and Clay. It was true enough that the young missus and her new husband were anything but cordial to each other. And that they hadn't spoken more than a handful of words since they'd uttered their "I do's." But that didn't mean that they didn't love each other. They were just two dang stubborn people who didn't know it right now.

"Don't be frettin' so, Mama. I seen the way Miss Eden's eyes follow Master Clay when he ain't lookin'. And he's a man in love if ever I seen one. Those two were meant for each other; they'll work out what's ailin' them. They jes need some time, that's all."

Ruby's look was skeptical, and she was about to disagree when her sharp eyes landed on a long, red tail sticking out from under the Chippendale loveseat. Bending down, her whole body shook in anger when she discovered Clay's dog fast asleep on Miss Charlotte's Aubusson rug. Swatting the animal's behind with her dusting rag, she shouted, "Get on outa heah, you red hussy. Iff'n Miss Agnes was to catch you, she'd have my hide."

The dog, with the unlikely name of Ruby, much to the old woman's annoyance, stretched lazily, as if she had all the time in the world, stuck her long snout in the air, cast an assessing gaze Aunt Ruby's way, then trotted out of the room in queenly fashion, bringing a bright flush to the old woman's cheeks.

Jewel giggled at the outrage on her mother's face. "I think that dog likes you, Mama. Truly I do. She's been following you around for days."

"*Hmph!* You jes finish puttin' on that beeswax and never mind about them dogs of Master Clay's. Who'd go and name a dog Ruby, anyways?" she wondered aloud, clearly indignant to have to share her name with a four-legged creature. "And the other one—Rory. What kind of a name is dat?" She shook her kerchiefed head, mumbling invectives under her breath.

"Them are Irish setters, Mama. Miss Eden done told me that Master Clay had them shipped all the way across the Atlantic Ocean."

"Well he can jes ship 'em back, 'cause iff'n that Rory attacks Miss Agnes's Desdemona one more time, there's goin' to be hell to pay."

Upstairs, Clay's intrusion into Beauclaire's normal routine was met with as much, or more, hostility from his new bride, who didn't appreciate sharing herself, or her bedchamber, with the overbearing brute.

"Hellfire and perdition!" Eden swore, hands splayed on well-rounded hips as she stared at the large accumulation of her husband's clothing which took up half the space in the walnut wardrobe. She shoved Clay's frilly white shirts aside in search of a suitable morning gown.

What right did Clay have to move all his stuff into her room, as if he belonged? Husband or no, he could just buy himself another wardrobe, and she intended to tell him so today. Retrieving her red and white calico gown, she donned it hurriedly, tying her hair back with a red satin ribbon.

Clay had gone to the fields to survey the tobacco crop, as if she really needed his help, she thought, sweeping out of her room to head downstairs. She had no intention of allowing him to usurp her authority where the management of Beauclaire was concerned. This was her plantation, and she would run it as she saw fit. So said, at least to herself, she slammed out the front door in the direction of the barn.

Unfortunately, when informed of her feelings, Clay wasn't at all inclined to agree with Eden, and he told her so in no uncertain terms.

"I've already explained to your overseer that after this crop of tobacco is brought in, we'll be planting this field in wheat, the other in clover, Eden."

Impervious to the dozens of field hands who were listening to the exchange with the utmost interest, Eden let loose with a shriek. "Wheat! Clover! Beauclaire is no ordinary farm. We're a tobacco plantation. We've always grown tobacco here; we'll continue to do so until the day I die."

Ignoring the puzzled looks that many of the slaves wore, Clay spoke to Isaac, issuing his final orders, before pulling his errant wife by the hand until they were standing beneath the shade of a tall catalpa tree, far away from inquisitive ears.

A thunderous expression clouded Clay's face; his words were pointed, and he stabbed the air when he spoke. "You will not gainsay my orders in the front of the hands, Eden. Is that clear? Do you want to undermine my authority? You'll not be allowed out to the fields if you continue to behave in such a rash manner."

Clay's position at Beauclaire was tenuous. It was important that he establish right from the beginning who was in charge. The slaves not only needed the authority, they needed the security of knowing that their lives and routines would not be interrupted by their mistress's marriage. Clay intended to provide them with both.

Eden gasped, her face turning red. "How dare you! This is my plantation. I will come and go as I please, where I please, and you will have no say. This plantation and everything on it is mine." Her words were pure bravado, for she knew, as did Clay, that everything she said was a lie.

As her husband, he ruled absolute, and that knowledge was a bitter pill to swallow. In fact, she wasn't sure if it would ever go down without choking the very life out of her.

Clay's smile was anything but kind, and his words were nothing more than she expected. "Oh, but you're wrong, Mrs. Braxton. As my wife, everything you own belongs to me. I am in charge of Beauclaire, as I am in charge of you. And if you don't mind what I have to say, I will lock you up in our room until you do. Is that clear?"

Like a teapot about to boil over, Eden sputtered with outrage. Counting to ten, she tried to regain control of her temper. Once she did, she said in as calm a voice as she could muster, "We have always planted tobacco here. Why would you want to change that fact? Your own family's lands are planted in the same way. If you want to change things, why don't you go back to Briarwood and do it?"

Patiently, he explained. "Beauclaire's soil is worn out. Your father never rotated his crops, and the tobacco has drained all of the nutrients out of the soil. If you continue on in this fashion, you will not be able to grow tobacco or any other crop, for that matter."

Her expression was clearly skeptical. "How do you know? Why . . . you haven't even farmed the land for over five years. What makes you such an expert?"

"Since I've been home, I've been attending some of the agriculture society meetings held in town. What I've learned makes sense. The other crops will put back into the soil what the tobacco takes out. We need to start a system of crop rotation to keep this land from playing out, and to keep this plantation running profitably."

"And do you have reading material that explains all this?" Her temper had cooled now, and she could see what Clay said made sense, though she didn't want to admit that to him. Fairchilds always made the decisions at Beauclaire, and she didn't see why that had to change just because she was married to a despot.

A handsome despot, she amended silently, allowing her gaze to flow over the tight buckskin breeches, the sweatstained shirt that clung to his chest. It wasn't fair that he had the power to make her want him. It wasn't fair at all.

"Probably," he answered her query, forcing her attention back to the matter at hand. "And if you're good, I might even let you read a couple of my agricultural journals." He grinned, causing anger to flare briefly in the violet depths again. Clay watched Eden fight to keep her temper in check, biting back a smile at the effort. If Eden could channel just a small portion of that emotion into their lovemaking... He shook his head, forcing the painful thought away.

They hadn't made love since that fateful morning when he'd found out just what the most important thing was in Eden's life. It had been a painful lesson to learn that these miserable acres of land meant more to her than he did. But then, why was he so surprised? She had married him only to save Beauclaire—not because she loved him.

And that knowledge hurt. In fact, it was downright wounding. For he had searched his heart, and found, much to his very great horror, that he was in love with his wife. Had always loved her. More fool he.

He gazed at her smooth features, the way the sunlight played off her face, the way a few loose strands of ebony hair clung to her cheeks, and his heart ached. Eden was so beautiful, and so very passionate. An unwelcome but familiar yearning stirred in his loins, but he forced it away. His pride would not allow him to play second fiddle to a piece of land.

Once, Eden had taken his heart and crushed it in her selfish hands. He would never open himself up to that kind of hurt again. Eden would never know how he felt about her, never know of his love. But she would know of his lust, and soon.

"I really can't say that I agree with your husband's decision to replant our fields in wheat and clover, Eden," James Wakefield said a short time later. He had come up to the house, eager to add his voice to the dissension Braxton had created. News of their disagreement had spread through the quarter like a plague, and it was the very thing he needed to drive a wedge into the chasm Braxton caused with his imperious demands and newfangled agricultural nonsense.

Eden sighed as she looked up from the row of

figures she added to gaze at James's earnest face. It wouldn't be proper to usurp Clay's authority with the overseer, no matter how much she might disagree with Clay. He was her husband, and they must always present a united front; her father had taught her that much in dealing with the help.

"Mr. Braxton is in charge of Beauclaire, James. It would do you good to remember that fact."

Of all the things James had expected Eden to say, that wasn't one of them, and he reeled on his heels as if slapped. Forcing down his anger, he replied, "Of course, Eden. I have no wish to gainsay your husband's edict. But I felt it my duty to advise you that I feel you're making a big mistake. We've always done well with tobacco. A change like this could ruin our profits."

"I intend to investigate Clay's methods, James, before I give my blessing to them, but in the meantime, we must acquiesce to his wishes. Mr. Braxton holds the reins at Beauclaire now."

"I can see that's not the only thing he controls," he tossed out, quickly amending, "I quite understand the situation, Eden, though I'm saddened by it."

The overseer's words hit close to the mark, bringing a rush of color to Eden's cheeks. The man had overstepped his bounds. But how could she correct him, when everything he said was true? She had no authority, and everyone at Beauclaire, including herself, knew it.

"I believe this discussion is at an end, James. Please be so kind as to drop off those invoices for the horse tack you purchased as soon as you're able. I need to reconcile my books. Friday begins the new month and the beginning of a new ledger."

He nodded, and as an afterthought said, "And, Eden, don't hesitate to come to me if I can be of any assistance. You know I'll always be here for you."

"I doubt my wife will require much of your assistance, Wakefield. She has me to help her now."

"Clay." Eden swallowed as her husband stepped into the room. He moved with such pantherlike grace, she hadn't heard him approach; and the expression on his face was anything but cordial as he stared directly at the overseer, his eyes as hard as his words when he spoke.

"I believe your services are no longer required this day, Wakefield. Get out to the fields where you belong. If you need to confer about anything else pertaining to the running of this estate, you're to seek me out. Do you understand?"

Wakefield's face grew florid. "Perfectly."

"Then go. I don't pay you to stand around and chit-chat with my wife."

"Clay!" Eden chastised, noting the animosity on the overseer's face. "James . . . Mr. Wakefield was only trying to help."

Slamming the door behind the overseer and locking it, Clay advanced on his wife. "You look awfully businesslike sitting behind that desk, angel. But your business is taking care of my needs, not interfering in the running of this plantation."

She gasped at his affront. "Taking care of your needs! Why . . . I'll do no such thing. I've kept my end of the agreement."

Crossing the room, he walked to the windows, pulling the drapery closed. Immediately, she grew wary. "What . . . what are you doing?"

"Once, when I was in Mexico," he began, seating himself on top of the desk directly in front of her, "I saw a general take a Mexican girl who'd been caught spying and drag her into his office."

Eden swallowed, not liking the provocative glimmer in Clay's eyes, nor where his story was headed. "I don't see what that has to do with me."

Without replying, he reached out, grabbing on to Eden's hand, pulling her out of her chair, until she was standing between his legs. "Do you know what he did to that girl?"

Her eyes wide, she shook her head, trying to swallow past the large lump that had formed in her throat. Clay's hands were gliding up and down her arms, his knees pressing into her hips to keep her firmly in place. "Well, angel . . ." he said, flipping her over his leg until she was sprawled on his lap, nearly lying on top of the desk.

"Clay, stop it," Eden demanded, squirming, trying to get free.

Ignoring her outburst, he continued, ". . . that general took that lovely señorita and laid her across his desk, much like you are now, with her tempting, firm fanny arched high in the air." He patted her buttocks with slow, circular motions, easing up her skirt all the while he talked. Undoing the tapes of her drawers, he eased them down off her hips until her lily white bottom was bare to his view.

"You're so lovely, Eden," he whispered, almost absently.

"Stop, Clay," Eden gasped, feeling his hands on her bare flesh. The caress of his fingers sent her senses soaring, as did the erotic pictures he created with his silken words.

"And do you know what he found when he inserted his finger deep within the soft velvet of her canal?"

Clay was demonstrating as he spoke, his finger entering her from behind, easing in and out, plying the bud of her desire until it was pebble-hard and throbbing. Eden couldn't form a response, only shook her head, as if to say that she didn't know anything at all except the way he was making her feel at this very moment, like a firecracker about to explode.

"He found a note hidden there," Clay went on to explain, "from Santa Anna, the Mexican general. We all speculated as to how it got there, and who put it there."

"Please," she cried out, as her woman's flesh rubbed against the rough material of his buckskin breeches, stimulating her, causing her to writhe and moan in painful pleasure. "Take me, Clay. Please!" she begged, unable to believe it was her voice asking for—demanding release.

Without hesitation, Clay flipped her over, bringing her hot flesh to his mouth. His tongue entered her, his lips and teeth biting playfully at the throbbing nub, as his hands went to the front of his breeches to undo the laces there.

Eden cried out as Clay penetrated her. Papers and ink scattered everywhere. The pair of brass candlesticks on the corner of the desk clanged to the floor as the desk shook from his hard pumping motions.

"Clay," Eden moaned, arching up to meet him.

"Look at me, Eden." Clay's voice was as hard as his shaft. "Look at me and tell me who is master of this plantation."

She opened her eyes, breathing deeply at the fierce look on Clay's sweatstained face. The effort to hold back was causing Clay as much pain as it was causing her. "Tell me," he demanded, grinding himself against her, torturing her with his words and body. "Tell me, or I will pull out and leave you to ponder the answer alone."

When she hesitated, he began to make good on his threat, but the throbbing ache between her thighs could not allow him to leave her unfulfilled. With tears filling her eyes, and a sob tearing from her throat, she admitted, "You are. Damn you! You are."

Smiling, he grasped her hips, pulling her onto him. And with one final, hard thrust, took her over the edge of her desire.

Eden screamed out at the intensity of her climax, clinging to Clay's muscular forearms as her body convulsed time and time again. When the spasms abated, she opened her eyes, but her euphoric state quickly evaporated at the sight of Clay's gloating smile. She turned away in shame.

But Clay would have none of it, and gently grasped her chin, turning her head back to face him. "You are mine, Eden. No man will ever taste of your flesh, or enter your hot core as I have done." He kissed her, and she smelled the musky scent of herself on his lips.

Eden's heart began pounding anew, but she refused to let Clay think she was completely his. She was her own woman, her own person, and she would let him know in no uncertain terms. "I am no man's slave, Clay. I belong to no one but myself. You can control my body's response, but you can't control my mind, my feelings. I am your equal in all things."

"You are my wife," he insisted, his gaze drilling into her. "As such, you will defer to me in all things. You will subjugate yourself to me. It is my right to expect this as your husband."

"No," she whispered, shaking her head. "I won't." But even as she spoke she could feel Clay's flesh growing hard inside her and instinctively she rose up to meet it, bringing a knowing smile to his lips.

"You have enslaved yourself, angel. You have conquered yourself with your own passion. And I will use that against you, to bind you to me for now and all eternity."

Clay's words, softly spoken, cocooned her, wrapped around her to steal her will, chain her to him with silken threads of bondage.

And she knew he had won. For she loved him.

But she would continue to resist. For her stubborn pride demanded no less.

But not now. For her body demanded even more.

The bayberry candles in the brass candelabra flickered softly, burnishing Clay's brown hair with gold and shimmering off the green satin of his waistcoat. The drapes at the dining room windows rustled softly as a cool breeze floated in to bring respite to the warm evening.

"I've decided to import some guano from Peru," Clay said, between bites of venison. "It's rich in nitrogen and will improve the fields immensely."

Eden, who'd been staring at Clay's lips in utter fascination as she replayed this afternoon's encounter over and over again in her mind, was jolted out of her perusal. She took a quick sip of her wine to help hide her embarrassment. "Guano? I don't believe I'm familiar with that substance."

"It's a new type of fertilizer," Clay explained. "Bird droppings. Very rich in . . ."

"I really don't think that the dining room is the proper place to be discussing bird droppings," Agnes piped in, setting down her fork. "Perhaps that discussion would be better left for the barn."

Eden's gaze slid to her aunt, who looked utterly vexed, then to Clay, who didn't bother to hide his annoyance when he replied, "I was under the impression that you were free from social constraints and decorum, Miss Agnes. And would appreciate me advising Eden of what I was planning to do to improve her plantation."

Eden and Agnes didn't miss the "her". Eden felt warmed by the admission, while Agnes reluctantly nodded her approval. "Very well," the older woman agreed, "you may continue. Since we are not having fowl this evening, I guess the subject of bird droppings won't be too intolerable."

Clay chuckled; Eden grinned; Aunt Agnes stifled her smile. And a silent truce began to form between Clay and Eden's aunt as they continued on with their supper.

Unfortunately that truce was not of a long-standing nature. For after supper, while seated on the front porch enjoying the evening air, the roar of the locusts, the persistent cry of a whippoorwill, the trio was treated to a display of Clay's dog, Rory, treeing Agnes's cat, Desdemona.

The dog's barking was so insistent, the cat's meows so loud, everyone's attention couldn't help but be drawn to the drama occurring in the front yard.

Eden knew the very moment when her aunt discovered that her precious Desdemona was in grave danger, for Agnes didn't bother to withhold the colorful epithets that spewed forth from her lips like a sailor's litany.

"Get that damn dog away from my cat or I'll cut off his you-know-whats and serve them up to the pigs for breakfast," Agnes screeched at Clay.

Eden gasped, unable to believe what her usually reserved aunt had just said, and turned to look at her husband. She was even more shocked, for she detected a glimmer of amusement in his eyes.

Clay fought down his laughter as a burgeoning respect for the outlandish older woman began to take root and grow. With a shrill whistle, he called off Rory, reprimanding the dog soundly, before sending him to the barn with his tail tucked between his legs.

Agnes breathed a sigh of relief as the cat slowly made its way back down the tree to scamper off into the night. She turned toward Clay and a grateful smile touched her lips. "Thank you for saving Desdemona. She's like a child to me; I could not bear to see her hurt."

"Rory wouldn't have hurt her, Miss Agnes. He doesn't have a mean bone in his body. He was just looking for someone to play with."

A gray brow arched. "Really? Dogs and cats don't usually play well together."

"I guess they'll have to learn to get along, the same as the rest of us," he replied, giving Eden a wink that brought color to her cheeks.

Agnes didn't miss her niece's reaction, and she smiled at the man who'd caused it. Clay was good for Eden, even if the stubborn child couldn't admit it just yet. She would eventually, for the passion between the two was palpable.

Rising to her feet, Agnes leaned over and gave Clay a peck on the cheek, startling both him and Eden. "Good night, children," she said, adding, with a twinkle in her eye, "And don't keep Eden up too late tonight, Clay. She was plumb tuckered out after this afternoon's discussion. Why, Aunt Ruby spent the better part of the day trying to get that black inkstain out of the carpet."

Eden gasped aloud, then blurted, "Aunt Agnes!" covering her cheeks in mortification.

But Clay only laughed, suddenly realizing how much he liked Eden's aunt—crazy cats, pants, cigars, and all.

Thirteen

Things soon settled into a routine at Beauclaire. Clay and Eden rode the fields early each morning to survey the tobacco crop and check on the progress of the fertilized field Clay was using as a test case of the guano.

Clay would then divide his time between his duties at Beauclaire and Briarwood, while Eden attended to the various chores that consumed each part of her day.

Mornings were usually spent touring the slave quarter to doctor those slaves needing medical attention, tending the vegetable garden, inventorying the foodstuffs, delegating the house chores for Jewel and Aunt Ruby, and conferring with Sukie on that day's menu.

Afternoons were occupied with keeping the accounts up to date, a chore which Clay had gladly allowed Eden to continue, since bookkeeping was not a task he relished nor particularly excelled in, whereas Eden was a wonder with figures.

At night, after supper was finished and Agnes

and the rest of the household had bedded down for the night, Clay and Eden occupied their time in the big tester bed, making love into the wee hours of the morning.

What wasn't expressed verbally was communicated by a kiss, a caress, finalized by an earth-shattering climax which left the two lovers shaken to the very centers of their souls.

Last night had been such a night, when the heavens had danced with a thousand stars, and Eden's heart had taken flight to soar high above the clouds.

And there were times like now, while she watched Clay work to mend a section of the paddock fence, observed the way his muscles grew taut beneath his shirt as he lifted a fence post, that Eden wondered what prevented her from telling Clay how much she loved him.

But she knew that many differences still stood between them. Only yesterday, those differences had been painfully pointed out when they'd disagreed about the way the overseer had handled the slave, Sam.

The problem began when Wakefield had ordered Belle to his house to oversee the cleaning of it, and Sam had openly defied the overseer's order by refusing to let his wife comply. Angered by Sam's defiant nature, Wakefield had been determined to flog the blacksmith, pointing out that Sam was setting a bad example for the others with his acts of aggression and insubordination.

But Clay had disagreed, stating that an intelligent man who loved his wife couldn't be faulted for trying to protect her from harm.

Eden didn't know what had prompted Clay's opinion that Belle might come to harm, but knowing of James's caring attitude toward the slaves, and Sam's dubious reputation when it came to arguments, she had sided with the overseer.

"If Sam's been argumentative and impertinent," she had told Clay, "then perhaps Mr. Wakefield is correct in instituting corporal punishment." She had never forgotten the horrible beating Belle had received, and was still not entirely convinced that it wasn't the huge black man who'd administered it.

Clay vehemently disagreed and told the overseer. "Sam will not be flogged. No man, woman, or child on this plantation will be whipped without my knowledge or consent. Is that clear, Wakefield?"

The blue eyes narrowed into thin slits. "Quite. But you're going to find that by allowing these blacks free rein, you'll not get a lick of work out of them, nor an inch of respect."

"Let me worry about that, Wakefield. You just follow orders. And by the way, Belle is not to clean your house again. She's too young for such an easy chore. I'll have one of the older women tend to it. From now on, Belle works in the laundry."

Eden's blood had run cold at the look on the overseer's face as he listened to Clay's edicts, but it had warmed a bit to see the joy reflected on Belle's. Up until yesterday, she had no idea that the young woman disliked her chores at the overseer's house. Perhaps Clay had been right after all, she conceded, though it was still hard for her to admit that to him.

"Hand me that hammer, will you, Eden?" Clay asked, propping the board up on his leg while he made ready to pound in the nail.

She handed it to him, asking, "Are you almost finished? Your family will be arriving soon for dinner. I need to get back to the house and change."

Perusing her attire, he grinned rakishly. "What for? You look damned appealing to me."

Though his admission pleased her, she couldn't help the outrageous comment that flew out of her mouth. "There are times, Clay Braxton, when I think a board with a hole in it would look damned appealing to you. You're insatiable." She colored fiercely at her own audacity.

Clay threw back his head and laughed. "Are you complaining, Mrs. Braxton? It seems to me that you're the one who kept me up until the rooster crowed this morning. I'll have to have Aunt Ruby fix me one of her heathen potions just to keep my strength up."

Eden blushed crimson. "You'll do no such thing, Clay. It's bad enough putting up with that old woman's snickers and snide remarks, without having you ask her for a potion. Why, she asks me every day if I'm with child as it is."

The pounding ceased and he paused, hammer in midair. "And are you?" Overhead, a flock of Canada geese honked loudly, as if demanding her answer, too.

Clay's question took her off guard, and she stammered, "No . . . no I'm not. At least, not that I know of." Was that disappointment flaring in the depths of his eyes? she wondered; she was surprised, for Clay had never mentioned having a child, and she'd never really even thought about the possibility. Though she guessed she should, for as often as they made love, she was bound to get pregnant sooner or later.

The thought of a child brought to mind her mother's journal. At Agnes's request, she hadn't read it again. But she wanted to—needed to. There were still many unresolved questions.

"Eden? Are you all right?"

Clay's question brought her back, and she nodded. "I'm fine, but I really do need to get back and change. I've no doubt Lucy will be arrayed in all her finery, and I don't want her to upstage me this afternoon."

Clay's eyes glowed with an inner warmth that sent tingles down Eden's spine. "That will never happen, angel eyes."

"Are you coming up?" she asked, unaware of the blatant invitation in her eyes.

"Is that an attempt to woo me?"

Her cheeks dimpled. "It might be, if you were to bathe first. You smell rather horsey," she said, her nose twitching.

"And would you consider doing the honors?"

Glancing down, Eden noticed the unmistakable bulge in Clay's breeches and her heart began to race. With a smile that held a wealth of promise, she spun on her heel and headed toward the house. Clay wasn't far behind her.

"Your handling of that nigger Sam is all the talk, Clay," Lucy commented during dinner that evening. "I swear, you always were too soft with the darkies. You never search their cabins for stolen goods or weapons, or check to see that they're safely tucked away before bedtime. It's a wonder we haven't been killed in our beds."

Clay's lips thinned in annoyance, but before he could form a suitable rebuke, Eden's aunt butted in.

"Slaves seldom wear their shackles lightly," Agnes advised, gazing over at Jewel, who stood unobtrusively in the corner of the room, a purposely blank expression on her face. Agnes had never been able to understand how whites could speak in front of the slaves as if they had no more feelings than a stick of furniture. "Perhaps when man realizes the inhumanity of the institution, he won't need to fear them."

Eden noted the fervor in her aunt's eyes and sighed inwardly. She had hoped to avoid a discussion on the slavery issue tonight, though Henry Clay's compromise was on the tip of everyone's tongue these days and abolitionism was gaining ground, even in the South.

"Perhaps we should choose another topic of discussion," Eden proposed. "Something not quite so controversial."

Wiping his forehead with his hankie before taking a sip of his wine, **Richard nodded** quickly in agreement. "Eden's right, **Lucy**. No one wants to hear your views on the slavery issue."

"I am not the one who invented the slavery system, Richard. The Athenians and Egyptians had slaves long before us Southerners," Lucy reminded him.

"That doesn't make the system right," Agnes argued.

"You sound like one of those Grimke sisters from up North," Lucy retorted, not bothering to keep the disdain out of her voice. "I vow, if I didn't know better, Miss Agnes, I'd suspect you were one of them abolitionists."

"It might interest you to know, Lucy, that the Grimke sisters are from a wealthy Carolina slaveholding family. They endured rather than endorsed a system based on slavery until their consciences couldn't bear it any longer. And it just so happens that I am a member of the American Anti-Slavery Society's Virginia chapter, though I don't attend the meetings. Most of the members are a bit zealous for my taste."

Lucy gasped, fanning herself, while Clay leaned back in his seat with a big grin on his face. It usually took an act of God to shut his big-mouthed sister-in-law up. And at this moment, Agnes was looking downright heavenly to him.

The rest of the meal passed in relative silence, and when they were through, Clay and Richard excused themselves to adjourn to the porch for brandy and cigars, leaving the ladies to retire to the parlor.

"We shouldn't leave them too long," Clay quipped, puffing contentedly on his cheroot. "There's no telling what Agnes might do if Lucy starts in on the slavery issue again."

Richard heaved a sigh. "I apologize for my wife's rudeness. She often speaks without thinking."

Clay was puzzled by his brother's attitude. Richard was usually the first to defend anything Lucy said or did. "Is there something wrong, Richard? I sensed some tension between you and Lucy this evening."

Richard smiled ruefully and shook his head. "Nothing that I didn't bring on myself." Taking a sip of his brandy, he confessed, "I led Lucy to believe that if she were to get herself pregnant, Father might be more inclined to leave us the plantation."

Clay's eyes widened. "But you know that's not true, Richard. Whatever prompted you to say such a thing?"

"Desperation, I suppose. Lucy was not what one would call demonstrative. Knowing her greed would lead her into my bed more often, I concocted the lie."

"And did it work?" Clay couldn't help asking.

Richard shook his head. "Only too well. The woman won't leave me alone. She's after me from morning till night. "I can't . . . I can't even take off my shirt and she's there, hounding my every step."

Clay stared at his brother's anguished face, then threw back his head and roared, falling into the wicker chair. Richard followed suit, but he was far from amused. "I don't see what's so damned funny. You wouldn't be laughing if you were in my position."

Wiping his eyes, Clay shook his head. "My God, man! Most men would consider your position enviable."

"Most men are not married to Lucy."

Clay's expression sobered, but his eyes still twinkled. "Does Father know?"

"God, no!" Richard said, horrified. "And you must promise not to tell him. He'll only lecture me on lying or some such."

Richard's comment brought to mind something that had plagued Clay all evening. "Why didn't Father come for dinner tonight? Eden said he would be joining us this evening."

"He's not been feeling well, Clay. He just sits in that chair of his all day, wasting away. Dr. Danielson's done all that he can, but nothing seems to help."

Clay frowned deeply, knowing that the words Richard spoke were true and fearing that if something wasn't done soon to help their father, he'd be dead within the year.

"I'll be over first thing in the morning to check on him. Perhaps I can convince him to seek another form of treatment." He'd been mulling over an idea for the past few days; perhaps it was time to speak to his father about it.

"What other form of treatment is there? I told you, Dr. Danielson's done everything possible."

"Aunt Ruby's quite adept at healing. Perhaps I can convince her to take a look at Father."

Richard's eyes widened in disbelief. "Father, take a slave potion? He'd rather roll over in his grave. Mammy Mae's tried to fix him up on several occasions, but he's refused all offers of help. Says she practices voodoo."

Clay sighed. "You may be right. Father can be obstinate when pressed." No one knew that better than Clay. "But I have to try, at least."

The next morning, after riding to Briarwood to see for himself how ill his father had become, Clay decided to approach Aunt Ruby about the possibility of tending his father.

But the old black woman had shaken her head at his request, saying, "Everything I knows about healin' I learned from Miss Agnes. She be the one to help yer daddy, Master Clay. She be the one wid the healing powers."

Agnes! Clay thought ruefully. Agnes hated his father. And Charles Braxton wasn't exactly enamored of the unconventional woman. Good Lord! Could nothing be easy?

Knowing he had no choice but to enlist Agnes's aid, Clay conferred his idea upon Eden, and after receiving her heartfelt blessing and a very passionate kiss that still had him reeling, he sought Agnes out. She was in the dairy, supervising the making of the butter.

"Churn harder, Lulu," he heard Agnes admonish the slave as he entered the cool brick building, standing quietly in the door frame, watching them. "That cream is not going to solidify by itself."

"Miss Agnes," Clay interrupted, waiting until she turned to face him, the wooden paddle held firmly in her hands. "I need a minute of your time."

"Just one moment, young man." She turned back to Lulu to demonstrate one more time the proper churning motion of the paddle, then relinquished her hold on the handle and approached Clay, wiping her hands on her apron as she walked.

"Do you mind if we take a stroll down by the river?" Clay asked. "I have something rather important that I wish to discuss with you."

Thinking it had something to do with Eden, Agnes followed Clay out of the building and down the oyster-shell path that led toward the river.

It was another cloudless day, the sky so azure it looked like a fine piece of blue satin, and it was far less humid than yesterday. A gentle breeze stirred the leaves, ruffling the cotton material of Agnes's bloomers.

"Is there a problem with Eden?" Agnes asked, grateful that Clay had slowed his pace to keep in step with her. "I know she can be somewhat stubborn. But give her time; she'll come around."

Clay smiled at the woman's astuteness. "That discussion must be left for another time, Miss Agnes, though you've definitely intrigued me."

Roses bloomed in the older woman's cheeks. "I wouldn't presume to interfere in your marriage, Clay. I hope you know that I only want what's best for my niece."

"My problem isn't with Eden, Miss Agnes. Not today, anyway," he amended, bringing a smile to her lips. "I've come to discuss my father."

"Charles?" Agnes's eyes widened. "I mean . . . is there a problem with Mr. Braxton? He certainly seemed his usual opinionated self at your wedding reception."

Pausing before the wooden bench that rested beneath a tall magnolia, whose shiny leaves were slowly turning from green to brown as September inched its way toward autumn, Clay assisted Agnes to sit, then lowered himself beside her.

"I realize that you and my father don't like each other much. But I was hoping that you could put aside your animosity to help him."

Agnes's hand reached out to cover Clay's, her face masked with concern. "Tell me."

"Father's been ill with malaria for years. There doesn't seem to be anything the doctor can do to cure him. I was hoping that you might be able to help him."

Agnes paled and her hands began to fidget nervously with the folds of her apron. "Me? Why . . . why, that's out of the question. It wouldn't be at all proper. It's quite an . . ."

"He's dying, Miss Agnes." There was a wealth of sadness reflected in his words; Clay's face was pinched in pain, and it touched Agnes deeply when he said, "You're his last hope."

She swallowed the anguish his words created. "I'm sure you must realize that I've just spent the better part of two years tending to Eden's father. My nursing did in no way help him, not that I didn't try my hardest. But I must confess, I'm not sorry Lawrence is dead."

Clay's head jerked up at the admission to stare quizzically at the older woman. He knew Agnes to be outspoken, often blunt. But for her to admit to what she just had left him speechless, and intensely curious to know why her feelings of hatred for Lawrence Fairchild ran so deep. He held his questions and allowed her to continue.

"Lawrence was a terrible individual who hurt many people," she began, by way of explanation. "My sister and I . . ." Intense pain crossed her face, and she paused to take a deep, halting breath. "Well, that's a rather long story.

"Anyway, you must realize that though I might offer to assist your father in his recuperation, there are no guarantees that I'll be able to help him. Charles is a stubborn man; his recent actions and words only confirm that fact."

Clay nurtured the growing suspicion that Agnes's animosity toward his father was due to more than just the old man's rudeness and outspoken ways. He wondered if the old rumor that had been floating about Agnes for years wasn't true: perhaps the woman just hated men. The thought didn't bode well for his father, and he pressed for an answer.

"You seem to be well acquainted with my father." At her blush, he added, "I thought as much. How did you come to know each other?"

Pulling her hankie out from her sleeve, she

wiped at the perspiration misting her cheeks and chin. "It was a long time ago. Hardly worth mentioning."

"I value your honesty above all else, Agnes. Don't fence with me; it won't work."

Agnes heaved a long sigh, her shoulders slumping in defeat as she admitted, "I knew your father before he married your mother. I came to live at Beauclaire when my sister Charlotte married Lawrence. I was sixteen, both my parents were dead, and I had nowhere else to go.

"Charles was the boy next door, so to speak. Eulalie was the sister of one of Lawrence's acquaintances. She visited here often, and we became best friends. It was I who introduced Eulalie to your father."

A knowing light entered Clay's eyes. "And he fell in love with my mother, and out of love with you?" The pain reflected in the depth of the blue eyes made Clay wish he hadn't been quite so blunt.

"As I said, it was a long time ago. And there were other factors which entered into it. Things I would rather not speak of."

Clay nodded. "As you wish."

"Though it will be very awkward attending to your father's needs, I will agree to nurse Charles, on one condition."

A dark eyebrow shot up. "And that is?"

"That he follows every one of my orders without fail and without argument. I'm too old to fight with a cantankerous old fool like Charles Braxton. And I'll not tolerate any of his rude comments about my wearing apparel. If you can get him to agree to my stipulations, I will begin his treatments first thing tomorrow."

Clay's expression exuded far more confidence than he felt. Surely defeating Santa Anna was far easier than convincing his father to be receptive to Agnes Peters's ministrations. "I don't see a problem. I'll ride over to Briarwood at once to speak to him."

Agnes smiled kindly, patting his hand, before pushing herself to her feet. "If you don't see a problem, Clay Braxton, then you're a better liar than I think." With a twinkle in her eye, she presented him her back and walked away.

Agnes was full of misgiving and far more nervous than she let on as she marched toward the house in search of Eden. Speaking of Charles, of her past, brought to mind, only too clearly, the necessity of speaking with her niece.

Soon, Eden would be demanding answers to things she would read in Charlotte's journal. And Agnes had no intention of allowing the young woman to be devastated by the news that Agnes and Eden's father had once been lovers.

Fourteen

Lovers! Ha! It had been rape, pure and simple, Agnes thought, her hands clenched into fists as she entered the rear of the house. But how was she going to explain that fact to Eden? To a child who had loved her father deeply?

Spying Uncle Beevis's white-haired head as he bent over the fireplace bender in the library, polishing the brass, Agnes inquired after her niece's whereabouts. She was informed, in Uncle Beevis's usual, slow, drawn-out speech, that Eden was up in her room, reading.

Panicked that Eden might be reading Charlotte's journal, Agnes fairly flew up the stairs, knocking once before entering the bedchamber. Much to Agnes's relief, Eden was seated in her rocker, reading one of those damned romances she was so fond of. Foolish nonsense, Agnes thought, but was gladdened nonetheless.

Eden's eyes widened in surprise at the sight of her aunt. "Why, Aunt Agnes, what brings you here? I thought you told me last night that you would be in the dairy all day. Have you finished so soon?" She shut her book, laying aside the leather volume of Emily Brontë's *Wuthering Heights,* sighing at the tragedy of Heathcliffe and Catherine's love affair. It was so romantic!

Taking a seat in the Queen Anne-styled wing chair opposite Eden, Agnes arched a questioning brow and said in a teasing voice, "I might ask you the same thing." She smiled at the bright blush suffusing Eden's cheeks. "Are you playing hooky from your chores today? Or aren't you feeling well? I noticed Clay was looking a bit ragged around the edges this morning."

"You spoke to Clay?" Eden asked, glad to be let off the hook. She had no intention of confessing that she and Clay had been "occupied" most of the evening, and that she had gotten only a few hours sleep.

Agnes nodded. "Yes, Clay's asked me to help out with his father. He's quite worried about him."

"And of course you said yes." Eden smiled, leaning forward to pat her aunt's hand. "I told him you would."

"Of course. How could I refuse? But the entire situation is going to be awkward for me." She went on to give a brief explanation regarding her former relationship with Charles.

"I knew your animosity toward the man stemmed from more than his rudeness, Aunt Agnes," Eden said, "but I wasn't aware that you grew up together. Thank you for telling me."

"I've more to tell you, child. And I hope when

I'm done, you'll still want me to live here with you."

For the first time since Agnes entered, Eden noticed the tautness about her lips, the pain in her eyes, which she tried so gallantly to hide. Apprehension for her aunt's welfare tickled her spine. "You're not ill, are you? I couldn't bear it if anything happened to you."

"No, child; I'm not ill. But I *am* sick of heart. I've kept secrets bottled up inside me for so long, they've threatened to consume me."

As Eden listened intently, Agnes went on to explain, "You know that I came here to live when I was but a young girl of sixteen. But what you don't know is that . . . that your father was strongly attracted to me."

"Papa?" Eden's brow furrowed in confusion. "But I don't understand."

"I wanted to tell you, Eden, before you read something in your mother's journal that would devastate you."

Devastate! What on earth was Agnes talking about? What could be so awful that it would cause such a powerful emotional reaction? What was Agnes hiding? she wondered. And did she really want to know? She bit her lower lip as her aunt continued her narrative.

"I was quite pretty when I was young, even lovelier than Charlotte, and just a little wild . . . like you." She smiled as her memories consumed her. "Your father was attracted to my independent ways. Charlotte was much more reserved. And, well . . ." She paused, unsure of how to broach the subject of frigidity with a young, healthy woman such as Eden. Finally, she said, "Charlotte didn't care to perform her marital duties."

"I know," Eden replied, causing her aunt's eyebrows to rise to her hairline. "I've read passages in Mama's journal about their wedding night and her feelings toward intimacy." Poor Mama, Eden thought, to have been so frightened of something so wonderful.

"I never encouraged your father. I was young, immature. I thought his interest in me was purely platonic—brother and sister." She took a deep breath. "One night, when your mother had retired early, your father came to my room. He said he wanted to talk, that he was depressed about my sister and needed someone to confide in."

Eden held her breath, unsure whether she wanted to hear what Agnes was about to confess.

"I let him in and we began to talk. He was despondent over your mother's rejection of him and began to cry. I tried to comfort him, to hold him, to tell him that everything would work out. But he took that comfort and turned it into something sordid. He began to kiss me, to fondle me. I struggled, but he was too strong and pushed me down on the bed." She covered her face as the memory of that night resurfaced to bring tears of anguish to her eyes. "Lawrence raped me."

Horrified, Eden covered her mouth to stifle her gasp of shock and outrage. Tears slid down her cheeks as she observed the torment on her aunt's face.

How could her father have done such a heinous

thing? How could he have been capable of so much brutality? But sadly, Eden knew he was. Lawrence Fairchild's treatment of his slaves had occasionally bordered on ruthless. His temper had gotten the better of him, time and time again. And his predilection for alcohol only worsened matters.

And then there was the deep, dark secret of his infatuation with the slave woman, Binna . . .

Without hesitation, Eden dropped to her knees to kneel before Agnes, taking the older woman in her arms. "What my father did was wrong. You mustn't blame yourself, Aunt Agnes."

Between choked sobs, Agnes explained, "You don't understand, Eden. Your mother heard my moans. Thinking I was ill, she entered my room to find your father on top of me. She saw us in the middle of what she thought was a lovers' tryst. Charlotte began to scream—awful screams, full of anguish and hurt at the betrayal she thought me guilty of."

"But it wasn't your fault. You weren't the guilty one; my father was."

"Charlotte never spoke to me again. I was allowed to continue living in the house. But I was forced to take my meals in my room. I was not allowed to mingle with my former friends, not allowed to tell anyone what had happened. I was treated as if I no longer existed; and to the rest of the world, I didn't."

Eden's heart was near to breaking as she studied her aunt's tearstained face, heard the raw pain in her voice—the pain of a young girl falsely accused. "Oh, Aunt Agnes, I'm so sorry. I had no idea that your life was so unhappy, so full of heartache. I would never have asked you to come back to help care for Papa if I had known."

Wiping her tears on her apron, Agnes tilted up Eden's chin. "I came back because of you, Eden. Your father's illness was a burden no woman your age should have to bear. As to my life . . ." She shrugged. "You have always made my life worthwhile, child. You, and my work with the womens' movement. I haven't been totally unhappy. But I would be, if I thought you'd blame me for what happened so many years ago."

"I could never blame you, Aunt Agnes. You were more mother to me than Charlotte Fairchild ever was. You and Aunt Ruby. I knew Mama was sick of mind, of heart. I always thought it was me that made her so distant, but I've come to realize that her problems existed long before I was born."

Caressing her niece's cheek, Agnes thought Eden quite perceptive for someone of such tender years. And very compassionate. But she needed to understand what had motivated her mother's unhappiness, lest she judge Charlotte too harshly. "That is why you must continue to read her journal, child. Through Charlotte's words, you will understand how she thought, what she went through."

Eden shook her head. "But I don't want to know. I don't want to read the unkind words she wrote about you."

"Your loyalty humbles me, Eden. But there are

other things in the journal that you need to know about. Things that happened here that none of us are proud of."

"You mean about Binna, the slave woman, and my father?"

Agnes's eyes widened. "You know? We tried so hard to keep it from you."

She nodded. "I was young, but I saw things, heard things. Eventually, I pieced it all together." Miscegenation and adultery were difficult revelations for a nine-year-old child to comprehend.

Rising to her feet, Agnes pulled Eden up with her and clutched her to her bosom. "For all your parents' faults, Eden, they loved you."

Eden was far less certain about that fact than was her aunt. But she was definitely sure of one thing: she loved Agnes. "I love you, Aunt Agnes. Never forget that."

Agnes smiled. "I won't, child. And I pray that Charles will be just as forgiving when he sees me again as you have been today."

"You loved him once, didn't you?"

Agnes's face softened. "As much as any child of sixteen can love a man. We were like two sides of the same coin. We had so much in common, like you and Clay."

"And he never knew why you quit seeing him? Why you no longer welcomed his visits?"

She shook her head sadly. "After a time, Charles transferred his affections to Eulalie. They were good for each other. Neither understood my defection, but they consoled each other."

"Perhaps you and Mr. Braxton can bring comfort to each other now," Eden suggested, her face brightening; but Agnes just laughed.

"Child, you are ever the romantic. You need to quit reading all those romance novels. True life does not always have happy endings."

"Life is what you make of it. Isn't that what you're always telling me?"

The blue eyes twinkled and she pinched her niece's cheek. "You're a saucy girl, with a quick mind and a sharp tongue. I often wonder who you take after."

Eden laughed gaily, then replied, "'Tis no secret, Aunty dear. No secret at all."

Cyrus gazed at the younger man seated across from him and shook his head. Wakefield was drunk. He'd entered the tavern on Water Street earlier this evening to find the Englishman well into his cups. Even a roll in the hay with the well-endowed whore Polly could not improve Wakefield's surly disposition. He truly was in a temper, for sweet Polly could do magical things with her mouth and hands that would leave a man smiling for weeks afterward.

The tavern was smokefilled and noisy, and Cyrus had to raise his voice to be heard above the din. "What ails you, James? You haven't spoken more than a handful of words since I first spotted you coming down the steps with that red-haired whore. What's the matter? Didn't she pleasure you with her tongue?" Just the thought made him stiffen.

"Leave me be, Long. I'm in no mood to discuss my problems or my passions, least of all with you."

Cyrus filled Wakefield's pewter tankard with ale, then filled his own. "I'm no fool, Wakefield. I know you're grieving about Eden Fairchild marrying that Braxton fella. But what's done is done. There's no use cryin' over spilt milk, as my mother used to say. 'Course, there was always a hearty smack that went along with her advice." Cyrus rubbed his cheek in remembrance.

Bleary-eyed, Wakefield replied, "You don't know what you're talking about, Cyrus, so keep your big mouth shut. I've lost everything I've been working for these past three years. Women are a dime a dozen. But Beauclaire—now, *that* was something worth possessing." He gulped down the ale, then banged the cup against the wooden table, causing Cyrus to start.

"And now you've lost it, thanks to Braxton."

"That bastard's been a thorn in my side since the day they married. Ordering me about. Taking away my pleasure with the slave women. He watches me like a hawk. I haven't had a good fuck since he's come."

"You ain't been able to, huh?" Cyrus quipped, pleased by his jest. But he could see by the deadly look in Wakefield's eyes, the overseer wasn't amused.

"You're crude, Cyrus," Wakefield slurred. "'Tisn't any wonder why Eden didn't want to take you up on your offer of marriage."

Indignation running rampant, he retorted,

"Well, you're not much better off. And one of these days I intend to get my revenge on the high-and-mighty Fairchilds."

James's head jerked up, and his eyes cleared as he stared at the older man across from him. "And how, pray tell, do you plan to accomplish that feat? Braxton has money . . . and influence. He holds all the cards right now."

"Really, Wakefield, you disappoint me. For such an intelligent, cultured man, you're quite dense. Braxton may hold the cards, but he hasn't been dealt a hand from the bottom of the deck."

As the light of recognition entered Wakefield's eyes, Cyrus smiled, pleased by the respect he saw on the younger man's face. "Ah. I see you get my meaning. I don't lose gracefully, James. Nor should you. Together we can get revenge on both Eden and Braxton, and possibly gain control of the one thing we both want: Beauclaire."

"You're suggesting a partnership?"

Cyrus nodded. "Fifty-fifty. And to show you that my heart's in the right place, I'll even throw in Eden. You can diddle her from now till Kingdom Come, then pass her on to me when you're through. I expect you'll get tired of her white little ass soon enough. It's the black meat you've got a hankerin' for. Once you get a taste of it, there's no going back, is there?"

Cyrus personally found the prospect of bedding a nigger wench highly distasteful. He hated blacks! Hated their kinky hair and foul-smelling skin. They were animals. And he didn't rut with animals. But he knew Wakefield did.

Long was very astute, Wakefield thought. He hadn't been able to get Belle out of his mind. Now that he couldn't have the black bitch, he wanted her all the more. He wanted her so bad his cock ached just thinking about it. He'd been her first; he'd busted her proper when he'd taken the job as Beauclaire's overseer.

And when he had Beauclaire in his possession, he would set her up as his mistress; maybe even move her into the master bedchamber. He smiled at the thought.

Flushed with need, James grabbed on to Polly's waist as she passed by, pulling the willing whore down on his hard erection.

"Oh, Mr. Wakefield, sir," she cooed, wiggling her generous bottom.

Thrusting his hand down the front of her dress, he fondled the pendulous globes, ignoring Polly's moans of delight while he and Cyrus finished their discussion.

"Are we going to be partners, then?" Cyrus asked, gulping, staring at the big, white mounds, now completely exposed to his view, and licking his lips.

Wakefield didn't miss the older man's reaction and chuckled. "Sure thing, Cyrus. Why don't we start now?" At the man's confused expression, he turned to the whore and said, "You can handle two, now, can't you, sweet Polly?"

She smiled enthusiastically and nodded.

Both men headed up the stairs with the woman between them. Stiff with resolve, they were ready and eager to cement their newly formed partnership.

"I never knew accounting could be such an erotic task," Clay teased, as he stared at his wife bent over the leatherbound ledger book in concentration. She tapped the end of the pen against her lips, drawing Clay's complete attention to their fullness as he stood staring at her from his position in the doorway. "If I'd known, I wouldn't have been so quick to turn the job over to you."

Eden's head snapped up, and she colored instantly. "You're quite welcome to the "erotic task," if you'd care to give a try to adding up these columns of figures."

Throwing himself into the wing chair in front of the desk, he grinned. "I think I'll leave you to your fun. I'll get my pleasure some other way." He winked at her.

"You are as randy as a stud in a pasture full of mares. I would think, after last night, you wouldn't have the energy to think of such things. I certainly don't."

"I was rather good, wasn't I?"

Shaking her head, and knowing that she wasn't going to best Clay at his own game, Eden changed the subject. "How are things at Briarwood? Did you ride over there this morning?"

"Of course. Did you think I would leave those two old people alone for any length of time? I fear your aunt's ready to kill my father. He hasn't been the best of patients."

Eden laughed. "That's an understatement. Aunt Agnes told me that Mr. Braxton was as cantankerous as a putrefied fever blister." Eden wrinkled her nose in disgust. "Now, that sounds pretty bad."

"Father's not used to taking orders from a woman. Once he resigns himself to his lot, he'll grow more tolerant."

"I guess his stubbornness just runs in the family," she said, smiling inwardly at Clay's affronted expression.

"What's that supposed to mean? Haven't I allowed you to keep the books? Haven't I kept you apprised of all the latest farming methods that I've learned?"

"Yes. But you've given me no real authority. You make me come to you as if I were no brighter than a little child who needs her papa's permission to do something."

"Naughty children get spanked." His eyebrow arched suggestively. "I can't recall that you've been spanked lately. Of course, you did seem to like it the last time . . ."

"Clay Braxton, there you go again. Always making light of whatever I take seriously. Until you recognize me as your equal partner, we are never going to . . . to . . ."

"To . . . what?"

"Get along. That's what. We'll just go through life tolerating each other. But until there's respect, there can be no . . . no . . ."

"No . . . what? Honestly, Eden, can't you complete a sentence?"

She was going to say *love,* but thought better of it, saying instead, "Happiness. We'll never be truly happy."

"Angel eyes," he said, rising to his feet to walk around the side of the desk. Pulling her to her feet, he wrapped his arms about her. "Aren't you happy? You've seemed quite content these past months."

Eden sighed deeply, pressing her head into Clay's shirt front. He smelled faintly of cigars and spice-scented cologne. "You make me deliriously happy in bed, Clay. But there's more to a marriage than mating."

"Nothing that matters."

Giving him a swift kick in the shin, she pulled out of his embrace. "You make me so mad, Clay Braxton, I could spit."

"Ow! What the hell'd you go and do that for? I was only joking." He rubbed his leg.

Anger flared in the amethyst eyes. "Get out! I have work to do."

"Don't go getting yourself all in a snit," he cajoled, pulling her back into his embrace. "I appreciate all that you do around here. I'm not blind to the fact that you're very competent at the tasks you undertake each day."

Her face brightened. "Really? You noticed?"

"Of course I noticed. There's nothing that goes on at this plantation that I don't notice. Including the fact that you work entirely too hard."

"Oh, Clay, I don't. And besides, there's just so much to do."

Ignoring her protestations, he said, "Come riding with me, Eden. I want to show you something."

"What is it?" she asked, her forehead wrinkling in concern. "Is there a problem with the tobacco? You never mentioned it."

"No, angel. Everything's fine with the crop. We should be cutting by the end of the week."

She breathed a sigh of relief, then said, "But I have at least another hour's worth of work on the books."

"You're coming with me, Eden, if I have to tie and gag you and throw you across my saddle."

"I think I can manage to sit a horse by myself, but thanks for the offer."

"I don't know. You might be a little sore after riding so hard last night."

He ducked as the brass candlestick sailed swiftly by his head.

Fifteen

Garbed in a deep purple velvet riding habit, a matching feathered hat tilted jauntily on her head, Eden followed Clay down the winding, tree-lined path toward their mysterious destination.

He had told her only that he had a surprise to show her, not where they were headed, nor why; and she had to admit, her curiosity had been piqued.

"How much farther?" she called out, raising her voice to be heard above the sudden gust of wind, which was tossing her skirts about her legs. The wind whipped through the tree branches, creating showers of leaves to fall about her. Several branches cracked, and Othello grew skittish. "Easy, boy," Eden crooned, trying to soothe his fears.

Clay glanced back over his shoulder, then up at the darkening sky, and frowned. "Not much farther. But we'd better pick up the pace. I don't like the look of that sky." He had no sooner uttered his ominous prediction than the sky opened up, releasing a heavy downpour of rain.

They hurried their pace, and just when Eden thought that the trail would never end, they came upon a clearing, and Clay reined his horse to a halt. As Eden came up alongside him, her eyes widened at the sight of the old log cabin that stood in the center of the clearing. There was smoke belching from the chimney, and colorful red gingham curtains hung at the window. It looked lived in. And welcoming. She felt like a drowned rat in her soggy habit, and wanted nothing more than to get out of the rain.

"Where are we? I feel totally lost," Eden admitted. "And who lives in that house?"

Dismounting, Clay helped Eden alight, then hurried her to the front door of the cabin. "We've been on Braxton property for the last hour, angel. This is an old hunting cabin that my father, brother, and I used to use years ago." Throwing open the door, he waited for her to enter.

It was little more than one large room, Eden noted, glancing about. But it smelled of pine and looked as if it had been recently cleaned. There was a large, crudely fashioned bed that stood in close proximity to the fireplace, a table, two chairs, and not much else. The interior was utilitarian rather than decorative—though there was a colorful starburst quilt upon the bed—but it had a definite charm of its own.

Clay was grinning like a schoolboy, and Eden smiled at his enthusiasm when he asked, "Do you like it?"

There was a large bouquet of wildflowers in the center of the scarred maple table, and she knew instantly that this cabin was her surprise, but was still confused as to why.

"It's lovely, Clay. But . . . what's it for? Are we going hunting?"

Clay's laughter was punctuated by the sound of thunder; torrents of rain were now lashing down upon the wooden shakes of the roof, sobering him instantly. "I need to see to the horses. There's a lean-to alongside the cabin. I'll be right back."

Without further explanation as to why they had come to the cabin, Clay slammed out the door, leaving Eden to ponder her questions alone.

Unbuttoning her jacket, she removed it and her hat, placing them carefully on the chair, then crossed to the fireplace, tossing a couple of pieces of wood onto the glowing embers. Lighting the oil lamp which rested on the small table near the bed, she sat down on the mattress to wait.

Clay returned a few minutes later, carrying another stack of firewood and his saddlebags. He slammed the door hard against the blowing wind, then dumped the wood into the box by the hearth, tossing the bags onto the bed.

"We're not going anywhere for a while, angel," he said, turning to face her, stripping out of his wet shirt and pants. "I suggest you take off those wet clothes before you catch cold. The storm's worsening; it's best to ride it out here."

The rain fell in sheets outside the window, and Eden, knowing the wisdom of Clay's words, began to take her clothes off as well. The fire was blazing now and the little cabin grew warm and cozy. Once they were both completely naked, Clay took their clothes and set them on a chair by the fire to dry.

"There's no telling how long this storm will keep up," he said, reaching into his saddlebags to remove a hunk of cheese and some bread. He smiled sheepishly at Eden's amazed expression. "I came prepared for a picnic. I guess we'll have to have it indoors."

It seemed totally outlandish to Eden that they were standing in a log cabin, out in the middle of nowhere, completely nude, conversing about having a picnic. She smiled at the absurdity of the whole situation.

"If I didn't know better, Clay, I'd say you arranged for that storm to come up." She took the bread and cheese he handed her, then sank down on the bed to eat, suddenly realizing she was famished.

Clay grinned erotically, walking toward the bed. "You look like temptation itself, with your hair draped about your shoulders like a black velvet mantle and your naked flesh shimmering like satin in the glow of the firelight."

She blushed, swallowing the cheese in her mouth as Clay climbed onto the bed. Thoughts of satisfying her hunger gave way to another kind when Clay's hands began to move up her legs toward her thighs. "Clay," she whispered. The thunder roared, but she was sure it was her own heart that pounded loud in her ears.

He lay down beside her and pulled her in to

the warmth of his embrace, stroking her back and buttocks. "I wanted to bring you here, Eden. This is a place I could always come to when I needed to sort out my feelings. It's a special place—a private place that I wanted to share with you."

She sighed in contentment, running her fingers through the soft hairs on his chest. "Thank you. I feel honored."

"When I was in Texas, I used to dream about this place—about bringing you here. There was so much death and destruction; I longed for our gentle world . . . for you. I missed you, angel eyes. I missed you so damn much." His arms tightened about her.

"Oh, Clay," Eden said, swallowing the lump in her throat at the words she never thought to hear. "I missed you, too."

Her admission pleased him and he smiled. "Did you?" Looking down into her eyes, he saw passion simmering there. Tenderly he kissed her, but soon the kiss became much more and he couldn't keep from exploring every inch of her flesh with his hands and mouth.

He drew her taut nipple in, delighting in her moan of pleasure as he sucked first one and then the other. "You're sweet, Eden. I can never get my fill of you."

"Nor I you," she whispered, her hand trailing down to grasp his throbbing member. "I want you inside me, Clay. I want to feel you deep within me."

With a tortured moan, he rolled her over until he was lying full on his back and she was on top of him. "Lift up," he instructed, easing her down onto his hardened shaft. "God that feels good, angel," he choked.

The feel of Clay deep within her, hard and pulsing, was a glorious sensation. She felt totally in control as she rocked to and fro, riding him hard, writhing up and down, up and down, bringing him deeper and deeper until she felt herself tighten and expand. The look of ecstasy on Clay's face intensified her pleasure, and she undulated uncontrollably, like some pagan goddess giving up her offering to the gods.

Outside the cabin the wind howled and the thunder roared. But it was no match for the fierce explosions pounding within Eden's body.

"Oh God, Clay!" she gasped, biting her lower lip as the feeling between her legs built. Every nerve ending in her body was on fire, and she felt as if she would burst into flame at any moment. Her breathing grew shallow, coming in quick, panting gasps, and a thin sheen of perspiration covered her burning flesh.

"Let it go, sweetheart," he urged, rubbing the engorged bud between her legs as she pushed hard against his hands, reaching for fulfillment. "That's it."

Grabbing onto her hips, he abetted her movements, urging her to go faster and faster until at last, with one primal scream, she shattered into her climax and he released himself within her.

Rolling her over, still deep within her, Clay smoothed back the dampened hairs from Eden's face and kissed her tenderly on the lips. "I love you, Eden. I've always loved you."

Tears trickled down Eden's cheeks at Clay's admission. Her own words of love were on the tip of her tongue, but she bit them back, afraid to give him that final bit of power that would forever subjugate her totally. And so, she caressed his cheek with her fingertips and said nothing.

She saw the hurt in his eyes, the question, but she couldn't bring herself to utter the words he longed to hear.

She loved him, but he could never know.

The journey back to Beauclaire the following morning was made in silence. Though the sun was shining brightly, dark clouds still masked Clay's face.

He'd been sullen and withdrawn since yesterday's episode of lovemaking, and Eden knew she was to blame for his sudden change in attitude. Though she had tried to make small talk after their encounter, Clay had pretty much ignored her, until, finally growing frustrated, she had turned over and gone to sleep.

This morning he had risen before dawn to saddle the horses for their trip home. And their conversation had been just as stilted as the previous day's.

"I expect Aunt Agnes and Aunt Ruby are going to be pretty upset that we didn't come home last night," Eden ventured, casting a sidelong glance at Clay, whose face looked as if it had been carved from granite.

"They'll get over it," he replied harshly. As would he, Clay thought, realizing how foolish he'd been to admit his love to Eden. What had possessed him to open himself up like that? he wondered, shaking his head. It would be a cold day in hell before she heard such an admission from his lips again, he decided. They rode for several more miles, and Clay was relieved when the big brick mansion came into view.

Eden breathed her own sigh of relief at the sight of her home, but grew instantly curious at the appearance of the black carriage parked in the drive. "Who do you suppose that is?" she asked. "We weren't expecting visitors."

Immediately concerned for his father's health, Clay took off at a gallop, not bothering to answer Eden, who was suddenly afforded a glimpse of his back. "Well, of all the rude . . ." She kicked Othello's sides gently, urging the horse into a trot.

When Eden reached the barn, she had every intention of telling Clay just what she thought of his high-handed departure, but he was nowhere in sight. Dismounting, she sought out the groom.

"Master Clay up at the big house, Miss Eden," Caleb supplied at her question. "He was worried that his daddy took sick."

Suddenly feeling foolish, Eden hurried toward the house, unable to squelch the feeling of unease that suddenly overtook her. When she entered, her aunt, Clay, and Aunt Ruby quickly ushered her into the dining room, shutting the door behind her. Fear darted through her at the furious expression on Clay's face and the worried one on her aunt's.

"What is it? What's wrong?"

"I think you had better sit down, Eden," Aunt Agnes suggested, pulling out one of the chairs from the dining room table. She began patting her hair nervously, and Eden knew Agnes was sorely vexed about something.

"There's something I must tell you."

Eden glanced over at Ruby, who looked fit to be tied, then at Clay, whose features had softened into one of pity. "You're all scaring me," Eden remarked, sitting down.

Clay heaved a sigh, unsure of how to break the news. "It seems we have visitors, Eden. A man and a woman who . . ."

Agnes placed her hand on his arm. "Let me tell her, Clay. It's really my place in Lawrence's absence."

At the mention of her father's name, Eden smirked. "Don't tell me one of Father's long-lost relatives has decided to show up and contest his will."

Agnes blanched and nodded, bringing Eden to her feet. "What!"

"I'm afraid it's even worse than that, child. You remember when we talked about the slave woman Binna? The one mentioned in your mother's journal?"

"Of course. Is she here?" That would be rather awkward Eden decided.

"No, child," Agnes said, shaking her head.

"She's not here . . . Binna is dead. But her son David is very much alive."

"Her son?" A feeling of dread was starting to eat away at Eden's composure. She felt her knees wobble and fell back into the chair. "She had a son?"

"I don't believe a word of it," Ruby said, crossing her beefy arms over her chest. "They is jes trash. Why, that woman looks like a hussy. All painted up, wid her hair dyed yellow as corn."

"It appears, Eden," Clay interjected, shooting the black woman a quelling look, "that your father sired a child by this Binna woman. That child has now come forth to lay claim to your plantation."

Eden's mouth dropped open, even as her eyes widened. "But he's black! He can make no claim on this property." The law was definite that a child born of a slave took the status of the mother, regardless of who the father was.

Agnes and Clay exchanged worried looks. "He may be half black, child, but he looks as white as you or me. And to make matters worse, he's a lawyer. He goes by the name of David Lawrence Fairchild."

Eden gasped. "How dare he!"

"Here drink this," Clay ordered, handing Eden a glass of sherry, a worried look on his face. "You're as white as a ghost."

Eden did, and feeling instantly revived, rose to her feet. "Where is this Mr. . . .Fairchild?"

"We put him in the parlor. I told him you were

gone, and that he'd have to wait. He's not alone," Agnes said.

"There's a woman with him," Clay added, frowning. "A companion by the name of Vera Marsden." Clay had almost exploded when Agnes had informed him upon entering the house that this mysterious half-brother of Eden's had brought along his paramour, who was nothing more than an actress.

"Is she his wife?" She knew that blacks often kept their own names when they married.

Agnes turned away to stare out the window and Clay wagged his head. "She's his mistress. And she's white."

"I see." But she didn't. She didn't know how any of this could be happening. A half-brother who had a white mistress. This was all so unreal, so incomprehensible. After a moment, she replied, "I must go up and change before I meet these people. I look a fright."

Agnes nodded. "You and Clay go upstairs and make yourselves presentable. I'll go in and tell this Mr. . . . this man that you'll be down directly."

Once Clay and Eden were upstairs in the bedchamber, Eden rushed to the nightstand and withdrew her mother's journal. Clay knew of its existence, but in deference to Eden's privacy, had never read it.

Disbelief registered on his face as he watched her. "You're going to read your mother's journal now? Don't you think you had better go down and face this man who claims to be your brother?"

"If what he claims is true, then the proof will be in this journal. My mother was very meticulous about recording everything. Clutching the leather book to her chest, she sat down on the edge of the bed and opened it.

Thumbing through the parchment pages, she came upon the first mention of the slave woman:

Beauclaire, June 15, 1828. I have seen the slave woman Binna. She is nothing more than an ugly black wench who Mr. Fairchild seems to take an inordinate amount of interest in. There has been talk of their alliance among the slaves. I am shamed beyond belief.

Eden read further, and her heart pounded in dread.

Beauclaire, June 28, 1828. I have witnessed with my own two eyes Mr. Fairchild's vile act of copulation upon the black wench Binna. They were in the barn, rutting like pigs, when I came upon them. Mr. Fairchild didn't notice my presence, but the black woman did. She smiled spitefully at me, then laughed as I fled.

"Oh, Mama," Eden whispered, tears filling her eyes.

"Eden, stop it. You're just making yourself upset," Clay said, coming to sit next to her on the bed.

She shook her head. "I have to read this. Don't you see, Clay? The truth is here in black and white. And no matter how much it hurts, I have to read it."

He sighed, draping his arm about her shoulders. "Go on, then. I'll be here for you."

She flipped forward through the book until she came upon the page for which she searched.

Beauclaire. February 13, 1831. The slave woman has borne a son. The son that should have been mine is now in the arms of Binna. May the good Lord take this child away and kill it, as He has taken away mine.

Eden gasped, unable to believe that her mother was capable of so much hatred. She continued reading.

Beauclaire. May 3, 1831. The slave child is as white as Eden. They call him David. There is no mistaking his heritage. Mr. Fairchild's stamp is upon this child, and I have no recourse but to kill it. Already there is talk in the town, and I am unable to hold my head up in church. Something must be done, and soon.

Eden reread the last passage aloud to Clay, then slammed the book shut. "It's true. What the man claims is true."

Clay took the book and threw it on the floor. The sound reverberated off the walls of the room and Eden's heart. "Eden, listen to me," Clay said, turning her to face him. "Even if this woman Binna had a child, there is no proof that this man who calls himself David Fairchild is really her son. And even if he is, he has no claim on Beauclaire. This is your plantation. Your father left it to you in his will."

Eden listened intently to everything Clay had to say. And though she knew legally he was right, morally everything that had happened was wrong.

"Let's get dressed and go down. There is only one way to be sure if what this man says is true. If he's not my half-brother, I will know immediately."

"And if he is?"

"I will know that, too."

Sixteen

The man who called himself David Fairchild was standing with his back toward her, staring out the window, when she entered the parlor. Eden could see that he was tall and lean, with brownish, curly hair. His blond companion was making a thorough examination of the Wedgwood figurines on the mantelpiece and didn't notice Eden when she entered.

"Mr. Fairchild," Eden said, watching intently as he turned. And then she knew, for he bore the unmistakable likeness of her father upon his features.

His blue eyes stared at her intently; his lips, fuller than Lawrence Fairchild's, turned up into a self-satisfied smile, as if measuring her reaction.

"Miss Fairchild?" he inquired, stepping forward to shake her hand.

Eden nodded. "I am Eden Fairchild Braxton. And this is my husband, Clay Braxton." She motioned toward Clay, who had come up behind her, and she was grateful for his presence.

"As I'm sure your aunt has made you aware, I am David Lawrence Fairchild, recently of New York." He motioned the blond woman forward. "And this is my fiancée, Miss Vera Marsden."

His words were cultured when he spoke, almost refined, quite in contrast to the brassy woman who stood on his right. Vera Marsden looked to be every bit the hussy Aunt Ruby had proclaimed her to be. She was garishly dressed in red velvet, which was cut much too low for daytime wear. She wore no gloves. And her use of kohl to darken her eyes and rouge to enhance the redness of her lips only emphasized her unsuitability.

"Miss Marsden," Eden said politely, acknowledging the woman's presence. The woman smiled slyly in response.

Eden instructed her guests to sit on the settee, while she and Clay took seats opposite on the loveseat. "My aunt has told me a bit of your background, Mr. . . . Fairchild." She had difficulty using her family name to address this stranger. "But I would like to hear the story from your own lips, if you don't mind."

"Which part would you like to hear first, Mrs. Braxton? The part where your father raped my mother, then sent her North with her small child? Or the part where we lived in shame for most of our lives?"

Eden gasped at the bitterness in his voice, bringing a flush of anger to Clay's cheeks.

"Now see here, Fairchild, or whatever the hell your name is."

Clay was about to rise to his feet when Eden

placed a restraining hand on his arm. She looked at her husband beseechingly. "Let's allow Mr. Fairchild a chance to speak, Clay. I'm sure he'll remember that we weren't the cause for his unhappiness." She looked pointedly at the young man and was surprised to note the pink tinge to his cheeks—cheeks that were nearly as white as her own. "Do go on, Mr. Fairchild."

"My mother was known as the slave woman, Binna. She lived here at Beauclaire until my presence proved too uncomfortable for your father to endure. We were sent north to live when I was six years old."

Six years old! Why had she never seen this child before? But then she thought of Agnes, and knew how good her father was at keeping secrets.

"And did my father provide for you and your mother?" she asked.

"Yes. We were given money and a note of introduction. My mother was able to find employment as a maid."

"And you were given your manumission papers?"

He nodded. "Yes. We were both set free. But that was no guarantee of anything. We were treated just as badly up north as we were here. You see, Mrs. Braxton," he said, his blue eyes darkening, "because my mother had a white child, she was considered a whore—a white man's whore. And I was nothing more than a bastard. A by-blow of some white man. I didn't fit into the white world, not after they realized who my mother was. And I didn't fit into the black world, either. They despised me for my white blood. Not everyone values white blood, you see."

"I hardly think you can blame your nonacceptance in the white man's world on my wife, Mr. Fairchild," Clay broke in. "It seems to me you were treated fairly by Lawrence Fairchild." At the sudden anger in the man's eyes, he added, "I'm not condoning the fact that he slept with your mother against her will. But at least he owned up to his responsibilities."

David's laugh was bitter. "He killed her."

Eden blanched at the accusation but kept silent, allowing him to continue.

"He might as well have strangled her with his own bare hands, after what he did to her. She loved him. My mother loved the bastard, and he swept her aside. I never knew my father, Mr. Braxton. Put yourself in my place—I didn't ask to be born. But when I was, I should have had the benefit of a family, of a home. Instead, I was ignored. I was the *massa's* embarrassment."

Hearing the hurt in David's voice, Eden's heart ached for the child he once was. How cruel it must have been to be denied the love of a father. "I'm truly sorry for what happened to you, Mr. Fairchild. What my father did was wrong. But I don't see how I can rectify what was done so long ago. As you informed my aunt, Binna is now dead."

"Yes, she died two years ago." A great sadness overcame him when he spoke of his mother. "But on her deathbed she made me promise that I would come back to claim what is rightfully mine."

Clay and Eden exchanged startled looks before Eden said, "If you're referring to Beauclaire, Mr. Fairchild, then you have made this long trip for nothing. Beauclaire is legally mine, willed to me upon my father's death. You may search the court records, if you like. But you will see that everything is legal and in order."

"I have already searched the records, Mrs. Braxton. And, as you say, everything is legal. But I'm not talking legalities, Mrs. Braxton. I'm talking about rights, what is rightfully mine. Half of this plantation is rightfully mine. I am Lawrence Fairchild's son. His only son, I might add. Perhaps, in a court of law, my claim would not be recognized. But under God's law, it should be. Morally, I deserve to inherit what is rightfully mine."

The entire time David Fairchild was talking, Vera Marsden was sending signals to Clay that a blind man wouldn't have missed. She postured and posed, batting her lashes and pouting her lips until Clay wanted to grab her by her long white throat and strangle her. Thank God Eden hadn't noticed, he thought. She had enough to contend with at the moment; his eyes narrowed as he studied David Fairchild.

Dressed in a somber blue serge suit, he looked every bit the gentleman, but there was something about the man he didn't trust. He couldn't quite put his finger on it. But he'd known enough dishonest lawyers in his time to know that most weren't much better than stage actors. Apparently, his liaison with the actress was a match made in heaven.

"I don't think we're going to resolve any of this today, Mr. Fairchild," Eden said. "And I'm sure you are both tired after your long journey. Why don't you and your fiancée remain as our guests for the night? Perhaps we can sort this out better in the morning."

Eden thought she heard Clay groan, but she wasn't going to look over at him for confirmation.

"Oh, that would be lovely," Vera cooed. "Wouldn't it, darling?" she said to David. "Imagine staying overnight in this big, beautiful mansion."

David cast an exasperated look at his fiancée and smiled politely at Eden. "We accept your hospitality, Mrs. Braxton."

"Fine. I'll have Aunt Ruby show you to your rooms. Dinner will be served promptly at eight."

"Yes, I remember," he said, a note of sarcasm in his voice as he rose to his feet. "My mother worked in the kitchen."

"Then you'll know to be on time," Clay retorted harshly.

The duo had barely excited the room when Clay turned on Eden, a fierce look lighting his eyes. "What the hell did you go and do that for, Eden? Are you insane? That man is trying to take your plantation away."

Eden heaved a sigh. "I don't expect you to understand, Clay. I barely understand it myself. But I feel sorry for David. He was a victim of my father's callous behavior."

Clay plowed impatient fingers through his hair.

"But that has nothing to do with you. With us. I don't trust him. I saw the way you looked at him, like he was a wounded puppy. You're too softhearted, Eden. He'll take advantage of you."

"Don't be silly, Clay. I'm perfectly capable of mastering my own feelings." She saw him flinch and wished she could take back her words. For though she knew they applied to him, she was thinking of David Fairchild. And she also knew that Clay was right. Her heart *had* softened toward the child the man had once been.

"You must do as your conscience dictates, Eden, but I want it known that I do not want those people under my roof for more than one night. Is that clear?"

The purple orbs narrowed at Clay's high-handedness. "Oh, it's quite clear, husband dear." She fairly spat the words. "But though you own Beauclaire lock, stock, and barrel, I am mistress here, and I will decide who I entertain." With that, she stuck her nose in the air, and with as much grace as she could, waltzed out of the room, leaving Clay to stare openmouthed after her.

"Damn," Clay muttered as the door slammed in his face. When was he ever going to learn not to back Eden into a corner? She was as stubborn as a mule when she made up her mind about something. And he feared she'd already made up her mind about David Fairchild.

"Oh, look, darling." Vera brushed her hand over the mahogany dresser. "Everything is so expensive, so genteel. Did you see that dress Mrs. Braxton had on? Why, all that taffeta must have cost a fortune." She couldn't keep the envy out of her voice.

David sighed. "Try to contain yourself, Vera. We don't own any of this yet. And unless I can convince my dear sister to welcome me with open arms, we won't."

Vera laughed and stepped forward to drape her arms about David's neck. "Darling," she said, pressing herself into him, "you were wonderful. Why, I think you missed your calling. You really should have joined me on the stage."

"Very funny, Vera. Why don't you make yourself useful and unpack my carpetbag? I have to think." He released her hold on him.

"But, darling, we have slaves to do that work now."

His lips thinned. "No black man or woman will wait on me—or you, for that matter. Is that understood? I'll not take advantage of their suffering."

"How will you pass yourself off as white, then, David? People will know if you act differently from everyone else."

He shook his head, wondering what had possessed him to bring Vera along on his quest. Most probably, her persistent nagging. "Are you forgetting that we come from the North? We're abolitionists, Vera. No one will think a thing about it."

She stuck out her lower lip. "Well, this visit is going to be just dreadful, then. It's hot and sticky here, and there's not a decent-sized town for miles and miles. If I can't play the lady of the manor, whatever will I do?"

"To act like a lady, you must first be one. Why don't you observe how Mrs. Braxton behaves, then you can emulate her." At her furious expression, he drew her into his arms, kissing her cheek. "Vera, you must remember that if you're going to be my wife, there are certain things you must learn."

She reached down to cup his crotch. "You seem to think I'm pretty clever in bed, darling." She gave a squeeze and heard his moan of desire, and smiled inwardly. She knew how to get her way. After all, she was the teacher and he the student when it came to lovemaking. David had been a virgin when he'd come to her that first time; a star-struck law student visiting the established actress. And she had delighted in introducing him to the fine art of lovemaking.

And the fact that he was a nigger only added to the excitement of their coupling. She'd always wondered what it would be like to bed a black man; their reputation for virility was well known. And well founded. She couldn't get enough of him and found herself growing stimulated.

"Shall I undress for you, darling? Shall we get up on that big bed right now?" She saw his eyes darken with passion as her fingers went to her bodice and she exposed her lush breasts to his view. She smiled seductively at his unspoken acquiescence.

It was going to be so easy to manage David once he had control of the plantation. He would become her very own slave. As his wife, she would no longer be Vera Marsden, actress and whore. She'd be Vera Fairchild, mistress of Beauclaire. And the respectability she sought would, at last, be hers.

Later that same evening, after an awkward supper where Clay and Agnes hadn't exchanged more than a few words with David and his fiancée, Eden had invited David to stroll about the grounds, so that they could converse by themselves without interruption from interfering relatives.

Clay had been furious at the exclusion, but had finally relented, locking himself in his office to go over the accounts. And Agnes, who'd been given the chore of entertaining Vera, was at the moment in the library, reading aloud to her from her least favorite book of poetry.

The air had a nip to it and Eden wrapped her shawl more firmly about her shoulders as they walked. She avoided the quarter, so as not to bring unpleasant memories back to her half-brother—funny, she didn't have nearly as much trouble getting used to that notion as everyone else in the family did. She guessed that had something to do with the fact that David looked so much like her father. They walked instead about the lawn of the rear yard.

"Tell me, David, what it is you hope to gain by your visit here? I already know your desire to control Beauclaire. But I'd like to know what motivates you beyond that."

Plucking a leaf off a magnolia tree they passed, David twirled it in his fingers and replied, "At first it was revenge. I won't deny that I've thought of nothing else but getting even with our father." Eden's eyes widened at the reference, but he failed to notice her reaction. "But it's more than that. I don't fit in up north. Though I'm a competent attorney, because of my race, no one will give me the opportunity to represent them. I am shunned by both worlds. I live in a land of gray that is neither black nor white."

They paused beneath a linden tree and Eden sat down on the wooden bench that surrounded it. "But surely you must know that to come back here to Virginia is dangerous for you. If anyone was to find out your true heritage, you would be put back into slavery. That is the law here, as I'm sure you are well aware."

He seated himself next to her. "I am. But I'm also aware that my skin is light enough that I can pass for white." At her shocked look, he added, "I know you must think me a fool for wanting to be something I'm not. But I yearn to come back to the state of my birth. To live here in the South again. To practice law and perhaps help those less fortunate than I have been."

"But to do so would be perpetrating a crime, David. And if we condoned your ruse, we would be guilty of the same crime. Harboring a slave is a serious offense."

His voice shook with suppressed anger. "But I

am a free man of color. I am not a slave. And I am your half-brother. Nothing you can do or say will ever change that fact."

Eden had already spent many hours pondering that truth. And she couldn't suppress the guilt that rose up every time she thought of what her father had done to this man—this man who was his flesh-and-blood; this man who was her brother. She swallowed at the look of anguish on his face and heard herself ask, "What is it you propose?"

"I would like to take up residence here, with my fiancée, of course. I would like to become part of your family, experience all I have missed by having been sent away."

Eden thought of Clay and knew what David suggested was impossible.

"I see your doubts, but I know it would work," he said. "I could pretend to be your cousin from New York. I look enough like your father that no one would question my connection to the family. I would work hard at establishing myself in the community as a lawyer. And I will do whatever it takes to learn the tobacco trade, so that I may help you run the plantation."

"Even if I were agreeable to letting you stay, David, you must know that there are other members of my family to consider. My aunt would have to be convinced. But she is not the problem."

His voice hardened. "I know that your husband does not like me. I sensed it when first we met. Does he hate all niggers, or just me?"

Eden jumped to her feet, her eyes flashing fire.

"Don't ever presume to judge someone, lest ye yourself be judged. My husband doesn't have a mean bone in his body. Our people are treated fairly. And though we recognize that the system of slavery is wrong, we are unable to do away with it overnight. Our whole economy is based upon it. It will take time to make the changes that we seek."

David reached out to take her hand. "I am sorry I spoke out of turn. My bitterness has made me harsh and judgmental."

"I can only guess as to how you feel, David. I have never been a slave; I have never been deprived of the love of my father. But if you are to live in the white man's world, if you are to pass yourself off as one of us, then you must learn to temper your anger with reason. A word spoken in anger will give you away quicker than anything else."

"Then you will consider my proposition?" There was a wealth of hope in his question.

She nodded. "I will discuss it with the rest of my family. This must be a joint decision. I cannot risk their reputations; they must do that themselves."

"And may I stay until you reach your decision?"

She thought of Clay's words and swallowed the lump of apprehension that formed in her throat. "Yes, for now, " she said, praying that she had made the right decision.

***

Aunt Agnes and Clay were fairly certain that she had not made the right decision and told her so after her guests had departed and gone up to bed. The trio were in the parlor, partaking of a cup of chocolate before retiring.

"You are making a big mistake, Eden," Clay advised, pacing the room like a caged tiger. He'd been furious when Eden had first related Fairchild's plan to pass himself off as her cousin. But seeing the uncertainty, the pain in her eyes, he had tried to remain reasonable. "Why should you risk your home and reputation for a man you don't even know? It doesn't make any sense."

"Clay is right," Agnes admitted, setting her cup down on the table. "If the authorities were to ever get wind of this man's true heritage, we could all be prosecuted. Are you forgetting your obligation to this plantation, Eden? Isn't it what motivates everything you do?"

The implied reference to her reasons for marrying Clay came across clear as a bell, and the angry look on Clay's face said he knew it, too. "Of course, I haven't forgotten. But you should know better than anyone, Aunt Agnes, how cruel my father could be." Her aunt paled, but Eden didn't relent. She had to make both Agnes and Clay see how important this was to her.

"How can I turn my back on my own flesh and blood? David Fairchild is my brother. Would you do less for your own family?" She turned toward Clay. "Would you?"

And so, without so much as another word being spoken, an agreement had been reached: no one outside the immediate family was to know about David's heritage. He would be welcomed into the family as if he belonged, for better or for worse.

Seventeen

"*'Fish and visitors stink after three days,'*" Agnes quoted. "It's been nearly ten, and the stench of Vera Marsden is proving overwhelming," she added, dipping the wicks, which hung suspended from a wooden candle-rod, into the large kettle of hot fat.

It was a cool, clear October morning, and Eden and Agnes had come outside to the rear of the kitchen to prepare the candles they would use to supplement their oil lamps for the coming winter. It was a time-consuming process, but on a good day two hundred candles could be fashioned.

"I don't care what anyone says," Agnes continued, "Vera Marsden cannot be trusted. I don't know what David sees in her. He seems to be a nice young gentleman, despite everything that has happened. But her . . ." Agnes shook her head. She'd seen the way Vera's eyes followed Clay whenever he walked into a room. And though she didn't want to upset Eden, who had much to contend with already, she thought her niece should be warned. Vera Marsden was a cat in heat, and she was definitely on the prowl.

Eden hung her dipped candles on the rack to dry. "David says Vera is just unsophisticated, Aunt Agnes. She's never been around genteel people before and doesn't know how to act."

"*Hmph!* Well, she certainly knows how to act around men."

Agnes's eyes trailed off to stare in the direction of the barn and Eden followed her gaze, her eyes narrowing at the sight of Vera watching Clay whitewash the fence. He was bare-chested, and she was fairly drooling over his muscular torso. A swift surge of jealousy poured through her.

"If you can spare me, Aunt Agnes, I do believe I'll go over and give Clay a hand with the fence. It looks as if he could use my help."

At her aunt's nod, Eden crossed the yard. As she approached the barn area, she could hear Clay and Vera laughing together. The sound of Vera's throaty laugh made hackles rise on the back of her neck, and she clenched her fists when Vera leaned unnecessarily close to hear something Clay was saying.

"My, my, don't you two look industrious this morning," Eden remarked, insinuating herself between the two people.

Vera straightened, smiling smugly. "Yes. I was just keeping Clay amused while he worked."

"Well, perhaps we should find something for you to occupy your time with, Miss Marsden. We wouldn't want you to become bored while you're visiting Beauclaire. And there's so much to do. We can always use another pair of hands."

Vera stared down at her soft, lily-white hands that had never done an honest day's work, at her carefully manicured nails, and blanched.

Clay could barely restrain his chuckle at the venom in Eden's voice. She was jealous, pure and simple, and the knowledge filled him with satisfaction. "Miss Marsden was just regaling me about her life on the stage. It seems she's quite an accomplished actress."

Eden forced a small smile to her lips. "I don't doubt it. It's always easier being something you're not than something you are." Eden was more than satisfied to see her barb had hit a nerve. Vera was blushing furiously.

"I believe I shall go find David. He's promised to take me on a ride today."

A dark eyebrow arched. "Oh? Are you an accomplished horsewoman as well as an accomplished actress?" Eden inquired.

She wrinkled her upturned nose. "Heavens, no! I wouldn't dream of getting near those filthy creatures. We are going to take the buggy."

"Pity. You can't really see the entire plantation unless you're on horseback."

A provocative smile crossed the blond woman's lips as her gaze lingered on Clay's body. "I've seen everything worth seeing on this plantation, Mrs. Braxton." She spun on her heel and headed back in the direction of the house.

"Did you hear that?" Eden asked after Vera was

out of earshot. "Why, that vile hussy! I ought to . . ."

"Now, angel," Clay cajoled, "there's no need to be jealous. I'm not . . ."

Eden's mouth dropped open, then snapped shut. "Jealous! Really, Clay, you do flatter yourself, if you think I'm jealous of that bleached hussy."

He grinned. "Vera Marsden isn't all that unattractive, Eden," he teased, watching her eyes darken in anger.

"I guess if you like that sort of woman. But then, I guess you've had your share of whores over the years."

"*Tsk, tsk*, Mrs. Braxton; I'm shocked to hear you speak that way. You—a gently reared Southern lady."

The sight of Clay's insufferable grin infuriated Eden. Without a thought to the consequences, she grabbed the paintbrush out of Clay's hands and smeared the whitewash over his face. He gasped in surprise as the white paint dripped from his eyelashes and chin, and Eden could barely contain her laughter. But noting the outraged expression that suddenly emerged on Clay's whitewashed face, Eden sobered instantly and ran as if the devil himself were on her heels.

Which he was.

Clay caught her just as she made to enter the barn. She screamed as he tackled her from behind, bringing her down on a soft pile of hay. "Clay, stop it!"

Ignoring her plea, he flipped her over, pinning

her body with his own. "Kiss me, Eden. Let me share the delicious taste of whitewash with you."

Horrified, Eden pressed her lips tightly together and wiggled, trying to escape. But Clay's lips came down forcefully, stealing away her determination to evade his "delicious," punishment and soon all thoughts of resistance fled.

"Clay," Eden asked the following morning, a beseeching look in her eyes, "would you be a dear and allow David to accompany you out to the fields? He's quite interested in learning all about the tobacco process, and I informed him that you would be supervising the cutting today."

Upon hearing his wife's question, Clay nearly choked on his coffee, but managed to swallow the hot liquid before turning to stare at the smug young man seated across the dining room table from him. He had no doubt that David had put Eden up to her request, and it rankled.

Clay had made no secret of his animosity toward Eden's so-called half-brother, though he'd tried his best to keep his opinions to himself, for Eden's sake. But he had no wish to be saddled with a man he didn't like and didn't trust.

"I doubt Mr. Fairchild would find the procedure all that interesting, Eden."

"On the contrary, Mr. Braxton, I'm anxious to learn all there is to know about Beauclaire's management."

"And it won't offend your sensibilities to observe slaves at work in the fields?" Clay pressed, observing the narrowing of the younger man's blue eyes.

"David is putting his past behind him, Clay," Vera interjected, smiling sweetly. "He's preparing for his new role in life."

Clay cast Eden an "I told you so" look, but she merely smiled.

"I doubt I will be able to remain completely unaffected, Mr. Braxton," David admitted. "But I will do my best to hide my emotions."

"Please, Clay," Eden asked again. The "for me" was left unsaid, but nonetheless came across as loud as a bell.

Clay sighed, pushing back his chair. "Very well. I'll meet you out at the stables, Mr. Fairchild. You do know how to ride a horse?" The man nodded and Clay made to leave, but not before saying, "Eden, perhaps Miss Marsden would like to accompany you on your chores today. I'm certain she would be vastly interested in learning how the plantation runs." He smiled inwardly at the horrified look on his wife's face.

Vera paled. "Oh, no. That's quite . . ."

"That's an excellent idea," David agreed, turning toward Eden and his fiancée.

The women stared at each other, then at the two men, who exited out the door, muttering curses silently under their breath.

"How does one know when the tobacco is ripe enough to be cut?" David asked, observing the yellowing stalks. They had dismounted and were standing in one of the tobacco fields already being harvested.

Clay handed David a grayish-colored leaf. "There's no set rule. You just get a sense of when the proper time is to cut. There are certain guidelines to follow, of course. When the tobacco is ripe, like the leaf you're holding, it turns a grayish color. The leaf feels somewhat thick, and if you press it between your thumb and forefinger, it will easily crack."

David performed the test, watching as the leaf cracked between his fingers. "And then you harvest?"

Clay shook his head. "We don't call it a harvest here in Virginia. That would indicate the procedure is near to completion, and it's not. There's still the curing and the sorting."

As David watched his black brethren work, he couldn't help but feel anger toward their white owners. "And this process is what justifies enslaving these men?"

Clay's eyes hardened as did his voice. "Look, Fairchild, I told you you weren't going to like coming out here to the fields. If you're going to pass judgment, then you might as well leave now. No one said the system was good, but it's all we have. We wouldn't be able to harvest the crop without slave labor."

"You could pay them a wage."

Clay nodded. "Eden and I have discussed that very thing. But Beauclaire has seen two years of drought and disease. Eden was in debt when I married her. It's going to take time to recoup her losses before she can implement a plan such as the one you've suggested. Now," he added, walking toward his horse, "I believe your lesson in tobacco culture is over. Why don't you go find something else to do that's a little more palatable." With those words, Clay mounted and rode off, leaving David to stare maliciously after him.

"You're not quite as smart as you think, Clay Braxton," David mumbled. "You might be married to Eden, but blood has always been thicker than water."

Agnes glanced at the feeble man sitting in the wheeled chair and hardly recognized him as the once-strapping beau of her youth. Charles was seriously ill, though he seemed to be responding to the treatment she'd been administering to him the last few days.

She'd been dosing him with a solution of quinine, preparing it from the bark of the cinchona tree, a plant indigenous to South America. A friend active in the women's movement had returned from her medical mission to Brazil, bringing the plant with her and extolling its miraculous healing powers.

It had certainly been effective in reducing Charles's persistent fevers, Agnes thought. His appetite had improved, and he'd been sleeping much more naturally of late.

"Quit staring at me, woman! I feel as if I'm some damn specimen in your collection."

Agnes smiled at Charles's indignation. "Feeling better, are we?" She crossed to the window and pushed it open, allowing a cool breeze to enter and diffuse the noxious odors in the room.

"Some. What's that heathen remedy you've been using on me? Not some voodoo medicine, is it?"

Wheeling Charles over to the window, Agnes took a seat near him on the windowseat. "You're still a cantankerous old fool. I don't know how Eulalie put up with you all those years."

"*Hmph!* She loved me," he replied, impaling her with eyes that said, "You once loved me, too."

Agnes stared down at her lap, unwilling to meet the question in his eyes. "Well, love is blind, they say." She looked up to find him grinning at her. And the most curious thing happened: her heart lurched madly in her chest.

"I guess I'm not much of a looker anymore. This damned disease has taken its toll."

She swallowed. "I still think you're a fine looking gentleman."

His eyes widened at the admission. "You do?"

She nodded and he reached for her hand. "I'm glad you came, Aggie. It's been a long time."

Tears filled her eyes at the use of the nickname she hadn't heard in forty years. "I'm glad, too."

Wakefield watched the young man ride off, and his eyes narrowed. Eden's cousin from New York was proving to be a bother. He didn't like the fellow. He was much too curious, much too nosy about the workings of the plantation.

Why would he need to know about the tobacco production? About the number of acres under cultivation? Supposedly, he was just visiting. But his questions were more indicative of a man who stood to inherit or join in the profits.

James's lips thinned, for he had no intention of allowing another usurper to interfere. He already had Braxton to contend with; he'd be damned if he was going to allow some hotshot lawyer from up north to cut into his plans. Of course, the fiancée was a different story.

Vera was quite the looker. The actress had sent him a few signals that seemed to indicate she wouldn't mind taking a tumble in the hay. That might bear looking into, James thought, smiling to himself. It had been a while since he'd had a whore. And Vera Marsden, for all her affected ways, was nothing but a whore at heart. She was older than Fairchild—and, he'd bet his last dollar, far more experienced in bed.

She was ripe for the plucking, and he hadn't had a prime piece of fruit in quite a while. And it just might be interesting to find out if her hair was really that white-blond color. And there was only one way to find that out, he thought, feeling himself harden.

Clay had stepped out onto the porch to smoke a cheroot before bed. Eden had already gone up, and there'd been a wealth of promise in her eyes that told him not to linger too long.

Absorbed in his thoughts of what he was going

to do to his lovely wife, Clay didn't hear Vera's approach until she was right up next to him.

"It's a lovely evening, isn't it, Clay?" she asked, her hand touching his forearm.

He continued to stare straight ahead, not wishing to encourage the foolish woman. Her motives were as transparent as glass, and he had no wish to become involved in whatever scheme she had cooked up to seduce him. "The weather's turning colder. You should go in before you catch a chill."

She inched closer to him, pressing her breasts against his forearm. "Perhaps we could warm each other up."

Extricating himself from her grasp, he threw his cheroot down on the floorboards and ground it out beneath his shoe. "I already have a bedwarmer, Vera. Perhaps your fiancé could use one."

"David is a mere boy compared to you, Clay. I've seen the way you look at me. I know you want me."

"You're wrong. I don't want anyone but my wife. Now, if you'll excuse me, I think I'll go up to bed."

Boldly, she reached down to touch his thigh. "Are you sure your wife can give you the same pleasure I can? I know ways of pleasing a man that could drive you wild."

He grabbed her hand as she made to caress his crotch and squeezed it none too gently. "Quite sure. Now, unless you want me to inform your fiancé of this meeting, you'll go into the house and up to bed."

Red-faced, Vera spun on her heel and re-entered the house. Clay stood on the porch a few moments longer, waiting for his temper to cool and the nauseated feeling in his stomach to subside. Eden was right: Vera was a vile hussy. Well, he hoped she had gotten the message that he wasn't interested. Next to Eden's shining beauty, Vera Marsden was tarnished brass.

As he made to leave, he didn't see the pair of hard blue eyes that stared at him through the dining room window. David hadn't heard what was said between Vera and Clay, but he sure as hell had seen the cozy exchange between the two. Braxton had a lot to answer for in trying to seduce his fiancée. And he'd see to it that he paid.

"I hesitated telling you this, Eden. But I thought that as your brother, it was my duty to inform you of what I saw last night."

Eden stared openmouthed as she listened to the accusations David was making about Vera and Clay. He had come into her office shortly after breakfast to confide his suspicions that Clay had attempted to seduce Vera into bed last night.

Eden found the whole thing extremely difficult to believe, especially in light of the way Clay had tenderly made love to her last night, confessing his love again at the height of their tempestuous climax.

"Are you sure you're not making more out of what you saw than what actually occurred, David? Clay is an honorable man. I find it difficult to believe that he would do such a thing." But she didn't find it difficult at all to believe Vera would.

His voice grew harsh when he said, "Your mother probably believed that your father was honorable, too, when he was bedding my mother. Or have you forgotten that little incident?"

Eden paled, for she hadn't forgotten, but had merely pushed it to the back of her mind. She'd been unable to read any more of the diary. Her parents' lives were too twisted and unhappy, and she didn't want to be reminded of their failed marriage.

But David was right: not all men were honorable. Her father had betrayed her mother right under her nose. And though Charlotte had known of his infidelity, she had never mentioned it to anyone.

David left, and Eden sat staring down at the columns of numbers; they blurred before her as the image of Vera in Clay's arms surfaced instead to take their place. A sharp ache entered her heart as suspicion stabbed into her.

Clay said he loved her. Would he betray her?

Tears streamed down her face at the uncertainty that filled her mind when she thought of Clay, but she brushed them away with the back of her hand.

As if conjured up by her thoughts, Clay entered the office a few moments later.

"What are you doing in here, angel? I thought you and Agnes were going to dispense the clothes and blankets to the slave families today."

Eden nodded absently, for it had always been

the custom of the mistress of the plantation to dole out the goods to the slave families. Every autumn, each man, woman, and child was given new clothing and supplies. The men each received two cotton shirts, two pair of woolen pants, new shoes, and a heavy wool jacket; each woman, six yards of cotton drilling, thread, buttons, shoes, stockings, kerchiefs, and blankets.

"I intend to see to it this afternoon."

He perched himself on the edge of the desk. "I saw David leave. Is there a problem?"

She shook her head, unable to ask the question that was uppermost on her mind. "He wanted to advise me about something."

"I hope he hasn't come to complain that I wouldn't let him help with the sorting yesterday. I just can't let an inexperienced hand attempt such an important job."

"David doesn't think you like him, Clay. Perhaps if you went out of your way to be nice to him."

Clay stood. "Christ, Eden! I've *been* trying. But he's right; I don't like him that much. How much longer are they going to be allowed to stay? We can't have a normal life with those two around."

Eden sighed. "You'd best get used to the idea that David is my brother. I can't just throw him out. I'm the only family he's got. And . . . and though I don't care for his fiancée, I can't very well ask her to leave."

"They're troublemakers—the both of them. I don't trust either one."

Was that true? Or was it that Clay didn't trust

himself where Vera was concerned? "I thought you told me that you found Vera attractive."

He wrinkled his nose in disgust. "That was before."

"Before?" Her heart started to pound when Clay's cheeks filled with color.

Clay's eyes shuttered and he turned away, heading for the door. "Just keep them away from me," he said, slamming it loudly behind him.

"Oh, Clay," Eden whispered, a lump forming in her throat. "What have you done?"

What have I?

Eighteen

The pounding on the bedroom door jolted Clay awake, and he glanced toward the window to discover it was still pitch black out. Who on earth would be disturbing them at this hour?

Pulling on his robe, he hurried to answer the door and found Uncle Beevis on the other side. The old, white-haired man was shaking so badly Clay thought he would expire on the spot.

"You'd best come, Master Clay," Uncle Beevis said. "Dere's a fire in de field."

Dread poured through Clay and he rushed to the window to stare out. Orange flames licked the darkened sky. "Shit!" was all he said as he watched his efforts going up in smoke. Then, "Send someone to fetch Wakefield, Uncle Beevis. Have him meet me at the north field." Lighting the lamp by the bed, he shook his wife awake. "Eden, wake up."

Eden awoke with a start, her eyes opening wide at Clay's ashen face. "What is it? What's wrong?"

Clay continued to dress while he talked. "One

of the sheds is on fire. I need to get out to the fields right away."

She gasped, bolting upright. "I'll come with you."

"No!" he said, fear for her safety uppermost on his mind. "It might be dangerous. You could get hurt."

"This is my plantation, Clay Braxton, and I'll be damned if I'm going to sit here while it burns down around me." When was he going to learn that they were equal partners in this venture? That she wouldn't remain on that damn pedestal he tried to keep her on?

He heaved a sigh at her obstinance. "Suit yourself. I don't have time to argue." With that, he fled out the door.

It took Eden a few minutes to dress, saddle Othello, and ride out to the north field. By the time she arrived, a line of men and women had already formed; they were passing buckets of water back and forth they'd fetched from the river to douse the burning flames which engulfed the tobacco shed.

Smoke filled the air, as did the sweet scent of the tobacco, burning Eden's eyes. Tears filled them, but she knew they were caused by more than the smoke. At least the other fields had been spared, she thought. It was only the one shed that had been torched.

Torched. She swallowed the lump of despair that formed thickly in her throat. Clay had confided that the fire had been deliberately set, with James adding that David had been seen in the vicinity not two hours before.

Sweaty, her arms aching from lifting the heavy buckets, Eden trudged wearily back to her horse. There was nothing more that she could do, and she knew it would be several more hours until Clay could complete his investigation of the incident.

No matter what Clay suspected, or how bad it looked, she refused to believe that David had torched the tobacco shed. What could he possibly hope to gain by such an action? No, she decided, mounting Othello. It wasn't David. Her gut feeling told her that much.

But then, why hadn't he come out to help?

She rode back to the house, the question still fresh on her mind when she spied David standing on the porch.

"Eden," he called, rushing toward her. "What happened? Aunt Ruby came to fetch me. Said there was trouble in one of the fields." He looked genuinely distraught.

"One of the tobacco sheds burned," Eden replied, sliding off the horse's back, allowing David to assist her onto the porch.

"How did it start? Does anyone have any idea?"

"Why didn't you come out to help, David? At times like these, family always pulls together." Her voice was tinged with accusation, his full of chagrin.

"I'm a sound sleeper. I didn't hear a thing until Aunt Ruby burst into my room and started shaking me."

Eden searched his face but could find no duplicity there. "They say the shed was torched—the fire was deliberately set. I have no idea who could have done such a thing." Pausing expectantly, she added, "Do you?"

"Me? How would I know?" His face paled. "You don't think I had anything to do with it?"

She placed her hand on his forearm. "I don't, David. But the overseer claims that you were seen out by the shed earlier this evening."

His face reddened in anger. "That's a lie. I've been up in my room reading. I wasn't feeling well and retired early. You can ask Vera if you don't believe me."

Eden heaved a sigh, for she had absolutely no desire to discuss anything with Vera Marsden, especially the woman's nocturnal habits. "I'm not blaming you, David. I'm sure the culprit will be found."

"Does Clay think it's me? He does, doesn't he?" David's mouth tightened grimly. "I can see it on your face."

She knew she had hurt him and was saddened by it. "Clay's just naturally suspicious by nature. Don't worry about it. Come," she said, reaching for his arm, "let's go on up. It's late, and tomorrow will be a busy day."

But despite Eden's reassurances, David did worry about it, and was determined to find out what he could about the burning of the tobacco shed. Someone on this plantation had framed him. But who?

* * *

Eden had almost been successful in convincing Clay that David was not responsible for setting fire to the tobacco shed when another incident happened a few days later that hit much closer to Clay's heart.

The day had started out crisp and cold. But despite the chilly weather, Eden had insisted on accompanying Clay on a tour of the fields to set her mind at rest that everything at Beauclaire was as it should be. She had challenged him to a race—Othello against Tempest—and Clay had been only too happy to make the wager.

"You're on, madam," he said, grinning. "But if I win, you have to make love with me whenever and wherever I want."

Eden blushed to the tips of her toes. "Clay, you're awful. Is that all you ever think about?" There was an erotic glimmer in his eyes that made Eden feel breathless, a little achy.

"I'll give you a head start. Whoever reaches the field first is the winner."

Eden laughed, kicking Othello into a trot. "Let's give them a run for their money, old boy," she said, urging Othello to go faster and faster, gazing back over her shoulder to see Clay closing the distance.

Leaning over the horse's neck to give him his head, she increased her lead. Then suddenly, without warning, her saddle began to slip from beneath her and she felt herself falling. Panic assailed her and she began to scream.

Clay watched horrified, as Eden struggled with her mount. "Eden," he shouted, as she flew through the air to land in the middle of the road. Fear for Eden's safety pounded through him as he rushed forward to aid her. Leaping off his horse, he bent down next to her unconscious body. "Eden, my God, Eden!" She was so still, so pale.

As gently as he could, Clay examined her body for broken bones. When he was satisfied that she didn't have any, he lifted her onto his horse and rode back to the house as swiftly as prudence allowed.

Agnes had been getting ready to leave for Briarwood when she saw Clay riding into the yard with Eden in his arms. Dropping her medicine bag, she rushed toward him. "What's happened?" she demanded, ordering Uncle Beevis to assist him.

"Eden's been thrown," Clay explained, laying her down on the porch as Agnes instructed.

It took the competent woman only a few moments to ascertain that Eden suffered from a sprain to her left arm, and a mild concussion. She had a lump on her head the size of a goose egg. But other than that, she appeared to be all right.

"Carry Eden up to your room, Clay," Agnes directed. "And quit scowling so; she's going to be all right."

An hour later, Eden opened her eyes to find Clay sitting next to her on the bed, hovering over her like a mother hen. Lines of worry etched his face, and he was holding on to her hand so tightly, he was cutting off the circulation to her fingers.

"I guess I'm not such a wonderful horsewoman after all," she quipped, trying to remove the concern from her husband's face.

Clay leaned over to kiss her forehead. "You're a terrific rider," he argued, relieved to find she was finally awake and behaving normally. "You would have beat me, too."

She smiled, but the effort cost her dearly and she winced as her temples pounded a cadence. "I never thought to hear you admit that, Clay." Instead of the teasing rejoinder she expected, Clay's face sobered instantly.

"Eden, listen to me," he began, his tone ominous, "your cinch was cut. That's why you lost your saddle and your seat. You could have been killed."

Eden paled white as the bed sheets, unable to believe what Clay was intimating. "Surely you're mistaken, Clay. Who would do such a thing?"

Clay stood and began pacing the floor, plowing agitated fingers through his hair while he walked. Eden was too damn trusting; she always had been. "You don't want to hear what I think, Eden. And I won't burden you with my suspicions now; but when you're well, we're going to have this out, once and for all."

"Clay," Eden said softly, "I know what you're thinking. But you're wrong. David didn't cut my cinch. He's not capable of violence."

His eyes hardened. "Your father was; you told me so yourself. And he *is* your father's son."

She thrust her chin out defiantly. "And I'm his daughter. Does that make me capable, too?"

Noting the hurt in her eyes, he moved to sit down beside her, reaching for her hand. "I love you, Eden. I couldn't bear it if anything happened to you."

Tears filled her eyes. "Oh, Clay," I . . . Tell him, her mind screamed. Tell him you love him, too. But she couldn't; not yet. Not until she was truly certain that he would accept her as his equal in all things.

Her parents had professed to love each other . . . Though she hated to make the comparison, it was there—always in the back of her mind.

The hope on Clay's face sent a knife straight into her heart. As did his resigned expression when he stood a moment later and said, "I'll leave you to rest, angel eyes. I'll be back later to see if you need anything."

"I'll be perfectly fine by tomorrow, Clay. You'll see."

Providing no one else makes another attempt on your life, he thought, but didn't voice his fears aloud. "So Agnes assures me," he finally replied.

Kissing her gently on the cheek, he quit the room, leaving Eden to ponder the very frightening truth that someone had tried to kill her.

With instructions to Uncle Beevis to keep an eye on Eden and to keep all visitors out of her room, save for Agnes, Clay rode over to Briarwood. With all the excitement the last few days, he hadn't had the opportunity to visit with his father, though Agnes had assured him Charles was doing much better.

He found his father, brother, and Lucy in the dining room, about to have their dinner.

"Clay," Charles said, smiling happily, his fork paused in midair at the sight of his son, "come in. We were just about to start dinner. Would you care to join us?"

Clay shook his head and sat down, pouring himself a glass of wine. "I'm too upset to eat. But I'll stay and visit, if you don't mind."

Charles's smile melted into a frown. "What is it, son? You look worried."

Lucy smirked. "Mercy me, Clay. Have you and Eden had a lover's spat? Is that what all this is about?"

Noting his brother's anguish, Richard turned on his wife and said, "Shut up, Lucy! Can't you see the man is upset?"

Lucy's alabaster cheeks flushed crimson. "Well, I never . . ."

"I heard there was a fire at Beauclaire, Clay. Is everything all right?" Richard asked, pushing his plate of ham and sweet potatoes aside.

"There's been another accident," he said. "Only I'm not sure it was an accident."

"Tell us, son. What can we do to help?"

"Eden was thrown from her horse this morning."

Lucy gasped, her hand going to her throat.

"Was she hurt?" There was genuine concern in her voice, which surprised Clay.

He shook his head. "Thankfully, no. Not seriously. Just a sprain to her arm and a mild concussion."

"Eden's an excellent horsewoman, Clay," Richard remarked. "How could she have fallen?"

"Her cinch was cut."

Charles and Richard exchanged startled looks while Lucy just stared openmouthed, for once having nothing more to say.

"I wondered why Agnes hadn't been by today," Charles said absently, realizing how much he had missed her visit.

"She's been attending Eden. She said to tell you she'll be by tomorrow at the usual time." Clay noted the pleased expression on his father's face and wondered at it. Apparently, his father and Agnes were getting along better than he'd expected.

He was relieved to note that his father once again had color in his cheeks and a clear sparkle in his eyes. Agnes had done that for him, and Clay was grateful.

Lucy fussed with the curls draped over her right shoulder. "I really don't see why that woman has to continue coming over here," she said. "You're much improved, Father Braxton. Surely I could take over your nursing duties." She smiled sweetly, but her smile disappeared at Charles's reply.

"Why don't you go on up to your room, Lucy? You're looking rather tired this evening. I think a nap would be in order." It was a command, not a question, and his tone brooked no refusal as he stared indignantly at his daughter-in-law.

Lucy knew better than to fence words with Charles when he was in a temper, and she excused herself from the room.

"Now perhaps we can talk without interruption about this situation," Charles said. Addressing his younger son, he added, "Perhaps you should consider a muzzle for that woman's mouth, son."

Richard smiled. "Believe me, I've considered it. But Lucy doesn't close her mouth long enough for me to put one on her."

Charles and Clay stared wide-eyed at Richard, then burst out laughing. The tension lifted and Clay finally felt his mood lighten, which is what he suspected was his brother's intention all along. He smiled gratefully at him.

"There's been problems at Beauclaire ever since Eden's cousin from New York showed up." He hadn't breached his promise to keep David's identity a secret, not even to his own family. "I don't trust the man. I think he has designs on Eden's property."

Clay's words brought a rush of color to Richard's cheeks. "I hope you don't think . . ."

Dismissing his brother's comment with a wave of his hand, Clay assured him, "Lord, no, Richard. I don't think any such thing."

Charles was pleased that Clay and Richard seemed to be getting along, despite the situation between them over controlling Briarwood. Family ties were strong bonds that weren't easily severed, which brought to mind Eden's predicament.

"I wasn't aware that Lawrence had a brother," Charles remarked, his brow furrowing in confusion. "Are you sure he is a legitimate relation? There are always shirttail relatives that come out of the woodwork when someone with property dies."

"If you saw David Fairchild, you wouldn't need to ask, Father," Clay remarked. "He's the spitting image of Lawrence, right down to the blue eyes. He's a Fairchild, all right."

Charles rubbed his chin thoughtfully. Something wasn't right; he'd bet money on it. Lawrence Fairchild had been an only child; he knew that for a fact. What was Clay keeping from him? He wouldn't press for details now, but he would certainly pull the information out of his son or Aggie at a later date.

"What is it you would like us to do, Clay? Father and I would be only too happy to help. You know how fond we are of Eden."

Clay was touched by the concern he saw in Richard's eyes and cast him an appreciative smile. "Just keep your eyes and ears open. If you hear anything from the slave quarter, let me know. The blacks have a far better information network than we do. If something's amiss, they'll hear of it first."

Charles and Richard promised Clay that they would, but even their assurances to assist weren't enough to put Clay's mind at ease. He couldn't erase the suspicion that nagged persistently at the back of his mind that David Fairchild wanted his half-sister dead.

Nineteen

"God damn it, Eden!" Clay shouted, as he faced her across the confines of their bedroom. The fire in the hearth blazed brightly, adding more color to Clay's already purplish hue. "How many more of these coincidences is it going to take before you realize that David is trying to cause you harm?"

"Keep your voice down," she said, moving to shut the window. The blast of cold that entered the room was as frigid as Clay's voice. "Do you want to wake everyone up?"

"I don't give a damn who I wake up. I want some answers and I want them now. Are you, or are you not, going to ask that brother of yours to leave?"

Eden bit her lower lip as she stared at the fury on her husband's face. Clay didn't lose his temper often, but when he did, it was a formidable sight to behold. And she could hardly blame him this time. Not after what they'd discovered tonight: two of Beauclaire's slaves had run off; apparently, after having been promised their freedom. Sam had confided that much to Clay, but he would say no more when pressed for details.

"I know you're upset, Clay, and with good reason. Beauclaire can hardly afford the loss of manpower. But it isn't fair to blame David. Just because the pair were supposedly headed for New York doesn't signify anything."

Clay took several deep breaths to calm himself. "Your brother has been here over a month. In that time, the tobacco shed has burned, you were almost killed from a fall off your horse, and now we have unrest in the slave quarter. Come on, Eden, admit it. There are too many coincidences."

Heaving a sigh, Eden picked up her hairbrush off the dresser and began to brush her hair with long, soothing strokes; it was an act which always served to calm her nerves, though she doubted it would have much effect this time.

"I won't admit any such thing," she said, turning back to face him, pointing the brush at him accusingly. "Why don't you admit that you haven't liked David from the moment he set foot through our door and announced who he was. You've never trusted him and have been willing to lay the blame at his door for everything that's gone wrong." She slammed the brush back down on the dresser.

"He's an abolitionist, for Christ's sake, Eden. And a former slave. Who would have more justification for helping the two blacks escape?"

With hands on her hips, she retorted, "Why

don't you just blame Aunt Agnes? She's an abolitionist. And she's spent time in New York. Perhaps she's out to do me harm, too."

Clay ripped at the buttons on his shirt as he started to undress. *Damn, but the woman was as stubborn as a mule!* "You know I would never blame Agnes for anything. If there's one thing I know about your aunt, it's that she loves you above all else. She would never do anything to cause you harm. I can't say the same for your half-brother, who just happens to covet this plantation."

Eden threw off her silk wrapper, pulled back the coverlet, and climbed into bed. "You're impossible to talk to, Clay. You're pigheaded and stubborn. And . . . and mulish. And I don't care to discuss this matter further." With that, she pulled the covers up over her head.

The muscle at Clay's jaw ticked ominously. "Mulish, am I?" He blew out the lamp before climbing under the covers. "Well, we'll just see about that."

"Clay," Eden said softly, turning back to face him, "let's not argue." But her plea was met by silence and the rigidity of Clay's naked back as he rolled on his side, away from her.

The purple eyes narrowed. "Mule!" she ground out between clenched teeth, before lying back down. "Stubborn, stubborn mule."

The night air was frigid, the black sky dotted with a thousand glittering stars as the two men stood whispering beneath the tree limbs.

Wakefield's breath came out like frozen mist as he exhaled into gloved hands. "Well?" He stared at Long expectantly.

"Everything went off without a hitch," Cyrus said, wrapping his arms about him to ward off the chill. "The two bucks were taken downriver. We should realize a tidy profit off their sale." He smiled. "A little added bonus, huh, James?"

"And you're sure no one saw you come here?" James didn't like the fact that Long had insisted on meeting him at the river's edge down by Beauclaire's dock. It was too risky. If someone should see them together, all would be lost.

Seemingly unconcerned, Cyrus replied, "I passed that burnt shed you torched a few weeks back. You really did a thorough job on it."

Wakefield smiled in satisfaction. "Braxton has all but convicted the Fairchild boy. It's only a matter of time before we rid ourselves of him. Then we can concentrate on getting rid of Braxton."

"And if the woman insists that her cousin stay, then what?"

"Then we proceed with our alternate plan. One way or the other, we'll get control of Beauclaire."

Cyrus looked skeptical. "But what about the woman? Eden isn't someone who's easily controlled." He hadn't forgotten her threat to shoot him. An angry woman was as dangerous as a loaded shotgun.

"Women can be subdued with a few drops of laudanum and a hard cock." He'd never forget the sight of her sprawled on the ground with her legs open in invitation. He knew what she wanted. And he knew how to give it to her. "Leave Eden to me. I'll be able to control her. Just like I'll control everything she owns."

"You mean *we'll* control, don't you? You're not fixin' to double-cross me, are you, Wakefield?"

An owl hooted, a dog barked in the distance, and James smiled, but the smile never reached his eyes. "Cyrus, old chap, I'm wounded to the quick." He wrapped his arm about the older man's shoulders. "How could you even think it?"

Agnes fairly floated into the house the next day, following her visit to Briarwood. But her smile smoothed, her feet hitting the Oriental carpet with a thud, when she entered the parlor and noticed the morose expression on her niece's face.

"Eden, honey, whatever is the matter? Your chin is hanging low enough to touch that book you're holding." Which, Agnes happened to notice, was held upside down.

Glancing up, Eden forced a small smile to her lips, but soon her eyes filled with tears and she couldn't hide her unhappiness a moment longer. "Clay and I had a horrible fight, Aunt Agnes. He's not speaking to me."

"Child," Agnes said, taking a seat next to Eden on the settee. She removed the book from her hand and patted it comfortingly. "Clay fears for your safety. It's only natural. He's in love with you."

"But he expects me to make David leave. How can I do that? The man is like a lost soul searching for a place to light. I'm his only kin."

"*'Quarrels never could last long, if on one side only lay the wrong.'*"

"Then you think I'm wrong in wanting David to stay?"

Agnes sighed. "I think you need to see what motivates Clay's harsh edict, as he needs to see what propels you to seek the course that you do."

Eden rose to her feet and walked to the window, pulling back the drapery. The sun shone brightly, but it didn't do a thing to dispel her gloomy mood. "I don't see that there's going to be a solution to our disagreement," she confessed. "I love Clay, but he can be so darn stubborn." She turned back to face her aunt, who was smiling widely.

"My, my, that doesn't sound like anyone I know, does it? Have you told Clay that you love him?"

Eden shook her head. "I can't. It would just give him more ways to control me. I want him to see me for who I am, not who he wants me to be."

Worry mixed with apology when Agnes said, "Eden, I fear I have done you a grave injustice with all my talk of women's equality."

"But you were right, Aunt Agnes." Eden rushed over to resume her seat. "A woman must assert herself; she mustn't just be an extension of her husband."

Agnes's own words came back to haunt her and she winced. "I don't think Clay views you as an extension of himself, Eden. I've heard him discuss plans for the plantation with you. And you're keeping control of the accounts. What more do you want?"

Eden shrugged. "I don't know. I just don't want to end up like Mama."

Agnes sighed at the despair and uncertainty she saw on her niece's face and sought to put an end to it. "Would it help if I told you that my views regarding the male species have changed?"

Eden's eyes widened. "Mr. Braxton?"

Nodding, Agnes blushed like a schoolgirl. "I've found that the feelings I once had for Charles have not completely died."

"Oh, Aunt Agnes!" Eden cried, throwing her arms about her aunt, "I'm so happy for you."

"Don't be happy yet, child. Just because I've discovered that I care, doesn't mean Charles has. He was very much in love with Eulalie."

"But he was also in love with you, once."

"But I'm not the type of woman he seeks. He's used to feminine graces and sweet-smelling ladies. Women who were trained to please a man. I'm just an old maid whose time has passed her by."

"Agnes Peters, shame on you. I thought you had more spunk than that. You're hardly old, and it wouldn't take much to make Mr. Braxton sit up and take notice."

Patting her hair nervously, Agnes said, "Do you really think so?" Then, a moment later, she shook her head. "No. This is absurd. I can't just do a complete turnaround. Everyone would think I'd gone crazy."

"Everyone would think you'd fallen in love," Eden countered.

Agnes glanced down at the bloomers she wore and frowned. Charles had always hated her unorthodox attire. "Would you help?" she finally asked.

Eden's cheeks dimpled, her eyes burning with excitement and determination as she did a thorough inspection of her aunt's assets, forgetting for the time being her unhappiness over Clay. "Try and stop me."

A short time later, Eden emerged from the attic with an armload of her mother's old dresses. Aunt Agnes was not going to be found lacking in the feminine frippery department, not if she had anything to say about it, Eden vowed silently. A few alterations and these dresses would be good as new.

Passing by the door to the plantation office, she heard voices and paused. Clay was most likely working on the books, and she knew how he hated that chore. Now would be as good a time as any to sort things out with him, she supposed. " *'Don't put off until tomorrow what you can do today,'* " Agnes had often advised her.

Smiling confidently that she would be able to patch things up with her stubborn husband, Eden opened the door, but was unprepared for the sight that greeted her.

Vera stood, arms wrapped about Clay's waist, looking up at him. And Clay was caressing the harlot's cheek!

She gasped and the two broke apart quickly.

"Eden!" Clay said, setting Vera from him, a guilty flush suffusing his cheeks.

Her own cheeks flaming red in anger, Eden said sarcastically, "Excuse me," and slammed the door shut behind her.

Clay rocked back on his heels at the venom in his wife's voice and the accusation in her eyes.

"My goodness, I do hope I haven't created a problem," Vera said. "And I do appreciate your helping me get that object out of my eye, Clay."

Disgusted with himself for having been taken in by the scheming little bitch, Clay's lips thinned. "Get out. And don't come around me again, Vera. You set this whole thing up, and don't try to deny it." He should have been suspicious the moment Vera walked in, complaining that there was something in her eye. She was an actress, after all. And she'd made no bones about the fact that she wanted him.

Her hand going up to cover breasts which were amply displayed by the low cut of her black taffeta gown, Vera said with wide-eyed innocence, "Really, Clay, I don't know what you mean." She smiled inwardly, thinking of the hurt expression on Eden's face. The uppity mistress of Beauclaire had certainly been taken down a peg or two.

And it was true; she'd planned the whole thing, for she'd seen Eden coming down the stairs with an armload of clothing just before ducking into Clay's office.

Things couldn't have worked out better—except for Clay's anger. He wasn't proving tractable. And she craved him in her bed, spent her nights thinking about him making love to her. Just the thought made her wet between her thighs.

Clay pointed at the door. "Get out, Vera. Go find your fiancé."

Placing her hand on his chest, she leaned into him. "I know you want me, and your wife knows it, too. Women sense these things, Clay darling."

"Well, sense this," he said, wrapping his hands about Vera's throat. "If you bother me or my wife again, I'll squeeze every bit of deviousness out of you. Is that understood?"

Wide-eyed, she nodded, gasping for breath when he finally released her. "You'll be sorry, Clay. I intend to tell David about this," she croaked, rubbing her throat.

Clay's smile was nasty. "No, you won't. For then he would know what a slut you are, Vera. And that wouldn't fit in with your plans, now, would it?"

Her eyes bright with fury, Vera slammed out the door, and Clay wondered how on earth he was going to explain to Eden what she thought she saw.

"God damn it!" he swore, cursing the day David Fairchild and his harlot-of-a-fiancée had entered his life.

* * *

"Did you tell the slaves what I told you to, Isaac?" Wakefield asked. "That I want them to refuse to work tomorrow? And if asked, they're to say Mr. Fairchild told them not to. Is that understood?"

David pressed himself against the wall of the barn and listened, unable to believe that he'd just discovered the perpetrator behind all his problems. He could hear the fear in the black man's voice when he replied, "I done told them, Mista Wakefield, but I don't know iff'n they's goin' to listen. They's scared they'll be whupped."

"You stupid, black bastard," Wakefield said, hitting the man across the face. The slap echoed loudly and David seethed with fury. "You didn't tell them right." The overseer shook his head in disgust. "You're as worthless as you are stupid. Why did I think a nigger could do a white man's job?"

Isaac hung his head and said nothing.

"Get out. And remember, if anyone hears of our conversation, I'm holding you responsible."

When the barn door banged shut and David was finally alone, he released the breath he didn't know he was holding.

James Wakefield was behind all the discord. But why? Why did the man want to cause him trouble? Since he'd been at Beauclaire, he hadn't exchanged more than a few polite pleasantries with the overseer. Perhaps he should confide what he'd overheard to Eden. But what if she didn't believe him? What if she asked him for proof?

When no answers were forthcoming, he made his way to the door. He would watch Wakefield, find out what the man was up to, gather the necessary proof. Then he would clear his name with Eden and her husband.

He exited the barn in time to see Vera walking across the yard toward the overseer's house. He was about to call out to her when he noticed Wakefield's approach. His confusion gave way to anger when he noticed the intimate smile crossing the blond man's lips and the provocative one on Vera's.

Was Vera the reason Wakefield wanted him gone?

His eyes narrowed into thin slits; he was certainly going to make it his business to find out.

Twenty

"Why, Miss Vera, what brings you out this way?" James smiled, his gaze riveting on Vera Marsden's generous display of bosom, which threatened to spill over the bodice of her gown.

She twirled her parasol, batting her lashes in her most coquettish fashion. "I was simply bored, Mr. Wakefield. There's not a lot for an active woman to do on this plantation. And I felt the need for a little *exercise*." Her eyes lowered to stare at the unmistakable bulge in his pants, and she licked her lips. Since Clay wasn't interested in bedding her, perhaps this handsome Englishman might be, Vera thought. At any rate, David was beginning to bore her.

"Perhaps you would permit me to entertain you." He moved closer, until their bodies touched, and heard a breathless gasp from her throat. Her need was palpable, filling his nostrils with her musky scent. "I was just about to have a glass of brandy. Would you care to join me?"

"Is that your house?" she asked, nodding toward the one-story white frame house that stood at the far end of the yard.

"Why, yes. Would you like to see it? I have many entertainments available there."

There was no mistaking the implication of his words, and Vera's heart began to pound; she licked her lips. "Such as?" she asked, latching on to his arm as he escorted her the short distance.

Bending down, he whispered, touching her ear with his lips, "Such as velvet ropes and a big bad whip."

His tongue snaked out to lick the whorls and Vera's center throbbed with longing and expectation. James Wakefield was a handsome man. His hands were strong and she imagined them cupping her aching breasts, petting her swollen mound. "And are you very good with your whip, Master Overseer?"

When they reached his door, he opened it, ushering her inside. Grabbing her hand, he placed it on his pulsing member. "What do you think, Miss Vera?"

She felt the power between his thighs and squeezed his rigid shaft. A wildness entered her eyes and her voice grew husky. "I want to be your slave, Master Overseer. I want to be your nigger wench." She loved being subjugated. But because of David's past, he had never indulged her fantasies.

Wakefield smiled, reaching for his whip, his eyes bright with anticipation as he pushed her toward the bedchamber. "And so you shall."

* * *

Entering the barn in search of Caleb, Eden pulled up short at the sight of Clay, naked from the waist up. His bronze chest glistened with the sweat of his labors as he prepared to disembowel the hogs which had just been killed, and the sight of him brought a familiar yearning deep within her belly.

She hadn't spoken to him in days, not after the spectacle she'd been forced to witness between him and Vera. Though he had tried to explain it away, she just wasn't sure she was ready to accept his reasons or excuses. But it had been torture, lying next to him night after night, wanting to reach out and touch him, yet not giving in to her weakness.

Stepping back into a dark corner, she let her eyes feast on him as he continued the yearly ritual of preparing the hogs.

The animals had been hoisted up and scraped, and she felt relieved to have missed the slaughter. Watching the hogs being stunned over the head with an ax, their throats cut with a knife, always made her feel a bit queasy. And lately, she'd been feeling that way quite a bit.

Clay, Sam, and Caleb began to disembowel the dead animals, removing the intestines, lungs, heart, and liver. The intestines would be saved, washed thoroughly, and hung on sticks to dry for later use as sausage casings.

After the carcasses were halved and left to hang for twenty-four hours, they would be cut into ham shoulders and bacon flanks and left to sit in a barrel of brine for three to four weeks. Then they would be transported to the smokehouse, where they would be cured.

The fat would be rendered down to make lard; the bristles from the hides used to make brushes. Nothing went to waste. Even the feet, ears, and head were soaked and stewed with meal gruel to make souse.

Clay's biceps rippled as he lifted the dead animal off the hook, and Eden knew that if she was to preserve her sanity and her pique, she had better leave immediately. She would talk to Caleb about Othello's shoes at a later time.

As she made to leave, she tripped over a piece of rope that was hidden in the hay and let out a little yelp. Clay heard her and called out.

"Eden." A hopeful smile lit his face as he made his way toward her, wiping his hands on his buckskin breeches as he walked, drawing Eden's attention to the large bulge centered there.

She swallowed, her eyes drifting up to his face. "Afternoon, Clay," she said, trying her best to act nonchalant. "You look industrious today."

"Just preparing the hogs for winter. What are you doing out here?"

She explained about Othello, and he nodded.

"I'll mention it to Caleb when we're done."

"Thank you."

He reached for her hand, but she pulled back, bringing a frown to his lips. "Are you still mad at me? I told you that incident with Vera was all a silly mistake." He moved closer to her, forcing her back into a secluded corner, away from prying eyes.

His nearness unsettled her, and Eden took a deep breath. "I . . . I don't know."

"Well, that's honest enough, I guess." He lifted the thick braid of hair which hung over her right breast and felt the hardening of her nipple as his finger brushed casually against it. "I've missed you, angel eyes. I hope you know, I don't want anyone else but you."

Her heart melted at the sincerity she saw in his eyes. "Oh, Clay . . ."

"Oh, Eden . . . ," he mimicked, pulling her hard against his chest as his mouth came down to cover hers hungrily.

Spirals of ecstasy swirled through Eden's body as Clay's tongue ravaged the inner recesses of her mouth. She gave in to her yearning, meeting each thrust of his tongue with one of her own. Tasting, touching, unable to get enough of him. When his head lifted, she felt bereft, but was quickly consoled by his admission. "I love you, angel eyes."

"Make love to me, Clay."

His eyes widened as he peered around the corner to see Sam and Caleb still hard at work. "Here?"

"There's a shed right behind you, where tools and supplies are kept." Her need made her words come out in a breathless rush.

Clay spied the door and pulled Eden toward it. They entered the dark room to find assorted gardening tools, sacks of grain and seed. Shutting the door behind them, Clay pulled Eden back into his embrace. "You drive me wild, angel," he whispered, capturing her lips again as his hands reached down to lift up her skirts.

Eden's hands went to the front of Clay's breeches and she heard his sharp intake of breath when she untied the laces. Insinuating her hands in the waistband, she pushed his pants down around his knees and began to caress his rigid shaft, stroking the velvet hardness as she licked the sweat from his chest with her tongue and nipped at his dusky nipples.

The taste of him made her mindless with wanting, and she dropped to her knees before him, taking him full in her mouth, letting her tongue caress the moist tip, tasting the saltiness of his maleness.

"God, Eden!" Clay cried out, his head lolling back in mindless ecstasy. Unable to withstand the exquisite torture a moment longer, he hoisted her up, laying her down against the large sacks of grain.

Pushing her skirts up to her waist, his eyes feasted on the wet and welcoming warmth. As Eden's legs came up to wrap about his waist, he plunged into her moist center, over and over, driving in and out, in and out. Their breathing quickened, their hearts and souls merging as one, as they climbed the pinnacle to their fulfillment. Eden cried out and Clay smothered her screams of ecstasy with his lips.

After the furor had subsided and both were breathing normally again, Clay smiled down into Eden's flushed face. "Still mad at me?"

"Just a bit." She smiled provocatively. "Do you

think you should try and make it up to me a little more?" She tightened her legs about his waist, pulling him into her, and felt him grow hard once again.

Cupping her buttocks, Clay's smile was wildly erotic. "With pleasure, angel."

"Miss Eden," Jewel said upon entering the parlor, her voice extremely agitated. She turned toward the older woman, who was seated on the loveseat next to Eden. "Excuse me, Miss Agnes, but I needs to speak to Miss Eden right away." The young girl fidgeted nervously with the folds of her apron strings.

"Come in, Jewel," Eden responded, casting a quizzical glance at her aunt. They'd been sharing a pot of tea and gossip about Agnes's latest visit to Briarwood. "You look fit to be tied. Calm down and tell me what's happened."

Jewel swallowed "It's that woman, Miss Eden; the fancy woman."

Eden looked surprised. "You mean Vera?"

"Yes'm, Miss Vera. She up and took off."

"What?" Eden bolted to her feet.

Jewel nodded. "Yes'm. I seen her myself, heading out the door with her bag. I asked if I could help, but she said no. Said she wasn't going all that far. Said she was going to live with Master Wakefield."

The purple eyes widened in shock. "James?"

Agnes gasped. "Merciful heavens! What about David? I thought they were going to be married."

Jewel got the most anguished look on her face at the mention of David Fairchild. "Mr. David's goin' to be mighty upset. He was out to the fields when she left, and he don't know a thing about what's happened."

"Merciful heavens!" Agnes repeated, patting her cheek in a distracted fashion.

Eden began to pace. "What on earth are we going to do? I suppose I could speak to James." But she knew that wouldn't set well with Clay, and she hated to mar their newfound truce.

"Well, I say good riddance to her. The woman is a tramp. And as far as I'm concerned, David is well rid of her."

"But David might not feel that way, Aunt Agnes. He loves Vera. I don't think he realizes what she is." Clay had gone out of his way to explain in agonizing and colorful detail just what Vera was, until her cheeks had flushed crimson.

"Mr. Fairchild be a mighty lonely man," Jewel said absently, shaking her head sadly.

Eden and Agnes exchanged knowing looks, then Agnes smiled, seeing the perfect solution to their problem standing right before her eyes. "Perhaps you could be nice to him, Jewel. Mr. Fairchild needs friends right now."

A definite blush crossed the young girl's cheeks as she admitted, "We have talked some. Mr. Fairchild helped me pick flowers for the dining room table the other day." And he'd given her a yellow marigold, which she'd hidden beneath her mattress.

Eden's smile was thoughtful as the wheels of

matchmaking churned feverishly in her head. Why hadn't she seen it before? Jewel would make the perfect mate for David.

"You like Master David, don't you, Jewel?"

Jewel nodded. "Yes'm, Miss Eden. He be a fine gentleman. I like him jes fine."

"Then perhaps you would consider doing me a favor." At the girl's questioning glance, she added, "Would you mind spending some time with David to help ease the pain of Vera's defection?"

The dark eyes rounded. "Spend time with Master David? But what about my chores? Mama will have a fit iff'n I don't get my chores done."

"You leave Aunt Ruby to me," Eden assured her. "From here on out, Mr. Fairchild will be your chief duty."

Agnes sighed. "But that still doesn't solve the problem of Vera running off to live with another man."

Eden nodded at the truth of her aunt's words. David was not going to be pleased to learn of his fiancée's betrayal. And she pitied Vera Marsden when he did.

Vera was in the process of unpacking her bags when David burst into the overseer's cottage a short time later.

"Vera!" he shouted. "Vera! Where the hell are you?" His angry shouts echoed off the plastered walls.

Vera emerged from the bedchamber, clutching

a silk dress she was preparing to hang in the wardrobe to her chest. Her eyes widened at the angry flush suffusing David's cheeks. She had never seen him quite this angry before and decided to brazen it out.

"Really, David, you're acting rather childish. It's obvious that I'm right here. And *here* is where I'm intending to stay." She couldn't get enough of James. Couldn't get enough of his stimulating sex games, his animal magnetism. She'd finally found a man who could match her voracious carnal appetite, and she wasn't about to give him up for a mere boy.

David held out his hands beseechingly. "I don't understand, Vera. I thought you loved me. I thought you wanted to marry me." He noticed the bruises on her wrists, on her chest, and frowned deeply. "Then I come home to find you've gone."

"Things have changed, David. I never really loved you, though I suppose you were adequate enough in bed. I just don't see us having much of a future together."

"But you see having one with the overseer, Wakefield?"

She shrugged. "I don't expect you to understand what a woman like me sees in a man like James. But we're two of a kind. Kindred spirits, so to speak."

The blue eyes hardened. "I know what kind of a man Wakefield is, Vera. Cruel. Vindictive. But I never thought of you in those terms. Perhaps I was too blinded by love to see the real you."

She laughed then, a mocking laugh that pierced David's heart. "You're such a boy, David. Why would I want you when I have James? He's a man. He makes me feel like a woman."

"Why, you . . ." He stepped toward her, his fists clenched.

She took a step back. "Don't come near me, you dirty nigger. Did you really think I would marry a low-born nigger like you, David? It only takes one drop of nigger blood to taint a body. And you've got more than a drop, David dear. Your daddy, Lawrence Fairchild, might have been white as snow, but your mama was as black as dirt."

David took a deep breath to tamp down his building rage. If the bitch said one more word, he would strangle her with his bare hands. "Stay with your lover, then, you whore. I might be a nigger, but you're nothing but poor white trash. And that's lower than the lowliest nigger."

"Get out!" she screamed, her teeth bared like a wounded animal's at the accuracy of his insult. "Get out this instant!"

"With pleasure. I can't abide the stench of this place a moment longer."

David slammed out of the house, leaving a shaken Vera to stare ashen-faced at the door.

No one noticed the tall man who stood off to the side of the porch, listening. Listening and plotting how best to use the information he'd just overheard: David Fairchild was a nigger.

* * *

"I tell you it's true," Wakefield insisted, taking another swallow of whiskey. He and Long were seated at one of the back tables in the Golden Goose Inn, sharing a drink and a conspiracy.

Outside, icy rain pelted down as the evening temperature dropped, but inside the fire and fervor of the discussion was enough to keep things warm.

A shrill whistle flew out between Cyrus's thin lips and his beady eyes widened in disbelief. "Fairchild, a nigger? This is too perfect." He steepled his fingers in front of his hands while he thought, a devious smile twisting his lips.

Wakefield leaned back in his chair. "I thought so, too. That bit of information will make it that much easier to rid ourselves of the Northerner."

"Northerner! Ha! He's black scum. You can dress them black bastards up, teach 'em fancy words, but beneath it all they're just niggers. And there ain't no changing that. I always knew Lawrence Fairchild had himself a taste for niggers. There was always lots of talk surrounding him."

"Well the nigger he sired just happens to look as white as you or me, and it's not going to be easy to dispose of him."

"Just you leave that part to me. I've got plenty of connections, not to mention my own sailing vessels. Them that wants to buy ain't that particular about where the goods come from. I've got a contact down in Georgia who'll be only too happy to take Fairchild off our hands. Besides, now that he's back in Virginia, he ain't a free man. He's as much a nigger as ever he was."

"You really hate blacks, don't you, Long?" Wakefield asked, taking a sip of his drink.

The brown eyes hardened. "You're damned right, I do." But he wasn't going to admit that it was because his mama had been caught fucking a black buck in his daddy's own bed. He would never tell anyone the shame of that tale. He smirked as he said, "Not all of us like black flesh, Wakefield. Though I hear you've replaced the black wench with a well-endowed blonde. Is that a fact?"

James nodded. Just thinking about Vera made his dick ache with longing. She was one hot woman. The harder he gave it to her, the more she liked it. And she had the cleverest little mouth; she'd nearly sucked him dry the last time she'd taken him.

"Belle was proving too big an obstacle. Braxton is very protective of her. And her husband," he sniggered, "would probably tear my head off if he got the chance."

Cyrus threw back his head and laughed. "I doubt it would be your head, Wakefield."

"Instead of worrying about where I stick my cock, why don't you worry about making a plan to get rid of Fairchild? The quicker we move, the quicker we get our hands on Beauclaire."

Cyrus puffed his chest out. "Never let it be said that Cyrus Long didn't have a plan. I'll make contact with a few friends down south and see what I can work out."

Filling the older man's glass with whiskey, Wakefield held up his glass in a toast. "To the successful completion of a well-executed plan." He downed the fiery liquid.

Cyrus refilled their glasses. "Here's to ridding ourselves of the nigger."

"And to the death of Braxton," Wakefield added. "May he rot in hell."

Twenty-one

The carriage plodded slowly down the icy road leading to Briarwood and Charles Braxton's sixtieth birthday celebration. The November wind howled a mournful tune, but the elements couldn't dampen the excitement of the trio who traveled in the velvet-lined conveyance.

"I swear, Aunt Agnes," Eden remarked, a teasing glimmer in her eyes. "You look as if you're ready to burst. If your smile gets any wider, your lips are going to crack."

"Hush now, child," Agnes said, patting her burning cheeks with her hands. She was flushed with excitement, but only because she shared a secret with Charles that Eden and Clay knew nothing about. "You promised you wouldn't tease an old woman like me."

Clay chuckled, patting Agnes's hand. "Agnes, you look as young as your niece and twice as pretty." He winked at Eden and received a grateful smile. "Is that a new dress? Blue certainly becomes you."

Agnes preened under the flattery, smoothing down the folds of her blue satin gown. It was one of Charlotte's old gowns that they'd remade, and it had turned out perfectly lovely, thanks to Aunt Ruby's skillful hands. "Why, thank you kindly, Clay. That's generous of you, considering what a beautiful niece I have."

Eden did look beautiful, too, in her gown of purple velvet with matching fur-trimmed mantle. It had been a surprise gift from Clay, and Eden had been beside herself with joy when she'd received it.

Eyeing his wife appreciatively, Clay smiled proudly. "I'm a lucky man, Aunt Agnes. No one knows that better than me."

"How you two do go on," Eden said, shaking her head and laughing. "I think you've both kissed the Blarney stone, that's what I think."

I'm just giving you a taste of your own medicine, Eden dear," Agnes replied.

"Which I know for a fact works; my father is living proof of that," Clay broke in.

Agnes beamed, barely able to contain the secret she was so eager to dispense.

"Well, I wish we had a cure for David's ailment," Eden said, her voice filled with concern. "Since Vera's defection, he's been brooding about the house, looking like a lost puppy."

"He's well rid of that one," Clay said, folding his arms across his chest. "Vera's a worthy mate for Wakefield."

"Clay," Eden chided at the mention of her overseer.

"I wouldn't worry too much about David," Agnes counseled. "Jewel has been keeping his mind off Vera. Why, only yesterday, I saw them strolling down by the river."

Clay's eyes widened at the news, then he looked disapprovingly at the pair. "You two haven't been matchmaking again, have you?"

Eden and Agnes nodded, proud of their accomplishments. But Clay, who was about to take them to task over their meddling, was prevented from saying anything further when the carriage drew to a halt.

"We're here," Agnes said, clapping her hands like a small child, and Clay and Eden exchanged amused glances.

The house was ablaze with candles when the group entered. Rufus was there to greet them in formal black attire, ushering them into the parlor.

"Master Charles says you ta wait here, folks."

The opulently furnished room with the rose damask covered chairs and drapery brought back a rush of memories to Eden. She could still recall Eulalie Braxton seated at the shiny black piano, her voice ringing out clear and sweet as she entertained her guests. She wondered if anyone had played the instrument since Clay's mother had died.

"Where's Richard and Lucy?" Clay inquired of Rufus, surprised that they weren't here to meet them.

The old man shuffled his feet nervously, coughing into his hands. Sidling up next to Clay, he lowered his voice in a conspiratorial fashion.

"They's still upstairs, Master Clay." He rolled his eyes. "Miss Lucy had something important to discuss with Master Richard."

Clay laughed, for he could just imagine what his determined sister-in-law was up to. He found out a few moments later when Lucy and Richard entered, the latter looking as weary as a field hand who'd been toiling laboriously.

While the women oohed and aahed over each other's gowns, Clay moved closer to Richard, hanging a comforting arm about his brother's shoulders. "Still working at getting Lucy pregnant, I see."

A miserable look etched Richard's face. "The woman is insatiable. I never thought I'd see the day. Why, I'm actually beginning to think she enjoys our lovemaking."

"No!" Clay teased, delighting in the red flush suffusing his brother's face, before Richard broke into a wide grin.

"It's tiring as hell; but a man's got to do what a man's got to do," Richard quipped.

Both men laughed uproariously, but as the room grew dead quiet, they ceased their laughter and turned toward the door. Charles stood there, on his own two feet, looking fit and happier than either brother had seen him in years.

Wide-eyed with pleasure, Richard was the first to speak. "Father, this is quite a surprise."

Swallowing the lump in his throat, Clay glanced over at Agnes and smiled gratefully. "Thank you," he mouthed silently.

"Well, you needn't stare as if you've seen a

ghost. I wasn't dead, only sick. Did you think I was going to die and give all of you your inheritance?"

"Oh, Father Braxton, you look so handsome this evening," Lucy gushed, crossing the room to place a chaste kiss upon his cheek.

"Well, come on, ladies." He motioned Eden and her aunt forward. "Aren't you going to give me a kiss, too?"

Eden complied, kissing Charles's cheek, but stared openmouthed as Agnes and Charles exchanged what could only be termed a very passionate kiss on the lips.

Four pair of eyes widened in surprise, then Clay remarked, "Well, well, it seems this evening is full of surprises."

Agnes and Charles broke apart quickly, and the embarrassed woman blushed; not so Charles, who merely laughed, swatting her gently on the behind, producing a loud gasp from Lucy, who stared at the older couple as if they had lost their minds.

"Well, my dear, shall we share our good news?"

Agnes nodded shyly, staring up at him with such open adoration it brought a lump of happiness to Eden's throat and tears to her eyes. *They love each other. Truly love each other*, she thought, her feelings confirmed a moment later, when Charles announced, "Miss Agnes Peters has done me the very great honor of consenting to be my wife."

Eden screamed her delight, running across the room to clasp both of them in her arms.

Richard and Clay smiled widely, nodding their approval.

Lucy, whose mouth was hanging down to touch her bosom, recovered herself long enough to say, "Rufus, get the smelling salts. I'm about to have a fit of the vapors." Then she proceeded to faint dead away on the sofa.

Back at Beauclaire, David and Jewel strolled slowly along the riverbank. It was cold, and Jewel shivered within the confines of the warm woolen cloak that Eden had provided for her. The blue cloak had been found among Miss Charlotte's old clothing, and though it was moth-eaten and smelled a bit musty, Jewel was delighted with it.

"Are you cold, Jewel?" David asked, wrapping his arm about the small woman's shoulders. "It's a bit brisk out this evening."

With David's arms wrapped about her, Jewel felt as warm as a flatiron, but she wasn't going to embarrass herself by admitting that to this nice man, who was most likely only showing her a bit of kindness. "I'm just fine, Master David. Don't you worry none about me."

David stiffened at the address. "You needn't call me Master, Jewel. I'm no one's master. And if you knew the truth about me, you'd see how wrong it is to do so."

They stopped beneath a linden tree, now leafless with the coming of winter, and Jewel's heart ached to see the despair on David's handsome face. "What's troublin' you so, Mas . . .

David? Is it because of that woman who up and left you? Cause iff'n it is, you shouldn't fret none. She's not good enough for you by half. And that's a fact."

David smiled for the first time that evening. "It is, is it?" Gazing down at the sincerity on the young woman's face, David's heart beat just a little bit faster. She was truly lovely. And so refreshingly honest compared to Vera, whose absence had been more of a relief than anything else.

"It doesn't have to do with Vera, Jewel. I'm just sort of at loose ends. I've been wondering if I shouldn't just pack up and leave this place. I don't belong here; I don't belong anywhere."

She clutched his arm, a fierce look on her face. "Now, you just hush that kind of talk. You belong here as much as anybody, and don't let anyone tell you different."

His eyebrow arched. "You know?"

"There ain't much that happens on this here plantation that we slaves don't find out about. Especially those of us who works in the big house. White folks tend to talk freely around us niggers. I guess they don't think we can hear because we's black."

He laughed aloud at that, saying, "Then you know that I'm as black as you are." He cupped her cheek, amending, "But your skin's not black; it's like rich coffee that's been lightened by thick cream."

Jewel felt the heat creep up her neck and center somewhere far below her belly. "You're a nice man, David Fairchild, and I like you."

"I like you, too," he whispered, before lowering his head to place a gentle kiss on her lips.

When the brief kiss ended, Jewel touched her mouth in wonderment. "I ain't never been kissed by no man before, white or black."

"Well, I guess now you've been kissed by both."

She smiled, blushing. "I guess so."

They resumed their walk and when they had gone a little farther downstream, Jewel paused by a large outcropping of rocks. "I needs to check my shoe, David. I gots a stone in it." She bent over to do so, and it was the last thing she remembered, for a large, meaty fist came down across the back of her neck to knock her unconscious.

David tried to break free of the hold the two men had on his arms. He had only turned away a moment to stare out at the water, and when he'd turned back, Jewel was lying prostrate on the ground. Seconds later, a black canvas bag had been forced over his head.

"Shut up, nigger, or the girl won't live to see morning."

Nigger. The word echoed loudly in David's head and fear shot through him. They knew. Whoever it was knew his true identity.

"Don't hurt her. I won't struggle."

"That's smart of you, Mr. Fairchild." The men laughed contemptuously, tying a rope about David's wrists and ankles. "All trussed up like a pig ready for roastin'," one of the men remarked.

David strained his ears to recognize the voices,

but with the hood, he couldn't hear them clearly. And their voices sounded muffled, like they were wearing masks, too.

Soon he was being hoisted up and thrown over the back of a waiting horse. And then an object hit the back of his head and everything went black.

All hell had broken loose by the time Clay and Eden stepped into Beauclaire's front hallway. Aunt Ruby was thrashing her hands wildly in the air, screaming that her "baby had been kilt." And even Uncle Beevis's calm assurances that she hadn't didn't seem to have any effect on the hysterical woman.

Caleb, who had found Jewel's body down by the river, could offer no reasonable explanation as to what had happened. He had gone with Isaac to check the grounds when they'd come upon Jewel quite by accident. She was unconscious and could offer no answers herself.

"Calm down, everyone!" Clay ordered harshly, handing Eden his coat before stepping into the office where Jewel had been placed. He took hold of the young woman's hand, which was cold and clammy, chafing it gently as he spoke.

"Tell me what happened. Tell me why Jewel was down by the river on such a cold night."

Tearfully, Ruby explained, "My baby went walking with Master David. He done asked her to accompany him on a stroll. And I told her it was all right. Miss Eden said she should go, iff'n he asked. Ain't that right, honey?" Ruby looked to Eden for confirmation and the young woman nodded guiltily.

Eden noted the angry look on Clay's face and shuddered. The word "meddler" seemed to be etched on his forehead, and she knew it was directed at her. Thank God Agnes had decided to stay over at the Braxtons'. At least she'd been spared Clay's wrath.

"I should have known that poor excuse for a man couldn't be trusted," Clay ground out, staring at the woman's still form. "God damn it, Eden! I told you something like this was going to happen. David Fairchild is not a man who can be trusted. Doesn't anyone but me see that?"

"Master David's always been kind to Jewel, Master Clay. I don't think he would hurt her," Ruby countered.

Clay shook his head in disbelief. Even faced with overwhelming evidence, everyone was still proclaiming the bastard's innocence. He pointed at Ruby's daughter. "Well, there's the proof, lying before you."

At Ruby's renewed tears, Eden finally found her voice. "Stop it, Clay. You don't know that David is responsible for this. Perhaps Jewel fell and hit her head. Did you ever consider that?"

He hadn't and blushed, turning to stare into the flames of the fire. A moment later a low groan emanated from the direction of the sofa, and Eden and Clay rushed back to the injured woman's side.

The brown eyes opened slowly; they were fearful at first, but then, focusing on familiar faces, grew calm. "My head hurts, Mama."

"Oh, baby," Ruby said, rushing to kneel down by the sofa. "I knows it, honey. But you is goin' to be jes fine."

Suddenly, Jewel's eyes grew wild. "David!" she screamed.

Clay cast Eden an "I told you so" look.

Jewel's eyes scanned the room. "Where's David? We was walking down by the river, and then I was hit from behind. Or I fell, I really can't remember."

"Did David hurt you, Jewel?" Clay asked, studying her face intently.

"No, sir." Her forehead wrinkled in confusion. "At least, I don't think so. We was talking, and I stopped to fix my shoe. Then everything went black." She moaned again.

"Quit interrogating her, Clay," Eden snapped. "Can't you see she's not feeling well?"

Clay turned toward Caleb, who hovered wide-eyed in the doorway. "Did you search for Mr. Fairchild, Caleb? Do you know where he's gone?" When he got his hands on that miserable bastard, he was going to break every bone in his body, Clay vowed.

"No, sir, Master Clay. Me and Isaac looked about after we brought Jewel home to her mama, but we couldn't find Master Fairchild."

"Odd, isn't it, Eden, that Jewel has been injured after walking out with David, and he's nowhere to be found?"

"I'm sure there's a logical explanation for all

this," she tried to reason. "Or perhaps David is hurt, too. Perhaps he's fallen into the river."

"No, ma'am," Caleb said. "We done checked the riverbank."

"Well, check it again in the morning," Eden ordered. "It was dark; perhaps you and Isaac missed something." If David had been hurt, he could be lying out in the cold. Or worse, he might have drowned in the river. That thought sent an ache straight to her heart. She had grown very fond of her half-brother in the short time she'd known him, not to mention protective.

"David's gone, Eden. Most likely he rode into town to get himself drunk, if he wasn't already that way. You said yourself, he's been mooning over that harlot."

Jewel wanted to contradict Clay's assertions, but her head was pounding too hard, making coherent speech impossible, so she said nothing.

"I guess we'll find out what we need to know in the morning," Eden maintained. "There's no use making further accusations and playing guessing games like we've been doing. It's time Ruby put Jewel to bed, and the rest of us followed suit."

But once in their room, Clay was not content to let things lie and began pacing the room furiously while Eden undressed.

"You always take his side, don't you, Eden? I can't believe it. I'm your husband, and you take the side of a virtual stranger."

A feeling of déjà vu swept over Eden. It seemed they had had this same discussion not long ago. "I'm tired, Clay. I think we should get some sleep. Things will look better in the morning."

"Why, because you think that sainted brother of yours is going to come riding back home with a reasonable explanation as to why an innocent young woman was lying in the dirt with a lump the size of a pumpkin on the back of her head?' "

Eden sighed, trying to hang on to what was left of her temper, though Clay wasn't making that easy to do. "I have never met a man who was so fond of exaggeration. First of all, Jewel was lying on the grass, by an outcropping of rocks, I might add. And the size of her lump more closely resembles an egg, not a pumpkin. Now, if you're through being unfair, unreasonable, and unrealistic, I am going to bed."

The green eyes glittered like emeralds and the pulse in Clay's neck throbbed ominously. "You'd better learn where your loyalties lie, Eden. I'll not play second fiddle to any man, including your precious brother." With those words, Clay slammed out the door, leaving Eden as shaken as the mirror still quivering on the wall.

The following morning they were no closer to an answer as to what had happened to Jewel and David than they'd been the night before.

Clay and Eden glared at each other from opposite ends of the dining room table as they attempted to eat their breakfast, but neither spoke.

Fortunately, Agnes had returned and, at the moment, was doing her best to mend the rift between the two stubborn children.

"*'Pride is as loud a beggar as want, and a great deal more saucy.'* And you two are as hardheaded and saucy a pair as ever I've had the misfortune to witness. Why don't you try being reasonable about this whole situation?" Agnes implored, staring at Clay's and Eden's implacable features. "I'm sure we'll solve the mystery that much quicker."

Clay stuffed a biscuit in his mouth, washed it down with coffee, then said, "There's no mystery, Agnes. David obviously took out his frustration on Jewel."

Before Eden could retort, Jewel entered the room, carrying a tray of sliced ham. She set it down on the sideboard, then said in a small voice, "I heard what you done said, Master Clay. And I think you is wrong."

Eden smiled spitefully at Clay, who looked none too pleased at Jewel's assertion, but said nothing.

"David was always gentle with me. And I think he harbored some affection for me." She blushed, wiping her hands nervously on her apron. "He told me that he was at loose ends. That he was thinkin' of leavin' this place. I don't think he felt like he belonged here." The young girl hung her head, hoping she hadn't spoken out of turn; but she wanted them to know that David wasn't the bad person Master Clay was making him out to be.

"Thank you, Jewel," Agnes said. "It was good of you to bring that information to our attention."

"Yess'm," Jewel said before turning on her heel and leaving the room.

She had no sooner shut the door when Eden turned on Clay, a furious look on her face. "I knew it!" she said, pointing an accusing finger at the middle of Clay's chest. "You're to blame for David's departure."

"Me?" Clay plastered himself against the back of the chair at the force of Eden's anger.

"Now, Eden, be reasonable," Agnes cautioned, but the shake of her niece's head told her she had no intention of being any such thing.

"Clay made it quite clear to David that he detested him. That he thought David's only mission in life was to steal Beauclaire away from me."

"Well, wasn't it?"

"No! And if you'd taken the time to get to know him like I did, you'd see that he was truly a gentle person. He only wanted to help those less fortunate than himself. He wanted to set up a law practice in town to help others, black and white, that weren't being treated fairly."

Clay's look of surprise made Agnes feel sorry for him. *'Hear reason or she'll make you hear her,'* Agnes thought, shaking her head sadly as she noted the resentment on her niece's face. Why did this unfortunate incident have to come about when everything was going so splendidly between the two young people? She wanted them to be as happy as she and Charles were.

"I was trying to protect you, Eden. And this is

the thanks I get?" Clay pushed back his chair, hurt and disbelief etched on his face.

"You're always trying to protect me, Clay. But I don't need protecting any more than I need to be placed on a pedestal and cosseted like a child. I have tried to make you see that over and over, but you refuse to listen, refuse to see me as the woman I have become. I am not that same child that you were engaged to once."

At the mention of their broken engagement, Clay's lips thinned and his eyes darkened in anger. "You have done your best to manufacture barriers to our happiness, Eden. From the beginning, you have acted spoiled and childish, refusing to marry me, accusing me of treating you like chattel."

At her surprised expression, he added, "Did you think I'd forget? Forget what you told me that day in the barn? Well, I didn't. Anymore than I'm going to forget how you've tried to keep me at arm's length since the day of our marriage. I love you, Eden. Doesn't that count for anything?"

Tears filled her eyes. "Of course, it does."

"But you've never once told me that you loved me." His accusation hung thickly in the air.

"I . . . I was afraid. Afraid to admit my feelings."

He jumped up so quickly, the chair behind him banged to the floor, making Eden wince. "I am sick and tired of hearing how you are afraid of me, Eden. Am I such an ogre, such a monster, that you would be afraid of me?

"I have tried to treat you with all the respect and love that is due my wife."

She glanced over at Agnes, who was looking ill at ease, staring down at the floor. "Clay, you don't understand . . ."

"No, I guess I don't. But I'm going to find that wayward brother of yours and drag him back here anyway, since he seems to be what's important to you, Eden. And when I get back, you'd better decide if you're going to make a go of this marriage. For if you're not, I'm leaving and I'm not coming back."

"Clay!" Eden said, staring at his retreating back as he stalked angrily out of the room. Her hands went to the slightly swollen mound of her abdomen and her heart ached, for she'd never even had a chance to tell him about the baby. Covering her face with her hands, she wept.

Agnes shook her head, hardly knowing what to say after the emotional outburst she'd been subjected to. Heaving a sigh, she reached out her hand to pat Eden's back. "There, child, don't be so distraught. It was only his anger speaking. Clay will return, you'll see."

Eden looked up, tears streaking her face. "And if he doesn't?" She shook her head. "Oh, Aunt Agnes, I've made such a fine mess of things. I love Clay, and I never had the courage to tell him."

"I never figured you for a coward, child."

"It's even worse than that. I'm going to have a baby."

Agnes's face lit up like a lantern. "Oh, Eden,

that's wonderful." She drew Eden into her embrace, hugging her to her bosom. "I'm so happy for you, for both you and Clay."

In a small voice, Eden admitted, "Clay doesn't know."

Agnes went slack-jawed, then she blurted, "Merciful heavens! You haven't told him that either?"

Eden shook her head as fresh tears began to fall. "No. And if I do now, he'll only be mad because I kept it from him."

Agnes grasped Eden's arm, hauling her out of the chair. "Hurry, child, you must go to Clay and tell him everything before he leaves."

For an instant, Eden fought the idea, but then, recognizing the wisdom of her aunt's words, she nodded. "I will. I'll go to him at once."

But when she grabbed her cloak and opened the front door, it was to see Clay galloping down the drive. She yelled at him, but he was too far away to hear her, and her heart sank.

Dispiritedly, she dropped down onto the steps and wept for her own stupidity that had brought her to this end.

She wept for David, who had left thinking no one cared.

She wept for Clay, who didn't believe she loved him.

And she wept for herself, because she knew she did.

Twenty-two

Still smarting from the argument he'd had with Eden, Clay took his time, walking his horse at a leisurely pace, as he made his way down the dusty, tree-lined road toward Port Royal.

There was a nip in the air this morning, and he was grateful for the buckskin coat and breeches he wore. Vivid leaves of red and yellow clung tenaciously to tree branches, though they soon would wither and brown, falling to the ground like most of the others had done. Fall would soon be nothing more than a memory as winter's claim on the weather grew more evident with every passing day.

Though the temperature was cold, it couldn't match the icy chill that lingered in his heart at Eden's defection. Her stubborn defense of her brother still hurt, and he was bound and determined to show her what a disreputable cad David Fairchild really was. David was as guilty as sin, and now that Clay had spoken to several of Beauclaire's slaves, he was even more certain of it.

For some inexplicable reason, David was headed for Cyrus Long's plantation in Port Royal. The blacksmith, Sam, had confided as much this morning, as well as the fact that he knew David was black. How many others knew? Clay wondered, recalling their conversation.

"I don't know why Master Fairchild has gone there, Master Clay," Sam said. "But there was talk of a white-looking nigger being at Long Acres."

Clay had puzzled over that piece of information as he rode. He wasn't even aware that David and Cyrus Long were acquainted. But knowing Long's reputation for unscrupulous behavior and disreputable business dealings, if they were connected, then David was up to no good.

Lost in thought, Clay never saw the group of hooded men that came out of the trees, riding swiftly toward him. Unarmed, he was no match for the guns that were suddenly pointed at his chest. He drew his horse to a halt.

"What do you men want?" he called out. "I have no money on my person. You're wasting your time, if your plan is to rob me."

"It's you we want, Mr. Braxton. We've come for you," the brawny man on his left announced in a deep voice.

Fear tingled up Clay's spine. These men knew who he was. And as he stared down the barrels of three rifles, he knew that whoever had sent them wanted him dead.

* * *

"It's been two days, Aunt Agnes! Two days since Clay left to find David, and there's been no word."

Agnes looked up from the lightly browned cookies she was lifting off the tin sheet to stare at her nieces's distraught face. Eden was wracked with guilt and regret, but Agnes knew no way to help her, short of going off to find Clay herself, which was highly impractical, considering she wasn't the most adept horsewoman in the county.

"Two days isn't all that long, Eden. You must give Clay time to locate David. After all, isn't that what you wanted?"

Without answering, Eden crossed to the window of the kitchen and swiped at the condensation on the glass with the heel of her hand. Outside, the sun shone brightly, despite the chilly temperatures. But inside, her heart was as gloomy as a cloud-covered sky. Even the smell of the cinnamon cookies—her favorite kind—hadn't been enough to lift her spirits.

"I feel so useless, just waiting for something to happen," Eden admitted, plopping down on the bench by the work table. "Do you need any help with the cookies?"

Agnes looked apologetic. "I'm afraid not, dear. Sukie and I were just finishing up when you entered."

Eden glanced at the cook and almost smiled at the woman's annoyed expression. Most likely, Sukie detested having Agnes meddling in her kitchen. If she had heard the old black woman say it once, she had heard her say a thousand times that the kitchen was "her private place."

Pushing herself to her feet, Eden crossed to the door, pulling her cloak off the hook. "I'm not going to remain idle one moment longer, Aunt Agnes. I've decided to walk over to Mr. Wakefield's house and see if he knows anything about David's disappearance. He may have heard something in the slave quarter that could prove helpful." She doubted it, though; she'd already quizzed several of the slaves, who had professed to know nothing.

Agnes felt uncomfortable with the notion that Eden was going over to the overseer's house by herself, and said so. "I don't like that man, Eden. Why don't you wait until I get back from Briarwood? I'll only be gone long enough to check on Charles and give him his medicine, and then we can go over there together."

Eden shook her head. "You're beginning to sound as protective as Clay. Honestly, why does everyone think that James is such an ogre? He's been nothing but kindness itself, and was really a help to me after Papa died."

Agnes had her own suspicions regarding James Wakefield, but she held her counsel. She knew Eden thought the man could do no wrong, and that her loyal niece had argued with Clay about the overseer in the past. But Agnes also knew that slave gossip was rarely wrong. And several of the older women had confided that Master Wakefield wasn't as kind as he'd let on.

"Please wait for me, Eden. I want to come with

you." There was a pleading note in her voice, but Eden ignored it.

"Now, Aunt Agnes," she cajoled, coming over to give the older woman a hug, "don't you be silly. You just go on and see to Mr. Braxton. If I have any problem, any problem at all, I'll come fetch you myself."

Agnes looked skeptical, but in the end, finally agreed, and Eden went in search of the overseer.

Drawing her cloak tight about her to ward off the afternoon chill, Eden crossed the short distance to the white frame house. Knocking on the door, she waited several moments for it to open. When it did, it wasn't James Wakefield who stood on the other side, but Vera Marsden, and the sight of her left Eden stunned.

Staring wide-eyed at the battered woman, Eden felt her entire being fill with revulsion. "Vera, my God! Who did this to you?" Vera's face was black and blue, her left eye swollen shut. There were ugly bruises around her wrists, and Eden was suddenly reminded of another incident with similar circumstances.

Vera tightened the sash on her satin wrapper and turned away as Eden shut the door. "I fell," she said, staring down at the floorboards.

When she looked as if she might collapse, Eden rushed forward to assist her to the sofa. "Shall I make you some tea?"

Vera wagged her head, licking her lips, which still showed evidence of dried blood, as did the white-blond hair, which clung matted to her cheeks. "No. Please, I just want to be left alone." James had told her he would kill her if she ever told anyone what he had done. And after witnessing the viciousness of his anger firsthand, she knew he wouldn't hesitate.

"You've been badly beaten. Was it James? Did he do this to you?" A feeling of déjà vu swept over her as she thought of Belle and the conversation they'd had that day in the garden. Though Belle had denied she'd been beaten, Eden knew, just as she knew now that Vera had been, too. Only then, she had thought it was Sam; now she knew better.

Fear lit the blue eyes and her voice was insistent when she maintained, "I said I fell."

"You might as well tell me, Vera. For when James returns, I'm going to ask him myself."

"No, you mustn't!" she blurted, her eyes rounding in horror. "He'll kill me. He threatened to do so."

Taking a seat in the faded blue velvet wing chair, Eden felt suddenly nauseated at the foolish trust she had placed in James Wakefield. She'd been a blind fool. Lord, how many of her people had the crazy bastard beaten? she wondered sadly.

"I'll protect you, but you must tell me everything."

"May I have a glass of water, please?"

Rising, Eden crossed to the dry sink and found a cracked pitcher and dirty glass that smelled distinctly of brandy. Wiping it as best she could,

Eden poured the woman a glass of water, handing it to her before resuming her seat.

Vera drank greedily, then swallowed hard. "It all started out as a game. One of many of James's perverse games we had played over the last few weeks."

Heat rose to Eden's cheeks at what Vera was alluding to, but she said nothing.

"But over the last few days, James has turned vicious. There's a wildness about him, a determination that has nothing to do with sex. He tied me to the bedpost, then beat me, first with his whip, then his fists. I blacked out. That was sometime Wednesday."

Eden's eyes widened. "Wednesday? But this is Friday. Didn't James come back to help you?"

She shook her head and Eden's gut wrenched. "He's been gone two days. Two days and good riddance."

Two days. Two days, Eden thought. Clay had been gone two days. It could be a coincidence, but somehow, she just didn't think it was. "You must tell me everything. It's very important."

Hesitantly, Vera began, taking another sip of water first. "James overheard the fight that David and I had. He knew David wasn't white. Said that he'd found a way to get rid of the nigger."

Eden covered her mouth, fighting back the bile that rose thickly to her throat.

"James was afraid that David was going to take Beauclaire away from him. He said that nothing and no one would prevent him from getting his hands on the plantation."

"Do you know if anyone was working with him?"

Vera nodded. "James said that a man by the name of Long was going to help him get rid of David."

Eden gasped, then her eyes narrowed. Cyrus Long . . . that miserable, greedy bastard.

"According to James, Long hates niggers and had arranged to sell David south. They were taking David to Long's place."

"My God!" Eden said, her face paling.

"I never thought James would actually go through with it," Vera said, almost absently.

Eden jumped up from her chair and rushed to take the seat next to Vera on the sofa. "Do you know if James saw Clay ride out two days ago? Try to remember, Vera; it's very important."

An unfathomable light shone in Vera's eyes, and her voice seemed almost wistful when she asked, "You love Clay, don't you, Eden?" She didn't wait for her answer, but said, "He loves you too, you know. He wouldn't give me the time of day."

Tears welled in Eden's eyes at the woman's admission. Please, God, don't let anything happen to Clay, Eden prayed silently. "I love him more than life itself, Vera, which is why I need your help. I fear James is out to kill him, though I'm not sure as to why."

"Your noble overseer is a very good actor, Eden. He fooled everyone, but he didn't fool me. I guess I've been on the stage too long. He wanted you to trust him. He told me that he once had plans to marry you, but Clay messed them up when he returned."

Eden gasped. "I knew he found me attractive, but I never thought he had marriage on his mind."

"No offense—you are an attractive woman and all—but James wasn't interested in your body. I daresay, you were much too conventional for him. He liked things rough, if you get my meaning?" Ignoring Eden's horrified expression, she continued, "He wanted you so he could gain control of your plantation. He told me that at one time, he even considered setting Belle up as his mistress here. Said that in England, blacks and whites mingled all the time."

"Belle!" Eden's heart ached at what the poor woman must have gone through. How could she have been so blind, when the evidence had been right before her eyes? Somehow, some way, she had to make it up to her.

"James blamed Clay for most of what went wrong with his plans. When he saw him ride out, he knew Clay was going after David. He plans to kill your husband, Eden."

Taking a deep breath, Eden pushed herself to her feet, crossing to the door. She paused and looked back to see Vera rubbing her wrists in an agitated fashion.

"Thank you for telling me this, Vera. I'll send Aunt Ruby over to tend your wounds. Whip lacerations can get infected if they're not treated properly. As soon as you're able to travel, you'll be taken into town and placed aboard a sailing vessel heading north. I will give you a small sum of money to tide you over until you can get settled."

The woman nodded, saying nothing.

"You understand that if you return here, I will be forced to go to the sheriff with the knowledge that you were James Wakefield's accomplice in all this. Though you didn't actually perpetrate the crime, you had knowledge. And under the law, that makes you just as guilty as James."

"Rest assured," Vera replied, her smile twisted, "I have no desire to return here. I intend to go back to New York. I'm sure I won't have any trouble finding another protector."

"I'm sure you won't, Miss Marsden. Like a cat, I fully expect that you'll land on your feet."

With that parting shot, Eden exited the house and hurried as fast as her feet would carry her toward the big house. As she walked, Vera's statement *"He wants to kill your husband, Eden"* echoed over and over in her brain, blotting out everything else.

Because of this, she failed to notice the pregnant black woman who lumbered slowly in her direction.

"Miz Eden, wait up. Wait up, Miz Eden."

Eden finally heard and turned to find Belle crossing the yard toward her. Guilt surged through her at the sight of the black woman.

"What's wrong, Belle?" she asked when the woman had caught up with her. "You looked sorely vexed about something."

"I needs to talk to you, Miz Eden. It's powerful important."

Torn between riding immediately to Briarwood or helping the distraught woman, Eden settled on the latter. "Come into the house and tell me what's wrong."

Belle shook her head, her eyes wide. "Oh, no, ma'am; I couldn't. It wouldn't be right. I ain't no house nigger."

"Well, maybe you should be," Eden said, pulling the reluctant woman forward as they climbed the porch together. Entering the house, she led Belle to the office and shut the door behind them, instructing her to sit. Taking the seat next to her, she said, "Now, tell me what's wrong."

Belle stared wide-eyed at all the pretty things, then blurted, "I'se going to have me a baby, Miz Eden."

Confusion wrinkled Eden's brow. "Yes, I know." She smiled. "I think that's wonderful."

Tears filled the black woman's eyes. "But Miz Eden, I ain't sure who the child's daddy is." She covered her face in mortification.

Tactfully, Eden asked, "You mean you've been with another man besides Sam?"

"Not by choice, Miz Eden. But . . . but the master done made me attend to his needs. And I just ain't sure iff'n this child is goin' to be black or white."

Tears filled Eden's eyes at the anguish on the young woman's face. "I'm so sorry, Belle. For everything."

Belle reached out to take Eden's hand, and it

was she who comforted Eden instead of the other way around. "Don't be, Miz Eden. You is a good person. You can't help it iff'n you always look for the good in people. Some folks is jes plain no good. Master Wakefield, he be one of dem."

"I've let you down. All of you. It was my responsibility to protect you, keep you from harm. And I was too stupid to see what was happening right before my eyes."

"Master Clay knew. Dat's why he shipped me over to da laundry. I'se a lot happier there. Things would be good, iff'n I didn't have to worry about this heah child."

Belle patted her swollen stomach, and Eden was reminded of the child she carried—Clay's child. She swallowed, touched by the woman's generosity. Despite everything she'd been put through, Belle didn't harbor any animosity toward her.

"Does Sam know about Wakefield forcing you?"

Belle nodded and shame filled her eyes. "He's happy about the baby. Says he'll love it no matter what color it is."

It seemed she had misjudged the blacksmith, too. Eden sighed heavily, searching for the right words. "If the child you carry is Wakefield's, then that is God's will, Belle. You must love it no matter what, for it is a gift from Almighty God." She paused, uncertain how to reveal her own family's shame.

"My father once did the same thing to another slave who lived here, Belle. The woman bore a son, and I'm sure she felt just as ashamed then as you must feel now."

"You talkin' about Master David?"

Eden's eyes widened. "You know?"

"We all know, Miz Eden. That ain't something you can hide, especially from a bunch of niggers."

Eden knew the woman's words to be true, for the slaves usually heard things much sooner than their white owners.

"Though David is half black, I love him like a true brother. I don't think any less of him for it, and you shouldn't think any less of your child if it is born half white. Perhaps someday, none of it will matter anymore."

Belle's eyes widened at that remark, but she remained silent.

"Starting tomorrow, you're to report to Aunt Ruby for your chores. I'm bringing you into the house to work."

The black woman's face shone like polished obsidian. "I'se goin' to be a house nigger?"

There was such pride in the question, Eden had to swallow the lump in her throat before answering. "Yes. That's right. Jewel and Aunt Ruby could use the extra help. Aunt Ruby's not getting any younger, though if you tell her I said that, I'll deny it."

Belle giggled. "You's a good woman, Miz Eden, and I thank you from the bottom of my heart."

Too choked up to reply, Eden thought it was a small kindness to bestow on a woman who had been so badly mistreated, and smiled her thanks instead.

***

With assurances to both Aunt Ruby and Jewel that she would be fine, Eden found herself in the barn an hour later, waiting for Caleb to saddle Othello. Despite the groom's offer to go with her, Eden knew she would find all the help she needed at Briarwood and set out immediately to recruit her rescue party.

When she entered the main house of Briarwood a short time later, it was strangely quiet. Rufus hadn't answered her knock, and glancing about the large entry hall, she saw no one about.

Hearing voices coming from the parlor, she swung open the wide double doors and stood wide-eyed in shock. For lying on the sofa, with most of their clothing undone, were her aunt and Mr. Braxton. Apparently, they hadn't heard her arrival. Easing the doors closed as quietly as she could, Eden waited a moment, then knocked. It took several moments for her summons to be answered.

"Come in, come in." Charles Braxton's agitated voice floated through the shut portal, and Eden's cheeks flamed at having interrupted a very intimate moment. Like father like son, she thought. Obviously, a propensity for lovemaking ran in the Braxton blood.

Relieved to find that her aunt and father-in-law were now sitting primly on the sofa, Eden rushed forward, unable to mask the concern on her face.

"What is it, child?" Agnes asked. "You look white as bleached muslin."

Quickly and efficiently, Eden explained her suspicions about David's disappearance and the fact that Clay had most likely ridden into some sort of trap.

"My boy's in danger!" Charles shouted, rising swiftly to his feet. "Rufus," he shouted, and when the black man appeared, ordered, "Tell Richard to come down immediately."

Rufus looked aghast. "But, Master Charles, he be upstairs with Miss Lucy."

Charles snorted. "I don't give a goddamn if he's upstairs with the President of these United States. Send him to me at once."

Wide-eyed, the old man nodded and hurried out of the room to do his master's bidding.

"What do you propose that we do, child? I don't think it's wise to follow David and Clay ourselves," Agnes cautioned. "We should summon the sheriff."

Charles stared at the older woman as if she were insane. "Sheriff Wallace is a good friend of Cyrus Long's. It's going to take quite a bit of convincing to get that lazy jackal to help us. We can't waste time waiting for him to come to us. We must ride into Port Royal and see to matters ourselves."

There was an animation on Charles Braxton's face that Eden hadn't seen in years. Not so Aunt Agnes, who had paled considerably at his proposal.

"You're in no condition to ride after a bunch of criminals, Charles. You've just recovered from a debilitating illness. You're bound to have a relapse if you try to undertake a rescue mission."

He waved off her objection. "Clay is my son. I must go after him."

Agnes stood. "Then I'm going with you. I'll not have you catch a chill and have no one there to tend you."

Eden's mouth gaped open. "Aunt Agnes, don't be ridiculous. You can barely sit a horse! No doubt we'd be tending *your* injuries, rather than Mr. Braxton's."

"Eden is right," Charles concurred. "You'll stay here, Agnes."

With a stubbornness that Eden recognized only too well, Agnes crossed her arms over her chest. "I'm going, and don't try to talk me out of it. I might be a trifle old for this sort of thing, but I can keep up. I'm certainly in better shape than Charles."

That comment produced a loud *"Hmph!"* from her father-in-law, and Eden almost smiled at the indignation on his face. It was, therefore, fortunate that Richard chose that particular moment to enter the room. His shirttail was hanging out of his pants, his shirt was buttoned incorrectly, and there was a definite aroma of lilac water floating about him.

Charles sniffed the air. "It smells like a goddamn bordello in here," he said, causing Richard to turn various shades of red.

"Rufus said you wanted to speak to me right away."

Nodding, Charles said, "Eden thinks Clay might be in danger. We need to ride for Port

Royal at once. That miserable piece of offal Cyrus Long may have kidnapped him."

Richard's eyes widened. "But why? Clay barely knew the man. And he certainly never had business dealings with him."

"I'll explain everything to you on the way. Saddle up your horse and have the groom bring the buggy around." He stared at Agnes, his lips pursed in annoyance, but she merely smiled in satisfaction.

In less than an hour, provisions were packed, horses readied, and the odd assortment of liberators were ready to depart on their rescue mission.

Eden wasn't entirely certain, viewing the motley crew, that she wouldn't have been better off taking Caleb and several of the slaves. The buggy was going to slow them down considerably, and time was something they couldn't afford to waste.

David might have already been sold and shipped south.

And Clay . . .

She shook her head. She wouldn't think of that. Clay would be fine. He had to be.

Twenty-three

"I might have known you were responsible for this," Clay said to the tall man towering over him. He was in some sort of underground dungeon at Long Acres—a slave holding cell, most likely—and though it was dark, he could still make out the blond hair and the distinctive English accent of Beauclaire's overseer.

Wakefield smiled in satisfaction. "I've dreamt of seeing you like this, Braxton. Your chivalrous attempt to rescue Eden's nigger is most commendable, especially since it played right into our hands."

Clay lunged forward, but the chains holding him to the rock wall held firm. "You bastard! I'll see you in hell if you've harmed Eden's brother."

"*Tsk, tsk*, Braxton. Your temper is showing. A most ungentlemanly way to behave. Actually, you won't have to worry about your troublesome brother-in-law much longer. In a day's time, he'll be sold south with the rest of Long's niggers. There's a buyer in Savannah who is anxious to get his hands on a white nigger. He's paying handsomely, too."

"I should have killed you when I found out what you'd done to Belle."

James nodded in agreement. "Probably. Belle was a nice piece of ass. Not as good as Vera, though. That woman knew more tricks than a magician. You should have taken her up on her offer, Braxton. She told me that she'd offered herself to you, and that you turned her down. She was heartbroken. We often discussed you and Eden while we were making love."

Clay's eyes darkened, but he said nothing.

"Oh, well. All of that is moot at this point. Water under the bridge, as they say. You won't be alive much longer to worry about David, Vera, or Eden, for that matter." Wakefield's smile was sinister. "I'll be sure to take real good care of your lovely wife, Braxton. I'm sure with the proper schooling, she can learn to service my needs quite well."

Clay pulled harder at his restraints, his nostrils flaring with fury. "You touch one hair on her head . . ."

Wakefield's demonic laughter echoed off the rock walls. "It's not the hair on her head that I'm interested in, old boy. Have a pleasant day. Your executioners will be arriving shortly to put you out of your misery."

The overseer climbed up the wooden ladder, then threw open the trap door at the top and climbed out, shutting and locking it behind him.

Clay took a deep breath, swallowing the lump

of fear in his throat. He didn't fear for himself . . . but for Eden . . . for David. God, how could he have been so wrong? How could he have let jealousy and anger blind him to the truth?

For the first time in a very long time, tears filled his eyes as he thought of his wife.

"Eden," he whispered, "I'm sorry."

Eden was at that moment climbing the stairs to the suite of rooms they'd secured for the night at Ewell's Ordinary. The plan was for her and Aunt Agnes to rest, while Charles and Richard scoured the various taverns in Port Royal to find out what they could about David's and Clay's whereabouts.

"Do you think that they'll have any luck, Aunt Agnes?" Eden asked, glancing dispiritedly at their surroundings. There was a large rope bed and mattress, clean but not too comfortable-looking, and a table and two chairs. The window looked as if it hadn't been cleaned in a decade, and there were cobwebs cowering in the corner. The brick fireplace blazed brightly, adding a bit of cheer to the otherwise drab surroundings.

The older woman sighed, removing her cloak and tossing it onto the chair. Lines of weariness etched her face. "I certainly hope so, my dear. I'm sure Charles will leave no stone unturned in an effort to find Clay. He loves his son very much."

The thought of Clay brought an ache to Eden's heart. If only they hadn't argued . . . If only she hadn't forced him away . . .

"There's no use blaming yourself, child," Agnes counseled, noting the anguish on the young woman's face. "*He that can have patience can have what he will.* You must be patient, Eden. We'll find Clay, and David, too. You'll see."

But as Eden sat staring morosely into the blazing fire, she knew that she didn't have the patience nor the faith that her aunt possessed.

And she also knew that if anything happened to Clay, she would never forgive herself.

Charles and Richard looked travel weary and bleary-eyed when Agnes and Eden faced them across the breakfast table the following morning. The two men had arrived back at the inn late in the night, and Eden was anxious to learn whether they had discovered anything useful.

"Well?" she prompted, as soon as Charles had taken his first sip of coffee. He didn't look at all well, and she felt guilty for having dragged him into this in the first place.

He swallowed a few more gulps, then said, his voice low, "There's been talk of a light-skinned Negro."

Hope blossomed within her. "David," Eden replied.

"He was seen yesterday at the wharf. The men I spoke to believe he's been taken aboard one of Long's ships that's ready to sail today."

"It appears," Richard interjected, "that Long has wasted no time in finding a buyer for your brother, Eden. He's to be shipped south to Savannah, Georgia."

Agnes gasped, exchanging a horrified glance with her niece. For both women knew that if David was sold south, there was an excellent chance that they would never see him again.

"Then we must hurry. We must find Sheriff Wallace."

Charles patted Eden's hand. "We will, my dear, never fear. But first we will finish our breakfast and make plans as to the best way to proceed. Going off half-cocked is not my style."

Eden nodded, realizing the wisdom of her father-in-law's words. Long and Wakefield no doubt had a well-executed plan. It only made sense that they should come up with one as well. "David entrusted me with his manumission papers. I've had them secured in Beauclaire's safe. I've brought them with me."

"Excellent," Charles said, smiling. "You're a bright young woman. Now, eat up; then we'll go in search of William Wallace."

Eden and the others arrived at the sheriff's office precisely forty-five minutes later. They were armed with David's manumission papers and a great deal of determination, which they found, after talking to the bull-headed man, they needed.

Sheriff William Wallace, after hearing their story about a white-skinned Negro, was not inclined to do much of anything.

"This is outrageous, Sheriff," Eden complained, eyeing the grossly overweight man with contempt. No doubt he would have to expend too much energy to go in search of David. She related the story they had concocted.

"Cyrus Long has stolen property which belongs to me. The man in question, David Fairchild, was set free by my father many years ago. I have his manumission papers to prove it. Now that he has returned to Virginia, he belongs to me once again. I have come to claim my property, Sheriff."

The sheriff leaned back in his chair, folding pudgy hands across a corpulent stomach. "It don't appear to me that you have much proof that this nigger of yours is being held by Cyrus Long. I can't arrest a man without proof. And just because you've got them papers doesn't mean anything. How do I know they weren't forged?"

"Now, see here," Agnes began, her blue eyes flashing fire as she stepped toward the sheriff. But Charles restrained her, saying, "I'm sure you are well aware of my influence in this county, Sheriff Wallace." He impaled him with a warning look, and the fat man began to sweat profusely. "And I'm sure that you're further aware that I am privy to much of what goes on in this area." The sheriff squirmed restlessly in his seat, nodding, and Charles continued. "I would suggest, unless, of course, you wish your private dealings with Mr. Long to be made public, that you assist us in our endeavors to find Mrs. Braxton's property."

It was a well-known fact that Wallace was taking money from Long to look the other way regarding Long's unscrupulous business dealings. It was also a well-known fact that Sheriff William Wallace was a spineless bastard. Charles was counting on that to aid them.

"I also insist that if David Fairchild is found aboard one of Cyrus Long's ships, that Mr. Long be incarcerated until he can be brought to trial. Is that clear, Sheriff?"

Sheriff Wallace removed his handkerchief from his back pocket and mopped his brow with it. "I'm at your service, Mr. Braxton," he said, pushing his massive bulk out of the chair. "Shall we proceed?"

Charles smiled and with a wave of his hand, said, "After you, sheriff."

It took only a few minutes to reach the wharf, which was bustling with activity. Several ships were in port, making ready to leave. Hogsheads of tobacco were being loaded, as were chained rows of slaves.

Long's ship, the *Southern Belle,* was at the far end of the pier. The group arrived just as the gangplank was being raised.

"Hold there," the sheriff shouted to the crewman who was yanking up the plank. "Lower it down. We wish to board."

"We're ready to cast off, Sheriff," came the sailor's reply.

Wallace pulled his gun, as did Charles and

Richard, and the sailor relented, lowering the gangplank once again.

Many crewmen milled about, attending to their various duties, but it wasn't difficult to spot Cyrus Long as he stood near the hatch, issuing orders for the loading of his human cargo. He was dressed garishly, as was his custom, in a brown and gold plaid suit. And the sight of him turned Eden's stomach.

"Step lively, you nigger scum," he shouted to the confused men and women, waving his whip menacingly. "Get your miserable black asses down this ladder."

"Mr. Long," Sheriff Wallace called out.

Eden observed with relish the moment Cyrus took notice of who had boarded his ship. His face paled as white as his shirt, and she couldn't resist smiling smugly up at him.

His voice filled with indignation. "What's the meaning of this intrusion, Sheriff? I'm getting ready to set sail for Savannah."

With no small amount of apology in his voice, Wallace replied, "These folks believe you have illegally taken a slave of theirs. I'm afraid we're going to have to search your ship, Cyrus."

Beads of sweat dotted Long's upper lip and forehead. "Search my ship? That is outrageous!"

Eden stepped forward, her voice as cold as the depths of the Rappahannock River. "You know perfectly well that you have stolen one of my slaves, Mr. Long. We are going to search the bowels of this ship. And if David is found, you, Mr. Long, are going to jail."

Long tried to edge his way toward the gangway, but Richard stepped in front of him, leveling his gun at his chest. "I wouldn't, if I were you, Long. Drop the whip, before I'm tempted to use it on you."

Sheriff Wallace and Charles entered the bowels of the ship. A few minutes later, they discovered David gagged and shackled in the ship's hold.

"Is that the man?" the sheriff inquired, gazing with derision at the light-skinned Negro.

Charles's lips thinned as he stared down at the bruised and bleeding man. "It is."

"You," the sheriff shouted to a crewman. "Unlock these chains. I'm taking this man into my custody."

A few minutes later, two of the crewmen carried David above decks, placing him carefully on the wooden planks.

"David!" Eden cried out, covering her mouth in horror as she stared at her injured brother. She turned on Long, her voice full of venom when she spoke. "You'll pay for this, Long. You and that vile Englishman."

Agnes was already tending to David's wounds when Eden approached. "Is he going to be all right?"

Agnes nodded. "He's bruised and bleeding. But he'll be fine once we get him bandaged."

Eden breathed a sigh of relief, staring sadly at her brother. She knew now with a certainty that David's plan to remain in the South could never be. Not as long as men like Cyrus Long and James

Wakefield existed. And they existed in very great abundance, she was afraid.

With Cyrus Long in custody, and the sheriff's vow that he would be placed in jail to await trial, Eden and her family of rescuers carted David back to the tavern.

Pacing nervously across the small confines of her room, Eden waited anxiously for David to awaken so she could question him about Clay. The sun was setting low on the horizon, and she knew that the longer they waited, the more difficult it would be for them to find Clay.

"He's awake, Eden."

She turned at the sound of her aunt's voice, and breathed a sigh of relief before rushing to the door of the connecting room.

David was propped up against the headboard, looking rested and not nearly as ill as she'd first surmised. With a nod of greeting to her in-laws, she took a seat on the edge of the bed, next to her brother.

"You look better, David," she said, holding on to his hand. "How do you feel?"

He smiled softly at the concern he saw on his half-sister's face. Being part of a family was a whole new experience for him. And he liked it.

"A bit bruised. But aside from that, I'm fine, thanks to Miss Agnes." He smiled at the older woman. "She's truly an angel of mercy."

"Glad you're feeling better, boy," Charles said.

Eden turned hopeful eyes on her father-in-law.

"Did you and Richard have any luck?" They had left shortly after bringing David to the tavern to search the entire area for Clay.

Charles shook his head, a worried frown creasing his lips. "No, my dear. We covered every square inch of the docks and the surrounding area, but there was no sign of Clay. Nor of that bastard Wakefield, either."

Eden's heart plummeted, and she heaved a sigh.

"Clay?" David said, staring wide-eyed at the occupants of the room. "Clay is missing?"

"He went in search of you, David," Eden explained. "We believe he's being held captive somewhere."

The light of understanding entered his blue eyes. "That explains what I heard on board ship. I overheard some of the crewmen talking. I didn't know at the time that they were referring to Clay, but it must be him."

"What is it, boy?" Charles asked impatiently.

"According to what I heard, Clay was severely beaten then taken to Long's plantation to await execution."

Eden vaulted from the bed. "Clay—my God, Clay," she screamed, throwing her hands wildly in the air as tears filled her eyes.

"Eden," David cried, pushing himself off the bed. He drew the hysterical woman into his arms, patting her head as if she were a small child. "You won't do Clay any good by becoming hysterical. We need to devise a plan to rescue him. And we need all our wits about us."

She took a deep breath, wiping the tears from her face. "You're right, of course. I'm sorry."

"We know that Clay has been taken to . . ." He paused expectantly, and Richard supplied, "Long Acres. That's the name of Cyrus Long's plantation. It's not far from here."

"We must go under cover of darkness." David glanced out the window; dusk was falling quickly. "We need the element of surprise on our side. With Long in custody, Wakefield is probably calling the shots." And that didn't bode well for Clay, knowing the man's vicious hatred for him. But though he didn't voice his fear aloud, he could see by the frightened expressions on everyone's face that they knew what he was thinking.

"Are you sure you are well enough to travel, David?" Agnes asked, not liking the pallor of his complexion. "Some of your cuts were deep and bled quite a bit."

"The man risked his life to find me," David argued passionately. "The least I can do is risk mine to save his."

It was pitch black by the time they reached Long Acres. There was none of the activity that David had expected, and as they made their way toward the slave quarter, he grew more confused as to why that was so.

"I don't like this, David," Charles whispered, grabbing on to his arm. "It's too quiet. Perhaps we're walking into a trap."

That was precisely what David was thinking,

but he refrained from voicing his concern, saying instead, "Stay here. I'm going to try and talk to some of the slaves. See if I can find out anything."

"I'm sure they know something," Richard said. "The slaves are always the first to know."

"But David," Eden protested, "you're as white as we are. What makes you think these folks will tell you anything?"

He smiled ruefully. "To you I look white. To them I'm just another nigger. I'll be back soon. Don't worry."

True to his word, David reappeared a few minutes later, bringing a collective sigh of relief to his companions.

"There's a man being held in the slave holding cell. It's out behind the barn, beneath the ground."

Richard's lips twisted in disgust. "Long was a clever bastard. I'll give him that."

"There's no telling how many poor unfortunates were incarcerated there," Agnes added, shaking her head sadly as she gazed at Charles. "It's an evil practice, Charles." She wiped the tears from her face.

He hugged her to him, nodding gravely. "I know, Aggie. I know."

They found the holding cell exactly where David's informant had said it would be. There was no lock on the hatch cover, which brought instant concern to the trio of men, who knew that dead men didn't require locks.

"I'll go down and see what's about," David said,

checking the gun at his belt that Charles had given him.

"We can't allow that," Eden argued. "What if there's someone down there? What if you're injured? I can't ask that of you, David."

He gripped her shoulders, staring into her pale face. "Eden, you don't have to ask it of me. It's what I want to do. Clay might have misjudged me, but he only had your best interests at heart. I'm going down after him. Now give me a kiss for luck."

She did, and he disappeared down the hatch.

It seemed like an eternity that David was gone. It was so quiet Eden could hear her own heart beating. It was as if everything had come to a standstill, as if the night creatures knew of the importance of their mission.

"There he is!" Charles called out, as he spotted David's head rising above the hatch. He and Richard rushed toward him.

"He's got Clay with him," Richard shouted.

Eden bit her lip as she watched the men lift Clay out of the cell. Agnes was holding onto her waist tightly, whether to support Eden or herself, Eden wasn't quite sure.

When they had Clay on the ground, Eden rushed toward him, kneeling down beside her husband. He'd been viciously beaten and was as lifeless and pale as a corpse. "Oh, my God!" she whispered, staring at the blood that oozed from his head.

"He's dead! Dear God, he's dead," she moaned, before keeling over in a faint.

Twenty-four

Clay was not dead, but he was bleeding profusely; the bullet had creased his scalp. Agnes ripped at her petticoats, grateful for once to have been wearing some, making a thick pad to staunch the flow. Tearing more of the skirt into several narrow strips, she bound the pad to the side of his head.

"He's lost a lot of blood," she said to Charles, who hovered over her left shoulder, tears in his eyes. "Head wounds always bleed a lot, my dear," she added, trying to comfort him.

"They left Clay for dead," David said. "When I went down into the holding cell, he was lying in the dirt; his chains had been unfastened. I guess they thought he wouldn't be needing them anymore." He didn't want to tell them that the rats had already gathered to divide up the corpse.

A low moan diverted everyone's attention from Clay to Eden, who was slowly coming to. When she did, her eyes grew wild once again, but Agnes placed a comforting hand on her shoulder. "He's alive, Eden. But just barely. We must get him home as quickly as possible. And you must be brave. Clay is going to need your strength, now more than ever."

Clay was alive! Eden clutched that thought to her breast as she turned over to glance at him. He'd been bandaged but was still bleeding. She grasped his hand, bringing it to her lips, kissing it, thanking God that his life had been spared.

"Come, my dear," Charles said, helping Eden to her feet. "Richard has brought the buggy around. David will drive you, Agnes, and Clay to the docks. Richard and I will borrow some horses from Long's stable and ride on ahead to make the arrangements. It will be much quicker if we transport Clay back to Beauclaire by river; and it will be a lot less difficult for him to travel that way."

Eden nodded, then walked over to David and took his hand. "Thank you for going after Clay."

He brought her hand to his lips and kissed it. "That's what families are for." At her pleased expression, he added, "Come on. Let's go home."

Charles had already secured a tobacco barge by the time Eden and the others arrived, and Clay was quickly transported onto it. The owner was assured a hefty bonus if he could get the group safely back to Beauclaire with all due haste.

Eden sat with her back propped against a hogshead, cradling Clay's head in her lap. Agnes sat beside her, looking weary and concerned. It was cold and damp on the river. The wind had come up, and the wooden barge bobbed up and down on the swift-moving current of water.

Stroking Clay's cheek with her fingers, Eden couldn't hold back her tears. "He's so pale, Aunt Agnes. He's lost so much blood."

Agnes wrapped her cloak more tightly about her, wishing for a pair of warm, woolen underwear and a cup of hot tea. "'Tis the nature of the wound, child. I'm not going to lie to you and say that Clay's injury isn't serious, for it is. But Clay is a strong man. And we're going to do everything possible to make him well."

"I'm so lucky to have you," Eden responded, glancing at David who was conversing with the captain of the barge. "And David, too. I don't know what I'd do without the love of my family."

"*'An empty bag cannot stand upright.'* So it is with people. We all need someone now and then to lean on—to hold us upright. Take heart, child. Clay's life is in God's hands now, and yours."

Eden was to relive her aunt's words over and over again in the following days as she maintained a constant vigil at Clay's bedside.

Though they had poured gallons of Agnes's healing herb broths into Clay, and sponged his fevered brow and body, he didn't seem to be getting any better. He hadn't regained consciousness, and his fever was rising, not abating.

The sun streamed into the bedchamber to land on Clay's sleeping form. It only served to illuminate the paleness of his complexion, the gauntness of his face, and it made Eden's heart ache to look at him.

She looked up as the door opened to find Agnes entering the room; she was carrying yet another bowl of broth.

"Has there been any improvement?" she asked, setting the bowl down on the nightstand, frowning at the purple smudges she saw beneath her niece's eyes, the listless droop to her shoulders, that told her more plainly than words that Eden needed to rest.

Eden shook her head and in a strained voice replied, "No. Nothing. He's not getting any better, despite everything we've tried. His body is raging with fever."

"I've brewed some boneset tea. I'll have Jewel bring it up. That might help bring his fever down."

"This is all my fault, Aunt Agnes. I'm to blame for everything that's happened to Clay. And now he's going to die because of my stupidity."

"Hush, child! I won't have you talking like that," Agnes scolded, hauling Eden to her feet. "You're exhausted. You can't spend every waking minute by Clay's side, watching for improvement. You've a child to consider. Have you forgotten?"

Eden's hands went to her slightly swollen stomach and tears filled her eyes. "I can't go on if anything happens to Clay."

Agnes dragged Eden to the rocker in front of the hearth and pushed her down into it, taking the seat in the wing chair across from her. "You can and you will. You are going to have Clay's baby. You owe that child the chance to survive by taking proper care of yourself. You look as sick as your husband, Eden. How long has it been since you've had a proper night's rest?"

The weary shoulders lifted, then dropped. "I don't remember."

Agnes heaved an impatient sigh. "You'll go into the guest room this very minute and lie down for a nap. I will stay with Clay."

"But what if he awakens? Calls for me?"

"I'll come get you. I promise. But it isn't likely that he will. His fever has to subside before he can begin the healing process. His body is fighting off the infection from the wound he received. Once his fever breaks, things will look a whole lot different."

"But I feel so helpless," Eden protested.

"Clay loves you, Eden. He will fight to live for you. You have the power to heal him. Your love can bring him back to us."

"But how?" She held out her hands beseechingly. "He doesn't even know that I love him."

Taking her niece's hands in her own, she said softly, staring into sad, violet eyes, "Then don't you think it's time you told him?"

"But he's unconscious; he can't hear me."

"How can you be certain of that? The power of love can work miracles." When Eden made to rise, Agnes added, "You may begin your new treatment this evening. For now, you are going to take a well-deserved rest."

Eden smiled for the first time in days. "You

should have been in the army. You issue orders like a general."

Agnes pointed toward the door, a self-satisfied smile on her face. "Then march. And don't you dare show your face in here until the sun sets."

Wearily, Eden trudged, rather than marched, to the door, and exited the room, leaving Agnes alone with her fears. She wasn't a particularly religious woman, but she did get down on her knees and pray.

Clay was as close to death as any man she'd ever seen, and it was going to take a miracle to bring him back from death's door.

Like a litany, Eden declared her love to Clay over and over again during the next few days. It was the first thing out of her mouth in the morning, the last thing she uttered before retiring to bed at night.

She'd taken her aunt's advice to heart and had been keeping more regular hours and eating properly. The weight she had lost the past week had been replenished, and she was feeling better than she had in days.

Clay's fever had finally broken last night. That had been the most dramatic occurrence to lift her spirits. And though he still looked pale, his head wound was healing nicely.

The sun was sinking into the horizon, and Eden reached over to turn up the lamp. Settling back into the rocker she had placed by Clay's bedside, she took up her knitting and began chatting with Clay as if he could hear her.

"I've decided that we're going to have a boy, Clay. That's why I'm making this blanket blue." The needles flew in and out of the blue yarn. "I know men set a lot of store by having sons, so I've decided that we're going to have one, too.

"Of course, you'll have to wake up if you're going to help name the child. Else I may come up with a perfectly dreadful name like Ulysses or Aristotle." She smiled to herself, thinking what perfectly awful names those would be to burden a tiny child with.

Pushing herself out of the rocker, she took a seat on the edge of the bed. Picking up Clay's hand, she pressed it against her abdomen. "Feel your child within me, Clay. It loves you as much as I do." She shut her eyes. "Oh, Clay, I love you so much. Please don't die. Please come back to me and the baby."

The hand on her abdomen moved slightly, as if in a caress, and Eden's eyes opened to stare at Clay's face. His eyes were open and he was smiling.

"Clay!" she exclaimed, unable to believe what her tear-filled eyes were telling her. "You're back!"

His throat was raspy when he said, "How could I not return when I have a wife who loves me? Is it true, angel eyes? or was I dreaming? I thought I heard you say that you loved me."

She kissed him tenderly on the lips. "I do love

you, Clay. I've always loved you. I was just too stupid to tell you."

"Ssh," he whispered, caressing her cheek. "We've plenty of time to talk everything out later. Now, I just want to look at you."

She fussed with her hair. "I must look a mess. I've been so preoccupied with . . ."

"You look beautiful, just like always."

"They say there's a glow that a pregnant woman gets."

His eyes widened. "I thought I was dreaming that part. You mean, you're with child . . . my child."

She took his hand and placed it on her abdomen again. "Your child rests within me."

Tears filled Clay's eyes. "I feel like I've died and gone to heaven."

She wagged a finger at him. "Don't you dare talk like that, Clay Braxton. Aunt Agnes and I have done everything in our power to prevent that from happening."

His eyes twinkled. "And was part of your treatment starvation? I'm so hungry I could eat a horse."

"Would roast turkey, cornbread dressing, and green beans do? That's what's left over from our Thanksgiving dinner."

Bringing Eden's hand to his lips, he kissed it. "We have much to be thankful for, you and I."

"Yes," she whispered. "And we have God and Aunt Agnes to thank for it."

* * *

"Eden told me what you did for me, David," Clay said, holding out his hand. "I want to thank you, and I want to apologize for all the false accusations and misunderstandings."

David stared down at the man in the bed and shook his head. "You don't have to apologize, Clay. I know you were acting in Eden's best interests. And I probably would have done the same thing if circumstances had been different."

"Shut the door, will you, David? I want to ask you something, but I don't want Eden to hear." Clay adjusted the bed covers, propping another pillow behind him.

Pulling up a chair to the side of the bed, David asked, "You want to know about Wakefield, right?"

Clay nodded, surprised by the man's astuteness. "Has he been spotted? Knowing the bastard, he won't give up his maniacal quest to get his hands on Beauclaire or Eden." Fear for Eden's safety had him chafing at the idea of spending two more days in bed. But Agnes had been adamant. And with both her and Eden against him, he could do no more than acquiesce.

"There's been no word, though your father has hired men to look for him. Long is in jail, awaiting trial. Charles had posted his own guard at the jail to make sure he remains there."

Clay had been quite surprised, and deeply touched, to learn of the role his father and brother had played in his rescue. They had risked their lives, as had David, to save him. It was a debt he could never repay.

His family was important to him, and he could see now why David was so adamant about having one of his own. "I'd like you to stay on here, David. Beauclaire is your home, and we'd like to be your family, if you'll let us."

Rather than the joyful expression Clay expected, he saw David's eyes fill with sadness. "I wish that were possible, Clay. I am happy here. I have found peace and contentment." And love, he added silently, thinking of Jewel. "But now that my secret is out, I'll be forced to leave this state. I can't run the risk of reenslavement." And he knew that if he were to marry Jewel, they couldn't remain safely in the South.

Clay nodded in understanding. "I understand. I only wish there was something I could do to help."

"Perhaps you'll bring Eden north for a visit, once I'm settled."

"We'd be pleased to come for a visit."

The young man's face beamed. "In that case, thank you. You don't know how much that means to me."

Clay sighed. "I think I do, David. I finally think I do."

The snow had been falling for hours, and Eden thought it was a perfectly delightful way to celebrate the beginning of the Christmas season. She and Aunt Agnes were in the kitchen, assisting Sukie with the baking chores for the upcoming holiday, despite the cook's protestations.

They had been quite industrious the past two days. Already, platters of fruitcakes, studded with nuts and dried fruit, sat soaking in rum, while piles of shrewsbury cakes, oatmeal cookies, and fruit tarts waited patiently in the pie safe to be devoured.

Seated across from each other at the old pine table, the smell of gingerbread and mulled cider surrounding them, Eden and her aunt were making preparations for the very special event that would take place on Christmas Eve: Aunt Agnes's wedding to Charles Braxton.

Absently, Eden ran her finger over the marred surface of the table, tracing all the knife cuts and dents years of use had put there as she listened to her aunt read the guest list for the reception.

"Do you think we've included too many people, Eden? After all, it's not like Charles and I are youngsters."

Studying her aunt, Eden noticed the warm glow about her cheeks, the way her eyes sparkled with happiness. "You look as young as a girl, if you ask me, Aunt Agnes. Why, folks will probably mistake you for my sister."

Agnes's cheeks glowed red, and it didn't have a thing to do with the rising temperature in the room. From the far corner of the kitchen came an amused chuckle as Sukie removed yet another batch of gingerbread men from the oven.

"Hush, child! You're embarrassing me to death," Agnes protested, covering her cheeks.

Eden smiled widely, a mischievous twinkle in her eye. "If you think you're embarrassed now,

Aunt Agnes, wait until I tell you about what I discovered you and Charles doing the day I rode over to Briarwood to fetch you."

Agnes gasped in mortification, her hand going to her throat, while Eden and Sukie released a simultaneous howl of amusement that could be heard for miles.

Later that same night, Clay and Eden snuggled beneath the covers, wrapped in each other's embrace, as they laid bare their souls to each other.

"I love you so much it hurts, Eden," Clay said, kissing her softly on the lips. "The worst part of thinking that I would die was contemplating not seeing you again."

Tears filled Eden's eyes and her heart ached with her love for him. "Oh, Clay," she whispered, trailing her finger across his firm abdomen, "I'm sorry it took me so long to come to my senses. I put Beauclaire and my own foolish needs above the one thing in life that really mattered: you. I've loved you forever, Clay. I was just afraid to admit it. Afraid it would give you too much power over me."

"Why would you be afraid of that, angel? You know how much I love you."

She told him about her father's visit just days before their first wedding, how his words about wifely duty had frightened her. And she told him about what she had read in her mother's journal.

"I didn't want to end up like my mother, Clay. She loved my father a great deal, but he chose another woman over her. She was miserably unhappy. Though I know now that she brought some of that misery on herself. She was unable to enjoy the physical side of their marriage and ruined their chances for happiness."

"You don't seem to have any such problem," he said, his hands coming up to fondle her lush breasts. Her nipples hardened in response and he smiled. "See what I mean?"

She cupped his swollen manhood and squeezed gently, making him moan softly in pleasure. "Nor do you."

"It would seem that we're well suited, then, Mrs. Braxton." He spread her legs apart, cupping her warm, wet mound. Gently, he inserted his finger and began a slow rhythmic motion as his tongue repeated the movement within her mouth.

Eden felt the familiar tension build within her, the urgent need to feel Clay pressed deep inside her, and arched her back, urging him to take her. Slowly, he entered her, plunging deep into her hot core, taking her higher and harder than he'd ever taken her before.

Her body began to vibrate with liquid fire as they rose to the top of the crest. She exploded in ecstasy, as did he, spilling his seed into her as they climaxed together.

They were one, she thought, smiling contentedly, hugging him to her, enjoying, needing the comforting weight of him pressed against her, into her.

He was hers. And she was his. And together they would always be one.

Twenty-five

"Are you sure I should be wearing a white gown, Eden?" Agnes gazed at her reflection in the mirror and frowned. "After all, I'm hardly in my first bloom of youth. People may think it's presumptuous of me."

Gazing at her aunt in the antique satin gown, Eden's eyes misted. Aunt Agnes looked truly beautiful, despite the worried lines streaking across her forehead. "Clarice Willowby would be devastated if you didn't wear that dress, Aunt Agnes; she's been working on it for weeks. Not to mention Clay, who paid a small fortune for it." It was Clay who had suggested surprising her aunt with it; it was his way of showing his gratitude for all Agnes had done for him.

Agnes's sigh held a wealth of uncertainty. "It is lovely, child." The seed pearls on the bodice twinkled brilliantly as the sun caught them.

"Aren't you the one who told me not to worry about what others think? That we should follow our own hearts? And isn't this your first marriage, which entitles you to wear white?"

Agnes blushed to the tips of her dainty satin slippers. "Yes. But I'm not . . . well, you know."

"I would hardly expect a fifty-six-year-old woman to be a virgin, Aunt Agnes!" Ignoring her aunt's gasp, she held out the skirt of her gown, asking, "Now, do I look all right? I don't look too fat in this gown, do I?" She looked down at her growing belly, patting it absently.

The violet satin matron-of-honor gown was stunning on Eden. It brought out the color of her eyes. And the fullness of the skirts hid quite well the fact that she was nearly four months pregnant.

"You always look lovely, child. Come and give me a hug."

Eden hung back momentarily. "But I don't want to mess up your dress. Clarice would kill me if it got wrinkled. And I know she's waiting downstairs to give you a final once-over."

"Stuff and nonsense. I couldn't care less. Now, give me a hug. I'm going to miss you, you know." Tears filled the kind blue eyes.

Choked with emotion, Eden admitted, "I'm going to miss you, too." She gave her aunt a heartfelt hug. "You've been so good to me over the years, Aunt Agnes. I don't know how I can ever repay you for all the sacrifices you've made on my behalf." She thought of this kind woman unselfishly nursing a man who had committed the vilest of acts upon her flesh, and tears misted her eyes.

"Merciful heavens!" Agnes wailed, dabbing at

her eyes. "You're going to make me leak like a sieve if you're not careful."

They both smiled through their tears.

"I won't be that far away," Agnes reminded her, patting Eden's cheek. "And chances are, you're going to see me just about every day."

"I'm so glad you convinced Charles not to leave for your honeymoon until day after tomorrow. I couldn't bear not having you here for Christmas. It wouldn't have been the same without you."

The sound of piano music drifted up, signaling the start of the processional, and Agnes paled considerably. "Oh, dear! I do think it's time for us to make our descent."

"Be happy, Aunt Agnes," Eden said, giving her one last hug. "You deserve it." Eden grabbed her bouquet of green holly and white poinsettia off the dressing table and preceded her aunt out the door.

After the last guest had finally departed, the entire Braxton family and David gathered in the parlor. The room had been decorated festively with greenery and ribbons for the Christmas holiday, and a tall, eight-foot fir tree stood between two windows. Tiny candles illuminated the conifer, while red velvet bows decorated the branches. Beneath it were dozens of gaily wrapped packages.

There was an air of anticipation among the occupants of the room. Clay had been quite mysterious about an announcement he wanted to make, and Eden was just as eager as everyone else to hear what it might be.

"I declare, your husband is being most mysterious, Eden," Lucy declared, smiling secretively. "Richard and I have our own announcement to make, but we're going to wait."

Eden smiled in genuine pleasure at her sister-in-law. "You mean it finally happened? You're actually going to have a baby?" She gazed over at Richard, who was seated next to Lucy on the sofa, and thought she saw a look of relief pass over his face.

Lucy nodded animatedly, squeezing her husband's hand. "We haven't told a soul, Eden. So you must promise to keep our secret. We thought we'd announce it tomorrow. We didn't want to intrude on Father Braxton's big day."

"That was thoughtful of you," Eden remarked, surprised that Lucy had restrained herself. The young woman usually relished being the center of attention.

Lucy gazed at her husband adoringly. "It's what Richard wanted." And Eden knew that the willful, selfish woman had finally been "handled properly," as Aunt Ruby was so fond of saying. And Lucy didn't seem to mind a bit.

Standing before the fireplace, a glass of eggnog in his hand, Clay cleared his throat, drawing everyone's attention to him.

"I wish to propose another toast to the happy couple." He lifted his glass. "To Father and Agnes. May they find as great a happiness as I have found with Eden." He turned toward his wife and his smile held a wealth of love and affection.

"I have asked you all here to make an announcement—several, actually. I know how tired you all are, and I appreciate your staying, especially the newlyweds, who, I'm sure, are anxious to retire." There was a chorus of giggles at that remark, and Agnes turned several shades of red. "So I won't keep you much longer. Traditionally, we've always exchanged our gifts on Christmas morning, but because I have some special presents to bestow, I'd like to hand them out now."

"Hurry up, Clay," Lucy encouraged, clapping her hands as she bounced up and down on the sofa. "We are all dying of curiosity."

Clay smiled indulgently at his sister-in-law. "Actually, Lucille, you and Richard are the first ones I'd like to gift." The woman's eyes widened in surprise, and Clay glanced over at his father, who winked in approval. "As most of you know, there is a stipulation in Father's will that states the eldest son shall inherit three-fourths of Briarwood upon his marriage. But," he turned toward his brother, "I have convinced Father that this is not totally fair to Richard, who has worked hard in my absence to make Briarwood everything it is today."

The younger man blushed, smiling his thanks.

"And so, with Father's blessing, I am turning over controlling interest in Briarwood to Richard and Lucy."

Lucy's loud screech sent the hairs straight up

on Eden's neck and she laughed, shaking her head at the happy woman.

"I don't know what to say," Richard began, his voice choked with emotion.

"How about thanks?" Charles retorted, and his son's blush deepened.

Eden couldn't have been prouder of Clay and beamed at him approvingly. Her pleasure increased tenfold at his next announcement. It was for David, and she couldn't wait to see her brother's expression.

"Eden and I present this next gift jointly to David, whom I suspect will have his own announcement to make rather shortly." David blushed and nodded, stepping forward at Clay's insistence.

"David is the newest member of our family, and we're quite proud to have him as part of our growing brood." Reaching into his breast pocket, he withdrew an official-looking document, handing it to David. "This is to new beginnings, my friend."

David's eyes widened in disbelief, filling with tears as he scanned the paper, bringing a similar reaction to Eden's. "This is a deed to five hundred acres of Braxton land in Connecticut," he stated, clearly astonished. He wiped his tear-stained face with the back of his hand. "I'm overwhelmed by your generosity."

Eden jumped to her feet and flung her arms about her brother's neck. "We couldn't leave the uncle of our first born child propertyless, now, could we?" She kissed him, dragging him back to sit down beside her.

"And now the final announcement," Clay stated, pulling another piece of paper out of his pocket. It was rolled and tied with a red satin ribbon. "This is for my wife—the mother of my child, who makes all things in life worthwhile."

Confusion etched Eden's face as she stepped up to take the rolled paper, and there wasn't a dry-eyed woman in the room as they listened to Clay's speech.

"Hurry, Eden, open it," Lucy encouraged, anxious as a small child.

Eden did, and when she gazed at the contents of the paper her mouth fell open, nearly hitting her chest. It was the deed to Beauclaire, signed over to her, making her sole owner of the plantation.

The gesture touched her heart, but after a moment, she handed it back to him, saying, "I appreciate the gesture, but I don't want it, nor do I need it." At his surprised look, she added, "Everything I own, including my heart, belongs to you." And then she kissed him, amidst a chorus of cheers.

Glancing about the room, Eden's heart filled to bursting, she was so happy. Everything was working out as it should. David had proposed to Jewel, and she had accepted. Though she would miss them, she knew that their happiness lay in the North, not in the present social climate of the South. With Jewel, David could start his own family. And perhaps one day, when things were different, they could return.

Lucy and Richard were now content to be landowners. And Charles's and Agnes's love for each other radiated out, touching everyone in the room.

Everything was perfect, including her marriage to Clay. And nothing could ever mar their happiness again.

James Wakefield stared out the window of his seedy tavern room at the happy Christmas revelers in the alley below and frowned.

Fools, the lot of them, he thought angrily, his lips twisting into a sneer. Making merry like they hadn't a care in the world. He spun away from the sight to stare into the flames of the fire.

At least the widow Braxton and her family were probably enjoying only a subdued Christmas celebration. But he was not happy to be holed up in an airless, filthy room, enjoying the sight of cockroaches clamoring over water-stained walls.

Warsaw was a nothing of a town across the river from Tappahannock. He had fled there as soon as he'd heard that Long had been arrested. Knowing that Cyrus wasn't likely to hang alone, he hadn't wasted any time in giving the order for Braxton's execution, then beating a hasty departure.

Damn Eden for ruining all his plans! If it hadn't been for her and that stupid rescue mission, David would have been long gone, and he'd have been around to console the weeping widow.

Of course, he hadn't counted on Vera spilling the beans. He'd heard she was gone. Run off to New York by Eden herself. The bitch had spilled her guts, even after he'd threatened her, ruining all his plans.

Well, Vera was out of his reach for reprisal. But Eden wasn't. Somehow, some way, he would make the bitch pay for all he had suffered.

Picking the knife up off the table, he ran the sharp, shiny blade against the palm of his hand until he drew blood; his face twisted in maniacal satisfaction.

Eden would pay. If it was the last thing he did, he would make the bitch pay.

Christmas morning dawned clear and cold, and Eden and Clay awoke to the traditional chorus of slaves, shouting, "Christmas gift, Christmas gift," as they lined up on Beauclaire's wide front porch to receive their annual reward.

Bolting upright, Eden glanced at the clock on the mantel. "Good gracious!" she shrieked, jumping out of bed to don her clothes. "We overslept and nearly forgot about handing out the presents."

Clay grinned, reaching out to grasp her hand, pulling her back down for a kiss. "Perhaps that's because you kept me up so late with your lascivious behavior, Mrs. Braxton." He chuckled at the heat rising to her cheeks as she pulled away from him.

With hands on her hips, she warned, "You'd best hurry, unless you want a mutiny on your hands, *Mr. Braxton*. Our people don't like to be kept waiting. This is as much their day as ours."

It was traditional at Beauclaire, as on many other plantations, to give the slaves small tokens of appreciation on Christmas morning. Usually gifts of clothing were presented, as well as tobacco, scarves, and toys and candy for the children.

Eden and Clay handed out the presents to the grateful recipients, who had such wide smiles on their faces at the small tokens they'd received, it brought a lump to Eden's throat. She couldn't wait to share the news with her people that they would soon be working to purchase their freedom. It was a decision she and Clay had been in total agreement on, and as soon as the holidays were over, Clay would present the plan to them.

But today was for merriment. Today the slaves' time was their own. And as long as they didn't venture beyond the plantation grounds, they could spend it as they saw fit.

Isaac, who'd been promoted to overseer, grabbed his fiddle and played a joyful tune, and several couples began to dance, paying no mind to the snow that still littered the ground.

Belle climbed up the porch steps slowly, dragging Sam behind her. She smiled shyly at Eden and Clay. "Me and Sam just wanted to wish you both a Happy Christmas and thank you for all you done, Miz Eden, Master Clay." She nudged Sam in the ribs and he shuffled his feet nervously, clearing his throat.

"I be wantin' to thank you for bringing my Belle into the house. It be much better for her and the babe." He stared down at the scuffed toes of his boots.

Eden's eyes twinkled as she stared at the big man's embarrassment and winked at the woman beside him. She could see that the love they shared was no less intense than the one she shared with Clay. It was obvious that love had no color lines.

"We pregnant women need to stick together, now, don't we, Belle?"

Giggling, Belle grasped her husband's hand and nodded, "We surely do, Miz Eden, we surely do."

The new year entered with a vengeance. The snow continued to fall with no relief in sight, and drifts as high as the office window piled up against the house.

The wind battered frozen branches against the brick, and the sound of cracking limbs was deafening against the stillness of the morning, bringing Eden out of her chair and over to the window.

"Hell fire and perdition!" she exclaimed, surveying the damage to the grounds. A huge oak limb, over thirty feet in length, hung nearly to the ground, broken by the weight of the snow.

Making a mental note to bring it to Clay's attention, she returned to the desk, and sat down, staring at the pile of ledgers before her and grimaced. It would take hours to enter all the purchases that had been made over the Christmas season. It wasn't that she didn't like doing the books—she was very meticulous about her work—she just didn't feel like doing them today.

At that moment, Clay stuck his head through the doorway. "Morning, angel." He frowned suddenly at Eden's morose expression. "Is there a problem? Your face is longer than that column of numbers you're adding up." Lately, Eden's moods had been as changeable as the weather. Moods which had been explained away by Aunt Ruby as merely being part of Eden's "condition."

Childishly, she stuck her tongue out at him, bringing a grin to his lips. "Testy, are we?" he teased, brushing the snow from his hat. He had just come from the barn, bringing a little surprise with him to present to his lovely wife. "I think I have just the cure for what ails you, angel."

She heaved a sigh and shook her head in exasperation. "Now, Clay, I don't have time for bedroom games right now. I'm up to my elbows in book work."

"Well, the books will just have to wait. I've decided that we need a little diversion. We're going outside to play in the snow."

Her mouth fell open, and she looked at him as if he were addled. "The snow? Are you daft?

There's a blizzard out there! Did you see the damage it's wrought to the yard? It's going to take weeks to clean up." If the snow ever ended, she added silently.

He held out his hand. "Come on, angel. I've hooked up the sleigh. We're going for a ride."

At the mention of the sleigh, Eden's eyes widened and she smiled in delight. It had been years since she'd been sleigh riding. Looking down at the pile of work, then up at Clay's smiling face, the decision was not a hard one to make—the books could wait.

The runners of the sleigh glided along the frozen road to Tappahannock. The harness, with its brass bells, jingled merrily as the horses trotted sedately along under Caleb's experienced hand.

They hadn't driven the old sleigh in years. Usually there wasn't enough snow on the ground to warrant its use, but this year was different. Already, three feet of snow had accumulated, and judging by the dark, heavy clouds on the horizon, more was on the way.

Clay and Eden snuggled together on the cushioned leather seat, the woolen blanket pulled up over their laps to keep them warm. The scenery surrounding them was breathtaking. The snow-covered trees and bushes took on whimsical shapes—fairies, dragons, and bears appeared out of nowhere, and Eden felt like a small child again, thinking back to the games she had played with her father.

Gazing at Clay, Eden felt her heart fill with joy. His face was chapped red from the cold, and crystals of ice clung to his eyelashes and hair. His deep laughter as the sleigh careened faster and faster sent tingles up her spine.

As if he could read her mind, Clay leaned over and kissed her lips. "If you keep devouring me with your eyes, angel, I fear Caleb will be quite shocked when we have to stop and run into the bushes."

"Clay!" Eden blushed, hoping Caleb hadn't heard the naughty comment.

Clay observed the two bright red splotches on Eden's cheeks and laughed. She still blushed like a virgin, though she carried his child, he thought.

Thoughts of the baby made him euphoric. He couldn't wait to hold his son or daughter in his arms. Sing to it. Play with it. He was truly the luckiest of men. If only . . .

He frowned as Wakefield came to mind. There had been no word of the Englishman, despite his father's efforts and his own. He had hired additional men to search out the ruthless bastard, but as of yet, there'd been no word.

Finding Wakefield had become an obsession. Though he had done his best to hide his need for revenge from Eden, it was there, lurking in the darkest depths of his soul.

Wakefield was out there somewhere, waiting. Waiting to make his move. And Clay was determined to find him first.

Suddenly, a large, wet flurry of snow caught

Clay full in the face, bringing an abrupt halt to his worry about Beauclaire's former overseer.

Eden laughed as she reached over and wiped the frozen snow from his startled face. "I'm ready for a hot cup of cocoa and some of Sukie's oatmeal cookies," she said, drawing the blanket up to her chin. "Let's turn back. I'm freezing."

Clay reached under the blanket, pulling Eden into his embrace. Placing his hot breath against her ear, he whispered, "I can think of some delightful ways to keep you warm, angel eyes."

A fire crackled in the hearth. The snow crystals clung to the panes of glass outside the bedchamber windows, which were fogged with condensation.

Eden lay immersed in a tub of hot, steamy water. Hundreds of tiny bubbles floated around her as she relaxed in the warm, soothing liquid, sighing contentedly, glad to be warm after the cold sleigh ride home. Raising her leg out of the water, she sponged herself, unaware she now had an audience.

Pausing at the door, Clay sucked in his breath. Would he never tire of gazing at Eden? he wondered. Her skin appeared soft, rosy in the glow of the firelight. Her ebony tresses were piled haphazardly on top of her head, exposing her long neck to his view. Her full breasts bobbed enticingly in and out of the water as she rubbed the sponge over her limbs, and Clay felt himself harden as he walked silently forward, bending down by the tub to place feathery kisses up and down her neck.

Eden gasped, dropping the sponge with a splash, then smiled when she realized who it was. "I didn't hear you come in," she murmured, her voice suddenly husky. There was no response, just more exquisite torture over her back and shoulders, causing gooseflesh to break out over her arms and neck; her skin tingled deliciously.

"Hello, angel," Clay said, his smile playing havoc with her senses. Rolling up his shirt sleeve, he reached into the soapy water.

"Clay!" Eden blurted, slapping at his hand.

"Ooops! I thought that felt too large and soft to be the sponge." He grinned. "Let me play lady's maid and give you your bath."

Eden smiled seductively. "Why not join me? The copper tub is large enough for two." She reclined against the back of the tub, her breasts rising up out of the water, the invitation too blatant for Clay to resist.

Stripping out of his pants and shirt, Clay fetched a bottle of Madeira and two glasses, setting them on the floor near the tub, then lowered himself into the water, positioning himself between Eden's thighs. Picking up the sponge, he began to gently wash her breasts, feeling the nipples grow rigid as he passed the sponge back and forth across them.

Eden moaned softly, arching her back, and her stomach started to flutter as Clay slid his soapy hands down her stomach and abdomen, paying careful attention to the mound between her thighs, kneading her flesh until she began to quiver. "Clay," she called his name softly, as she felt the tautness between her thighs escalate.

"Let go, angel," he urged. "Let go."

Her passionate cries filled the room as she climaxed into his hands. Lifting her to sit on his lap, Clay entered her then, impaling her with his need as he took her again to a place that was magical in its beauty and intensity.

When they were both sated, they wrapped themselves in each other's embrace, love and contentment washing over them in gentle waves of rapture.

Twenty-six

The beginning of February brought the return of Agnes and Charles from their honeymoon trip to New York, and the family had gathered around Briarwood's dining room table for a special welcome-home dinner.

The candles on the table flickered softly. The conversation sparkled with tidbits about Agnes's forays into some of the more expensive stores on Park Avenue, and everyone was having a wonderful time, except Clay.

Though the partridges were succulent, the wild rice cooked to perfection, Clay could hardly concentrate on the festive occasion or the meal. His mind was preoccupied with thoughts of James Wakefield, as it had been since the day of his abduction. And his preoccupation had by now put a strain on his relationship with Eden, who was eager to put the whole, unpleasant episode behind her.

"Clay," she whispered, noting that he'd hardly touched his dinner. She clutched at his arm as he reached for his wine glass. "This is a special occasion, can't you be a little less dour?" she pleaded. "You're ruining the mood for everyone else."

Agnes had noted the tension between the two young people and remarked sagely, " *'Enjoy the present hour, be mindful of the past; and neither fear nor wish the approaches of the last.'* "Eden rolled her eyes and heaved a rather loud sigh, prompting Agnes to add, "One does not need perfect vision to see that there is a problem at this table, children. Would you like to tell us what it is, Clay?"

Clay glanced about the table, an apologetic look on his face, saying in a voice filled with frustration, "It's been months, and there's been no word of Wakefield. I can think of nothing else except bringing that animal to justice. And I can have no peace of mind until I do so."

Charles frowned deeply as he stared probingly at his son. "'Revenge can eat away at a man, son. Though no one knows better than I that you have a valid grudge to bear, perhaps it is time to put it aside. For all we know, Wakefield is dead."

"Your father is right, Clay," Eden was quick to concur. "It's time to get on with our lives. Wakefield has already ruined time enough. Why let him spoil our happiness now?"

The green eyes hardened. "Wakefield is not dead," Clay insisted. "Like cream, the bastard will rise to the top. You'll see. And if we pretend that he doesn't exist, we're going to leave ourselves open to his vindictiveness."

Pushing herself up from the table, Eden threw

down her napkin, glaring at Clay. "I refuse to listen to any more talk about that man." Tears filled her eyes and she said, "I will leave you to discuss James Wakefield to your heart's content. It seems to be your only topic of conversation of late." With that, she rushed from the room with Agnes and Lucy following discreetly behind her, leaving Clay to stare openmouthed after them.

Richard chuckled at Clay's crestfallen expression. "I would think you'd be used to a pregnant woman's moods by now, brother. Lucy is even more of a shrew than she used to be; and I didn't think that was humanly possible."

"You boys have got it easy," Charles interjected, trying to lighten the mood. "When Eulalie was pregnant with you boys, my life was a living hell. She would only eat certain foods, and no meat, whatsoever. I nearly starved to death during those nine-month periods."

Absorbed in his own thoughts, Clay ignored the repartee. "I'm concerned for Eden's safety, though I haven't let on to her about my worries. If Wakefield is out there—and I feel certain that he is—he's not going to rest until he exacts retribution against Eden. A man like Wakefield doesn't like to be thwarted. And I have felt the brunt of his anger firsthand."

Charles paled at the reminder. "But he thinks you're dead, Clay. Why would he want to harm Eden?"

"I'm afraid that I have to agree with Father, Clay. Wakefield's hatred was directed at you.

Surely you don't think he would lay a hand on an innocent woman."

Clay thought back to what Eden had told him about Belle and Vera and shuddered inwardly. Wakefield was a crazy bastard. And there was no doubt in his mind that he wouldn't hesitate to strike at anyone who he thought had done him an injustice, man or woman.

"I have each of the fieldhands on special alert. Isaac and Caleb have been instructed to shoot first and ask questions later. Does that tell you what I think about Wakefield?"

Taking a sip of his wine, Charles stared thoughtfully into the burgundy liquid for a moment, then said, "So you firmly believe that Eden's life is in danger?"

Clay's expression was ominous as he stared at his father and brother. "I haven't a doubt in my mind that Wakefield won't be satisfied until Eden is dead."

The object of Clay's consideration was at the moment saddling his horse as he made preparations to ride back to Tappahannock.

Wakefield checked the cinch, then tightened it a fraction more, eager to put his plan into action. He'd been cooling his heels for weeks, waiting for just the right moment. Now that moment had arrived.

The mistress of Beauclaire would soon be making her annual trek into Fredericksburg to purchase supplies for the coming spring. Eden had been doing so since he'd worked there, since the age of seventeen, according to what her aunt had told him on one of those rare occasions when the old bitch deigned to speak to him.

He really should take care of the old biddy, too, he thought. Maybe he'd luck out and she'd be riding into town with Eden.

The blue eyes glittered, and a smile of confidence crossed his lips. There was no doubt in his mind that Eden would make the trip this year. And he would be waiting for her. Waiting to give her just what she deserved.

"I will not be cosseted like a baby, Clay!" Eden insisted, tossing her petticoat into the portmanteau. "We have been over this a thousand times; I am going to Fredericksburg, with or without your blessing."

Clay rubbed the back of his neck in agitation, staring at the stubborn woman across the room from him. "Then I'll go with you."

"You most certainly will not! I refuse to give in to your paranoia about James Wakefield's nefarious scheme to do away with me. Really, Clay, can't you see how silly you're being? It's been months since your rescue. And none of those expensive thugs you and your father hired could find out a thing about him." She waved her hand in the air as if the matter was already decided. "I'm going, and that's final."

Clay clenched his fists and the pulse in his neck throbbed to reflect the pounding at his temples.

Eden was giving him a full-blown headache. "You are as stubborn . . ."

"As a mule?" She smiled. "Yes, I know. You've told me so at least a hundred times before. And like a mule, I'm digging my heels in and refusing to budge on my decision. Tomorrow I leave for Fredericksburg."

"And what if it snows?"

She laughed, glancing out the window. The sun shone brightly, sending streams of light into the room. "The sky is as blue as your mood, my darling. Spring is definitely on the way."

"You know how changeable the weather can be in February." He wanted to add "like your moods," but didn't.

She hauled several wool dresses out of her wardrobe to the bed and began folding them. "I'm going."

Clay banged his hand atop the valise. "Damn it, Eden! Think of the baby. You could be endangering its life!"

Eden heaved a sigh, and her eyes softened. Patting Clay's cheek, she said, "I promise to be extra careful, darling. Caleb will be driving. And the baby is part of the reason I'm going; you know that. I want to buy some pretty things for the nursery to add to those I've already knitted."

"You've already made enough garments to outfit a dozen children."

She ignored him and continued packing. There was just no reasoning with Clay when he made up his mind about something. Just no reasoning at all.

***

Agnes paced across the parlor, lines of worry etched on her face. "Was there any reasoning with her?" She'd been waiting for Clay to come downstairs. From the angry look on his face, she feared the worst.

Clay shook his head. "None whatsoever. Eden is determined to go. And her trip will afford Wakefield the perfect opportunity to exact his revenge."

Her face paled and she plopped down on the settee, deflated by his comment. "That girl is too foolish and stubborn for her own good. I should have punished her more as a child. I can see now, I was far too lenient with her."

"I've told her as much, but it went in one ear and out the other."

"Perhaps I should go with her. There is oftentimes safety in numbers."

Clay shook his head. It would be difficult enough to protect Eden as it was; he wouldn't put Agnes's life in jeopardy, too. "I have a plan, which I intend to put into action immediately."

Hope filled her breast. "May I know?"

"It's better if you don't. Eden is too perceptive for her own good, and I have no intention of letting her think anything other than that she's going to Fredericksburg by herself."

Agnes smiled knowingly. "*'One good husband is worth two good wives; for the scarcer they are, the more they're valued.'* And I do bless the day you came back into Eden's life, dear boy." She patted his cheek. "I will pray for you. *'Prayers and provender hinder no journey.'*"

Clay gave the older woman a hug and a tender kiss on the cheek. "Aunt Agnes, have you ever thought of writing down all those expressions of yours and publishing them in a book? You could probably make a lot of money."

She seemed astounded at the suggestion. "But they already are, dear boy. Haven't you ever had the privilege of reading *Poor Richard's Almanack?* Surely you don't think that I could come up with all those clever things by myself." She laughed at his dumbfounded look. "I'm flattered, but the credit must go to the Yankee Benjamin Franklin. A nobler man has yet to be born."

He shook his head. "You continue to amaze me, Aunt Agnes."

"And your dear father, as well. *'Tis a wife's duty to keep a husband on his toes.'*"

Clay's eyebrow arched in question. "Dr. Franklin?"

She wagged her head and smiled proudly. "Agnes Peters Braxton."

Through with her packing, Eden took her mother's journal out of the nightstand and ran her fingers over the rough-grained leather. She hadn't wanted to read it, not since David's arrival had prompted her to learn about her mother's irrational desire to kill the half-breed child. But now, on the eve of her journey, she felt compelled to finish it.

Perhaps Clay's ominous warnings had had more of an effect on her than she wanted to believe. She'd scoffed at the notion that Wakefield wanted her dead. But somewhere in the recesses of her mind, she believed it. One had only to think about the brutality that he'd heaped upon Vera Marsden and Belle to know that the man was totally insane, a monster of the greatest proportions.

A shudder rushed through her and she crossed to the rocker and opened the journal.

Beauclaire, March 26, 1828. Today my life has new meaning, for it is the day that the good Lord has seen fit to gift me with a child. A daughter was born, and I shall name her Eden, for the name denotes my state of bliss, my extreme felicity at the notion that Mr. Fairchild's seed has borne fruit. Perhaps the birth of this child will bring us closer together. Perhaps we will finally be happy.

Eden could barely read the finely penned cursive with her eyes so full of tears. She swallowed with difficulty and took a deep breath, flipping ahead several pages.

Beauclaire, March 26, 1838. Eden's tenth birthday. She's a beautiful child, but alas, a girl. I so wanted to provide Mr. Fairchild with a rightful heir—a son to carry on his name. I seek solace in the elixir that the doctor has provided. It soothes my frazzled nerves, and this world is too cruel to be borne without it.

Laudanum, Eden thought. The magic elixir her mother had mentioned; the one Aunt Agnes had said Charlotte had grown so dependent on. Was it the reason her mother had died so young? Or had the unhappy woman taken her own life, as she'd heard intimated? Dreading the answer, but needing to know, she read on, turning the pages until she reached the final passage. The handwriting was barely legible; the words rather incoherent.

Beauclaire, May 3rd, 1843. My 17th wedding anniversary. Mr. Fairchild came to visit, brought me a bouquet of white roses, but didn't stay long. He never does. My mind is palsied by the amount of laudanum I have taken today. I feel sluggish, disoriented, sad. Eden brought me a lovely shawl she crocheted. I am wearing it now and will treasure it always. I have been remiss in my duties to Eden. She seeks love, but I am unable to express how great my love is for this child of my heart. Nothing else in my life has been worthwhile, except my daughter. Sleep is overtaking my body, and my hand grows too weary to write. And so I go to my slumber with the image of my lovely Eden firmly embedded in my mind. Good night, my darling daughter.

Tears poured forth from Eden's eyes as she shut the book and sobbed softly for the woman whose life had ended so sadly. Thirty-five years old and gone. But she didn't die by her own hand. Eden was positive of that fact. Her mother's death had been an accident. A tragic accidental overdose of the laudanum.

"Goodbye, Mama," Eden whispered, knowing she would be able to lay her mother to rest at last.

Tenderly, she placed her hands on her abdomen and felt the baby stir inside her. If it was a girl, she would name her Charlotte.

Charlotte Eulalie Agnes Braxton. It was quite

a mouthful for so tiny a babe. But Eden knew that her child would be worthy of carrying the names of the women she revered most in the world.

Charlotte meant little and womanly; Eulalie—fair of speech; Agnes—pure. And her child would be all those things and more. Much more. And she would be loved.

Twenty-seven

The sun was barely up when Clay leaned over and pressed a kiss to his wife's lips. "Eden, I have to leave. I wanted to say goodbye before I go."

Sleepily, Eden opened her eyes, surprised to find Clay fully dressed. A look of disappointment passed over her face when she realized he was leaving before her departure. "Go? But I'm leaving for Fredericksburg this morning. Aren't you going to be here to see me off?"

Clay shook his head. "Father and I are riding into Port Royal this morning. The magistrate is presiding over Cyrus Long's case today, and we must be there to present evidence."

Confusion etched her brow. "But don't I need to be there, too? I was a witness."

"No. Father has explained your condition to the magistrate, and he has agreed to waive your testimony." His expression turned grave. "Promise me that you'll use extreme caution on your journey this morning. I've given Caleb detailed instructions that he's to stop for nothing and no one."

Placing her hand on his cheek, Eden smiled softly. "I will miss you. This is the first time since our marriage that we've been separated."

"Are you forgetting my abduction?"

She sighed. "I'd like to; it was such a dreadful experience."

His voice hardened. "Well, I'm not likely to, which is why I must leave at once." His features softened then. "Father may decide to climb back into bed with Agnes, if I don't get over there."

"That sounds like a wonderful idea." Eden's smile was full of promise. "Why don't you climb back into bed with me. I'll postpone my trip for another day."

Clay chucked her under the chin. *"Tsk, tsk,* Mrs. Braxton. Duty calls. Though your offer is a tempting one." He kissed her then, long and hard. "I will see you in three days' time."

Tears misted her eyes. "We will miss you."

A dark eyebrow arched. "We?"

"The baby, silly. He goes everywhere I go."

A measure of fear coursed through his body, and he quickly turned toward the door before Eden could notice. "Take care, angel." He blew her a kiss, then was gone.

A great emptiness settled over Eden at the prospect of not seeing Clay for several days.

"Hellfire and perdition!" she chastised herself, throwing back the covers before jumping out of bed. "I've turned into the very thing I feared all these years: a weepy, dependent housewife."

She shook her head in disgust and rang the bellpull for Jewel.

As soon as she was on her way, she'd feel better about the whole situation, Eden decided. But still an uneasiness gnawed at her that she couldn't seem to shake loose.

"You sure you doan want me to come wid you, Miz Eden?" Aunt Ruby asked, clucking her tongue in disapproval as she bustled after her mistress. Deep lines of worry etched her forehead. "I can't believe Master Clay is letting you go all the way to Fredericksburg with no chaperone. It jes doan seem right to me." Placing her hands on ample hips, she frowned fiercely. "Doan seem right a'tall."

Eden patted the woman's cheek soothingly. "I'll be perfectly fine, Aunt Ruby. You're not to worry. Clay was finally convinced that I could take care of myself. Caleb is perfectly capable of providing protection." She stepped toward the carriage and opened the door.

"*Hmph!* That useless boy can barely take care of hisself. How's he goin' to take care of you?" Ruby's eyes widened as she glanced up at the driver's perch and caught sight of the man who was driving the carriage. It definitely wasn't Caleb. He motioned for her to keep silent, and she swallowed her surprise. "You be careful now, honey, you heah?" She helped Eden into the carriage, feeling an immense measure of relief. "I'se goin' to miss you."

Giving the old woman a kiss on her leathery cheek, Eden winked at Jewel, who was standing in the doorway waving, and noted her radiant smile. Jewel had been giddy with joy over her upcoming wedding to David. David, who had gone north to prepare a home for his intended bride, would return in summer to marry Jewel and take her back north with him. Eden sighed happily, grateful that everything was working out as it should, and settled back against the velvet cushions.

A moment later the coach took off. She was finally on her way, Eden thought, smiling to herself in satisfaction that she'd been able to make her departure without incident.

Pulling back the drapery, she gazed out the window to find clear blue skies. Even the weather was in favor of her going, she thought happily.

Winter still held a firm grip on the landscape, however, despite the azure sky. The trees were devoid of leaves, except for the pines and cedars that mingled intermittently with oaks, elms, and sycamores. Patches of unmelted snow could still be seen frosting the boxwood bushes and ground in places. But the majority of the earth was barren and brown.

Closing the curtain against the chill, Eden picked up the book by Edgar Allan Poe she had brought along and began to read. Soon the rocking motion of the coach lulled her to sleep.

An hour passed before Eden was jolted awake by the sound of gunfire. Her hand went to her throat, and she took a deep, calming breath, smiling at her foolishness, as she remembered that hunters were often out shooting at game this time of year.

But pulling back the drapery, her eyes widened in fright as she saw the horse and rider emerge from the thick stand of trees on the left. His gun was drawn, and he was bearing down hard on the carriage.

Eden stuck her head out the window to yell up to Caleb, and when she did, she saw that the gunman wasn't just an ordinary highwayman. The distinctive coloring of his blond hair told her with sickening clarity that every one of Clay's dire predictions had come true: James Wakefield was shooting at her carriage. He was trying to kill her!

Fear made her heart beat faster as another shot rang out. She yelled up to Caleb, "Hurry, Caleb, we're being fired upon. Go faster."

She leaned back against the seat, bracing herself for the surge she expected to feel when the carriage increased its speed. And was unprepared and horrified when she realized that the carriage was slowing down rather than speeding up. Clay had told Caleb to stop for nothing. Why was he disobeying a direct order?

She gazed out the window again, her face paling to find Wakefield closing up the distance between them. She banged on the roof of the carriage with her fist. "Caleb," she shouted at the top of her lungs, "go faster. We're going to be killed."

Wakefield drew close to the carriage, brandishing his weapon at the driver as he screamed, "Pull up, you stupid nigger! Before I shoot you where you sit."

The man bowed his head low, as if in deference, his hat shielding his face. "Yessir, boss!" came the muffled reply as the carriage drew to a halt.

Wakefield smiled in satisfaction, ignoring the driver, who he knew would be unarmed. Niggers weren't allowed to carry weapons. White folks were afraid they'd be shot dead in their beds.

"Open the door, Eden, and come out," he ordered. "We have some unfinished business to attend to."

A feeling of dread washed over Eden. Mustering every bit of courage she possessed, she pushed open the door and climbed out. Wakefield was still sitting atop his horse, looking as smug as a cat who'd just cornered a mouse. His attitude ignited her anger, and her eyes flashed fire.

"What do you want, Mr. Wakefield? Haven't you caused my family enough trouble?"

He laughed at her audacity. "You always were a spirited little thing, Eden. Too bad I was never able to bed you." At her shocked gasp, his voice grew hard. "Of course, I could still remedy that . . . before I kill you."

She swallowed her fear. "I'd sooner die than have a rabid dog like you touch me. You aren't a man. You're nothing more than a snake who preys on the weak and unsuspecting. A viperous piece of trash."

The man on the coach sucked in his breath as

he saw the angry glitter in Wakefield's blue eyes. But pride surged through his breast at his wife's courage. Clay eased the gun from beneath the blanket on his lap.

"You high-and-mighty bitch!" James sneered. "You always *did* think you were better than me. I was just the hired hand, never good enough to consort with the mistress of Beauclaire."

His eyes glowed with fervor, and Eden shuddered at the insanity she saw in their depths. She threw back her head and laughed in his face. If she was going to die, she was going to have her say first.

"Vera told me of your grandiose plans to marry me." Her look was clearly contemptuous. "Did you really think I would sink so low as to marry my overseer? Ha! You really are insane. I would sooner wed one of the slaves."

He went on as if he hadn't heard her. "My people in England were landed gentry. For centuries, Wakefields held positions close to the Crown. It would have been beneath me to marry an American. Your race is an inferior breed."

His supercilious sentiment angered her. "It was good enough to defeat you stupid British bastards in the Revolution!" she countered. When he made to dismount, she backed up next to the coach, fingers of fear tingling her spine.

"That's far enough, Wakefield."

Recognizing her husband's voice, Eden's heart lurched. "Clay!"

"Stay back against the carriage, Eden," he ordered. And then, to Wakefield, "Dismount. I'm taking you into Port Royal to stand trial."

Wakefield's eyes widened in surprise at the sight of the man he thought dead, then his lips curled like an animal's and he fired the gun he was holding. But anger had made his aim poor, and the bullet went high, hitting the top of the carriage. Clay fired simultaneously, his aim true, hitting Wakefield in the shoulder.

Eden stood watching as Wakefield dropped his weapon to clutch at his shoulder; blood oozed out between his fingers as he tried to staunch the flow of blood with his hand. She was too stunned to move or utter a sound.

"I'm bleeding, Braxton. You've got to help me."

Clay's grin was menacing as he jumped down from his perch, his gun still trained on Wakefield. "My heart goes out to you, Wakefield. It would be a real pity if you bled to death. Eden," he yelled, "fetch the rope from the boot of the carriage."

Clay's order finally penetrated and she did as he instructed. Handing Eden his gun, Clay said, "Hold this on him. And if he moves one muscle, shoot to kill."

"You think you've won, Braxton, but you haven't. I'll escape, and I'll come find you."

The gun in Eden's hand began to shake.

"Australia is lovely this time of year, I'm told," Clay replied. "And they have such a wonderful penal colony there."

The Englishman blanched, his eyes widening in fear.

Eden listened to the exchange as Clay took the rope, tying Wakefield's hands and feet securely. He then gagged Wakefield's mouth with his handkerchief; it was one of the ones she had made him for Christmas, she thought absently.

When Clay was finished, he lifted the man into the carriage, dumping him on the floor. Removing the woolen scarf from around his neck, he wadded it up, pressing it against the Englishman's shoulder until the bleeding slowed.

"Enjoy the ride, you ruthless bastard. There's a small contingent of concerned citizens waiting for you in Port Royal." Clay slammed the door at the muffled curses being hurled at him and walked toward his wife, who was shaking like a willow in a heavy wind.

Taking the gun from Eden's hand, he stuck it in the waistband of his breeches and drew her into his arms, patting her back in a soothing fashion. "Are you all right, angel eyes?" Her pallor alarmed him.

Eden finally found her voice, but it was weak and thready. "I . . . I was so scared, Clay. I tried to be brave. But I was scared." She wrapped her arms about his waist, needing to feel the solid comfort of his body pressed against her.

Kissing the top of her head, he replied in a voice filled with admiration, "You were very brave, Eden; I'm quite proud of the way you stood up to that bastard."

She looked up at him with tear-filled eyes. "Is it truly over, Clay? Can we really get on with our lives now?"

"Yes, angel, it's over. Father and Richard are waiting for us in Port Royal. The hearing is set for this afternoon. Father has already talked with Judge Willis, who assured him, after hearing my testimony and David's, that Wakefield will be placed on a ship tonight and transported to Australia. Apparently, the judge has friends within the British Admiralty."

"Is this the same Judge Willis who happens to be your godfather?"

Clay grinned. "One and the same. Good old Uncle Willy; I knew he'd come through in a pinch."

Eden caressed Clay's cheek. "Do you forgive me for being such a stubborn fool?"

Helping her onto the driver's perch, so she wouldn't have to ride with Wakefield, he said, "I think I'll be able to devise a suitable punishment for your obstinate ways while we enjoy a brief honeymoon in Fredericksburg."

Eden's face lit with pleasure, her voice filling with excitement. "Oh, Clay, do you really mean it? A real honeymoon?"

He nodded. "As soon as we're done with the trial, we'll continue on to Fredericksburg and you can begin trying to convince me of how sorry you are."

She smiled and her cheeks dimpled. "But that could take days, Clay," she said, her hand coming to rest on his upper thigh as she squeezed it suggestively.

"I'm counting on it, angel eyes," he said, leaning over to kiss her. "I'm counting on it."

Epilogue

It was a perfect day for a wedding. The sun was shining, and a warm summer breeze ruffled the leaves of the magnolias outside the white-columned Methodist church. Everything was perfect, Eden thought, clutching two-month-old sleeping Charlotte to her breast.

"Are you ready to go in, Eden?" Clay asked, coming up next to her, kissing her and his baby daughter on the cheek.

She smiled and turned toward Aunt Ruby and Uncle Beevis, who stood on her other side. "Well?" she asked them.

"Dis be about the happiest day of my life, Miz Eden," the old woman confessed, sniffing into her hankie. "Me and Beevis is as proud as we can be about our Jewel marrying Master David." Beevis nodded, but as was his usual custom, said nothing.

"You're free now, Aunt Ruby," Clay reminded her. "You don't need to call anyone 'master' again."

She waved her hankie at him. "Oh, I'se too old to learn new tricks, Master Clay. And even if me and Beevis is free, you still our family, and we loves you."

"You're going to make me start crying even before the wedding starts, Aunt Ruby," Eden confessed, escorting the older couple into the church, which was already filled with guests, mostly blacks from their plantation and Briarwood.

Aunt Agnes and Charles were seated in the first pew on the right, and Eden and Clay slid in next to them, while Ruby and Beevis took their places right up front in the pew on the left.

"I thought you two would never get here," Aunt Agnes scolded. "What took you so long? The ceremony is due to start at any moment."

Eden blushed, glancing over at Clay, who was grinning stupidly at her. She wasn't about to explain to her aunt what they'd spent the better part of the morning doing. What they'd spent the better part of every day of the last two weeks doing, she amended.

"Charlotte was a bit fussy. I needed to get her fed before we came." At least that much was true, Eden thought. But she could see by the twinkle in her father-in-law's eyes that he didn't believe her for a moment.

She was spared further embarrassment when Lucy waddled up the aisle, looking like she was going to give birth at any moment. She was very, very pregnant. More pregnant than anyone Eden had ever seen. And there'd been speculation on Agnes's part that Lucy was carrying twins.

"Hello, you two," she said, waving, easing herself into the pew behind them. She plopped down heavily onto the wooden bench.

Richard looked more haggard than Lucy, Eden noted, and she smiled sympathetically at the deep, dark circles she observed beneath his eyes. Eyes that were trained on his wife's swollen belly.

"I told you we shouldn't have come, Lucy," Eden heard Richard say. "You're too pregnant to be out in public. What if you were to have the baby?" There was definite panic in his voice.

"Oh, pooh," Lucy retorted. "Jewel and David are about to get married, and I just love weddings. Besides, Agnes says it will probably be a few more days."

Richard heaved a sigh of relief and settled back, and Eden couldn't help thinking what a drastic change in attitude Lucy had developed toward Negroes. Her sister-in-law was definitely turning into someone Eden was beginning to like.

At Ruby's loud wail, all heads turned to find David and Jewel strolling arm-in-arm down the aisle. Portly Reverend Sproull, who'd been sympathetic to the black couple's plight and had agreed to marry them, stood waiting at the altar, impatient to begin the service.

"Jewel looks so beautiful, Clay," Eden whispered. "It was so thoughtful of Aunt Agnes to lend Jewel her wedding gown. And look how happy she is! Why, her cheeks are fairly glowing."

"Your brother looks like he's on his way to the

gallows," Clay quipped, noting David's somber expression, the way he fidgeted nervously with his collar.

She cuffed his arm. "Don't be silly. He's just nervous. I'm sure you were nervous on your wedding day, too."

Clay grinned, leaning over to brush his lips against her ear. "The only thing I was nervous about, angel, was trying to figure out how I was going to get you into my bed."

Eden looked about quickly, hoping no one had heard her husband's outrageous comment. She blushed deeply. "Ssh! Don't say such things. Everyone will hear you."

At that moment, much to Eden's great mortification, Clay stood up and announced to the hushed assembly who were waiting for the Reverend Sproull to begin, "Ladies and gentlemen, this is my wife, Eden, and I'd like everyone to know that I love her very much."

Agnes and Charles exchanged amused glances. Lucy giggled loudly and Richard snorted.

The folks in the church stared at each other and smiled, then began to clap.

"See?" Clay said to his wife, who was now weeping with joy and laughter, as he resumed his seat. "No one minds a bit that I love you."

Gazing into his eyes, she confessed, "I love you, too."

"Do you want to stand up and make the announcement?" There was a definite challenge in his voice.

"Is that a dare?" she asked, her eyebrow arching in question.

It was.

And she did.

About the Author

Award-winning author of six historical romances, Millie Criswell lives in Fredericksburg, Virginia with her husband, two grown children, and one neurotic Boston Terrier.

An avid collector of books, she has an extensive library and combines book research with her hobbies of haunting used bookstores and traveling to exotic places.

Millie has twice been nominated by ROMANTIC TIMES for their prestigious Reviewer's Choice Award—for *Brazen Virginia Bride* and *Desire's Endless Kiss*—and is the recipient of the Bookrak Award for *California Temptress*, Bestselling Romance Author, Series Romance, 1991, and the ROMANTIC TIMES K.I.S.S. Award, 1993.

Her four previous Zebra novels are *Brazen Virginia Bride, California Temptress, Desire's Endless Kiss,* and *Temptation's Fire*.

PINNACLE'S PASSIONATE AUTHOR—

PATRICIA MATTHEWS

EXPERIENCE *LOVE'S* PROMISE

LOVE'S AVENGING HEART   (302-1, $3.95/$4.95)
Red-haired Hannah, sold into servitude as an innkeeper's barmaiden, must survive the illicit passions of many men, until love comes to free her questing heart.

LOVE'S BOLD JOURNEY   (421-4, $4.50/$5.50)
Innocent Rachel, orphaned after the Civil War, travels out West to start a new life, only to meet three bold men—two she couldn't love and one she couldn't trust.

LOVE'S DARING DREAM   (372-2, $4.50/$5.50)
Proud Maggie must overcome the poverty and shame of her family's bleak existence, encountering men of wealth, power, and greed until her impassioned dreams of love are answered.

LOVE'S GOLDEN DESTINY   (393-5, $4.50/$5.50)
Lovely Belinda Lee follows her gold-seeking father to the Alaskan Yukon where danger and love are waiting in the wilderness.

LOVE'S MAGIC MOMENT   (409-5, $4.50/$5.50)
Sensuous Meredith boldly undertakes her father's lifework to search for a fabled treasure in Mexico, where she must learn to distinguish between the sweet truth of love and the seduction of greed and lust.

Available wherever paperbacks are sold, or order direct from the Publisher. Send cover price plus 50¢ per copy for mailing and handling to Pinnacle Books, Dept. 778, 475 Park Avenue South, New York, N.Y. 10016. Residents of New York and Tennessee must include sales tax. DO NOT SEND CASH. For a free Zebra/ Pinnacle catalog please write to the above address.

PINNACLE BOOKS HAS SOMETHING FOR EVERYONE—

MAGICIANS, EXPLORERS, WITCHES AND CATS

THE HANDYMAN (377-3, $3.95/$4.95)
He is a magician who likes hands. He likes their comfortable shape and weight and size. He likes the portability of the hands once they are severed from the rest of the ponderous body. Detective Lanark must discover who The Handyman is before more handless bodies appear.

PASSAGE TO EDEN (538-5, $4.95/$5.95)
Set in a world of prehistoric beauty, here is the epic story of a courageous seafarer whose wanderings lead him to the ends of the old world—and to the discovery of a new world in the rugged, untamed wilderness of northwestern America.

BLACK BODY (505-9, $5.95/$6.95)
An extraordinary chronicle, this is the diary of a witch, a journal of the secrets of her race kept in return for not being burned for her "sin." It is the story of Alba, that rarest of creatures, a white witch: beautiful and able to walk in the human world undetected.

THE WHITE PUMA (532-6, $4.95/NCR)
The white puma has recognized the men who deprived him of his family. Now, like other predators before him, he has become a man-hater. This story is a fitting tribute to this magnificent animal that stands for all living creatures that have become, through man's carelessness, close to disappearing forever from the face of the earth.

Available wherever paperbacks are sold, or order direct from the Publisher. Send cover price plus 50¢ per copy for mailing and handling to Pinnacle Books, Dept 778, 475 Park Avenue South, New York, N.Y. 10016. Residents of New York and Tennessee must include sales tax. DO NOT SEND CASH. For a free Zebra/Pinnacle catalog please write to the above address.

MAKE SURE YOUR DOORS AND WINDOWS ARE LOCKED!
SPINE-TINGLING SUSPENSE FROM PINNACLE

SILENT WITNESS (677, $4.50)
by Mary Germano

Katherine Hansen had been with The Information Warehouse too long to stand by and watch it be destroyed by sabotage. At first there were breaches in security, as well as computer malfunctions and unexplained power failures. But soon Katherine started receiving sinister phone calls, and she realized someone was stalking her, willing her to make one fatal mistake. And all Katherine could do was wait. . . .

BLOOD SECRETS (695, $4.50)
by Dale Ludwig

When orphaned Kirsten Walker turned thirty, she inherited her mother's secret diary—learning the shattering truth about her past. A deranged serial killer has been locked away for years but will soon be free. He knows all of Kirsten's secrets and will follow her to a house on the storm-tossed cape. Now she is trapped alone with a madman who wants something only Kirsten can give him!

CIRCLE OF FEAR (721, $4.50)
by Jim Norman

Psychiatrist Sarah Johnson has a new patient, Diana Smith. And something is very wrong with Diana . . . something Sarah has never seen before. For in the haunted recesses of Diana's tormented psyche a horrible secret is buried. As compassion turns into obsession, Sarah is drawn into Diana's chilling nightmare world. And now Sarah must fight with every weapon she possesses to save them both from the deadly danger that is closing in fast!

SUMMER OF FEAR (741, $4.50)
by Carolyn Haines

Connor Tremaine moves back east to take a dream job as a riding instructor. Soon she has fallen in love with and marries Clay Sumner, a local politician. Beginning with shocking stories about his first wife's death and culminating with a near-fatal attack on Connor, she realizes that someone most definitely does not want her in Clay's life. And now, Connor has two things to fear: a deranged killer, and the fact that her husband's winning charm may mask a most murderous nature . . .

Available wherever paperbacks are sold, or order direct from the Publisher. Send cover price plus 50¢ per copy for mailing and handling to Zebra Books, Dept. 778, 475 Park Avenue South, New York, N.Y. 10016. Residents of New York and Tennessee must include sales tax. DO NOT SEND CASH. For a free Zebra/Pinnacle catalog please write to the above address.